Queen Vashti's DREAMS

Queen Vashti's DREAMS

A NOVEL

by

Alison Buckley

Queen Vashti's Dreams
by Alison Buckley

Published by Nenge Books, Australia, November 2025
ABN 26809396184
nengebooks1@gmail.com
www.nengebooks.com

1st revision, Jan 2026

This book is available to purchase online at www.nengebooks.com and through booksellers worldwide.

ebook ISBN 978-1-7644052-1-8

ISBN 978-1-7644052-0-1

To Zors Ciwana,
the very beautiful woman warrior
who looked after me in the mountains
of Queen Vashti's lands.

Table of Contents

Acknowledgements x
Preface xi
Introduction 1
Chapter 1 3
Chapter 2 9
Chapter 3 17
Chapter 4 25
Chapter 5 34
Chapter 6 44
Chapter 7 49
Chapter 8 60
Chapter 9 66
Chapter 10 74
Chapter 11 82
Chapter 12 93
Chapter 13 99
Chapter 14 108
Chapter 15 117
Chapter 16 125
Chapter 17 130
Chapter 18 135
Chapter 19 139
Chapter 20 145
Chapter 21 152
Chapter 22 156
Chapter 23 162
Chapter 24 168
Chapter 25 181
Chapter 26 187
Chapter 27 195
Chapter 28 199

Chapter 29	204
Chapter 30	211
Chapter 31	217
Chapter 32	226
Chapter 33	238
Chapter 34	243
Chapter 35	245
Chapter 36	254
Chapter 37	269
Chapter 38	274
Chapter 39	281
Chapter 40	288
Chapter 41	295
Chapter 42	300
Chapter 43	306
Chapter 44	314
Chapter 45	319
Chapter 46	324
Chapter 47	332
Chapter 48	339
Chapter 49	347
Chapter 50	352
Chapter 51	360
References	369
Glossary	370

Preface

Who was Queen Vashti? Many believe she was Persian, the fifth century BCE wife of King Xerxes of Persia. But others think she might have been a Mede, ruling one hundred years before, and married to King Ahasuerus the Mede, known in history as Astyages.

It has been acknowledged that the Medes were ancestors of today's Kurds. At their greatest extent, the Medes' territories covered much of the regions of today's Iraq, Iran, Syria, and Turkey continuously inhabited and claimed by Kurds as their ethnic homeland, which they call Kurdistan. If Vashti was a Mede, she stands in the tradition of Kurdish women who still struggle to protect their gender and reclaim their ancient lands.

This work of historical fiction tells part of the Medes' story according to Queen Vashti.

Acknowledgements

Debbie, PPJ, Zardasht, Mike, Susan, Jotham, Ciyako, Chad and Evin – my heartfelt thanks to your all for contributing in various ways to the manuscript, cover design and publishing of this book. Most of all your encouragement kept me going when challenges arose.

Alison Buckley

Introduction

Some linguistic, archaeological, and written evidence now indicates that the Medes' forbears could have been among the founders of the Sumerian civilization approximately six thousand years ago. These people have been credited with establishing agriculture and the first writing, and inventing baked bricks, the wheel, weaving, metallurgy, architecture, irrigation systems, and geometry. Taking advantage of reliable food sources, they developed complex judicial, economic, and food production and distribution systems.

Ancient sites such as Gobelke Tepe, the Lalish temple complex, and a possible resting place of the patriarch Noah's boat after the Great Flood are all found in Kurdish lands. According to the ancient Hebrew record, Noah's sons Madai, Gomer, and Magog, and their descendants, made their homes in what are still the Kurdish regions of the Middle East. In the Zagros Mountain region, the Medes became known as Gutians, or Mannaeans. Rising in 750BCE, the Median dynasty flourished for two hundred years until King Cyrus, a Persian of Median ancestry, conquered the kingdom.

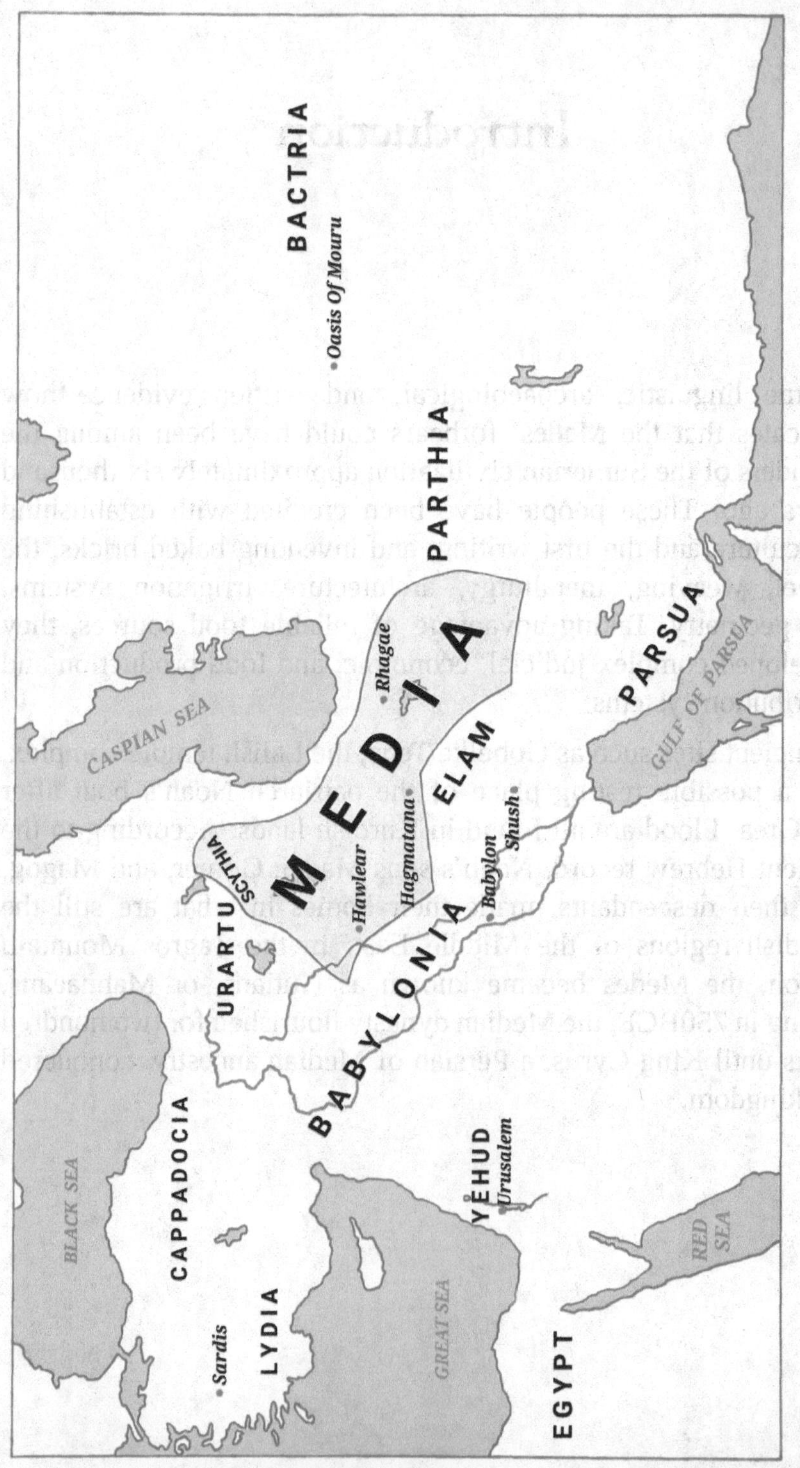
BACTRIA
Oasis Of Mouru
PARTHIA
CASPIAN SEA
Rhagae
MEDIA
PARSUA
GULF OF PARSUA
ELAM
Hagmatana
Hawlear
SCYTHIA
URARTU
Shush
Babylon
BABYLONIA
CAPPADOCIA
BLACK SEA
YEHUD
Urusalem
RED SEA
GREAT SEA
LYDIA
Sardis
EGYPT

Chapter 1

Horses' hooves pound hard turf past stately palm groves.

The head of Vashti's horse bobs up and down as she furiously urges him on. Somewhere ahead her father, General Cicataxma of the Medes, leads shield-clad warriors wielding iron battle-axes toward a vast, high-walled palace.

Flash.

Against the darkening sky, hundreds of airborne metal arrowheads fly.

Row upon row of chariot wheels crash over blooming shrubs.

Flash.

A single lance flies by and disappears.

Bathed in sweat, Vashti woke from her dream with a start, her eyes roaming wildly. Her sacred parchments were still on the shelf, and pinprick stars were fading from the dimly lit sky just visible between the parted curtains of her open bedroom window. Shivering despite the heat still radiating from her body, she swung her feet onto the woolen floor rug beside her bed. Quickly, she slipped on a brightly woven *chokha* jacket, secured a loose silk skirt with a colorful sash, and hurried downstairs, the silver discs on her headdress jangling.

Something must have happened to her father.

Lamp light threw dark shadows on the cold stone of her home in the castle wall, but Mother Shamin's warm hug and loving smile did little to ease Vashti's anxiety. Rubbing her hands together above the tendur stove's comforting heat, she wondered why she had been unable to reach her father in her dream.

"Where is your maid, dear?" Shamin asked, her gentle voice drifting through the chilly air.

"Father didn't rescue Khezmet from our enemies to enslave her, Mother," Vashti replied, grabbing a piece of flatbread and dipping it in creamy *mast* offered by Gulah, the cook. "I've promised her a free day to visit her friend Daro in the stables."

"Dear, you are too kind," Shamin protested, sitting down beside her daughter and kissing her lightly on the forehead.

"Not at all, Mother," Vashti replied. "Khezmet can buy ceci beans from the markets for Gulah's *terkhena* soup. But now I must hurry to the palace."

"Why dear?" Shamin asked. "It is too early to bother Aunt Ardela."

"I had a dream last night," Vashti explained, taking a sip of chai tea from a steaming ceramic cup.

"Perhaps Auramazda has sent you a message," Shamin suggested. "Can you tell me about your dream?"

Not wanting to worry her mother with the details, Vashti shook her head impatiently. "I was with the army. I must tell Aunt Ardela straightaway."

Shamin's smooth brow wrinkled. "Then go quickly, find out what your dream means," she urged. "And remember your manners," she called as her daughter rushed out.

Outside, the sweet, strong scents of roses and jasmine brought from the far-flung lands of Ariavarta wafted from the gardens hanging down the palace's stone walls. Kitchen hands hurrying to the servants' entrance emerged from a soft mist rising from the courtyard as donkey drawn carts laden with bags of grain creaked by. Quickly climbing the palace's stone steps, she recalled the excitement of her first formal visit when her father had explained that the carved bears at each end were their national symbol. It seemed like only yesterday that he had left with her uncle, Shahan Shah Hovakhshatra of the Medes, to fight the Athorayans.

The guard at the great oak doors of the palace nodded recognition, and she slipped into the cool quiet of the silver-lined grand entrance hall, her leather boots softly tapping the creamy marble floor. Relieved no grim-faced officials were in sight, she hurried past wall reliefs of birds, animals, and cuneiform wedged notations of her language. Suddenly, the doors at the end of the hall flew open and Shahjin Ardela, queen of the Medes, appeared, closely followed by her fourteen-year-old son, Ishtovigo.

"Vashti dear," Ardela cried, opening her purple-clad arms to hug her niece, "what brings you here so early?"

The awe Vashti usually felt for her tall, graceful aunt vanished as she recalled her early morning vision.

"Dear aunt, I had a dream," she blurted. "Is there any news of the army?"

"No, dear, but follow me to my chamber. We must find out what your dream means," Ardela replied briskly, flicking back her thick mane of wavy auburn hair as she led the way. Inside her oil lamp-lit reception chamber, she sank into a cushioned silver couch, waved her son and niece onto brocade floor bolsters, and invited Vashti to explain her dream.

"Our army was riding across a field toward a palace surrounded by gardens," Vashti began.

Ardela frowned, called a guard outside the chamber, and ordered him to summon the Piree Magush immediately. Soon a white-clad figure in a felt triangular hat appeared apparition-like in the doorway.

"Come," Ardela beckoned the chief priest. "Vashti has had a dream."

The Magush listened intently. "The troops are inside the city of Nineveh," he informed them solemnly.

Vashti's heart leapt. "Are they safe?" she asked anxiously.

The priest stared out the flax-curtained window. "Yes, but our army has faced its biggest battle yet. I must consult the bansom wands."

"Please petition Auramazda for their victory," Ardela entreated, her almond eyes flashing a desperate appeal.

"And ask him to send their *yazata* angels to protect them," Vashti implored. The priest nodded, the ribbons and lappets of his headwear trembling. Not satisfied, Vashti asked permission to leave and marched out, unwilling to wait till the priest had consulted tamarisk bush sticks to discover her father's fate.

Out in the shiny hall, a disheveled, panting soldier headed toward Shahjin Ardela's council room at the end of the hall, but still thinking about her dream, Vashti took little notice. Soon, other quick footsteps approached from behind. Expecting an official, she turned to find Ishtovigo.

"Do you want to go hunting?" he asked.

"No," she replied. "I want to know what my dream means."

"But this is the fourth time I've asked in two weeks," he whined. "You're just angry at the Magush because he didn't interpret your dream."

"I am not," Vashti replied hotly, turning to face him squarely. "I will wait for his answer." But her anger was evaporating at the sight of her cousin's winning smile, and she paused to think. "Yes," she answered dispassionately, regretting that she had never been able to withstand the grin animating his perfectly symmetrical face. "But we will have to prepare the horses ourselves. Daro is not here today."

"I'll insist Father dismisses that lazy stable hand when he gets back," Ishtovigo replied.

"No. He will be needed to care for the troops' horses when they return," she countered.

"Not after Father comes back," he maintained.

She shook her head. As usual, she and Ishtovigo could not agree about anything.

Ignoring him, she strode ahead into the cool, dark recesses of the stable. He followed, his nose wrinkling at the pungent smell of manure. In the corner, her horse, Nzdar, whinnied and nuzzled her for his usual citron apple. By the time she had thrown a riding rug over him, attached his bronze bridle, and tied some green, yellow, and red woolen *golang* ribbons to his mane, Ishtovigo was calling impatiently from the courtyard.

"Race you to the bottom," he yelled, kicking his horse's flanks.

Opening the golden gate of the uppermost wall of the Medes' citadel, the guard stood back as Ishtovigo flew through, the hard hooves of his sturdy mountain-bred horse breaking shards off the cobblestones. Vashti followed the path around the gold-trimmed wall at a more measured pace with two of the Shahan Shah's customary guards not far behind. On reaching the silver gate of the next circular wall, she could not see Ishtovigo, but the clatter of hooves on the path beneath the wall just below indicated he was farther down the hill. After guiding Nzdar round each of the blue-, scarlet-, and black-trimmed walls, she glimpsed Ishtovigo breaching the white gateway in the lowest of the seven walls protecting the palace, treasury, barracks, and Atashkedah temple of the Medes' citadel.

"You always were a little slow," he taunted when she caught up.

"Better slow and sure," she shot back, patting Nzdar's neck. Pressuring his flanks, she eased the dappled gray into a trot. "Race you to the markets," she called as the horse broke into a gallop.

Arriving ahead of her companion, she carefully steered Nzdar past blacksmiths clanging foundries, odorous tanneries piled with skins, and hot coal pits firing clay pots in the city marketplace. Suddenly, Khezmet and Daro emerged from a nearby stall displaying silver and gold jewelry.

"Hide quickly," Vashti yelled.

Startled, Daro grabbed Khezmet, and they disappeared behind a pile of straw, just as Ishtovigo's horse knocked over a barrel of wine.

"Watch where you're going, you fool," the owner cried, whereupon Ishtovigo grabbed his lance to throw at the angry vintner, who instinctively ducked.

"Leave him," Vashti cried, seizing the lance. "You shouldn't ride so fast through the markets."

"And you shouldn't tell me what to do," Ishtovigo yelled. By this time, the vintner had disappeared into the crowd and a woman had righted the barrel. Ishtovigo scowled. "Let's go," he snapped, digging his heels into his horse's side. The animal shot off, scattering marketgoers and shopkeepers alike.

As Daro and Khezmet sneaked away, Vashti fumbled in the leather bag around her waist for some silver coins, which she handed to the woman. "Please accept these with apologies for my friend," she requested. "He's not his usual self today."

Allowing Nzdar to pick his way through the marketgoers, she felt her face flush. "Such a weak excuse for telling the *druj*," she fretted, "and against the prophet's teachings. I should have told her Ishtovigo was his usual self."

Chapter 2

Vashti soon caught up with Ishtovigo, who had apparently forgotten his displeasure. After crossing a stone causeway over the River Yalfan south of the city, the couple headed southeast. Only the steady clip-clop of their horses' hooves broke the silence as they passed harvested millet and barley crops patchworked with ripening wheat and spelt fields. Eventually, Ishtovigo spoke.

"It feels like Father is never coming home," he lamented, staring intently ahead to the triple peaks of distant Mount Alvand towering above the Shahan Shah's hunting grounds.

Vashti nodded. "I can hardly remember what Cica's voice sounds like," she confessed sadly of her own father as a flock of sheep scattered before them. To distract herself from her dream, she disputed Ishtovigo's boasts of the trophies acquired on his last hunting trip. Their banter continued as the road wound through foothills to a village of simple stone and wooden houses.

Not long after riding through a stream pooled by late-summer drought, they arrived at the two stone pillars topped by carved bears marking the cool, forested lands of the ruling family. Eyeing the hunters from above, hawks and vultures hovered, their cries calling for future meals.

"Load up," Ishtovigo called. Clutching his bow and pulling two flint arrows from his quiver, he dashed into the greenery just as Vashti spied the jagged antlers of a stag darting in the opposite direction. Squeezing Nzdar's flank firmly, she galloped off in pursuit. Moments later, her first shot was a clean hit, and she motioned the guards to mark the location of the dead animal. The crash of another quickly sent Ishtovigo into a copse of young oak trees. She watched as he ran down a mature doe and fired, his arrow coming within a spear's width of her head. Then the doe turned and vanished into thicker bushes.

"I will get you next time," he shouted and cantered back. "Another of my near misses," he admitted sheepishly.

"And such a big, vicious animal!" Vashti cried, grinning widely.

"Let's head for the other end of the park," Ishtovigo suggested, "and see if we can find some even bigger game." Wondering if this was another of his ruses, she raised her eyebrows questioningly.

"You'll see," he replied confidently. After a short ride along animal trails through lush undergrowth, they arrived at a bush-covered cave entrance in the side of the mountain, which seemed too low for a man to stand in. Nearby, a narrow stream trickling down rough, worn stone steps filled the balmy air with its effervescent song, but all else was still and hushed.

"Quiet," he whispered, signaling her to dismount and the guards to wait as a low growl came from the cave. Treading carefully, he led the way to a path up the mountain. When they had climbed to treetop height, he stopped, carefully removed a rock in the roof of the cave, and looked down. Below was a mother tiger lying next to three young cubs playing with a stick. Her mouth agape, Vashti watched while Ishtovigo grinned satisfaction. Suddenly, the mother tiger stood up, and he stepped back.

"Time to go," he murmured and began to scramble back down the path.

"Amazing!" Vashti exclaimed when they reached the bottom.

"Yes, but Father will not allow them or the lions to be hunted anymore," Ishtovigo complained, a ring of disappointment in his voice. "Except if they are attacking domestic animals."

"What about the bears?"

"No. He has decreed that we can't touch them either even though they often raid the beehives."

Something rustled in the bushes nearby.

"There's a gazelle," Vashti shouted, jumping onto Nzdar as a brown, darkly striped animal crashed through the undergrowth. Sensing the hunt, the horse almost galloped from under her, and the lithe gazelle shot out in front of her arrow. Branches whipped her face as Nzdar bravely followed the prey, but she drew while he maintained his pace. Another *whoosh* and the weapon found its mark, stopping the animal dead in its tracks. Halting Nzdar, she dismounted and stood over her prize, panting, while the horse, too, heaved from exertion.

"Now that deserves a reward," Ishtovigo remarked when he drew up beside her. "We'll ask the guards to pick it up later."

"The Shahjin will be holding a banquet tomorrow," Vashti predicted, pointing to the young beast.

"Yes, but she will probably give most of the meat to the servants," Ishtovigo replied.

"But now it's time for us to eat," he continued, pointing to a clearing in the forest. Waving the guards away, he untied a flax cloth from his riding rug, spread it on the springy grass, and took walnuts, cheeses, and bread from a leather bag. Two small clay flasks of new wine completed the feast. Then, asking to be excused, he disappeared into the forest. Thinking he was relieving himself, Vashti lay down on the cool grass and gazed up into the brilliant blue dome above framed by huge, overhanging oak trees. Soon, footsteps squelched thick grass and Ishtovigo appeared overhead. Startled, she sat straight up.

"For you, my dear," he declared, handing her a bunch of violets. Accepting the flowers with a shy smile, she inhaled their sweet fragrance, her face tensing as she suddenly recalled the garden in her dream and the lance flying to its unknown destination. Without commenting on her frown, Ishtovigo urged her to eat.

Enjoying the peaceful buzzing of bees raiding flowers, and the warmth of mottled shade in the clearing, the young hunters chatted, happily recalling previous hunts at the park with their families before realizing the sun was well past its zenith. Ishtovigo summoned the guards and Vashti suggested they return the next day for her trophies. He agreed, and they headed for the road back to the city.

They had not long left the hills behind when a fuzzy line of foot soldiers and blurred cavalry horses appeared ahead in the distance with the banner of Kawa the Blacksmith barely visible in front. "The army is back," Ishtovigo yelled, spurring his horse into a gallop.

"Cica," Vashti cried, urging Nzdar on. But as they drew closer, she realized something was wrong. Shahan Shah Hovakhshatra, flanked by his two eldest sons, Shawish and Artaspaya, led the mounted Bear regiment, but Cica's horse pulled a red chariot. Her heart thumping hard, she drew up to her uncle, who could hardly be distinguished from his dusty troops. He halted.

"Vashti, dear," he greeted, his voice gravelly. The subdued tone scared her, and she looked around wildly.

"Where is Cica?" she yelled. Then she saw it. A long box in the chariot, draped in a red, white, and green banner.

"He is martyred, my dear." Hovakhshatra's gentle words full of compassion floated past her, like the visions in her dream.

"No, not my Cica," she cried, gazing unseeing at the box. "He said he would come back."

"He is with our other beloved warriors." She hardly heard the Shahan Shah's commiserations; the dark hole opening up inside her all but blanketed his words. She drew her arm away as he reached over to pat it then froze. The lance in her dream must have been on its way to Cica! And the disheveled messenger she had passed in the palace must have been the bearer of the dreadful news. Engulfed in an ever-widening black hole of shock and dismay, she brushed away angry tears. Why had she not been told by the messenger?

Ishtovigo dismounted and bowed to his father, who indicated he should ride in front of the chariot with his brothers. Suddenly, Vashti noticed that the whole army had stopped. The men were waiting to see their families, so she turned Nzdar, nodded to the

Shahan Shah, and slowly edged her horse behind the chariot. His rhythmic steps carried her effortlessly through the warm afternoon, but she could not feel his movement. Her only thoughts were of Shamin and her brother and sister waiting for Cicataxma.

Slowly, the sad procession made its way to the white gate of the citadel. Women's ululations of joy dissolved into cries of anguish when they saw the chariot's burden while others scanned the ranks, searching for their husbands, fathers, and sons. From an open window in the uppermost wall, Shamin looked out and saw her brother, Shahan Shah Hovakhshatra, and her nephews leading the lone chariot.

"The army is home," she cried and raced outside with her son, Ferhad, and youngest daughter Parwin, almost falling over each other and the servants in their haste to follow. From the golden gateway, the family caught glimpses of Cicataxma's Bear regiment slowly making its way up the circular path.

When the Shahan Shah rode through the gateway, Shamin rushed to him. "Where is Cica?" she cried. Then she saw the box in the chariot, and Vashti dismount and walk stiffly toward her, her arms open wide.

"Father has given his life for our freedom, Mother," she said, hugging Shamin tightly. "But Uncle Hovakhshatra has brought him home to us," she choked through sobs. Shamin and Vashti clung to each other, their wails echoing across the courtyard while little Parwin wrapped her arms around both in confusion.

Ferhad walked up to the Shahan Shah and stood to attention. "Your father, the great general of the Medes, sacrificed his life most nobly and bravely in battle for his family and our people," Hovakhshatra told his nephew before resuming the path toward his wife, Shahjin Ardela, her maid, and their daughter Shelna waiting on the palace steps. Bowing his head to Vashti and Shamin, Ishtovigo followed while Shawish, the heir to the throne, and his next youngest brother, Artaspaya, dismounted and expressed their sorrow to Shamin, Vashti, and the children.

The subdued column of soldiers fragmented and walked toward their quarters as Daro and other stable hands appeared to care for their tired horses. After the soldiers uttered their final battle cry, silence descended to be punctuated only by the quiet sobbing of the little family hovering beneath the oak tree outside their home like fluttering birds blown off their migration course. But Shamin's eyes never left the lone chariot as it paced the six stade wall of the palace compound.

Shamin's cook and housemaid, Gulah, who considered herself a family member and acted like one, was the first to speak. Enfolding Ferhad and Parwin in her ample arms, she urged them to come inside for chai while Debyar, the children's tall, willowy teacher, ushered them all into the house. Vashti's maid, Khezmet, took her mistress's hand and squeezed it, remembering the loss of her own father in battle with wild Scythian tribesmen from the north.

"Where is Cica, Mother?" asked four-year-old Parwin.

"He is resting now after his big fight, dear. He got badly hurt and he…"

"Is he dead?" Parwin asked.

"Yes, dear," Shamin whispered, hugging her youngest daughter tightly as tears flowed freely down her full cheeks.

"But we will meet him again after Frashokeriti when the world will be remade with only kindness and goodness," Vashti assured her little sister.

"Then I will wait for him," Parwin declared defiantly, folding her arms.

"Yes, but till then we must be brave like Cica," Shamin replied.

Gulah appeared with a tray of chai tea glasses. "Everyone must drink," she urged. "Too many tears shed."

After they had all sipped silently for a while, Vashti sniffed and looked around at the tear-streaked faces. "Father taught us how to do good deeds from good thoughts. He spoke good words to us and others. Let's write down everything we can remember about him, so we never forget," she suggested. "Even though it is not yet forty days since his death."

"Wonderful idea!" Debyar exclaimed, reaching for her basket of reed parchment sheets and finely honed charcoal sticks. "You first, Shamin," she suggested.

Sustained by warm milk and honey, long into the evening the family members talked and wrote as all their thoughts and sadness tumbled out.

Shamin: "Dearest husband, when Vashti was nearly ready to enter this world, you returned early from military training. You were so worried about me when I had fever after she was born that you went to the Atashkedah temple to consult the priests and then to the city for some medicines. My darling, you will always be my husband. I am yours forever."

Ferhad: "Father Cica, the Shahan Shah told me how courageously you led the troops when we defeated the Scythians who had ruled us for eight long years. Obeying our smart Uncle Hovakhshatra, you waited until all the enemy became drunk at their celebrations then shouted the battle cry, 'Ahasuerus,' and the Bears attacked and overcame them."

"So that is why the Shahan Shah is affectionately called Ahasuerus," Vashti commented.

"Dear Cica, you will always be alive to me," she wrote, "and always with me through Spenta Mainyu, the ever-loving spirit of Auramazda." Wondering if this message was too short, she added more, "Father, please forgive me for climbing the wall in my new shiny slippers that you gave me to wear to the palace. I'm so sorry the silver got scuffed with gold. And I promise to be more patient with Ishtovigo."

Parwin dictated to Debyar: "My father, I love the wooden bear and lion you bought for me when you were fighting a long way away. I take them to bed with me every night, but I will miss your hugs and kisses."

Debyar also wrote for the servants.

Khezmet: "General Cicataxma, I am forever indebted to you for rescuing my family from the Scythians. Serving your family is my freedom."

Gulah: "General, I know you loved my *terkhena* soup, that's why I always left a pot on the stove for you, and I always will."

Debyar then thanked the general for giving her such clever, curious students. "I will continue to teach them your ways and those of the prophet," she promised.

When everyone else had gone to bed, Vashti and Ferhad agreed they had one last family duty to carry out. Creeping out of their home, they raised the freedom banner of Kawa the Blacksmith above the gold-trimmed wall where it hung limply from a sentinel-like pole below the crescent moon.

"Just like Cica, it is resting now," Ferhad whispered, "but soon a strong wind will wave it proudly."

Chapter 3

The next day, Vashti awoke to the clump of boots on the cobblestones outside followed by a knock on the door of her home in the castle wall. Drawing aside the flax curtains, she craned her head to catch sight of the banner of the Blacksmith flying briskly above her home in the stiff breeze.

"The Shahan Shah has sent his chief advisor to discuss the funeral details," Gulah called from downstairs.

Catching Shamin's muffled reply, Vashti called Khezmet, who offered her a wet cloth for her puffy eyes and a black robe, which she refused to wear in favor of the scarlet *chokha* and *pantol* of her father's regiment.

"But we are in mourning," Khezmet protested, her light blue eyes blinking in consternation beneath wisps of fair hair escaping from her headscarf.

Vashti grimaced. "I will not dress like the desert peoples. It will dampen my spirit even more," she replied firmly.

"Then let me make up your face," Khezmet offered.

"With red poppy powder on my lips to match my eyes?" Vashti replied in a forlorn attempt to dispel the raw sadness that gnawed away at her whole body.

"No more tears, dear, or it will run," Khezmet mumbled, squeezing her mistress's hand.

Dressed and determined to represent the courage of her father, Vashti hurried downstairs to where Shamin was listening to the advisor. "The Shahan Shah and Shahjin wish the ceremonies to be held in the city, so all the people can attend," he informed her. "They will lead the funeral chariot with their personal guard, followed by the general's regiment and the other two generals. All three regiments have been given permission to return to their families, but not one of the Bears has left the barracks."

"That is as it should be," Shamin replied stiffly, "in honor of my husband."

"The Shahah Shah and Shahjin have decreed a national week of victory celebrations over the city of Nineveh after the general's funeral," the advisor continued. "He trusts you will agree."

"Yes, and since my husband's body was preserved for its journey home he will later be buried in the family tomb," Shamin declared.

The advisor nodded. "Of course. If his body does not touch the earth, it will not contaminate the soil," he conceded. "You and your family will follow the funeral chariot in procession," he added hastily.

Instead of lessons that day, Debyar took the children for a long walk around the citadel walls. Although hot, the clear, sunny day lifted their spirits, and it wasn't until they were circling the silver trimmed wall that Parwin asked why her father had died. Debyar sighed and hugged her small pupil.

"In the year that the Shahan Shah and your father won control of our nation from the Scythian tribes, Shah Nabopolassar of Babylonia defeated the Athorayan army, but the Athorayans continued to attack us, stealing our people, our land, and our animals, and destroying our homes," she explained.

"But didn't Kawa the Blacksmith kill the evil Athorayan Shah Azhdahak who was murdering our children?" Vashti asked, holding Parwin's hand.

"Yes, dear, but that was long ago in the land to our west between the Two Rivers, Ufratu and Idigna. Later, the Athorayans became strong there again." The teacher stopped and gently took the hand of each child. "Your father died to protect us. The enemy is all but defeated," she assured them, looking each in the eyes.

Ferhad stood straight, his other fist clenched as though gripping a lance, while Vashti tried to suppress her trembling lip as she cuddled Parwin, who had begun to sob. Overcome with grief herself, Debyar's heartstrings tightened as she enfolded all of them in her arms and sang soothingly of the victory of Kawa.

When the children's sobs subsided, and Debyar had dabbed their faces dry with her headscarf, the little group paused at the silver gate. Sadly, they gazed at the unusually quiet city below ringed by nomads' goat's hair *dwars* and oak trees beginning to drop burnished leaves of orange, red, and brown.

"The trees are weeping for Cica," Vashti lamented. Watching the leaves gently float to the ground, the children couldn't help but shed more tears.

The next day, the Shahan Shah and Shahjin invited Shamin and the children to the palace. Draped in a saffron-yellow robe woven with patterns of roses, inverted tulips, and stripes, and secured with a red sash, Shahan Shah Hovakhshatra sat splendidly on a well-padded golden couch. He waited patiently while Shahjin Ardela's maid arranged her scarlet Mukryani robe before she seated herself beside him on an identical couch. Their two eldest sons, Shawish and Artaspaya, then took their places on silver couches either side of their parents while the children were asked to sit next to Ishtovigo on cushions at their feet. Ardela's maid ushered Shamin to a silver couch next to her sister-in-law's as the Shahan Shah's two other generals were admitted by a young man armed with a short-handled lance and a dagger sheathed in his sash. Bearing a golden scepter, he took his place between the ruling couple.

After a servant brought chai, freshly pressed wine, and honey-pistachio sweets, Hovakhshatra asked the family if they were ready to hear the story of Cicataxma's last day.

"Of course," Shamin replied stiffly, and the children nodded.

Hovakhshatra cleared his throat and surveyed the faces around him, the tightly curled hair beneath his tribal headband bobbing above his kind eyes. "After the city of Ashur was captured, Cica built a wall to keep out the Athorayans at Rajaw where he secured the fort before and proceeding with the Bears," he began. "As the countryside was subdued, he commandeered camels to upset the enemy's horses, then joined me and my forces marching to Nineveh. On arrival, we camped outside the city to plan our final strategy."

"I knew Father would use the camels," Ferhad cried. "He told me they could be weaponized against the Athorayans."

"Hush, dear," Shamin urged.

"No. The boy is right. We planned to put them in the front line," his uncle concurred. "Over the summer, with our Babylonian allies, we besieged Nineveh, giving sufficient time to plan an assault just after Norouz New Year's festival. General Taxmaspada directed his lancer regiment in the building of earthworks topped by equally spaced wooden planks along the perimeter of the city's walls. Then our siege machine bombarded the wall with the stones we had removed to make the earthworks, and the siege tower was run up against the wall to knock the top off. When the enemy dropped torches on the tower, we put the fires out with large water ladles. Slowly, through the Athorayan months of Simanu to Abu, we increased the size of the holes in the walls, particularly near the earthworks."

The Shahan Shah stopped and looked at the listeners again. All eyes were upon his benevolent face, which was usually lit by a wide smile on his generous lips; but this time his mouth was pursed, and his jaw was clenched.

"During this stage of the campaign, Shah Sin-shar-ishkun of Athoraya was killed and was replaced by his brother, Ashur-uballit the Second," he continued. "When the enemy cavalry outside the walls attacked, Cicataxma's Bear regiment dispatched them quickly." Hovakhshatra paused again to glance at Shamin, who beamed proudly. "The enemy troops seemed to lessen in numbers and resolve," he went on, "but perhaps they were keeping their best for last."

Noticing the Shahan Shah's hesitancy, General Biraxeas asked to continue the account. "Finally, sections of the wall were sufficiently damaged for our best mountaineers to scramble up the sides like monkeys while my archers showered the enemy above them," he explained, the fringes of the Tiger regiment's emblem on his *chokha* rippling as he emulated the climbers. "Despite the Athorayans raining arrows, stones, and boiling liquids on our mountaineers, most reached the top where our bombardment continued. In this way, we breached the city's defenses with Cica leading his regiment into the central city and the palace where our battle cry once more assailed the ears of our enemies."

Vashti clapped her hands. "If only I had been there!" she exclaimed then slapped her hand over her mouth as she remembered the charging army in her dream. Her mother and the Shahjin frowned, but General Biraxeas, who had been training her in archery before he left, smiled approval.

"Our casualties were mounting," the Shahan Shah continued, "but the men were spurred on by the thought of ridding us of the Athorayan scourge. There were days of hand-to-hand fighting while we took the outer precincts of the palace. Through all this, we hardly slept or ate, but we were advancing on our goal, the imperial residence, near the place of my father Kshathrita's untimely death. We had used up all our reserve troops when we struck the Athorayan Shah's guard, giants of men, covered in metal armor." The Shahan Shah paused and looked at the children's expectant faces and then at Shamin who nodded. Vashti cuddled Parwin closely and put her hands over her little sister's ears, but Parwin pulled them off, insisting she wanted to hear about her father.

"Then it happened," Hovakhshatra went on. "Cica charged at a wild-looking Athorayan whose arrow targeted his heart. The enemy also lunged at him with his spear. Cica weaved to avoid the arrow, but the spear caught him in the side of his chest, which was not quite protected by his armor. He fell immediately and was dead by the time I reached him. One of Cica's officers shot his assailant." Hovakhshatra turned to Shamin, who held his gaze. "When my brother Cica died, I promised on his body to take care of you and the children," he declared, his hand over his heart.

"This is my lifelong pledge."

There was silence as the Shahan Shah's face contorted with emotion. "That afternoon, we took the palace," he resumed, his voice breaking while unrestrained tears flowed down his face. "We captured all the officials and the shah's family, but Ashur-uballit escaped. We think he is in Harran with Egyptian protection. Harpagos put his household to the sword to eliminate any other successors," he added, glancing at Ardela, who winced. "But at last, I had avenged the death of my father," he concluded, his voice now gritty.

While the Shahan Shah recovered, General Biraxeas took up the account again. "The men were so enraged by the loss of Cicataxma that they rooted out and destroyed all Athorayan resistance in the palace precinct," he explained. "The only people left were the slaves and other captives, whom we freed and sent home. Some chose to join us."

General Taxmaspada then rose, straightened his Lynx regiment emblazoned vest, and asked permission to speak. "For ten days, we took gold and silver from the palace and surrounding buildings sufficient to fill our chariots," he explained when it was given. "The men were also permitted to take what they could carry on their horses, except for the replicas of the Athorayans' gods."

Hovakhshatra then signaled his general to stop and turned to Shamin, who remained stone-faced, while the children wept quietly. "Dear, please excuse us for a short while," Ardela requested of her husband, placing her hand gently on her sister-in-law's arm. "Harpagos, General Cicataxma's army bag for Shamin, please," she requested of the young man guarding the leading couple.

Shamin took the worn bag and opened it to find a dusty roll of reed parchments. Hastily closing the bag, she stood, and Ardela took her hand. Thinking only of entertainment, Ishtovigo waved a haichin ball in front of his father and asked if he and his cousins could play. Glancing carefully from child to child, Hovakhshatra clucked like a distressed mother hen over her small flock of upset chicks then nodded. The children wiped their eyes, rose silently, and filed out. All except Vashti, who hurried out to the stables to recall Khezmet from her visit with Daro.

Ardela and Shamin dangled their feet in one of several warm pools spilling down the gently sloping gardens beneath the palace's Great Hall.

"Do you want to open the bags now?" Ardela asked gently.

"No, I must do it alone. No one can bear this burden but me," Shamin replied, her tears dropping silently into the water.

Ardela squeezed her sister-in-law's hand. "My dear, take courage, the Prophet has declared that one day war will be no more."

"May that day be tomorrow," Shamin whispered.

On the women's and children's return, Hovakhshatra unrolled a tattered deerskin scroll that had been found at the home of one of the Hapiru captives in Nineveh. General Taxsmaspada read:

An attacker advances against you, Nineveh…

The shields of his soldiers are red,
The warriors are clad in scarlet.
The metal on chariots flashes

On the day they are made ready

The spears of pine are brandished.
The chariots storm through the streets,
rushing back and forth through the squares.
They look like flaming torches,

They dart about like lightning.

He summons his handpicked troops,

yet they stumble on their way.

They dash to the city wall,

the protective shield is put in place.

The river gates are thrown open,
and the palace collapses.

It is decreed that the city

be exiled and carried away.

Three days later, the Magush informed the palace that Cica's soul had safely reached its spirit guide, confirming its passing. Shamin, Vashti, and Parwin rose early the next day, cut their hair, then wound the long tresses around Cicataxma's horse's neck, and tied the shorter pieces to its rug. Following the Shahan Shah's carriage, Shamin and the children rode down the hill behind the chariot bearing Cica's body. The discs of the women's silver *sarwains* jingled above their bare necks in concert with their horses' hooves as the procession passed through each of the gateways. Only the sight of Khezmet and Daro riding behind her brightened Vashti's day and reassured her of the loyalty of the citizens of the shahdom.

Down in the city, men with mud-smeared faces beat their heads with their hands and shouted, "*Baw-kah roo roo*" (our father is gone), while women with multicolored goat's hair from their *dwars* tied around their necks trilled, "*Li-li-li. Li-li-li,*" from their tongues to the back of their throats. As Cica's chariot passed, a concert of deep howling wails rose in agonized symphony up to the heavens.

When the procession reached the city center, the Bears lowered their weapons, and the women stopped their wails to chant hauntingly to the rippling tones of the tanbur strings. But the pain was over for Cica; his bones would later be laid to rest with his ancestors in a stone tomb carved into Mount Alvand.

Chapter 4

Alone that night after the children had gone to bed and the servants had retired, Shamin took the scroll out of Cicataxma's army bag and read:

My darling Shamin,

I write trusting that you and the children are in good health and spirits. As the advance regiment, we moved out from our base by the city of Medaktoo along village-dotted roads toward the Gehwar region, passing Mount Behishtan and the southern part of the Mahi-Dasht plain. After taking a few weeks to travel from Gahvareh to the Rajaw district, we built a strong wall at the front line on the other side of Mount Dalaho to stop the Athorayan forces. When the enemy retreated, I marched my men across the Sirwan River near Sherwaina toward Arrapkha.

Stationed there, we awaited the Shahan Shah's orders. Apparently, this abundant land is not so cold in winter as our mountains. The fruit trees and vines are heavy with figs and grapes, ripening fields of grain wave in the warm breeze, and fat cattle, sheep, and goats graze contentedly. I wish so much that you were here. Perhaps one day we will take a trip to these western lands of Ariavarta, and even venture further west to the Land of Karda once we have won it back from the Athorayans.

We are very close to the border of our present territories; this letter might be the last I send before we return.

I miss you every moment.

Forever your husband,

Cicataxma

Shamin put the letter back in Cicataxma's bag, grabbed her cloak, and raced out the front door of her home, her unshod feet pounding the cobblestones. When she reached the golden gate, the half-moon hung over distant Mount Alvand.

"Cicaaaaa," she cried, her scream ringing out across the city. But there was no reply. Through her tears, the opaque moon seemed to quiver above the silent landscape. Utterly wretched, she collapsed in a sobbing heap onto the cold stones.

In the weeks following Cica's death, Shamin and Vashti took long rides through the tall, silky grasses and blossoming wild almond trees of the high summer mountains, admiring the last of green crowned, red-frilled inverted tulips and glimpsing the occasional cheetah on the trail of alpine sheep. As they lunched one day on a rocky outcrop, a cool breeze coming up the valley below sent Shamin shivering.

"What is it, Mother?" Vashti asked, wrapping some cheese and walnuts in a piece of bread.

"Ferhad is continuing his military training under General Biraxeas," she answered flatly. "Your father was so delighted to have a son…and now he is preparing for battles. I fear he too will leave and not come back alive."

"Do not worry, Mother. We have peace now," Vashti assured her although they both knew war could break out any time.

“And Cica thought your birth was very special too, even a sign,” Shamin continued wistfully. Vashti smiled, remembering her father’s pride in General Biraxeas’ prediction that she would ride and hunt not only on Mount Alvand, but in other lands.

“Once you were walking, it was hard to keep you inside when you heard horses’ hooves,” Shamin went on. “You would run out looking for Cica. When he finally came, you would put your arms up to be lifted onto his horse. And whenever he left, you would ask to go with him.”

“‘Soon, Vashti girl, one day soon,’ he would say,” Vashti recalled sadly. “It seems like only yesterday that he spoke to me.” Gazing at the distant rows of mountain ranges piled on top of each other, she breathed in deeply. “I must resume my cavalry and archery training.”

Shamin sighed. “Yes, Cica’s appointment of Scythians loyal to the Shahan Shah has improved the Bears’ archery on horseback considerably. But now Ferhad wants to succeed his father as general of the Bears, and you are learning the art of war…” Shamin’s voice trembled and trailed off. Blinking back tears, Vashti reached over and hugged her mother.

Nothing seemed to take away the pain of Cica’s loss.

One day months later, when summer had been swept away by bitterly cold winds, and Debyar was teaching the children about their forbears, Vashti asked how Nefertiti of the Mitanni became Shahjin of Egypt. Debyar smiled and patted her oldest pupil’s head.

“A long time ago, after the Hittites destroyed the Amorites in Babylon and captured Babylon itself, the Mitanni came to power in the area west of Nineveh,” she replied.

“Who were the Hittites?” Ferhad asked.

“They were a powerful nation who lived west of the region of the Hurrians, a people of several city states in the region of the Mountains of Tur north of Carchemish, extending to the country of Namar around Lake Chauon. The Mitanni succeeded them before the rise of our Median dynasty. We are related to them."

"Did they live east of Lydia?" Ferhad queried.

"Yes. Good guess, dear," Debyar enthused.

"Why were the Amorites destroyed?" Vashti asked.

Debyar hesitated, wondering if she should tell the awful truth. "All nations that commit *druj* eventually fall," she answered, grimacing. "The Amorites were no different. They sacrificed their babies and sometimes older people to their gods."

"Why?" Khezmet, who had been listening carefully, gasped.

"They thought it would make their crops grow and bring them riches and that they would avoid punishment for offending their gods."

"That is not our way," Vashti insisted, hugging and kissing Parwin, whose face had fallen in horror.

"Yes," Ferhad chimed in. "Cica told me about the ugly gods of stone and wood he saw in Ashur. But we follow the light of Auramazda," he added with wisdom beyond his age.

"Sadly, when the Hittite empire grew," Debyar continued, "the Mitanni became afraid of them and ran away. They built forts all the way down to Egypt, who had become their friend. Eventually, many Mitanni were driven into Egypt by the Hittites and the Athorayans. But some stayed here and in the land of the Parsu."

"That explains why Nefertiti was in Egypt," Vashti commented. "Did she really teach the Egyptians to worship one god only?"

"It's hard to be sure, dear, but we think so," Debyar replied.

"I wonder what she looked like," Vashti pondered.

"Perhaps…" Debyar smiled cheekily at Vashti. "Perhaps… like you," she ventured, and all the children laughed. But Vashti couldn't imagine how her angular jawline, pronounced chin, high cheekbones, and fine, straight nose could be likened to those of a shahjin or even seen as beautiful.

When the merriment had stopped, the teacher's smile faded. "Now we must talk about *asha* and *druj*," she continued, and the mood suddenly became solemn.

"What is *druj*?" Ferhad asked.

"*Druj*," replied the teacher, "means double-faced. You are behaving like a good person on the outside and everybody trusts you, but on the inside, you are thinking like a bad person who cannot be trusted."

"And then you will probably do bad things," Khezmet interjected, "like the Scythians did to my father." All the children nodded.

"What is the most important lesson Prophet Zarathrustra taught?" Debyar asked.

"Follow *asha* with good thoughts, good words, and good deeds," the children chorused.

"Correct," the teacher enthused. "Which bad things come from *druj*?"

"Disobeying parents," Vashti volunteered.

"Killing people," Ferhad answered, "unless in self-defense."

"Hurting mothers and children and other people who need protection," Khezmet added.

"What about stealing or taking things that are not yours?" Debyar asked. The children nodded again. "Shahan Shah Daia-okku followed *asha*, that is why his people loved him, and he was strong enough to establish Media," she continued.

"Tell us about him," Vashti urged.

"About ninety years ago, Chief Daia-okku brought all the tribes from this mountain region together in a council."

"What were their names?" Ferhad asked.

"Much the same as now," Debyar replied, holding up a parchment sketch of the lands and pointing to the tribal areas within the Median triangle. "The Pareteceni were from Aspadana to the southeast, the Arizanti lived nearby in Kashan, and the Budii and

Struchates occupied villages between here, Aspadana and Rhagae, from where the Magi tribe brought their fire altars. The Busae tribe still lives around our city, which they named Hagmatana, 'the gathering place.'"

"How did the tribal chiefs make decisions?" Ferhad asked.

"They gathered all the people before them and asked what was important to them. When the people had decided, they were represented by elders of their tribes, all of whom met in Hagmatana to choose the Shahan Shah."

"Then everyone could say what they wanted," Parwin commented.

"Exactly dear," Debyar replied.

"Were the magi priests the first to use fire altars?" Vashti asked, changing the subject.

"We think the Saka to our northeast taught the people of Ariavarta about the essences of earth, air, fire, and water. Then they informed the priests of the Magi," Debyar answered.

Vashti's brow creased in thought. "Was that the way of Prophet Zarathrustra?"

"Again, we can't be sure because many of the scrolls and tablets recording his words were destroyed by our enemies, but we know he gained wisdom by observing the natural world," Debyar replied.

"Tell us about Grandfather Kshathrita," Ferhad requested.

"After rising from village chief of Kar Kashi to leader of our tribes, he tried to end the war between us and the Cimmerians in the northwest by making a treaty with them to fight our common enemy, Athoraya," Debyar explained.

"Did he succeed?" Vashti asked.

Debyar nodded. "Before dying in battle fighting Shah Ashur-uballit the First of Athoraya, he subjected the Parsu to the south and the Parthavans to the east and defended us from the Scythians, who took control of Media about twenty-five years ago."

Ferhad whistled in admiration. "Grandfather Kshathrita was just as brave as Uncle Hovakhshatra."

The other children agreed and Parwin yawned.

Debyar looked around at her attentive pupils. "Time to run in the courtyard before lunch," she announced. "Then Gulah has prepared a large pot of *terkhena* for the midday meal."

A few days later, lessons were interrupted by the clack of animal hooves in the courtyard where weary drivers led heavily laden donkeys and camels toward the treasury. The children crowded around the window trying to get a glimpse of the long train.

"It is the rest of our share of the plunder from Athoraya," Debyar told them. "Nineveh was around three hundred and fifty stade square, so it gave us much more than the temples of Ashur."

"What will the Shahan Shah do with all this wealth?" Vashti asked, wondering why taking plunder was not *druj*.

"The Magush says he will build masonry and brick works to improve housing for city dwellers and permanent shops at the marketplace," Debyar explained.

"What about the farmers?" Khezmet, whose brother grew crops of lentils and ceci peas, a new crop recently brought from western Athoraya, wanted to know.

"More canals will be built from the river and the springs to supply extra water for food production."

"General Biraxeas says the Babylonians continue the fight against the rest of the Athorayans," Ferhad announced. "They are campaigning against Shah Ashur-uballit in Harran. Mother, how long before I can go into battle with the army?"

Noticing Shamin's bottom lip quiver in dismay, Vashti decided to distract her with Daro's story about the travels west to Nineveh of his friend in the Shahan Shah's Guard.

"Excellent idea," Debyar enthused. "We will draw it as though we are birds, flying high above the countryside." Reaching for a large sheet of reed parchment and some finely honed charcoal sticks, she began to sketch little mountain peaks and parallel lines for rivers. Vashti closed her eyes to recall. While she described the troops' journey from Mount Alvand through bear-, tiger-, and wolf-infested country and past Piree Magroon Mountain of the Magi, the girls drew houses, wells, gardens, and other settlement symbols on the map; and Ferhad represented the army with little shields. When the drawing was complete, the children surveyed their work with satisfaction.

"General Biraxeas told me he went another way with the chariots," Ferhad volunteered. "After he found shallow river crossings, the scythes were attached to them."

"Another of our secret weapons," Vashti commented. "Besides exacting tribute, how will Uncle Hovakhshatra make sure the Athorayans will not rise up against us again?"

Debyar smiled approvingly. "Vashti thinks with foresight about the future," she told Shamin. "Our Gutian ancestors fought to protect us in the mountains. Now we will do so on our ancestral Mitanni lowlands we have taken back from Athoraya," she replied.

"I think Uncle Hovakhshatra has a big hole under the palace to store all the gold and silver, but he just throws the bronze away," Parwin remarked, and everyone laughed. Everyone except Shamin, who found she could no longer enjoy anything.

"Why such a perplexed face?" Khezmet asked Vashti a few days later upon finding her mistress looking worried again.

"Shamin is not well. I sometimes hear her crying at night. She looks after us, but she is always sad."

"Yes, and she is quite thin. Have you asked Gulah about this illness? She knows of foods to make sick people better."

"She has been feeding Shamin *danola* but thinks we should

consult the Magush. He is experienced in all the healing arts."

"Nothing can take the place of Cicataxma," Shamin replied disconsolately when Vashti suggested the idea later.

"True, but Mother, you must get well. We children don't want to lose you too," Vashti implored.

Shamin sighed, her kindly brow wrinkling below her dull brown headscarf. "Then we will visit the Atashkedah temple tomorrow."

A chilly breeze blew, and the winter sun shone weakly as mother and daughter walked the length of the palace to the Atashkedah. As they drew closer, Shamin slowed her pace.

"What is it?" Vashti asked.

"Cica and I came here regularly to seek the wisdom of the Magush before you were born," she reminisced sadly. "The priest never told me that…" Her voice broke off.

"Dear Mother, believe that you will be healed through the words of the Magush," Vashti pleaded. Shamin nodded but did not reply.

After bowing homage to the fire burning in a shallow stone pit beneath the arched entrance to the Atashkedah, Vashti left Shamin with the Magush in a room smelling strongly of musk and cloves.

Outside in the wintry sunshine, she took her kusti beads from her sash and prayed. Her pleas were answered when Shamin emerged a little later, her face peaceful.

"I am ready to return now," she informed Vashti calmly, "to whatever else awaits us."

With a sigh of relief, Vashti hugged her mother's comforting frame, took her arm, and led the way back to their home.

But an iron band of grief still gripped her own heart.

Chapter 5

Khezmet bustled into Vashti's room carrying a ream of creamy linen cloth and asked if she liked it. "Yes, but I do not need any more robes," Vashti replied firmly.

"It's for me, dear," Khezmet explained. "My mother spent all her silver…I am getting married."

Vashti flung her arms around her maid and kissed both her cheeks. "Is the husband to be Daro?"

"Yes," Khezmet admitted shyly.

"So that's what you two were doing when I saw you at the—" She stopped, remembering the fateful day she learned of Cica's death. "When is the wedding?"

"The month of Serxwerban."

"Then we have plenty of time to get ready. I think the color is a little dull, but you will also need a cloak, a sash, and a headdress."

"And I already have a necklace," Khezmet exclaimed, pulling a fine silver chain with little discs on it from underneath her scarf.

"Such a well-kept secret, dear!" Vashti exclaimed, vowing privately not to let marriage get in the way of her army training to ultimately avenge her father's death.

"Yes. Daro didn't want anyone to know in case Ishtovigo found out. The Shahan Shah's third son does not like him," Khezmet replied warily.

"Don't worry about my cranky cousin. I will not allow him or anyone to mar my beloved maid's happiness," Vashti assured her.

Having taken Vashti's mind off whatever was bothering her, Khezmet hugged her and was rewarded with a kiss.

"Special delivery for you from the palace," Khezmet announced later that morning after lessons had finished, handing Vashti a silk-wrapped parcel.

"Who sent it?" Ferhad asked mischievously, leaning over the parcel. "Shawish or…Ishtovigo?"

Vashti blushed as she unwrapped the parcel to reveal an intricate mosaic of a young woman on a horse poised to shoot an arrow. The chestnut horse was unmistakably Nzdar in full stride, and the rider was clearly herself in her hunting *chokha* and *pantol*.

"Ohhh, your eyes are so green," Parwin cried. A delicately embossed parchment note fell on the floor, and Vashti snatched it up. It read:

Dear Vashti,

It's been so long since we have seen each other. I've heard you've been training. Let's practice archery together as soon as your mourning is over.

Your faithful,

Ishtovigo

"What does the note say?" Ferhad wanted to know.

"It's just for me, little brother." Vashti smiled.

"We will ask one of the palace attendants to hang the mosaic after Cica's official entombment next week," Shamin offered. Vashti nodded but her face quickly crumpled, and she burst into tears.

"Dear, whatever is wrong, don't you like the picture?" Shamin asked. Vashti could only shake her head between sniffles. "Bring some chai, Khezmet," Shamin ordered. "Daughter, come out into the sunshine, and we will talk."

Outside, the pair seated themselves on the stone bench under the now-bare oak tree. Drawing their cloaks about them against the cold, they sat until Shamin broke the silence. "You've been as strong as a marble pillar, dear," she said, patting Vashti's hand, "but you don't have to attend Cica's burial. Khezmet will keep you company while we are away."

"No, Mother. I will come to my dear Cica's farewell. But…now it is I who needs to know the message the Magush gave you that day at the Atashkedah."

Shamin hesitated. "The Magush told me that Cica's *fravashi* gave him his *urvan* to help him fight the battle for *asha* against *druj*. Four days after his death, his *urvan* returned to his *fravashi*, which now aids us in that battle," she explained. "He said we will see Cica again in the Frashokeriti."

"Every day is too long to wait to see Father again," Vashti cried, her tears falling quickly. "But I will fight to keep us safe like he did."

Shamin shuddered at the thought of her eldest daughter going off to war, but she put her arm around Vashti and squeezed her hand. "May peace continue to rule," she breathed.

Six months after Cica's funeral, the chariot bearing his remains drew to a halt in front of a tomb cut into the side of Mount Alvand. The gaping hole of the entrance guarded either side by pillars with scrolled capitals was no comfort to Vashti until she noticed the multi-winged *faravahar* sculpted above.

Guarded closely by Harpagos, the Shahan Shah and Shahjin arrived with their family and greeted Shamin and the children as they alighted from their carriage. Cicataxma's Busae tribal chiefs and extended family lined one side of the tomb, and the generals and the Shahan Shah's chief advisors flanked the other. A lone piper's plaintive tune interrupted the silence as her father's silver bear-embossed ossuary was carefully placed inside the tomb above carvings of an Atashkedah fire urn attended by two harp-bearing magi.

As a singer began the mournful song of parting, Vashti looked up into the deep blue sky, and her heart lifted. Despite her sadness, at last she too felt ready for whatever the future would bring.

But glancing down, she caught the eye of Ishtovigo watching her intently.

"Mother, I am going to the palace after lessons today," Vashti informed Shamin a week later. "Ishtovigo has invited me to view his treasure collection."

"I've heard his personal artifacts are impressive," Shamin replied. "Ardela says he enjoys them much more than army training."

Vashti frowned. "Debyar told us Media is second only to Babylonia in power now. We must be ready to defend our position in the region."

"She has taught you well, dear," Shamin declared, kissing her daughter on the forehead. "Go to the palace with my blessing."

After lessons, Vashti felt strangely nervous as Khezmet tied the sash beneath the silver beaded vest complimenting her blue silk robe.

"I have never seen these before," her maid remarked, clasping a string of jade gemstones around Vashti's neck.

"Shamin has lent them to me. They were a gift from Father, but she gave me this brooch," she explained, handing Khezmet the matching jewelry to fasten the folds of her robe.

"You need a little more glow on your face," Khezmet advised, rubbing rose oil into her mistress's sculpted cheekbones. "And some color on your eyelids to make your eyes look bigger," she added, dipping a feather brush into malachite green powder on a colorfully embossed palette.

"Dear, this is not a state occasion," Vashti protested. "And please don't make my lips any fuller or I'll look like a Mossala priestess."

Khezmet sighed and put down the red lipstick she was holding. "One more thing," she insisted, picking up a blue hare's pelt *sarwain* with silver discs suspended and fitting it snugly on Vashti's head. "You are ready now," she declared.

Just then, Shamin walked in and smiled approval. "I think I hear a knock on the door," she announced, her eyes dancing with anticipation.

Ishtovigo was waiting outside and stepped back when Vashti appeared, shifting his head to one side admiringly. Khezmet followed, linking arms with the tall form of Daro, who had also been waiting, but for her, and tousling his unruly hair.

"Meet me at the palace at the sixth hour," Vashti reminded her maid as the two disappeared around the corner of the stables to plan their wedding.

"Good evening. You are looking as serene as the Caspian Sea, dear cousin," Ishtovigo greeted.

"I trust you will provide me with nothing less," Vashti replied jauntily.

"Than the Caspian Sea or a good evening?"

"Both," was the emphatic reply.

"Even though I am the son of a shah of the world's strongest alliance," he boasted, "that is a big request, but not for a man of my stature. Maybe we will visit Caspian one day."

❖

At the entrance to the palace, the couple sprinkled themselves with rosewater offered by a servant. Ishtovigo then led the way to a long hall lined with twenty marble columns on each side.

"Father has enlarged the Audience Hall to accommodate foreign emissaries and their entourages from Cappadocia in the west and east as far as Bactria, bringing tribute of gold and silver vessels, vases, weapons, woven fabrics, jewelry, and animals," he explained. "Urartu to the north and Parsua to the south also send representatives."

Vashti acknowledged the Shahan Shah's ingenuity and ran her fingers down the smooth cream, gray, and sandy-colored columns. "Where did these come from?" she asked.

"Some from as far away as Lydia, but most are from our own quarries. Come see the shahdom's collection," he urged. "It's much more impressive than these lumps of stone." As he led the way past small anterooms, the flicker of a flame in one of the chambers caught her eye.

"What's in there?" she asked.

"It's Father's and Mother's worship room," he replied. "They come here if they are too busy to go to the Atashkedah." Vashti stepped into the small, white-washed room lined by shelves littered with parchment scrolls. Luxuriously thick cushions occupied each corner.

"Father comes here every day to read the Avesta," Ishtovigo continued. "He probably wants to get away from all those people asking him questions and telling him things."

"Do you come here every day too?" she asked.

"No" was the quick reply. "Once a week with Father, Mother, and little sister Shelna is enough," he stated emphatically. She wondered why but thought it best not to ask. "How much of this is your own collection?" she inquired after they had entered a gold-trimmed, pink-washed gallery displaying fine ceramics and statues acquired from Nineveh.

"Only the cream, buff, and light red ceramic pieces tempered with gold or silver mica," he replied. "The rest is kept near my quarters.

The two sculpted men represent our grandfather Kshathrita and our great-grandfather Daia-okku."

"You don't look like either."

"No. I'm like my mother."

"She's a fine-looking lady."

"So I'm beautiful, am I?"

"No. You're…" Vashti surveyed her host's high cheekbones, pointed chin, and dark, deep-set eyes. "Different."

"That could mean anything."

"You have your mother's traditional Ariavartan looks, only in a manly way," Vashti finally conceded.

Ishtovigo smiled. "Your generous words surprise me," he quipped, flashing another of his winning smiles. Not to be further distracted by his handsomeness, she admired a lifelike mosaic portrait of the Shahan Shah, hung between the sculptures of his ancestors, for which Ishtovigo took credit.

"The cobalt-blue tint for the tiles comes from Egypt," he explained. "And we have mines nearby supplying the iron and copper dust to make yellow and bluish green. "But there is something special from Bactria you must see," he added, leading the way to a small chamber beside his quarters. "The Bactrians claim these parchments traveled a long way from a land far to the east. The writing is even more peculiar than the hieroglyphs of the Egyptians." He unrolled several oversized scrolls of pictographs beneath drawings of temples with their roofs curled up on the edges and a strange black-and-white bear.

"This is a very different country," Vashti commented. "The women wear long *chokhas* over their robes, but they must not ride as I cannot see any pictures of them on horses."

"That's so their husbands can restrict them to domestic duties," Ishtovigo replied, but she wasn't sure whether he was joking or not. "The shadows are drawing on, and the dinner hour is approaching," he continued nonchalantly, glancing out the window to the sundial in the courtyard. "Let us prepare."

In the women's quarters of the palace, Khezmet rearranged Vashti's hair around her *sarwain* and refreshed her perfumed oil. "Do you have any court gossip?" her maid inquired.

"Shh, dear. Shamin has told me the Shahan Shah has ordered strict secrecy to prevent infiltration by spies. General Harpagos and the rest of the guard must inspect all visitors and their entourages no matter how high their position."

"So, he was the redheaded soldier who questioned me at the palace servants' entrance," Khezmet remarked.

"Yes, I don't know much about him, but he has risen quickly in the Shahan Shah's favor," Vashti replied, "I suspect he is a Busae tribe member with outstanding military prowess and a reputation for trustworthiness."

She was soon to confirm Harpagos' permanent position in the leading couple's guard when he later opened the door to the official dining room for her and Ishtovigo. "The other diners are already present," he stated solemnly, indicating she should sit with Ishtovigo and his two older brothers, Shawish and Artaspaya, on cushions around a low-carved Lebanese cedarwood table.

Shawish smiled broadly at her. "Welcome, cousin. I appreciate your presence with us this evening. I trust my brother has been showing you the best of our treasure collection."

"He has. Thank you. I particularly enjoyed the Far East exhibition," she replied. "Their civilization seems very different to ours." Privately, she thought the Shahan Shah and Shahjin should send an emissary to such a rich and complex shahdom, but an official was announcing their arrival. Everyone stood as Hovakhshatra and Ardela entered, followed by Harpagos and their cupbearer. As they sat down, Ishtovigo winked at her from the other side of the table, and she replied with only a polite smile.

Finding herself seated next to Shawish, Vashti asked him about his experiences at Nineveh with her father's regiment while servants brought in courses of roast venison, herbed millet, fresh sprouted greens, fine wheat bread, and a range of sauces. The cupbearer safely tasted the leading couple's food then everyone else placed their meal on the plates assigned them. When Shawish received only one dish less than the Shahan Shah, Ishtovigo grunted his displeasure.

The dinner conversation began with the availability of horse rugs from nearby provinces and shifted to the need to root out the last of the Athorayan resistance in northern Mesopotamia, Urartu, and Asia Minor east of the Halys River.

"We are almost ready," Shawish commented. "A few more weeks of our best Scythian archers teaching General Biraxeas' regiment their special technique of firing backwards while riding uphill should complete the Bears' weapons training. Then some camps in the mountains should bring them to peak condition."

"But why the mountains?" Artaspaya asked. "Harran, where we will soon join the Babylonians for an assault on the remaining Athorayan forces, is on the plains."

"The mountains have always been our friends. We must be ready to defend them," Shawish replied. "But General Taxmaspada's lancers will also be preparing to fight on flat, open spaces."

"You are both right, my sons," the Shahan Shah concurred. "The Babylonians have asked for our assistance, and we are bound by the alliance to help them. However, we must also attend to some domestic matters while keeping the borders of our territories to the north and east secure."

"Which domestic matters, Uncle?" Vashti asked.

"More metalwork foundries for making agricultural implements and transport and military equipment."

"They will help us hold the territories won from Athoraya and Mannaea," Artaspaya, the more talkative second son, explained.

"Is your mother willing to allow your brother Ferhad to join his father's regiment for more advanced training?" Hovakhshatra asked Vashti.

"Shamin knows that Ferhad wants only to become a member of the Bears, but it's too soon after Cica's death. I will ask her to consult with you on this matter if you wish," she replied, and the Shahan Shah nodded.

"Ferhad seems to have a very straight eye with the bow and arrow," Artaspaya remarked.

"So the generals have observed," Hovakhshatra replied.

"Dear, too many of our women are getting sick or dying after childbirth," Ardela interrupted. "We won't have enough future troops if this goes on. What can be done about this pressing problem?"

"I will ask the Magush," her husband replied.

"Shouldn't the midwives be consulted?" Vashti suggested.

"Excellent idea. Just as we use our military experts, so we must use our learned civilians to protect our people, especially those most exposed to possible harm. I will make sure the Magush asks the midwives about the best care for our mothers," Hovakhshatra replied.

"Well said, most wise Shahan Shah," Ardela commented with satisfaction and a wink at Vashti.

When everyone had finished eating, keen to find out about Khezmet's wedding plans, Vashti wiped her hands on her napkin, thanked her hosts, and asked permission to leave, whereupon Ishtovigo suggested they go hunting the next day.

"Don't you have archery training tomorrow?" Shawish reminded him.

"Not if I have other official business," Ishtovigo replied testily.

"As your elder, I insist you fulfill your military duty," Shawish maintained. Ishtovigo scowled, turned suddenly, and raised his fist to his brother. Instantly, Harpagos leaned over, caught the wayward arm, apologized to the Shahan Shah and Shahjin, and marched their offending son out.

"Put him under house arrest," Hovakhshatra called out. "We will deal with him tomorrow." Ardela opened her mouth to protest but closed it quickly at her husband's raised eyebrows. Her only weapon of response was a frown.

Hovakhshatra abruptly dismissed all the guests. Led by Vashti, they rose and slipped quietly away.

Chapter 6

A few days after the upset in the palace, the postal rider from the city of Babylon arrived with a letter for Vashti from her cousin Amytis. When they were young girls, Amytis had told her about a dream she had of marrying a powerful soldier from the west. The dream came true several years later when Amytis' betrothal to Nebuchadnezzar, heir to the throne of Babylonia, sealed Media's treaty with his father, Shah Nabopolassar of Babylonia. Although her cousin accepted the arrangement without complaint, Vashti could not forget the day she was driven away in a silver-plated iron carriage with her retinue, bound for her new home in the strange city of Babylon. The sight of Amytis waving her green, yellow, and red scarf to her weeping family as her vehicle bearing the banner of Kawa passed through the golden gateway still haunted her. So did Amytis' letters from Babylon revealing her homesickness until she wrote that Nebuchadnezzar had ordered his engineers to build a mountain-like structure from which to suspend gardens like those adorning the palace in Hagmatana.

"They are a little piece of home, and I spend much of my time there when I'm not learning how to behave in this foreign court," Amytis had written.

"Her maids were courageous too. Their love for Amytis meant they would follow her to a distant land," Khezmet remarked when Vashti told her the story.

"Would you follow me to another shahdom?" Vashti had asked without really thinking about the implications of her question.

"Of course, even if you become Shahjin of a faraway land."

Vashti shrugged. "The only rule I want is over enemy forces," she had declared.

Breaking the seal of the lion on the scroll of Amytis' latest letter, she read:

My darling Vashti,

Spring is here and once again the dust from date palm flowers is making me sneeze terribly! The warmer weather has made it easier for several thousand Babylonian soldiers to travel west for military exercises in the desert. I sometimes wonder if Nebuchadnezzar considers the impracticalities of so many men and animals trying to survive the fierce heat of summer in such a harsh place.

However, since our Median forces aided the Babylonian victory over the Athorayans at Harran, Shah Nabopolassar has switched his campaign to Urartu. Apparently, he left recently for the mountains. Nebuchadnezzar has since become worried about Egypt aligning with the remaining Athorayans…

Vashti gasped. Urartu was on Media's northern border! Was Amytis' message code for a possible threat to her homeland? Nebuchadnezzar was becoming known for his irrational fear of anyone, such as the Scythians, he considered an enemy; but Babylonia also could benefit from Urartu's verdant, river-fed land which the Medes wished to protect. Plus, Amytis seemed disturbed.

"Ask the palace guard to summon General Harpagos immediately," she told Khezmet.

Her maid raced out the door and soon returned with the flame-haired young general, brandishing his dagger. "Where is the threat?" he demanded.

"Not here," Vashti replied as Harpagos vanished into the kitchen to the screams of Gulah.

"Where then?" he yelled.

"Amytis has written something I think important," Vashti explained calmly. "The Shahan Shah and Shahjin should be informed." Harpagos glanced at the letter, quickly bade Vashti and Khezmet goodbye, and rushed out. "I can see why he's known for his efficiency," Vashti remarked, and they both burst out laughing.

In the palace, with Ardela busy in the city making sure war widows and orphans were being looked after by their families, Hovakhshatra read the letter passively.

"Reply to Vashti that I am not concerned," he told Harpagos. "Our forces are still in the mountains and will always be ready to defend our territories. Nebuchadnezzar will soon be busy contending with Pharoah Necho, who is moving his army northwards into Sham. General Taxmaspada, who is stationed near the land of the Hapiru exiled to our cities by the Athorayan, has sent word that Necho is trying to fill the void in the region left by the Athorayans, but I do not think he will succeed."

Harpagos nodded and exited as quickly as he had entered to be met by Shawish, dressed in battle armor. "Father, I wish to marry Vashti," he blurted without even bidding his sovereign good morning. "As your eldest son and heir, I seek your permission in the absence of her father," he added breathlessly.

Hovakhshatra surveyed his firstborn. Tall and thickset, Shawish's fair hair tumbling down his shoulders resembled the locks of the wild but now loyal Scythians who had trained him. Was Vashti a match for him? She was steady and straight, not only with the bow and arrow but with everyone. However, she was still young and had much to learn. The Shahan Shah cleared his throat.

"Son, wait a while," he advised then hesitated. "It was hard seeing my daughter leave for Babylonia and marriage, but she did so willingly to protect our people. We are at peace now. Let us concentrate on rebuilding the army before attending to civil matters such as marriage."

Shawish's eyes flickered impatiently. "Yes, Father, but at least tell Ishtovigo to stay away from Vashti. He has no right to her," he implored. "I love her, and as a member of the family, she is first in line to be my wife."

"I will speak to him," Hovakhshatra promised, "but you know your brother is not inclined to listen."

"True, Father. Auramazda willing, he will never have the throne of Media," Shawish replied fervently. Hovakhshatra grunted his reply, and Shawish turned on his heel and marched out.

The next night, Vashti awoke with a start from a dream about an attack on a city with a huge, colonnaded temple. The city wasn't Hagmatana, Nineveh was already destroyed, and from what Debyar had told her about her hometown of Rhagae, it did not have such a grand temple.

Perhaps Amytis will know, she thought. I will reply to her letter and ask.

Rising early, she wrote:

Dearest cousin,

Even though it was years ago, I am still sorry we could not attend your wedding due to the war. I do so miss you and am forever grateful for your sacrifice for us.

All praise to you for adapting to your life in Babylon so courageously. What is it like being the future Shahjin of Babylonia? Do you have to sit demurely for endless hours receiving the women of the court and the provinces? Whatever your duties, I know you will always perform them with the service of our people in your heart.

Since Father Cicataxma fell at Nineveh, I have been training with the army even though your father might object to my ambition to join the Bears. But I am determined and getting stronger every day.

Ishtovigo is his usual self, pestering me to go hunting with him when he isn't creating artworks. Your dear brothers, Shawish and Artaspaya are busy rebuilding the standing army with Harpagos, the new general of the Bears, who are still our number one army regiment.

My dear, I had a dream that an unknown city with a temple very different to ours was being attacked. Do you know which city it might be? Please reply soon and tell me what you think the dream might mean. I still find it hard to trust the Magush's interpretations.

Remember, if your husband should be lost on one of his military campaigns, you must return to us. We could never leave you in the strange land of Babylonia.

May your yazatas watch over you and keep you safe.

All my love,
Vashti

Chapter 7

Khezmet set down Vashti's chai on her bedside table and turned to leave, but not before Vashti noticed her maid's red-rimmed eyes and asked why she had been crying. Khezmet sat down on the end of Vashti's bed and stared out the window, her lip trembling.

"Daro's family want to delay the wedding," she replied despondently. "I don't think they will accept me into their family."

"How stupid," Vashti replied indignantly. "Forget them. You can stay with me."

"But, dear, I love Daro—"

"And you don't love me?" Vashti shot back with a little grin.

Khezmet looked pained. "I do but—"

"You want to have a family?"

"Yes, and one day you will too…perhaps with Ishtovigo. He seems to very much appreciate your company."

Vashti took a deep breath. "Not with him…He's too irresponsible and doesn't really care about Media. Besides, Shawish will be first to marry, probably someone from our cousins in Parsua. All I want is to be ready to defend our lands."

"But we have the strongest ally in the region."

"For now, but alliances can change."

Khezmet frowned. "According to stable gossip from Daro, Shawish likes you, and he's often on the target range. Maybe you should spend more time there yourself if you want to be a warrior?"

"I'm interested in training, not courting," Vashti replied firmly. "Especially since Babylonia will likely be led by Nebuchadnezzar, who keeps trying to expand his territories. If he threatens ours, we will need to be fully prepared." She took another deep breath. "Where does Daro's family live? I will visit them to find out why they do not think my maid is good enough for their son."

Khezmet waved her hand in protest. "Oh, please no, dear. That might make matters worse."

'Do you think I can't persuade them?" came Vashti's determined reply.

"No, but…please let me talk to Daro again," Khezmet pleaded.

"Not until I have gone to the city. Stay here. I will take one of the Shahan Shah's guards with me." Khezmet shook her head in consternation. But her mistress had decided, and it was no use trying to stop her.

"The Shahan Shah's other guards are busy with the army," the palace door guard replied to Vashti's request for an escort. "But he is sending General Harpagos."

Vashti sighed. She was hoping for a relaxed ride down the citadel hill instead of being accompanied by the equivalent of a crouching tiger ready to pounce. "And my knife is enough protection," she reasoned. "Nevertheless, I must follow Uncle Hovakhshatra's orders. Not all the people in the city can be trusted."

Halfway down the hill, Harpagos broke the silence. "Ishtovigo wanted to accompany you, but the Shahan Shah refused. Do you know why?" Vashti shrugged, although from the rumor Khezmet had heard, she could guess. "He is not for you," Harpagos stated bluntly. She looked away and nodded agreement. "The Shahan Shah is planning a strong future for Media," he added, staring straight ahead.

"So am I," she replied firmly, lifting her head. It wasn't that the men were not capable of defending her nation, it was more the frustration of knowing that as a woman there would be barriers to her joining the army. But if she did marry and have children, the palace would become a village, with their grandmothers, aunts, and Khezmet delighted to raise them in her absence even though some of the men would insist she put motherhood before the defense of Media. The pride of men who believed that their archery, lance, battle-ax, slingshot, and dagger skills were superior would keep her from the battlefield.

Her meeting with Daro's family was a big success. They accepted her offer of a wedding on the city common below the citadel, to which both families would be invited, but which Harpagos protested, claiming there would be too many people of unknown allegiance close to the citadel. Vashti replied firmly that Harpagos would have to use the army as well as the Shahan Shah's special guard and promised to speak to her aunt and uncle about it.

When she asked Harpagos if she could approach the Shahan Shah a few days later, Hovakhshatra and Ardela were deep in conversation with their advisors on the city expansion plans, which a scribe was recording on wax-covered wooden boards with a reed stylus. A circle of men and women were sitting cross-legged on brightly embroidered cushions surrounding a large sheet of reed parchment on which the city streets had been outlined.

After Harpagos cautiously interrupted his sovereigns on Vashti's behalf, Hovakhshatra and Ardela halted the meeting and told him to invite her to the next chamber. A few minutes later, Vashti appeared in the hallway grinning after receiving permission to hold the wedding at the chosen site.

"I will order some of our cooks to assist," Ardela promised as her niece passed Harpagos, who shook his head.

"Don't worry, dear friend," she assured him. "We will all be safe and happy."

As she waited for the carriage her mistress had ordered for her wedding day, Khezmet arranged the sash on the blue, scarlet, and bright yellow silk robe Vashti had given her, claiming the cream linen did not befit her maid. In the early spring sunshine outside, the clip-clop of horses' hooves announced the arrival of the groom. Vashti led her maid out, and they both climbed into the carriage to be greeted by an excited Daro in black *chokha* and *pantol*, a multicolored sash, and a black *kulaw-u-dastmal* fringed in fuller's white. The smile animating his face lit up his wide brown eyes and beamed the happiness of the day as he proudly flicked his dark wavy hair against the fringe. As the carriage creaked into motion, other hooves followed. Vashti turned round to see Shawish and Harpagos resplendent in official costume, their gold necklaces, bracelets, and earrings flashing in the sunlight. When they raised their crowned felt hats, Vashti smiled and squeezed Khezmet's hand.

"It's going to be a perfect day," she declared as her maid blinked away happy tears.

Down at the city park, many more than the bride's and groom's families had come to celebrate their union. True to her word, Ardela had supplied baskets of bread, walnuts, cheeses, and dried figs for the crowds. Seated on picnic rugs scattered across the park, the guests and their friends feasted. But soon the park was ringed by dancers stepping to the melody of *shimshal* pipes and the beat of *daf* drums. It was not until the shadows were drawing long and the air sharply cool that Khezmet and Daro left with their families for the Atashkedah where the Magush confirmed the union.

Occupied with the safety of the Shahan Shah and Shahjin, Harpagos had entrusted Shawish to escort Vashti back to the palace in a carriage at the end of the festivities. Handing the reins of his horse to one of his men, Shawish folded his tall physique into the vehicle. "Shahan Shah's orders," he quipped when Vashti asked why she couldn't join the leading couple's retinue, "but we are taking a different way home."

"This isn't a kidnapping, is it?" Vashti laughed, declining to improperly resist the bidding of the first in line to the throne.

"Certainly not," Shawish replied, a smile of satisfaction softening his penetrating blue eyes. "The sweet stall please," he instructed the driver. Soon a row of stalls appeared in the eerie quiet of dusk. Shawish told the driver to stop, slipped out, and returned with a small silver bowl covered with a flax cloth. "Sweets for a charming lady," he mumbled awkwardly. Under the cloth, little bunches of dried grapes swam in dark brown syrup. "Amytis sent seeds of sweet date fruits from Babylonia," he explained of the syrup. "We can't grow them in the mountains, but our people have learned to cultivate them in the Shiraz region. They are delicious with smoked almonds," he added, handing her a ceramic jar of the cured nuts.

"To the old canal," he directed the carriage driver.

Fringed by willow trees, the deserted, grassy banks of the canal made Vashti uneasy. Why had Shawish brought her here? They had enjoyed many pleasant times at hunts, horse races, and other family gatherings in the past, but he had changed since returning from the war, become more serious. Now he too seemed anxious.

Watching a mother duck with her brood swim up the canal, the couple ate in silence until Shawish asked Vashti how she had enjoyed the wedding.

"With pleasure," she replied, "Khezmet and Daro deserve much happiness." Shawish cast his eyes across the canal and toward the citadel as though wondering what to say. "Are you still keen to co-command the military?" she ventured after another awkward silence.

"Of course, while Harpagos guards Father and Mother at home, I will continue training the troops in the field with our loyal Scythians," he replied enthusiastically.

"Our women should learn how to defend themselves too," Vashti commented, relieved that the conversation was at last progressing smoothly.

Shawish grinned in disbelief. "Do you think they could use weapons?"

"Of course. They are strong from working in the fields and harvesting crops. Throwing a lance would be easy with enough target practice," she claimed, flexing her lance arm. "And they use knives every day, not much difference between carving a meat carcass and thrusting a dagger into an enemy soldier is there?"

Shawish stifled a gasp. "Daggers and lances are not for you, Vashti," he said quietly, his voice insistently low. "Nor will they be needed by the future Shahjin of Media. She will be protected by me and my guard."

Realizing it was pointless to differ, and not wishing to consider Ardela's successor, Vashti sighed, finished the last of the grapes, and licked the delicious syrup from her fingers. The rest of the outing was spent in another awkward silence as the reflection of the waning moon tracked the surface of the canal.

Ishtovigo kicked a piece of broken pottery across his workshop floor. Palace gossip that Vashti and Shawish had left the wedding alone together had infuriated him.

"She cannot be trusted," he yelled to himself. "And Shawish was probably planning his bid for her at dinner a few weeks ago, and I never noticed. Father was no help. He never has been. I could appeal to dear Mother but—"

Footsteps in the corridor outside alerted him to an approaching guard. Grabbing his cloak, he rushed out of the palace to the stables, keeping ahead of his pursuer. Without stopping to throw a rug on his horse, he flung himself on the animal and headed for the golden gateway.

At the doorway to the stables, Harpagos stood watching. Calling to a stable hand for a mount, he waited several minutes before the rattle of hooves quickly descending the citadel faded then rode through the golden gateway on the Shahan Shah's orders. Having been instructed to monitor Ishtovigo's movements, Harpagos followed him to the Mossala temple and returned to inform Hovakhshatra of his belligerent son's whereabouts.

Vashti awoke next morning still feeling uneasy. After Shawish's strange behavior at the canal and his subtle hints, she wondered if marriage plans were being made for her.

"If they are, I will go back to my village and live with my tribal family," she vowed.

Later that day, from the window of her home, Shamin observed her daughter sitting deep in thought on the stone seat under the oak tree outside their home. It wasn't long before she joined her.

"What's on your mind, darling?" she asked.

"Time has gone by so fast, dear Mother. I feel I am still Parwin's age," Vashti replied earnestly, fixing her eyes on the palace entrance. "But I am not. Do you or Uncle Hovakhshatra and Aunt Ardela want me to marry soon?" she asked turning to face Shamin squarely.

"No, dear, I have no such plans, but I cannot speak for my brother," Shamin replied, her frown belying assurance as she put her arm around her daughter.

"I fear there is a long path ahead of me," Vashti confessed, resting her head on Shamin's shoulder. "If I had the courage of Amytis, I would be ready to take it. But I do not, and I am not."

Vashti wasn't surprised when Shawish appeared on her doorstep that afternoon. The silver clasps on his *chokha* shone and so did his pink face. He held a small bunch of magenta violets in his damp hand, which he offered her with a mumbled greeting. She had just invited him for chai when Shamin appeared. After chatting to his aunt amiably for a few minutes about the campaign against the last of the Athorayans, Shawish rose, nodded to Vashti, and left.

"Why did he come here to talk to you about our enemy, Mother?" she asked as Gulah closed the door behind him.

Shamin shrugged. "Dear, I don't think he did. I think he came to see you. Do you like him?"

Vashti wiggled her head indecisively. "He is kind and noble, but as you see, he cannot say what he feels and neither can I. Please, Mother, I don't want to marry. But if I must, let me be free a little longer," she pleaded.

Shamin seated herself heavily on a cushion beside her daughter and sighed. "Yes, dear," she replied, patting Vashti's arm sympathetically. But her tone of voice said otherwise.

"Tell me about your courtship with Father," Vashti asked. Trying to put the thought of her inevitable nuptials out of her mind, she snuggled up to her mother's warmth.

Shamin beamed. "On our Father Kshathrita's death, my brother Hovakhshatra was entrusted with the responsibility of finding me a husband. He was looking for men of valor to join the army and met Cicataxma at a council of chiefs just after he had become chief of the Busae tribe. When he noticed Cicataxma's archery skills on a hunting trip, Hovakhshatra immediately asked him to train the troops. But it wasn't until after I came first at the Norouz horse races that I met your father. He was very gracious in defeat!"

"Did you like him?" Vashti asked.

"Yes, so much that I paid one of the palace guards to let me sneak out and meet him on my own in the city."

"And so, the story continued until…," Vashti added sadly.

"It wasn't long before Hovakhshatra approved our marriage," Shamin added, her eyes quickly misting, "but we truly loved each other. It was a match meant for *bahasht*."

With their daughter Shelna visiting her cousin Parwin, their two eldest sons at the barracks, and Ishtovigo once again absent, the Shahan Shah and Shahjin were dining alone together and, once more, deep in discussion.

"What should we do with our third son?" Hovakhshatra asked. "I don't know where he is tonight, and Harpagos tells me he's been to the Mossala temple again."

"Why don't you have that evil building torn down?" Ardela replied indignantly. "You know women are used there to please the gods."

"We do not prevent worship of other gods, my dear," Hovakhshatra replied firmly. "We want to keep the peace with all our peoples, including exiles."

Ardela shook her head and wagged her finger. "That place will only bring trouble," she complained. "You should speak once more to Ishtovigo about it."

"Perhaps you should. He doesn't listen to me," Hovakhshatra replied.

Ardela sighed. "Nor me. Now that he is older, he does just what he likes."

Hovakhshatra nodded sadly. "I know he ran wild while I was at the war, but I'm planning to appoint him assistant governor of Susiana."

"But dear, he has no experience," Ardela protested.

"He will learn when he gets there. The governor is very capable… and loyal."

"The governor will need patience too," Ardela added. "But our son might forget about Vashti if he is kept busy in the province of Susiana."

Hovakhshatra nodded again. "Ishtovigo knows Shawish will be given first choice of a bride. I don't know why he deceives himself about Vashti."

"Even so, there should still be a role for the third son," Ardela conceded.

"Then it is settled. I will have him drafted into the remainder of General Taxmaspada's Lynx regiment in preparation for his posting. It might teach him some discipline."

"I am concerned about the children's lessons," Debyar told Shamin one cool early spring day. "If they are to lead Media in the future, their reading and writing and their numbers must be improved, and they should learn more about the story of our peoples and the natural features of our lands."

"Then their lessons should continue throughout the month of Nisan, except for Norouz," Shamin replied.

"And they should also visit the Magush to learn about the sun, the moon, the stars, and the other celestial bodies of the cosmos," Debyar added. "The Magi have told me that they know when a Saoshyant will appear."

"Tell me," Shamin asked eagerly.

"Five years after the planets Enlil and Ninurta line up in the sky with our planet, Enlil will be overshadowed by Regulus, the brightest star in the Lion constellation, and move through Pisces, the Hapirus' constellation. Two years later, a Saoshyant and true Lion of Righteousness will be born in Yehud as Enlil hangs over that land."

Shamin had always wished a Saoshyant would come to Media, but her eyes still shone in excitement, and she danced around the room.

"Wonderful news," she cried. "Perhaps then we will have peace. The children must study this knowledge and work hard till summer. And next year you should prepare the older ones for their hardship tests."

Sharing Shamin's happiness with a hug, Debyar agreed and went out to find her pupils.

"We have already named the six tribes of Media," the teacher began a little later when the children had settled under the oak tree. "But our story is much older. Once they learned how to grow enough food to feed everyone using irrigation, our ancestors in Kiengi, the southern land between the Two Rivers, built structures, devised machines and laws, and wrote about them and the natural world. Later, our people of the Hurrians came from the north and settled as far south as the land of Elam."

"The Shahan Shah is now building a new palace in Shush," Ferhad remarked.

"Yes. The province of Susiana was in Elam and became part of our empire over a hundred years ago when Chief Daia-okku led our tribes to the Zagros Mountain tableland and the Parsu settled farther south near the Gulf of Parsa."

"Near the Great Sea?" Parwin asked.

Debyar smiled. "Good question, dear, but the Great Sea is thousands of stades to the west of the Gulf of Parsa. I will draw you a map of these places for our next lesson," she promised.

Parwin smiled back. "What is a tableland, dear teacher?" she asked.

"It is a high flat area of mountains and gentle valleys. Hagmatana is on the Zagros Tableland."

"Where did the Scythians come from?" Vashti wanted to know of those who had been both enemy and friend.

"They are an Ariavartan tribe who settled far to the east, near Bactria. They were some of the first invaders of our region."

"And hopefully the last," Ferhad commented.

Vashti nodded. "According to Aunt Ardela, the Scythians are still a threat north of Bactria where they are called Saka."

"Yes, but originally they moved across our northern boundaries to Athoraya where their Shah Partatua married a young Athorayan woman," Debyar continued. "From then on, they fought with Babylonia."

"But they didn't stop attacking us until the Shahan Shah and Father conquered them," Ferhad added triumphantly.

"Exactly, dear," Debyar concurred. "Thank you for reminding us."

"I think we should be very careful of those tribes," Vashti warned. "They cannot be trusted."

Debyar agreed and so did the other children.

Little did they anticipate the trouble rebel Scythians would once again cause to the leading family of Media.

Chapter 8

"Nebuchadnezzar has defeated the Egyptians at Carchemish," Hovakhshatra informed his generals and advisors in his lamp-lit council chamber a few months later. "And they are finally finished in Sham."

The men all cheered. Following the Shahan Shah's cue, they raised their horse head rhytons and drank deeply of the best Athorayan wine, despite the Piree Magush's frown of disapproval. "Now that the Babylonians are absolutely the most powerful force in the region, we must affirm our treaty with them and clearly outline our territorial boundaries," the Shahan Shah stated.

"Have you heard from Amytis?" Harpagos asked.

"Yes, our daughter is now Shahjin Amytis of Babylonia," Hovakhshatra announced proudly, "and has informed us through the ambassadorial pouch that Nebuchadnezzar's father died not long after the Babylonian victory over the Egyptians. The heir apparent was in such a hurry to return and secure his throne that he conducted his inauguration very quickly with little respect for his father's very successful reign." He turned to the scribe recording the proceedings on a wax-covered tablet. "Note our congratulations to Shah Nebuchadnezzar and inform him we are looking forward to meeting his emissaries," he instructed. "Tell him we will also accept any of the conquered peoples he finds unsuitable for his building program and his farms," he continued.

The Shahan Shah then rose, raised the golden scepter to dismiss his guests, and ordered Harpagos to deliver a letter to Vashti from the ambassadorial pouch. "Perhaps Nebuchadnezzar will invite us to honor his accession at the end of his inaugural year," the general commented as he stuffed the letter into his sash.

Hovakhshatra grunted and shook his head, wondering at the impatience of the new young ruler.

Vashti broke the seal of the lion quickly. She hadn't heard from her beloved cousin for over a year. Amytis' letter read:

Dearest Vashti

How are you, my darling? Have you been able to tame Ishtovigo? How are my dear brothers, Shawish and Artaspaya? I long to be home for Norouz, the celebrations here to Marduk and other gods in spring are endlessly long and boring, and I so miss the fires our people jump over and the long dances of Norouz. I also wish I was free to roam the cool mountains with you in summer. It's dreadfully hot on this marshy, insect-ridden plain at that time of year.

Now that I am Shahjin of Babylonia, I have many new duties, which keep me very busy and my mind occupied. But when Nebuchadnezzar's forces recently arrived with captives from Yehud, including members of the shah's family and other high-ranking officials to ensure the nation's loyalty to Babylonia, and discourage it from aligning with Egypt, I remembered your dream. They must have come from Ursalim, their city near the Great Sea.

Four of the young Hapiru men of high status in their nation have already been brought into the shah's service after he allowed them to eat separately of their national diet while they were being schooled for service. Following a trial period, he found them wiser and more knowledgeable than all the other students preparing to enter his court, especially in the interpretation of dreams and visions. I am astonished that these young men from such a small, weak country know so much. Their leader, Belteshazzar, is very intelligent, quite the most proper young man, and already highly regarded by my husband.

Even though the gardens Nebuchadnezzar made for me are lovely, I still miss the Hagmatana palace and everyone at home and our rivers and lakes.

I trust it won't be long before I visit you all, dear, or you come to see me.

Your

Amytis

Vashti sighed. It was unusual for Amytis to complain, and she hadn't confirmed whether a city of Ursalim had the temple that had been attacked in her dream. She would ask again and seek Amytis' true feelings in her reply.

Although Hovakhshatra and Ardela kept Vashti busy with palace affairs, she soon found the protocols of receiving emissaries and their yearly tributes from throughout the Median lands quite tedious. However, if any acted at all suspiciously, she immediately notified Harpagos, who removed them for interrogation as possible spies or even assassins. When all the visitors had gone, she would inspect the treasury and citadel storehouses to make sure bulky goods such as industrial metals, grain, and wool, had been accurately recorded and securely stowed.

Currency was taken directly to the treasury.

Every year after Norouz, the Shahan Shah hosted the governors of his provinces in a weeklong feast and tours of the citadel and city sites. The vigilance of Harpagos' team of specially trained guards made Vashti joke that he never rested from seeking out armed foreigners. At the end of the week, the Shahan Shah hosted a banquet for the men while Shahjin Ardela entertained their wives in her quarters. Anticipating meeting women from other lands when she was asked to assist, Vashti soon discovered that not all were friendly.

"The Parsu and Athorayan women were loud and scowled when I mentioned that Ishtovigo would soon be stationed in Shush. I think the Athorayans were angry that we took their territory of Susiana, and the Parsu want it themselves," she complained to Khezmet. "But the Cappadocians from the west, the Urartans from the north, and the Bactrians and Parthavans from the east are very friendly, love riding, and wear simple gold earrings and bracelets as do the Ariavartans whose headdresses are just like ours."

"What about the Scythians?" Khezmet asked.

"They don't come anymore. The Shahan Shah suspects rebellion and is taking steps to…I can't tell you anything else," Vashti replied, lowering her voice to a whisper. "And even though the Shahan Shah introduced Shamin to the Parthavan and Bactrian governors—both tall, very handsome men despite their graying beards—she didn't show any interest in them."

"Did you?" Khezmet asked.

"Absolutely not," Vashti retorted. "General Biraxeas says my archery skills are sufficient to join the Tigers, but it is not yet time to approach the Shahan Shah to obtain his permission, or Shamin's."

"Ferhad has been admitted to the Bear regiment," Khezmet remarked.

"I know, but I will have to wait. Until I can join the army, I will work to give our women back their traditional place beside our men," Vashti vowed. "Debyar told us that hundreds of years ago, all women in our lands not only grew food and made clothes and shelter for their families, but also made their own decisions and were free to rule their families."

Khezmet nodded. "But I am thankful to be here in Hagmatana in your service, dear."

"And I am thankful for you, dear. But if not for Cica's bravery, you would have been another victim of the competition between the powers around us for land to grow crops and pasture flocks and herds. Debyar also told us that once men armed themselves for war, women were left to care for the children by themselves, but the men took women's independence from them when they returned. Now we are at peace, we must give women back their natural place in their families, clans, and tribes," she declared emphatically. "And manage our surplus produce carefully to feed everyone, including foreigners and the poor."

Nodding again, Khezmet smiled in awe of her mistress' wisdom.

After Ishtovigo moved to Shush, Shawish began inviting Vashti on weekly rides into the mountains. Vashti politely agreed but remained quite disinterested in his attentions.

"He's easy company," she told Khezmet. "But nothing more."

One high summer's day, with two guards keeping a discreet distance, the couple ventured deeper into the range to a waterfall, which emptied into a pool at the bottom of an oak tree covered valley. After stopping at the pool to fill their water bags and let their mounts drink, Vashti and Shawish gazed across the sleepy valley with its river rushing noisily over worn gray boulders. Shrouded in heat haze, it beckoned them to explore the moist depressions below for butterflies, but a strange lethargy had overcome them.

Suddenly, much to her surprise, Shawish seized Vashti with a surprisingly carefree chuckle and dragged her into the water. Quickly surfacing and spluttering from the cold, she laughed and grabbed his boot, upon which he hurled himself into the pool. Coming up, he pulled her down a second time and sank into the water beside her. When they arose together, each stared at the other in silence before Shawish drew her to himself and kissed her.

The warmth of his mouth on her cool lips was strangely pleasant, despite her muffled objections, but a bird's cry in the distance reminded her that she was acting improperly, and so was he.

She drew back, wanting to kick him or, much more strangely, hug him. Instead, she splashed out of the pool, called Nzdar, and mounted hastily, shivering despite the heat rising from the valley. With an embarrassed cough, Shahwish followed. Sincerely hoping the guards had not witnessed the indiscretions of their charges, Vashti shook her head, trying to make sense of the mixed emotions she had experienced in the pool. But like the hazy day, nothing was clear, and she became aware that her heart was beating differently.

The ride back to the city was devoid of conversation as she scolded herself for not letting Shawish know that she did not feel the same way about him as he did about her. But it was difficult—she was not at liberty to refuse the heir to the throne, and both sides of her family seemed to approve the match. The only problem was, she didn't.

So, it wasn't until they were riding the well-trodden city streets that she spoke. Still thinking about the cold pool of her disgrace, she basked in the hot, low-angled rays of the late-afternoon sun beaming into the homes of workers soon to take their rest. Joyous *shimshal* pipe strains drifted over the pleasantly warm streets, to which the deep call of the shofar ram's horn boomed replies.

"Debyar told me that sound is from the Hapiru," she commented. "And see, they are burning a seven-branched lamp!" she cried, pointing to a window. "We will return soon to practice our Aramaic with them. The Shahan Shah has insisted Debyar teach us their language to learn more about our subject peoples. But for now, we must hurry home. Gulah will be lighting our lamps."

Not knowing if he had been forgiven his passion, Shawish patted his horse and led the way up the first citadel path with his usually straight posture a little bent. At the golden gate, with one more longing glance at Vashti, he uttered a wistful goodbye.

Chapter 9

Heading south toward the city of Shush in the province of Elam, also known as Susiana, Ishtovigo and his entourage crossed the hills and passes of the Zagros Mountains to rolling hills watered by full-flowing rivers. Hosted generously by the Bakhtyari people, they made steady progress until reaching the drier regions north of the city, inhabited by the less-welcoming Parsu.

With donkeys and packhorses still loaded for several days' journey, Salya, the guard assigned by Harpagos to protect Ishtovigo, insisted they stop to rest in the middle of the day. "How much further in this wretched heat?" Ishtovigo complained.

"Only a hundred stades," Salya replied, grimacing and regretting his decision to accept the role of protecting the third in line to the throne in the hope of securing a higher position in the guard service.

"Look, there's a temple!" Ishtovigo suddenly cried, pointing to a multitiered building in the distance shimmering in the heat haze, despite the surrounding lush grove of trees.

"The Elamite people have ruled as far west as Yehud and have been here for many years, but they have kept the Dur Untash temple in good condition," Salya explained. Ishtovigo only grunted in reply and urged his tired horse on, forcing the exhausted party to keep up. A couple of hours later, as the building's square, stone-pillared entrance appeared, Ishtovigo began to ask questions about the temple, leaving Salya suspicious as to why.

Finally, as the light began to wane at the end of the next day, the entrance to the city of Shush through a gap in the mountain range appeared ahead. Inside, a collection of mud-brick huts surrounded the central citadel overlooking the Karun River. As Salya led the party through the streets, much to Ishtovigo's dissatisfaction, no one bowed or even took notice of them.

"We'll soon see how these people change when I am governor," he informed Salya before viewing the burnt brick foundations of his father's palace, which, when completed, he was determined to make his own.

Not long after declaring the governor's rough stone house and stables in Shush beneath his station as the Shah's son, Ishtovigo promptly commandeered the home of the richest merchant in the city and the "household" services of his unmarried daughter. The merchant's protests prompted Salya to send a message to the Shahan Shah explaining the trouble his son was causing and that the Medes could not afford to insult their friends in the city.

"Leave him," the Shahan Shah wrote in reply. "Your report on the road between Hagmatana and Shush is more important. Shush, Elam, and the western provinces should be well-connected so we can easily defend them. Tell Ishtovigo if his behavior does not reflect my shahdom, he must return and will immediately be sent to the desert to complete his hardship test." Salya sighed and headed for the merchant's house.

The following night, the guards invited Ishtovigo to a backgammon game played on a wooden board inlaid with pieces of bone, lapis lazuli, black limestone, and black mortar. Absorbed, they failed to notice that his indulgence in wine was contributing to his losses. The next day, Ishtovigo's aching head made Shush seem much less attractive. Angry about his father's threatening message, he called for his horse and headed for the Dur Untash temple where he hoped to find some ritual consolation. After being denied entrance to the local chief's private quarters, and the Magush's complaint to the governor about his misbehavior with the women attending the temple, Ishtovigo was reported again by Salya in another message to the Shahan Shah.

A few weeks later, Harpagos arrived with Debyar and an official to assist the governor. On the Shahan Shah's orders, Harpagos told Ishtovigo to get on his horse, and the three began the journey back to Hagmatana. Debyar recited the Avesta most of the way, and by the time they all reached the city, the teacher's instructions on how to live "good thoughts, good words and good deeds" had been firmly embedded in the mind but not the heart of the third in line to the throne.

The day before their arrival, Vashti and a small troop of the Bear regiment left Hagmatana. Appointed by the Shahan Shah to visit the northern and eastern provinces, she was to inspect the condition of the subject peoples of the region and the cultivated and wild lands and send reports of unrest or rebellion immediately to the palace. Shamin had protested her daughter's travels with an all-male escort, but Vashti relished the idea of such an adventure, despite leaving her family and Khezmet and her two children behind. Flushed with excitement, she hugged Shamin tightly and assured her all would be well while Ferhad and Parwin kept asking if they could go too. Vashti's reminder that she would be doing her hardship test on the trip and that they would be expected to soon do theirs did little to dampen her siblings' quests to accompany her.

Nzdar settled into an easy gait on the road south as Vashti and her guards passed the Mossala temple, an abominable building of the *druj* on which she longed to spit and stomp. As the days wore on and they turned northeast, agricultural lands gave way to thick forest. Chief guard Godel, who had traveled to Bactria before, then ordered the little group to tighten its ranks against ambushes by robbers and wild animal attacks. The pace was occasionally slowed to protect the cart carrying copper and tin to make bronze for the fort gates at Zadraka, a distant town on the edge of the desert.

Several days later, as the last rays of the sun hit the highest snowy peaks of the distant Alborz Mountains, the troops found a small clearing off the road suitable for camping. After dinner, the first rotation of two guards was stationed, but on this night, with the outline of the mountain range clearly visible for the first time, Vashti felt the loneliness of being a long way from home in a wild place with only a few men to protect her. But still excited about her adventure, she fell asleep easily, dreaming of leading her own troop of women warriors over snowy ranges against an unidentified enemy.

She awoke the next day to a clear but chilly dawn sky. The guards had lit a fire, and the horses and donkeys were stamping restlessly. After breakfast of barley bread and ceci bean paste laced with ground sesame seeds, they crossed a wide, green-carpeted plain scattered with the black woolen goat's hair and willow *dwars* of nomadic sheep and cattle herders. Later the next day, pastureland yielded to crops, vineyards, and pomegranate groves.

At the provincial town of Caspian, closest settlement to Hagmatana on the eastern trade route, foundries supplying the army and farmers with weapons and implements belched smoke into the balmy air. After purchasing a cream silk scarf, in her riding bags, she stowed handfuls of hard little cakes containing tiny parchment pieces with writing characters like those in Ishtovigo's collection and instantly forgot about them.

That evening at their quarters in the town's barracks, Godel and the men produced some numbered dice cubes and invited her to join them in a game of chance. The other soldiers' disapproving glances did not spoil her fun, but her disturbing dream that night of Shawish beckoning her to a dark place awakened her in a sweat. Was he in danger like her father had been? Or did the dream mean she should decline his invitations even though it might not bode well for her family or her plan to join the army? She lay awake for what seemed like hours, wondering if she should return to

Hagmatana to warn Shawish.

But in the morning, her dream seemed vague and unimportant, and she felt impressed to continue her journey east. Leaving the Caspian region, Godel led the party up the Ganjah Valley where they stopped to buy freshly picked almonds and walnuts. Following the Sefid River down the other side of the range, with its lush, silt-nourished wheat crops, they entered another narrowing valley at the head of which towered snowcapped Mount Zamawand.

"When smoke, fiery stones, and rocks come out of the mountain, the local farmworkers scurry for their houses because they think Angra Mainyu will come from the mountain to destroy them," a farmer told them. "But the ash makes the trees and crops grow."

The next day, they began to climb the tree and branch-strewn path to the Nowshahr Pass. Myriads of birds flitted through forest vegetation and the soldiers shot several pheasants and partridges for the evening meal. Closer to the pass, eagles and falcons wheeled through the sky, uttering their lonely cries as if lost in the wilderness. Camped just below the snow line, Vashti and her men secured the horses, donkeys, and cart in a circle around the fire they had lit for safety as well as warmth.

"Panthers and lynxes inhabit the higher slopes of the mountain," Godel warned. "The fire should repel them, but we must sleep close together."

After a cold night's sleep huddled between horse rugs and their cloaks, the little company resumed its journey up the lower slopes of the volcano. Smoke billowed from the crater and rising heat steamed snow clinging to its rim. Spooked by rumblings from deep within the vast bowl of ash and fiery rocks, the horses and donkeys had to be coaxed through clouds of yellow gas and thick dust.

"Tie your sash over your face," Godel called out as everyone began to cough.

In cleaner air on the other side, they washed off gritty ash in a cold stream flowing through juniper and beech trees. Further down, thick, wet forest gave way to a view of a warm, luxuriant plain lined by the smooth welt of the Caspian Sea. As they descended, the forest soon yielded to citron orchards, and fields of purple petalled flowers whose crimson spikes Godel explained were used for spice and coloring cloth. The rich deep color reminded Vashti of Shahjin Ardela's court cloak.

On reaching the shore of the Caspian Sea that evening, Godel secured rooms for them all in a simple village caravansary. Early the next morning, hoping none of her party were awake, Vashti crept past the animals tied to rails in the central courtyard. Making her way on foot to the gently lapping waters of the sea, she removed her boots and padded over a gray sandy beach to gentle wavelets curling crisply on the shore.

Bahasht is a garden, she thought, breathing in the fresh, mildly salty air. Just then, the sun broke the flat blue horizon, and the golden ball haloed light over the dull sky. Inspired by the crisp morning, she thanked Auramazda for his life and light giving energy.

"I could stay here forever," she whispered.

But she had arranged a meeting with the local chief and his wife and keeping them waiting would shame the Shahan Shah. So after snatching a few more minutes' quiet contemplation, she hurried off to her hosts' greetings, a sumptuous breakfast, and their gifts of a bag each of pomegranates and pistachio nuts. After listening to their requests, she promised to speak to the Shahan Shah on their behalf, and soon her little party was reluctantly farewelling the coast.

Once more they led the animals and cart across a mountain pass to green slopes. Dry scrubland drained by wadis into marshes and salt lakes soon appeared, but by evening, nomads watering their sheep at the base of another mountain range urged them to stay overnight. Vashti and Godel gratefully accepted their invitation and, after agreeing with the nomads' pleas to stay longer, remained a few more entertaining and endearing days. Then, with many grateful farewells, the little party filled their water bags, loaded bread and dried fruits on the donkeys, and set out early as the herders led their flocks to pasture. The sun was already hot, and a warm wind was drying the travelers like last year's preserved figs. But half a day's march later, they came to a welcome spring where a herdsman watering his goats told them the fort of Zadraka was only a few days' journey away.

At sunset the following day, another small oasis appeared. Relieved he would not have to push the thirsty animals any further, Godel ordered his dusty, sweat-stained men to make camp.

"Not far to go tomorrow," he informed Vashti, who longed to bathe in the oasis pool but couldn't, due to the presence of so many men. Shamin and Ardela had urged her to take a maid on her trip, but she had insisted she could manage quite well by herself and that she did not want to expose a servant to hardship.

That evening around their campfire, munching bread and cheese provided by the nomads, Vashti and her men were startled by the harsh laugh of a jackal in the depths of the approaching gloom.

"At least the snakes and lizards will be too cold to bother us," one of the guards remarked as the chill of night descended, "but be very careful of scorpions."

Waking early the next morning, Vashti crept out from under her sleeping rug to the sight of a huge fort looming on the horizon. The structure's morbid gray walls were as dreary as the desert they had just passed through, but she was drawn to its majestic splendor rising from the wilderness, like a huge rock sprouting from the landscape. Later, following the creaking cart toward its destination, she wondered about the reception she and her men would receive from the governor and the people of a territory known for its fierce independence.

But her doubts were soon dispelled when a cloud of dust appeared from which a band of bushy bearded warriors armed only with shields emerged.

"Peace," the leader called when the two parties met. "Welcome to Zadraka. I am the governor," he explained, whereupon Godel raised his lance and offered him the Shahan Shah's greetings. Vashti sighed in relief, and the men of the Bears all smiled and nodded.

Closer to the city, the people joined the party, beating their *daf* drums and ululating. Outside the fort, a bronze statue of Kawa the Blacksmith wielding the hammer with which he had slain the evil Shah Ahzdehak displayed the people's metalwork. Vashti gazed up at the legendary figure, wondering if Ahzdehak had really killed children and used their brains to feed snakes growing painfully from his shoulders. She doubted the snakes' supposed home but shivered at the thought of children being killed to satisfy the appetite of a shah. But the cart driver was asking her for directions about the delivery of its load, and she snapped back to attention.

The next morning, the governor, a short plump man whose balding head was fringed comically by gray curls escaping from his headband, hosted Vashti for breakfast with his wife. Freshly roasted goat meat, *mast*, and bread with olive paste washed down with cinnamon-spiced chai reminded her how far she was from the green valleys of home. After accepting a gift from the Shahan Shah and Shahjin of a gold bracelet, and a pair of gold earrings for his wife, the governor thanked Vashti, who presented him with orders for the fort repairs.

"Now that we have materials for the new gate, we must fortify the walls against the raiding desert tribes," the governor informed her before unrolling a parchment sheet of plans.

"Do you need more troops to defend the area?" she asked.

"We need reinforcements to build our numbers and to instruct our men," the governor replied. "They are mostly untrained farmers and herdsmen, but they want to be ready to protect their families, crops, and flocks."

Vashti agreed the population needed the assurance of stronger defense forces and promised to speak to the Shahan Shah about the matter.

Chapter 10

After farewelling her hosts and the fort dwellers, who raised their metalwork tools in salute, Vashti and her men returned to the nomads' camp. They spent a few more idyllic days with their generous new friends, then once more loaded the donkeys with food and filled their water bags before commencing their journey to Bactria, the farthest-flung province of the Shahdom of Media.

Not long after, the party reached the eastern fork in the road which would take them through the arid lands of Parthava, across the great salt plain of the east, through the region of Parthava known as "the land where the sun comes from."

"Robbers and dangerous animals inhabit the region," Godel warned Vashti gravely, his forehead crinkled with doubt beneath his dirty, sweat-stained *kulaw-u-dasmal*. "Do not trouble yourself to go through this untamed land. Many strong men have died trying to cross it."

"How long does the desert crossing take?" Vashti asked.

"Three weeks, perhaps a month, depending on how many oases we find, and if there is water suitable for drinking," Godel replied, looking sideways at her from dark brown eyes set in clear whites. "The people at Zadraka told me it has not rained here for two years," he advised, turning to face her squarely. "You can go back to Hagmatana if you prefer. I will ask my second-in-command to accompany you. Then I will proceed to Bactria with the rest of the men and the Shahan Shah's orders."

Vashti took a deep breath, glanced up at the searing sun, and then to the horizon. Nothing but sand and pebbles lay before them, sprinkled with a few hardy bushes. The Shahan Shah had told her of the treasures of a distant city his grandfather, Daia-okku had brought under the Medes' control over seventy years ago. How could she come this far without visiting such a renowned jewel of the east? She exhaled slowly and stared resolutely ahead.

"We will do it," she vowed. "We will cross this barren place. And may Auramazda guide us through it safely."

Godel nodded and gave the signal to mount. Vashti patted Nzdar, took his reins, and did likewise. Ahead, the barrenness of the endless horizon stretched before them, and she wondered if this hardship test would be her last. But as Nzdar settled into his steady gait, she promised herself that she would not countenance failure.

For days, the little party trudged a sand dune wasteland, the animals eating only some of the salt marsh bushes in between oases. When thirst played with her mind, Vashti thought she saw *yazatas* hanging above distant clouds, beckoning her to keep going. Once all the food had been eaten and she had shared the hard little cookies in her riding bags, it wasn't long before hunger began to plague them all. The desert tribes whom Godel believed would feed them along the way were nowhere to be seen.

But the oases that replenished their strength were grand little lakes of *bahasht*. Filled with birds, including fat, skinny-legged bustards, larks, desert warblers, and finches, they were visited by wild cats, foxes, and wolves who came to drink at night, some of which were necessarily killed for food. With little fuel for fires, the travelers suffered bitterly cold nights under bright starry skies in which the Great Bear star formation shone clearly. It was on those nights that Vashti most felt the warm spirit of Auramazda.

I might die in this dry, harsh land, she thought, but I will be content.

Before long, the big red sand dunes over which they trudged were interrupted by the shallow banks of a wide, dry lakebed. "It fills with water when rains come," Godel explained as the animals scrambled up the other side. Vashti looked down at Nzdar, straining to get to the top. Lacking the energy needed to urge him on, she let the horse make his way at his own pace. When he reached the crest, she patted his neck.

"Not far to go now, my darling," she whispered into his ear.

Just when the exhausted travelers thought their parched, fallen, lifeless bodies would soon be covered by wind-blown sand, a film of green appeared on the horizon. Vashti halted Nzdar and dismounted, determined to walk the last few stades to sustenance with her beloved companion. But soon, only a treeless expanse of short grass became visible.

"Where will we get water now?" she asked Godel calmly while trying desperately to hide her panic.

"There should be one more oasis," he replied hesitantly, gazing into the distance. Vashti wasn't convinced. All she could see was endless fading grass.

"I…I don't think the animals can go much farther," she told him when the horses and donkeys slowed their pace even more a stade or so later.

"Rest here with the others. I will find the oasis and return with water." Godel's tone was confident, but his eyes darted anxiously. She agreed and, hoping he would be able to get up again, allowed Nzdar to lie in the dry grass. Godel moved off, leaving the little party in the iron grip of relentless heat and tinder-dry air. The slow plodding of his horse's hooves growing fainter over hard ground sounded like the fading death drum of a funeral march, and she wondered what they would do if he did not return.

Too weak to forage, the horses and donkeys collapsed one after the other, and the men cut a few spindly blades of grass for them. When the animals had eaten, after unsuccessfully searching for one last morsel of bread in their bags, everyone lay down, waiting for Godel's return. Dozing in Nzdar's shadow, she listened to his rhythmic, labored breathing. At last, the merciless sun went down, and the animals' groans lessened. It seemed that their lives and those of their riders were seeping into the parched soil.

Sometime later, something rustled in the grass. Vashti opened her eyes to see the yellow-eyed stare of a jackal, its mouth locked in a greedy smile. Jumping up, she drove it away but fell into blackness to the faint sound of pounding horses' hooves. Then someone was holding her head, pouring cool water into her mouth. She looked up hazily into a man's frowning face.

"Don't drink too much," he warned in a strange accent.

"My horse," she croaked, sitting up and motioning the stranger to give Nzdar a drink. The man lifted Nzdar's head and poured the life-giving fluid down his throat.

Once Godel had offered the men a little water, the stranger began watering the rest of the animals, but one would not move. She glanced at Nzdar. His chest was rising and falling, but his eyes were closed. Hugging his neck, she whispered into his ear again.

"My darling, please do not leave me. We have not finished our journey yet." Nzdar lifted his head a little and whinnied weakly. Precious tears fell from her eyes. Whatever happened, she would never leave him in this desolate place.

The stranger had brought extra rugs which the men wrapped around themselves to relieve the cold. Hooded by his cloak, the whites of the stranger's eyes were all she could see of his face until he lifted the torch he had brought, and his noble, rugged features were lit against the darkness. Gently, he urged Vashti and her men to drink small doses of water and slowly chew the nuts and dates he had brought. The animals still could not stand up, so the men lay down beside them for warmth. As they settled, Vashti found herself between Nzdar and the stranger, who shared his cloak with her. Too exhausted to protest such impropriety, she drifted into a restless sleep.

In the morning, the stranger was gone but returned a few hours later with another horse laden with water bags and fodder for the animals, some of whom were still lying down. After a drink, Nzdar struggled to his feet, and Vashti picked more grass for him. The stranger had also brought bread and olives, which slid down her throat like honey. Godel fed the surviving horses with the fodder, and eventually, they were all strong enough to stand.

Vashti caught the stranger examining Nzdar's legs.

"He is fine," he commented in a dialect she barely understood, "but he should not be ridden today. You may ride with me," he half-offered, half-insisted.

The stranger looked up at her, his thick black hair falling untidily from his gray *kulaw-u dastmal*. Beneath bushy eyebrows, his brown eyes regarded her steadily as if trying to penetrate her thoughts. Embarrassed, she looked down.

"Thank you," she replied cautiously in what she guessed was his Aryo language. Her hesitancy was justified; she was yet to determine whether this stranger was friend or foe.

Godel soon informed her that the oasis was not far away and that the men would lead the horses and donkeys there slowly. The stranger helped her mount his sturdy mare, and taking Nzdar's reins to lead him, she settled herself behind her rescuer. She had not asked his name nor had he asked for hers; the dire circumstances had not required such formalities. He seemed trustworthy; she would have to find out who he really was, but not till she and her party were feeling better.

As the sun rose, weakened by their ordeal but grateful for Auramazda's deliverance, the depleted party made its way across the dry plain in single file. Much to her dismay, for the first time on her trip, Vashti found herself weighed down by the unfamiliar burden of discouragement. The stranger had informed her that Bactria was still many stades distant, and she wondered if she really would complete her hardship test.

Much to her delight, the oasis the stranger led them to was another *bahasht*. Hardy Moringa trees and tamarisk bushes around a deep, clear pool protected date palms bearing sweet fruit.

"We have a channel leading to a smaller pool for the wild and domestic animals," the stranger explained as they walked around the little settlement.

Still unsure about him and his motives, Vashti expressed her admiration of the oasis and appreciation for his rescue of her and her troops. “And thank you, for…bringing us food and water,” she stammered, embarrassed by her attempts to use his language. “The Shahan Shah is indebted to you for saving his niece and his men. I am Vashti, council representative of Hovakhshatra of Media.”

The stranger’s eyes widened. He stopped and held her gaze, the light breeze rippling the fringes of his *kulaw-u-dastmal*. “I am Mithridates, chief of the local Parthavan tribe,” he replied. Turning to his men nearby, he called out something quickly. “You are very welcome to attend my quarters for chai and a meal,” he informed her, “so is your commander.” One of his men then hurried to a striped pavilion behind the date palms, spoke loudly to someone inside, and took a pile of dried date leaf bases into the shelter. Soon clanging and chopping sounds drifted across the placid oasis. “Refresh yourself in the pool,” Mithridates suggested after Vashti thanked him again. “We will see you shortly.” With a quick nod, he turned and strode toward the pavilion.

Wandering toward the pool, she let her eyes adjust to the cool shade. Her men were chatting to the tribesmen on the other side of the pavilion, so she felt safe in dropping her cloak to wash her face and arms and, after removing her boots, raising her *pantol* to splash her legs and feet in the clean pool. It seemed a shame to ruffle the perfectly still surface of the water, but it enlivened her parched skin. Unsure how many days had passed since she had washed at Zadraka, she longed to launch her whole grit-covered body into the pool.

Her face and extremities clean, she searched her riding bag for the scarf she had bought in the Caspian village. Wrapping the cream sheath around herself, she secured it with her family’s purple sash and fastened a ruby necklace, for which she had paid a high price in Zadraka, around her neck.

Without the bronze mirror she used at home, she gazed into the pool’s reflective surface and was shocked by the sight of her matted, untidy hair. Shaking out sand and dust, she brushed the knots out, coiled thick strands into a neat knot on top of her head, and secured them with a large silver clasp. Her headdresses were all dirtier than her hair, so she hoped her uncovered head would not offend. But approaching the tent, she was relieved when a young woman came out with a jewel studded *sarwain*.

"My brother offers this to you as a gift. You may wear it to meet with him," she advised. "Now please follow me."

Vashti returned thanks, quickly fitted the ornament around the topknot on her head and stepped under the brightly tasselled pavilion entrance into cool dimness. The light of a single lamp throwing shadows mysteriously over the hexagonally patterned walls framed the dark outline of Mithridates, who stepped forward.

"Welcome to my humble home," he said, motioning her to sit on thick cushions lining the pavilion walls. "I see you have met my sister, Kani." Instantly comfortable, Vashti nodded acknowledgment.

Kani brought tea and water and Mithridates sipped, placed his glass on the floor, and regarded her, his eyes again lingering.

"Do you like the *sarwain*?" he inquired.

"Yes, very much. Thank you," Vashti replied, unable to decide whether to meet his gaze or avert her eyes. "Your sister has great wisdom. I accept this fine gift on behalf of the Shahdom of Media."

He smiled. "It was my wife's, but I am giving it to you as a token of my appreciation for the Shahan Shah's representative. We do not often have an important visitor of such…beauty and bravery."

Vashti felt her face flush. "And I have not had the privilege of meeting such a chief as yourself in this excellent country of many natural wonders," she replied.

Mithridates smiled again. "Perhaps I will have the pleasure of showing you more of our lands," he suggested. Squirming with embarrassment at his unabashed stare, she was relieved when Kani placed trays of boiled lamb, bread, and young water lily leaves on the star-patterned floor rug. "But now it is time to eat," he said, as Vashti glanced out the pavilion doorway for Godel, who had stayed with the rest of the troop.

"Do not worry," Mithridates assured her. "Your commander and his men are also eating."

When it was time to retire, Mithridates offered Vashti his place in the pavilion, but she shook her head. "I greatly appreciate your hospitality, but I too will remain with my men. We have endured much together."

"Then please let me accompany you to your camp," Mithridates offered, and she assented.

The moon shining over the silvery surface of the oasis pool threw date palm shadows as Mithridates led the way over fallen fronds. Covered in their cloaks, her men were all asleep at the camp and the animals rested quietly. A slight breeze rustled nearby tamarisk bushes. Once again, Vashti felt Mithridates' eyes on her, searching for she knew not what. Suddenly, he seized her hand and kissed it.

"Sweet dreams, Vashti of the Medes. The Parthavans also protect you."

Shocked by his audacity, she withdrew her hand and turned her back. It wasn't until the sound of Mithridates' footsteps had faded that she lifted her hand to her nose and smelled smoke mingled with the musty pine fragrance of frankincense oil.

Chapter 11

The next morning, Vashti awoke to the bleating of sheep as Mithridates' herdsmen led their flocks toward the rising sun. She waited till the noise subsided then rose and wandered down to the oasis pool. Mist swirled across its placid surface. The only other visitors were a small flock of saxaul sparrows, poking their short beaks into the muddy edge. To avoid disturbing them, she walked slowly to the opposite side and sat down to watch the birds' busy search for food. Despite the cold and lack of privacy, she still longed to wash her whole body. After deliberating for a few minutes, the longing outweighed her fear of being seen. Shedding her cloak, *chokha* and riding *pantol*, she stepped into the water and dropped beneath the surface of the crystal-clear pool, hardly making a ripple. When she came up, the birds squawked and scattered. Then she saw him.

Squatting at the other end of the pool, Mithridates was watching her, a curious little smile crossing his face. She had no idea how long he had been there, but it was now impossible to get out of the pool and keep her modesty. Gasping, she turned her back to him, folded her arms across her chest, and splashed out, her flimsy silk underrobe clinging to her legs and torso. Quickly, she flung her cloak over her shoulders, grabbed her clothes, and ran up the bank.

Her men had lit a fire, and though her body was soon warm, Vashti's mind remained frozen in horror at the sight of Mithridates on the side of the pool.

“I will apologize for disrespecting his hospitality,” she decided, “then if the men and animals are ready to move, we will say goodbye and leave this morning.”

But her plan was soon swept away when a strong wind began to blow from the south, bringing great clouds of whirling sand. One of Mithridates’ men emerged from the storm and told them to cover their faces and join the chief in his pavilion.

“First, water the animals at the second pool and take them to the shelter of the date palms,” he instructed Godel. “They will lie there safely with their backs to the wind.” Vashti grabbed her riding bag containing documents for the provincial governors and patted Nzdar briefly before her men hurried the animals away. Wrapping a scarf over her face, she ran toward the pavilion, the wind ripping at her cloak.

Inside, the pavilion was crowded. “Please sit here with me,” Kani offered after greeting her. “My brother is with the shepherds. Thank Auramazda they have been found with the flocks and are safe.”

Kani rose when Mithridates entered a little later followed by several sand-riddled shepherds. After telling her to give them food and drink, he ordered one of the shepherds to tighten the pavilion ropes as a strong gust tugged at the walls. Turning to Vashti, he grinned mischievously, like he had at the pool that morning.

“Good morning. I trust you are now warm after your cool dip,” he said jauntily. “And your skin is radiant,” he added as she blushed.

Annoyed by her impulsiveness at the pool, and his comment heightening her discomfort, Vashti didn’t return his greeting or his smile.

He is quick to claim victory, she thought irritably, but he does not yet know his opponent.

“Kani, our esteemed guest is still recovering from her ordeal, please bring fresh chai, bread, and *mast*,” Mithridates requested, interrupting her thoughts, and still smiling as though oblivious to her discomfort.

Godel appeared and informed her that their horses and donkeys were securely settled near the flocks. "We will share watches with the chief's men," he informed her. "The storm might continue for days." She thanked him and some of the shepherds left to take their turn whereupon, much to her surprise, Mithridates promptly lay down and fell asleep.

Despite the howling wind outside, peace settled over the pavilion interior.

"My brother likes to tease," Kani whispered sympathetically. "I often wash in the pool, and he never says anything. Forget about him. I have something much more interesting to show you." With dry date palm stalks, she stoked the smokeless fire under an iron grate oven and poured chai from a tin kettle. Then she rolled back her *chokha* sleeves, took a big copper bowl, partially filled it with flour, and tipped some water in.

"Now we make bread," she explained. "*Shire-ye-korma* is my special ingredient," she elaborated, holding up a jar of dark liquid. "I will mix it into the dough and let it grow all morning."

While the date syrup was doing its mysterious work and the remaining men smoked and played *kevci* with a marked board and a small number-dotted cube, Kani reached behind a curtain for a basket full of date palm leaflet fibers. Taking a handful, she began separating them into two long skeins, which she lightly twisted. After folding the fibers in half, she curled them around each other to make a strong rope.

"Please strengthen the pavilion wall facing the wind," Kani requested, handing one of the men the new rope. "Now you try," she urged Vashti, handing her a bunch of fibers.

By the time more ropes were finished, the bread dough was rising over the top of the bowl. Soon, the sweet smell of baking filled the tent, providing welcome distraction from the howling wind. After everyone was served a meal of goat's cheese on fresh bread, Kani filled the kettle and threw in another handful of chai leaves, a stick of cinnamon, and some cardamom pods.

"From the land of Hindush," she explained. "Very strong."

Once the chai had brewed and everyone's glass was full, the storytelling began. Vashti told of Hovakhshatra's victories, and the shepherds described a tiny star that had recently appeared low in the eastern sky.

"It moves a little toward the west each month," they claimed, "between the Great Bear and the Little Lion."

"Perhaps it is the sign of a Saoshyant?" Kani suggested, and Vashti agreed.

Mithridates, who had shaken himself from sleep, reached for a glass of chai and recounted a dream he had just experienced. "I saw the Parthaavans in battle against the Saka to our north," he said, his intense eyes darting to Vashti. "Perhaps this means we should formalize an alliance with Media."

Vashti hesitated. She still wasn't sure of Mithridates' allegiance. "I will speak of this to the Shahan Shah and Shahjin," she replied neutrally. "You should be aware that any agreement we make within the Shahdom of Media must be based on the Mitradat covenant."

"We keep the ways of Mitra but worship only Auramazda," he replied, still watching her closely, she thought, for a reaction. "We recognize that an agreement between the Parthavans and Media would be unbreakable."

"Your promise on behalf of the Parthavans should perpetuate the peace between us," she replied, returning his gaze unflinchingly. "But always the Shahan Shah and Shahjin have the final word on such proposals," she added, congratulating herself on her diplomatic answer and smiling sweetly.

Mithridates smiled back appreciatively. "I will hold both you and the authority of your rulers to your declaration," he stated flatly.

"By the word of the Mitradat, we honor our commitments to all our subject peoples," Vashti promised just as sincerely.

The fire under the stove was dying down, so in the absence of a magi priest, Mithridates closed the evening with a recitation from the Avesta and praised Auramazda as the Shahan Shah of all, the Life, and the Rewarder. With the pavilion walls still flapping and the wind whistling through the date palms, twenty or so human souls settled for the night. Vashti once again found herself protected by Mithridates while Godel guarded the entrance.

By the following morning, visibility had increased but the wind was still blowing hard, making travel very uncomfortable. So out of respect for Mithridates' suggestion the previous evening, Vashti proposed that they discuss the terms of a possible treaty between the Parthavans and Media. He readily agreed, and after tedious negotiations, a tentative agreement protecting the independence of the Parthavan within the Median Shahdom was formulated.

"Of course, it would be best if a marriage between the Shahan Shah's family and the Parthavans were arranged," Mithridates concluded, his imposing eyebrows raised in expectation. "To allow your textile and horse merchants more access to the far eastern trade route, of course," he added hastily.

"We do not have any women eligible to seal such an agreement," Vashti replied just as quickly, surprised by his impertinent suggestion that she might consider marriage to him.

"And I do not have any men of sufficiently high rank to enter the Shahan Shah's family," he replied, his voice tinged with regret. "The agreement will have to be confirmed another way. But let us now prepare to travel to the Oasis of Mouru," he proposed, quickly recovering his equanimity.

Once the storm abated, accompanied by Mithridates and some of his men and still in inhospitable country, Vashti and her party resumed their journey east. To the north, distant mountains hemmed the horizon. Later, as the sun began to sink behind them, Mithridates pointed south to another mountain range.

"There lies Ariavarta, one of the sixteen perfect lands Auramazda made," he explained, "and which Prophet Zarathrustra named. Mouru is another."

Vashti nodded and grinned. "My teacher has told me little about these lands," she replied. "I will have so much to tell her on my return."

Mithridates glanced over at her, his expression relaxed, easy, and self-assured.

He's going to be a friend, she thought, letting the tension that had accumulated in their conversation go and inhaling the piquant desert air scented with dust and dry wood. As she pressured Nzdar's flanks to signal forward, she began to feel more confident about their prospects of reaching their destination.

Over the following days, Mithridates asked Vashti questions about the male heirs to the Median throne, and the Medes' alliance with Babylonia. She replied circumspectly, weaving tales of the Medes' conquests into the conversations. Then one afternoon, in the hazy light of dusk, she was relieved and pleasantly surprised to experience the Prophet's description of Mouru as herdsmen led their sheep, cattle, and goats past verdant fields to night pens in the sublime settlement. Sniffing the lush grass, Nzdar lifted his head and whinnied, and Vashti stroked his mane.

"We will find a comfortable stable for you this evening," she promised him.

Inside the town, Mithridates led the way along unpaved streets past mud-brick houses, some with a wooden upper floor and small courtyard, to the walled compound guarding his permanent home.

"Most of the townspeople can seek shelter here if we are attacked," he explained, "but Mouru is usually safe, the local tribes are peaceful, and the Saka mostly stay north of the mountains."

The gatekeeper let them into a courtyard fragrant with blossom-laden pomegranate bushes and cherry trees in small leaf bud. Entering through a heavy wooden doorway, Vashti found herself in a stone-floored reception room with an iron stove emitting comforting heat. Calling to his servant in his dialect, Mithridates ordered chai, dried fruits, cheese, and bread. Godel brought in her riding bags, and Mithridates showed her to a sweetly scented room hung with delicate pastel-colored silks.

"It was my wife's devotional chamber," her host explained, picking up a limbless, rounded female figurine in an intricately carved cloak. He passed it to Vashti, who ran her fingers over the statuette's soft stone cap. "The power of the goddess did not help her," he continued. "She did not have children."

"I am sorry," was all Vashti could reply, sad that the woman had not achieved her desire.

"She died when her horse fell beneath her," Mithridates added, his voice strangely empty of emotion.

Vashti lowered her eyes before his intense gaze. When she looked up, his eyes were glistening. This time he avoided her gaze.

"Tomorrow we will go to the citadel of Gonur," he announced abruptly, "but now we must rest. My mother occupies the next room. Please ask her for anything else you need."

Fatigued from the exertions of her long journey, Vashti thanked Mithridates and bid him good night. Host and guest retired early to the silence of the sleeping town while her men slept in his stables.

The following day, she ordered the party's second-in-command to stay with the rest of her men and asked Godel to take the trip with her and Mithridates to nearby Gonur, where Mithridates claimed secrets of their civilization would be revealed. As they passed through the gateway of the citadel's two circular walls, Vashti remarked on the impressiveness of the rectangular-shaped temple supported by huge, round corner towers and half-towers midway along the walls.

Leaving Godel with the horses, Mithridates led the way to the temple where he and Vashti silently followed the priest to pay homage to the sacred fire. Vashti then offered the Magush the Shahan Shah's gift of a small carved incense-filled box and praised the building, both of which he thanked her for profusely.

"Your wife did not follow the Prophet?" she asked Mithridates as they were leaving.

"She did, but she also had her own ways," he replied. "I did not try to prevent her, and she sometimes accompanied me to the Atashkedah." He turned to her then lifted his eyes to the temple towers. "I loved my wife," he confessed. Much to Vashti's astonishment, he suddenly marched briskly to his horse, mounted, and rode off, leaving her and Godel behind in a cloud of dust. Vashti shook her head, puzzled by her host's sudden lapse in hospitality but not surprised that he held his feelings close to his heart.

Back in Mouru, Mithridates apologized for his desertion, and Vashti ordered a rest day in preparation for her party's trip to its furthest easterly destination.

Two days later, she informed Mithridates that she would resume her journey whereupon, despite her protests, he insisted on accompanying her and her men.

"We will be leaving my territory, but I have an agreement with the local chiefs that guarantees safe passage through Bactria for myself and my caravans," he assured her. "It is my duty to escort the Shahan Shah's representative safely to the city of Baxtri," he explained.

Unable to resist his gracious offer and having learned to ignore his attempts to tease her, she agreed.

Crossing a wide plain bordered by increasingly close mountain ranges, the travelers eventually reached a valley richly clad with vegetation, from which numerous wells appeared.

"They are the entrances to qanats, the tunnels that feed water from the foothills to the closest villages," Mithridates explained. "The shepherds and cattle herders follow them," he added, pointing to a trail of animal droppings.

Soon another range of green-topped mountains patched with gray loose rocks appeared to the north.

"The Prophet called them 'water mountains'," Mithridates remarked, as Vashti gazed in awe at the sunlit silver snake of a river flowing from the mountains onto the plain before them. Closer to the city, the travelers passed neatly planted grain crops and grape vines watered by lily-graced canals.

"The capital of another perfect land?" she inquired of Mithridates.

He smiled. "Beneath the great Hindu Kush," he proclaimed, pointing to the ridge of snowcapped mountains behind the city.

"What a treasure Grandfather Daia-okku acquired for Media," Vashti marveled of the white towers. But Mithridates was waving at an approaching caravan of fully laden two-humped camels. Quickly, she steered Nzdar to the side of the road. "They have come through the valley of Balkhab," he explained. "But if you wish to visit the land of Sina far, far to the east, you will have to cross the Oxus River and journey through Samarqand."

"To Sina to buy silk? We will have to go there another time!" She chuckled.

Mithridates smiled broadly, his face lighting up at her suggestion of further travels. "Not before you discover the city of Baxtri," he maintained. "The Prophet Zarathrustra taught here. It is a sacred place, but it is not well-protected." Vashti looked up at the fortified city walls arrayed against the mountains. She had achieved her goal, but she was a long way from the safety of Hagmatana and her only strong friend in this foreign land was a tribal chief, whom she was only just learning to trust. She sighed inwardly.

"All praise to Auramazda," she said to herself. "We have reached our destination."

"Would you like me to find a caravansary for you and your men?" Mithridates offered, interrupting her thoughts.

"Yes. Please inform the proprietor that we will require all the rooms and the stables," Vashti replied. She wanted to give her loyal men comfortable accommodation, and Nzdar and the other animals, who had faithfully brought them all the way to this exotic city, a good rest.

After ensuring that Vashti and her party were settled into the caravansary's mud-brick rooms built around a central courtyard, and Godel had fed the horses and donkeys and watered them from the spring-fed fountain, Mithridates left to negotiate the price of an evening meal of bread and cooked beans from a vendor outside the establishment.

She awoke the next day to the gentle splashing of the fountain in the courtyard, and Mithridates knock on her door. She opened it to find him with a bag each of fresh apricots and pistachio nuts. Grabbing last night's pile of leftover bread and sending one of her men to ask for a pot of *mast* from the caravansary manager, she suggested they breakfast around the fountain. Soon the bowing proprietor appeared with glasses of chai and some cushions. Gazing at the fountain's bubbling cascade, Mithridates turned to her with an impish grin and warned her not to venture into the pool, lest she be observed by himself and any of her men. Laughing, she picked up a cushion and threw it at him. Startled by her impulsive response, she suddenly realized that the Parthavan chief was becoming more than a guide and silently thanked Auramazda for him.

Both knew how to take care of her.

After Godel and the men had examined and treated the animals for sores and lameness, some rest days were declared for both travelers and beasts. At Vashti's request, Mithridates then sent his chieftain to request an audience with the Governor of Baxtri. Returning with information about the purchase of new horse rugs to replace their worn ones, he announced that the governor would meet them in two days' time.

When she dismissed her men the next day, Vashti warned them to honor the Shahan Shah in all their dealings. Godel insisted he stay with her, but she told him Mithridates had once again volunteered his guard services and that she wished to maintain the diplomatic relationship by keeping his company. Her guard reluctantly agreed and went off to inform the men of her instructions.

Instead of touring the city as expected, Mithridates engaged fresh horses for himself and Vashti to ride to the foothills of the mountains. A cold wind blew off jagged peaks as they drew closer to the impenetrable barrier.

"What is beyond?" she asked.

"The land of Hindush," he answered. "Some of our people settled there many years ago and took our civilization with them."

"Do they follow the Prophet?"

"Some do, but others worship many gods."

I have even more to tell Debyar, Vashti thought, wrinkling her brow.

Mithridates regarded her intently. "Is something wrong, dear?"

Startled, she glanced back. It was the first time he had used such an expression of close friendship, and she didn't know whether to be offended or appreciative.

"No, thank you, but I am learning how extensive the Ariavartan territories are to the east and that there are many more fascinating lands beyond," she replied. "I have also discovered how much the Shahan Shah, the Shahjin, and I value our good friends and allies."

He smiled broadly, his teeth flashing white beneath his full moustache. "It is my wish that your audience with the governor will yield the same result," he replied. The Parthavan chief's formality belied the sudden softening of his eyes, and she couldn't help wondering what he really thought of her.

As the Shahan Shah's representative, it was a question she could probably never ask.

Chapter 12

"Baxtri is at the crossroads of many lands," Mithridates commented as he and Vashti passed stalls selling gold and silver vessels and other metalwares on their way to the governor's residence.

"These come from the east," he said, pointing to the shiny displays.

"I wish to purchase some embroidered silks for the women in my family," Vashti requested of the piles of fine fabrics painted with colorful floral, bird, and animal designs.

"We will return to them later," he promised.

The gatekeeper admitted them to the compound of the governor's stone, wood-framed house, and they were ushered into a dim reception room lit by mounted oil lamps and warmed by a tendur fire oven. The governor's tasselled cloak swished as he bowed to Vashti and offered her a seat on a carved wooden chair next to himself. His wife then lit an incense burner of earthy frankincense resin and gifted Vashti with a small alabaster jar of myrrh oil, which she accepted with many thanks. As translator, Mithridates sat legs folded on a large cushion in the middle of the rug-covered floor.

A servant brought chai, roasted sunflower seeds, and fresh figs as the governor turned to Vashti.

"Welcome to Baxtri, capital of the *bahasht* of Bactria, Vashti of the Medes. I trust you are enjoying another of Auramazda's sixteen perfect lands of the Ariavartan people?" he inquired enthusiastically, his neatly clipped and curled beard jiggling beneath his weathered face.

"Thank you for your welcome. I am enjoying their warm hospitality," Vashti responded warmly. "Shahan Shah Hovakhshatra and Shahjin Ardela send their greetings and gratitude for your maintenance of peace in the region."

"We accept their most gracious messages and patronage," the governor replied, grinning widely, "and are honored by the visit of their ambassador. I trust you have had a safe trip to this corner of our world?"

Vashti smiled and caught Mithridates' eye. "Due to the diligence of your ally chief Mithridates, and Auramazda's protection, I have the privilege of meeting you in your splendid city," she replied before briefly describing her travels.

"Many thanks," the governor replied. "You are welcome to attend one of the fire temples we have in honor of Prophet Zarathrustra's birth in Bactria and his work in the city. I will ask my personal magi priest to accompany you."

After accepting the invitation, Vashti directed the conversation to state business. "Do you have any concerns about the protection of the region and especially the city?" she asked, recalling Mithridates' comment about its vulnerability.

"We are exposed to attack on this wide open plain but rely on our friends the Parthavans and their allies the Dahae to come to our aid," the governor answered, glancing at Mithridates, who nodded agreement. "However, if our enemies break through the Pamir Mountains, we will struggle to defend ourselves with our local garrisons."

"Would you like the Shahan Shah to send specialized fighters to defend the strategic mountain passes?" Vashti offered.

The governor beamed. "We would be most grateful. It would help ensure our trade with the land of Hindush to the southeast and safe passage of goods to Hagmatana and beyond. And we will continue to maintain the road across the northern foothills. We call it the Silk Road."

"It's a beautiful name for a route bringing many luxury goods," Vashti noted of the spices, precious stones, and porcelain products that had begun to trickle in from the east. "The Shahan Shah plans to build a road between Hagmatana and Susiana, which he hopes will extend all the way to Sardis, the capital of Lydia. But at present, the Lydians are not cooperating with us, in fact quite the opposite. However, I will speak to him about improving the road from Hagmatana to Rhagae and farther to the east. Perhaps one day it too will join the Silk Road."

The governor looked pleased. "We trust peace will prevail, and that trade from the east can be extended throughout all the Ariavartan lands," he replied enthusiastically.

The servant offered citron cakes, *mast*, bread, and wine; and the governor produced a parchment sheet marked with the area's garrisons. By the time the meeting had finished, a scribe had made a fresh copy for Vashti to take back to the Shahan Shah. From her riding bag, Vashti took instructions for the governor to count the people and record crop yields and animal increases.

"They will only be taxed in time of war," she explained. "Your yearly tribute is enough in peace time. Please return the records with your emissary."

With the discussions almost finished, the governor's wife, Anahita, who had sat silently throughout the meeting, seized Vashti's hand. "Come, dear, I will show you my collection of furs."

By this time, the men had lit long *galyan* pipes and were laughing and telling stories in the bliss of pungent smoke.

In her chamber, Anahita opened a chest of animal skins. "This is fox," she explained, wrapping a red fur around her neck, "and this is lynx." She revealed a vest of light brown fur tipped in black. "But my favorite is the snow leopard," she boasted of another light-skinned *chokha* with large black dots.

"Do they keep you warm?" Vashti asked coolly, not wanting to voice her displeasure at the destruction of the wild animals. "We are increasing our sheep flocks. The wool trade with lands to our west is growing, especially in the regions of Romanus and Hellas, north of the Great Sea islands."

Anahita looked puzzled. "Furs are preferred by the leading women here," she sniffed. "They are very warm, plentiful, and do not cost much. Killing the wild animals protects our people and our domestic animals."

"That's why we have shepherds. Ours fight bears and wolves," Vashti replied evenly.

Anahita scowled, closed the chest, and waved Vashti to the door. "We will return to the reception room," she announced coldly. Scolding herself for her insensitivity, Vashti apologized, took the silver chain from her neck, and handed it to Anahita, who accepted it with a bow.

Back in the smoky reception room, the governor and Mithridates were still conversing gaily in their dialect. Vashti and Anahita chatted amiably until Mithridates stood unsteadily and bid the governor a slurred farewell. Unhappy about hastily saying goodbye to her hosts, Vashti followed Mithridates.

Outside, a cold wind blowing off the mountains quickly snapped him to attention. Breathing deeply, he apologized, mounted his horse slowly, and led the way back to the markets, where many colorful banners and shoppers buying smoked meats, fruits, and bread-making grains signified the approach of Norouz.

After purchasing the pretty fabrics she had previously admired, Vashti couldn't resist a carved, creamy colored lion.

"Do you know which animal it is made from?" Mithridates asked, a frown crossing his brow.

"An ox?" Vashti replied.

"No. It is from an elephant."

She gasped. Debyar had told her about the huge gray animals with long teeth growing beside even longer noses called trunks, and Amytis had written that Nebuchadnezzar kept some in his animal park.

"Yes. They are killed in the land of Hindush for their long tusks known as ivory," Mithridates continued.

"Then I must return this," Vashti replied quickly.

"Don't," Mithridates advised. "It would not be good for a visitor to reject the craft." Not wanting to create an international incident, she wrapped the carving in her cream silk scarf and stuffed it in her riding bag.

That evening, the governor invited Vashti and her party to a musical evening around a huge fire in the town. Under a moonless sky, the star sign of the warrior shone brightly as the people ate, drank, and watched Gosan minstrels in colorful, textured tunics play musical instruments, dance, and recite poems proclaiming the worth of the Kayaniam shahs, Shahan Shah Hovakhshatra, his family, and his ancestors. They told of a golden age in the past when Shahan Shah Yima-yima-khshaeta left his land of harsh winters to rule a perfectly happy people in the secluded land of Ariavarta. The inhabitants were not overbearing, mean-spirited, stupid, or violent. There was no poverty or *druj*, nor were there any physical weaknesses or deformities in the people; all had perfect teeth and well-proportioned bodies. The *daevas* did not affect them, and they lived amongst fragrant trees and golden pillars with fat, healthy cattle, and sweet fruits, which made them grow tall and beautiful.

Vashti listened in rapture, yearning to help her uncle and aunt make Media such a land, a place where *asha* flourished and *druj* could not survive. Seated beside her, Mithridates occasionally sought her approval with a quick glance, which she caught from the corner of her eye. However, she only responded once. On her last night in this exotic city of many different peoples, some strange and some known to her, she didn't want to seem too familiar with someone she might never have any dealings with again.

As the evening drew on, Mithridates called to the lead minstrel and whispered in his ear. The performer looked at Vashti, grinned, strummed his *tanbour*, and sang:

How can I tell your voice is sweet?
Well, it enters my heart and takes me,
Off in the air where I dance like a leaf,

What do I know about you?

Well, you shake me when you are with me,

And I get restless till I see you again,

Till I see you are for me

Always for me, over and over, again.

This time, she could not avoid Mithridates' eyes firmly fixed on her. Realizing her hot face was red with embarrassment, she didn't know where else to look.

Chapter 13

With the horses and donkeys well rested, it was time for Vashti and her party to begin their long journey home. But this time, Mithridates led them along another road west from Baxtri through green valleys and rivers spilling from the foothills of the northern range they had seen on their inward journey. Two weeks later, he announced that he would turn south to his own land.

Thunderclouds were gathering over the mountains when the time for parting came. Mithridates gave Godel his last instructions and handed Vashti a small leather pouch. "For you…to keep in remembrance of our travels," he explained haltingly, his eyes averted. Recalling his bold engagement of the minstrel at Baxtri, she wondered what the pouch contained but, instead of opening it, quickly stowed it in her riding bag. Then she dismounted Nzdar and stepped toward the man who had guided her and her men safely over thousands of stades.

"How can I thank you?" she asked.

"Tell Shahan Shah Hovakhshatra and Shahjin Ardela about my great land," he requested, "and that my people stand in peace with them."

Vashti held out her hand. "*Zors spas,* friend of the Medes."

Mithridates took her hand in both of his and held it tightly. "Restless till I see you again. Always for me," he said softly.

Vashti looked away from his eyes willing her to stay, as Godel stealthily approached.

"Stop," she cried. "Do you think he would harm me after all this time?" She turned to Mithridates and met his gaze.

His eyes are deeper than Lake Zrebar, but he is not hidden from me, she thought. Even though we have touched for the first time, I know this man.

Her fingers on his wrist covered his steadily beating pulse. She wanted the life within him but would not take it. Media called and she would return to Hagmatana. Slowly, she withdrew her hand.

Nzdar whinnied as if to hurry her. She took his reins, mounted, squeezed his flanks, and signaled Godel and her party to follow. Her tears dropping onto Nzdar's rug continued as the gulf between her and the man she had learned to trust grew.

A few long minutes later, she looked back. The Parthavan chief stood alone watching her, his cloak flapping in the light breeze. She lifted the hand he had held and waved. Mithridates sank to his knees, his head bowed, his hand on his heart.

She turned around quickly so he would not see her tear-streaked face glistening. As the stades between them grew, she fought the urge to turn Nzdar round, gallop back, and accept his veiled offer of marriage.

While traveling with him, the only dreams she could remember were sweet. Her sleep was always deep and her body soft; each morning, she awoke peacefully to pleasantries like the twitter of birds, the sigh of wind in date palms, the bleating and neighing of animals, or the sounds of people moving in a camp, a dwar, a house, or outside on city streets. Her transition into daytime was always smooth, and there was no stiffness in her body. But on leaving the Parthavan chief, she began to dream again. At first fleeting visions of her home, her family, Khezmet, and Debyar. The mere smell of Nzdar's mane created pictures in her mind of the stables, Daro, and Ishtovigo angrily throwing bronze horses' bits at the stable wall. Sometimes she would see the Shahan Shah and Shahjin receiving visitors in the palace. The tightness in her body began to return.

Back in the citadel, Shahan Shah Hovakhshatra paced the floor of his chamber. His eldest son and his second son had not returned from their hunting trip in Azadia, and Vashti and her escort had been away longer than expected.

"Take a small search party and find Shawish and Artaspaya," he ordered Harpagos impatiently. "I want them back before Vashti returns."

Harpagos frowned. "But Shahan Shah perhaps they have found plenty of game and are enjoying an extended trip, especially since they were accompanied by our most skilled Scythian archers," he protested. "And we do not know when Vashti will return."

"Yes, it is all quite uncertain," Hovakhshatra replied. "Nevertheless, I want my sons back home. In case there has been foul play, arm the search party so that it looks like another training exercise. Leave before dawn tomorrow. We do not want to let any internal enemies know about our troops' movements."

"Certainly, Shahan Shah. I will send my second-in-command to guard you." Harpagos turned on his heel and went straight to the barracks to prepare. Daro and his assistants had just finished fitting the last rugs and reins for the expedition when the clack of horses' hooves on cobblestones distracted all the stable hands, who rushed outside. Godel and Vashti were leading their horses through the golden gateway, in honor of the beasts who had taken them safely to and from their destination. Daro beat a *daf* drum to announce their arrival; and Shamin, Parwin, and Khezmet, followed by her two children, raced outside to see what the noise was about.

Shamin hurried to Vashti and hugged her tightly. "My darling, I thought I would never see you again but here you are…at last."

"Dear, Mother, I am back…with so much to tell you. And I finished my hardship test," she declared triumphantly. Her voice trailed off as the others tried to hug her while Khezmet picked up her crying children.

"They are wondering who you are, stranger," she laughed.

"Have I been away so long that they have forgotten me?" Vashti cried.

"Five months."

Vashti looked across the citadel compound. Nothing had changed in the buildings, but she was different. Mithridates had imprinted memories even more enduring than the stone bears lining the steps to the palace. But her weary mind was still struggling to sort through those memories…and what she thought about Mithridates.

Little hands were tugging at her dirty cloak. "Shireen remembers you," Khezmet announced of her eldest whereupon Vashti picked up the child and hugged her.

"Dear," Khezmet cried as Vashti stumbled over a cobblestone, "you are very tired. Come inside now." Leaning on Shamin and Khezmet, she tottered toward her home.

"Thank Auramazda you are back," Shamin exclaimed when they sat down inside, "but my brother still awaits the arrival of his sons."

"Where are they?" Vashti asked.

As Shamin explained, Vashti realized that neither of her two older male cousins were in her recent dreams. Then she remembered her dream about Shawish weeks ago and shuddered, hoping nothing serious had happened to him.

"You know how much they love the chase of the hunt," she told Shamin, trying to console her. "They have probably gone through Azadia, deep into the region of Urartu."

That night, Vashti had another dream. She was hunting with Shawish when suddenly he disappeared; she rode up and down the park but failed to find him. Sometimes she thought she saw his shadow disappearing into the forest, but Nzdar could not go fast enough to catch him. She was home, but where was Shawish? And what did her two dreams about him mean?

When Khezmet entered Vashti's room next morning, she found her putting on formal robes. Outside, horses whinnied as Harpagos issued orders to his departing troops.

“Mistress, you should rest after your long journey,” Khezmet protested.

“I must see the Shahan Shah to report on my trip,” Vashti explained. “Where is Ferhad?”

“Still with the Bears. He wanted to go to Azadia with his cousins, but General Biraxeas would not allow it.” Vashti sighed. At least her brother was safe and surely nothing could happen to the heirs to the throne with such experienced fighters in attendance, except, perhaps for a wild animal attack.

“Come for chai, dear,” Shamin called from downstairs. “The Shahjin will be here soon. You must prepare.” When Ardela arrived with her daughter Shelna, Shamin hugged and kissed her, and Vashti called Parwin to play with her cousin. Ardela responded calmly, but her expression was grim, and her eyes were bloodshot.

“Let’s discuss the menu for the next women’s banquet,” Shamin suggested to distract her sister-in-law. “I think the *terkhena* should be made of—”

Vashti interrupted her mother to excuse herself to the Shahjin, explaining her mission to the Shahan Shah. Then she called Khezmet to help her finish her preparations. The governors of Zadraka and Bactria expected her to faithfully represent their requests, and no matter what she thought of Mithridates, those of the Parthavan chief could not be ignored.

Stopping regularly to change horses, Harpagos’ search party traveled fifty stades a day west along the Shahan Shah’s Road for several days to overnight in the town of Hawler. They then proceeded northeast to the foothills of the Qandil Mountains and made camp in the region of Azadia. Searching the sparsely wooded region the following day, they saw plenty of game but no hunters. In villages nestled in valleys, they questioned the inhabitants, but no one had seen any strangers.

"It's as though our men have been taken by the *daevas,*" Harpagos told his troops, scratching his head in puzzlement. After a villager reported recently seeing a caravan of strangers heading west, Harpagos and his party followed the mountain trail they were said to have taken. Early the next morning, in another remote village, they encountered an elderly man herding goats.

When Harpagos inquired about the hunters, the man wrinkled his brow. "Yes, I recall a friendly young man with some hunters who asked me where to find gazelle, ibex, and wild ass. I told him farther up the mountain. He smiled kindly and gave me a gold coin. I asked him what a fine young man was doing out here with such wild-looking warriors, and he said that he and his brother were on a hunting trip." The old man paused. "Scythians from the steppe region between the Caspian and Aral Seas have been raiding us for months. Their families follow when their soldiers have taken what they want."

Harpagos cursed. "What did the young man and his party do then?"

"He thanked me for my help and invited me to visit him and his companions in his camp, but I had my goats to care for, so I did not accept," the old man answered, smiling apologetically.

"Did you see him again?" Harpagos asked.

"No, but when I later became uneasy about the Scythian caravan, I left my goats with my son and went with some of the young men from my village to a sheltered place I knew farther up the mountain. I found a campsite, but I couldn't tell how long the occupants had been gone," the villager explained.

Harpagos nodded appreciatively. "What is your name?"

"I am Reband, at your service."

"Reband, can you take us to the campsite?" Harpagos asked, handing the man some silver coins.

"Yes, Commander," Reband replied, pocketing the coins, "it is not far."

After leading them to a cleared site on the mountainside, Reband headed back to his village. Brushing away leaves in the middle of the clearing, Harpagos and his men found ashes, dead coals, and charred animal bones. Horse manure under nearby trees signaled recent occupation.

"Scour the area," Harpagos ordered. After cutting away light undergrowth, the men fanned out from the spent campfire, prodding the ground with their lances in search of disturbed soil. Suddenly, a cry rang out from a dell below the campsite.

"General, over here." Harpagos raced down to where a pointy-toed boot with three eyelet holes on each side was sticking out of the ground. "It looks like one of ours," he breathed.

"The soil around it is loose," the soldier who had found the boot noted.

"Dig it out," Harpagos ordered. Using their hands and daggers, the soldiers loosened the earth around the leg still in *pantol*. Another soldier appeared holding a rounded felt hat trimmed with a single lappet. "He is one of ours," Harpagos declared. "There might be more. Keep working in circles from the fire two paces apart."

"Here," came another urgent call from farther down the dell as more troops furiously dug the loose soil with their hands.

"He is tall, and his sash is the Shahan Shah's regimental scarlet," the soldier's voice echoed up the hill as Harpagos crashed through the bushes. On reaching the mutilated body, Harpagos slammed his lance into the ground. "It is Shawish," he stated bitterly. "Media has been attacked."

"This one has a triangular-shaped arrow in his back," yelled the soldier at the top of the dell. "And, General, his sash means he must be the Shahan Shah's second son."

"So it was the Scythians," Harpagos muttered to his second-in-command, "but which ones?"

By the time the men had searched the area within a half stade of the fire site, all the hunting party members had been found, killed by the same sorts of weapons. Harpagos assembled his men.

"It probably wasn't the Scythian caravan," he surmised. "And if the villagers had been suspicious of them, they would have driven them out. This was a cunning ambush, probably by Scythians whose families followed them, but clearly our Scythians were loyal. They died defending our men and themselves."

"Do you want us to try to pursue the attackers?" Harpagos' second-in-command asked.

"No. The Shahan Shah is awaiting news, and we must hurry home with the bodies of his sons. We will let him decide how he will avenge their deaths. Ride now with this message," he ordered his most hardy warriors. Taking a deerskin patch and metal writing rod out of his riding bag, Harpagos etched the message that he had long dreaded.

Reband wrung his hands when he heard the news. "Commander, this has nothing to do with the people of our village," he pleaded. "We are the loyal subjects of the Shahan Shah and are very sorry for the loss of his sons and his men."

"I believe the Azadians would never do this," Harpagos assured him. "It is the work of highly skilled archers, most likely a raiding party of Scythian warriors from the north."

"Please stay in our homes and eat with us," Reband offered. "I will notify the village chief so we can all help with the bodies of your dead."

"Many thanks, Reband. We will buy a cart from you for the Shahan Shah's sons and leave the rest of our dead in your care," Harpagos replied.

"We will give you a cart in honor of the Shahan Shah's sons," Reband insisted. "And be assured we will treat his soldiers as our own." Harpagos nodded, and his men took the bodies from their horses and carried them into the homes of Reband and his neighbors.

Ten days later, the exhausted bearers of the terrible tidings breached the uppermost gate of the citadel. Stumbling from their mounts, they brushed past the palace guards who offered no resistance. The Shahah Shah and Shahjin were farewelling the Piree Magush when the messengers arrived. Recognizing them, Harpagos' second-in-command guard notified the leading couple of their arrival.

"My dear, I think you should leave," Hovakhshatra told his wife when they reached their private chambers.

"No, dear, I want to hear the message," Ardela replied firmly. The men bowed before the golden scepter and one handed the Shahan Shah Harpagos' note. As Hovakhshatra read it, his hands began to tremble, but his face stiffened.

"Our sons are gone?" Ardela whispered.

"Yes. Harpagos thinks rogue Scythians from north of Azadia took them in a well-planned attack."

Ardela gasped, and her face blanched.

"Summon the generals," Hovakhshatra bellowed to the guard. "We are at war."

"Dear, wait till Harpagos returns," Ardela urged, placing a restraining hand on her husband's arm. "We should get all the information before taking such action."

"Be sure, my love. I will avenge those murderous dogs if it takes my life," Hovakshatra yelled as Ardela stifled her sobs.

"No, my Shahan Shah, not yours as well," Ardela cried. "It is enough that we have lost our precious sons," she added before collapsing on a nearby couch.

"Quickly, bring the Shahjin chai and herbal mixtures," the Shahan Shah roared. "And order the Piree Magush to attend her immediately."

The guard called for one of Ardela's maids just as her sobs turned to wails.

Chapter 14

Peering through her bedroom window, Vashti saw the two messengers stagger up the palace steps as Daro led their weary mounts away. Wondering if Shawish and Artaspaya had been found, she stepped outside, sat on the wooden seat beneath the oak tree, and waited. Soon Khezmet joined her, and they rested in silence.

"Dear, your face is pale. Have you had another dream?" Khezmet asked.

Vashti fixed her gaze on the palace steps. "Yes, but I still don't understand it." She took Khezmet's hand. "And I am afraid I do not want to know."

"Dear, do not say such things," Khezmet replied. "You are tired after your long trip. Soon you will be strong again." She squeezed Vashti's hand. "You are cold. I will get a glass of hot chai for you."

In the palace, when the generals arrived the Shahan Shah held out the golden scepter, informed them of the attack, and gave everyone permission to speak. Harpagos' appointed guard had ushered in the Magush, who sat quietly in the corner of the war room.

After condolences were given, Hovakhshatra detailed his response. "We must consider the possibility of an alliance between the Scythian tribes north of Urartu, and the Lydians west of our territory in Cappadocia since we have no treaty with them," he began.

"Generals Biraxeas and Taxsmaspada, you will accompany me to the site of the massacre with fifty men from each of your regiments. I will send messengers to the provincial governors to summons all capable men for war. The Bears under my nephew Ferhad will remain here on full alert until Harpagos returns."

"But, Shahan Shah, who will till the fields if our men are fighting Lydia?" General Taxsmaspada asked.

"Who grew our food when we fought Athoraya?" Hovakhshatra replied.

Taxmaspada looked down. "The women…they sowed, cultivated, and harvested in the war with Athoraya."

"And they will do it again," General Biraxeas added, "along with the children. Our people taught the Salmat Qaqqardi lowlands people between the Two Rivers to grow crops. They will never starve."

"The destruction of my sons and their forces is an act of war against Media," Hovakhshatra continued. "The messengers to the provinces will remain as spies to gather information on any suspicious activities against Media, which will be reported back to us."

"Shouldn't something be done about the remaining Scythians in the shahdom, at least those in Busae lands?" General Taxsmaspada asked.

"Not necessarily," the Shahan Shah replied. "It appears that our Scythians were not involved."

"But which people other than Scythians could possibly overcome our troops?"

"We will wait till Harpagos returns to determine that," Hovakhshatra insisted, taking his wife's advice, but the generals were not convinced.

"Shahan Shah, this sort of atrocity must never happen again.

Not only have we lost your precious sons and heirs but also some of our finest young officers," General Biraxeas implored. "The Scythians in Media cannot be trusted. They must be either placed in captivity or deported," General Taxsmaspada insisted.

"I disagree," Hovakhshatra replied indignantly, "but if that is what you want, the Scythians will be given three days to either leave our territories or work without pay on our farms. If we find that foreign Scythians are responsible for the attack, our Scythians will be allowed to return or be released. Now you are dismissed to your regiments."

When they had gone, the Magush rose from the corner of the room, his expression grave. "Shahan Shah, if I may offer advice?"

"What is it?" Hovakhshatra snapped.

"Do not seek hasty revenge. Auramazda has his way of peace. Try to find it." Without asking permission to leave, he strode out. Hovakhshatra then rose and asked his guard to call the Shahjin, who had been helped from the room by her maids.

"All is lost," Ardela cried on returning. "Two sons gone and the other almost completely disinterested in his nation!"

"Do not worry. We still have Vashti," Hovakhshatra replied confidently.

Ardela stared at her husband. "No. She is not for Ishtovigo."

"She is the only one who can succeed you and provide an heir from us," Hovakhshatra insisted.

Even more stricken, Ardela could only reply with the ululation of mourning.

"The palace guard is outside," Gulah informed Shamin that afternoon. "He says the Shahan Shah and Shahjin are here to see you."

Shamin jumped up. “Let them in,” she ordered. Gulah hurried to the door and admitted the waiting couple with their daughter, Shelna. “How pleasant to see you all,” Shamin greeted, wondering about the solemn expression on her guests’ faces.

“Shamin, you look well. Are the children here?” her brother asked.

“Yes. They are all here except Ferhad. Gulah, please call them,” Shamin instructed. Vashti appeared with Khezmet and greeted her aunt and uncle, and Parwin crept in and sat beside Shelna.

Hovakhshatra cleared his throat. “There has been a vicious attack,” he began.

“It’s Shawish, isn’t it?” Vashti cried. “He’s been injured or—”

“We’ve lost both our boys,” Ardela cried.

Parwin hugged Shelna, and Shamin and Khezmet each took one of Vashti’s hands. “My dreams came true again,” Vashti replied. “In all of them, Shawish either disappeared or couldn’t be found. How did they die?” she asked, wringing her hands in anguish. After her uncle explained they were waiting for Harpagos to return to find out, Vashti acknowledged that her cousins would never provoke such an attack, and everyone agreed. Gulah brought chai as Ardela and Shamin tried unsuccessfully to persuade Hovakhshatra not to venture to Azadia.

“Vashti dear,” Ardela continued, sniffling, “we understand you and Shawish were…good friends. We know you brought him happiness. To us you are both niece and daughter.”

Vashti smiled weakly. “Aunt, it was a privilege to be Shawish’s friend and companion. He always practiced good thoughts, good words, and good deeds toward me and upheld *asha*.” Her compliments brought fresh tears from everyone except the Shahan Shah, whose grim expression indicated his steely resolve to avenge the killers of his sons.

❖

Forty days of mourning throughout Media followed the return of Harpagos with the bodies of Shawish and Artaspaya. Taking the Magush's advice, Hovakhshatra set aside his plans for war and employed hunters from the Azadia region to follow the trail of reports about the caravan mentioned by Reband. After tracing the caravan's journey to the border with Lydia, the hunters returned without any evidence that Lydia harbored the murderers. Hovakhshatra subsequently sent an envoy to the city of Sardis inquiring about Scythian activity in Lydian territory near the border with Media but received no reply.

"Uncooperative as usual," Hovakhshatra complained of Shah Alyattes at a meeting of his advisors. "He thinks his new gold and silver alloy coins will become the currency everywhere and dominate trading so that he can build his army with the proceeds and expand his shahdom."

His advisors nodded. "It's very unwise to ignore the ally of Babylonia," the Magush commented. Hovakhshatra grimaced, vowed not to forget Alyattes' snub, and resolved privately to order the hunters to go deeper into the region on Media's northwestern border that Scythians were known to frequent.

In the following months, yellow, orange, and red leaves of oak, cypress, and elm trees fell on the fertile lands of the Median triangle in sympathy with their human occupants while the Shahan Shah and Shahjin took no hunting trips, canceled the traditional autumn horse races, and did not consult the Magush. After the remains of Shawish and Artaspaya were buried in the rock tomb on Mount Alvand, Vashti and the children resumed their lessons with Debyar, whose headdress studded with rare red garnet stones fascinated them. When Vashti asked her about it, the teacher blushed and replied that it came from a market town on the Shahan Shah's Road.

"Do we trade with that town?" Vashti asked.

"No. This headdress was given to me by a friend," Debyar replied shyly. Vashti nodded, wondering how her teacher had found such a friend. Her question was answered when a few days later Harpagos appeared at Shamin's front door, asking for Debyar and bearing a bunch of lilies.

"Lessons are just finishing," Gulah informed him.

Trailed by her pupils and carrying her basket of writing implements and scrolls, Debyar greeted her visitor with a radiant smile. Accepting the flowers, she handed her basket to Khezmet, threaded her arm through Harpagos', and walked out with him into the courtyard, the light specks in her headdress's gemstones flashing in the afternoon sun. Debyar's pupils and the servants stood watching, their mouths agape. All except Vashti, who was reminded of the jewelry stalls at the markets of Baxtri.

"Vashti spends much time reading the Avesta," Debyar told Shamin sometime later. "Have you noticed she no longer goes to the palace, the city, or the hunting grounds?"

"Yes. She is still in mourning and won't entertain any guests. Ishtovigo keeps calling but she says she is too tired. The Magush claims it will take at least six months…"

Shamin sighed. "Loss is strange and unnatural," she commented. "But at least her reading is improving." Debyar nodded agreement, wondering what else might be causing the behavior change in her favorite pupil.

At the end of a lesson on the lands dependent on the Medes the next day, Vashti began to ask questions.

"Is Lydia west of Urartu?"

"Yes, but many hundreds of stades away."

"And if you were fleeing from crimes committed in northern Media, would you go there?"

"Yes. You might go through Cappadocia to hide in Lydia," the teacher answered.

"Thank you, Debyar. I must finish my lesson now. I have something important to do," Vashti declared.

Before her teacher could answer, she headed for the door. Out in the stables, she inspected Nzdar's reins and rug before sneaking back into the house to stuff food, gold coins, and extra clothing into her riding bags. When Khezmet brought Vashti her warm drink just before bedtime, she found her once more reading her Avesta parchments.

"It helps me sleep," Vashti explained. "And not dream."

Early the next morning, clad in her thickest cloak and a long *kulaw-u-dastmal* draped around her head and neck, Vashti rode Nzdar out of the stables, down through the citadel gates and onto the northwestern road. Believing that if she could find the place where Shawish and Artaspaya had died, she would not dream of them again, she rode on. Since she had not warned them of their fate, it was the least she could do to honor their memories.

When Khezmet realized Vashti was missing, she immediately informed Shamin and checked the stables. Finding Nzdar gone, she returned to the house to tell Debyar, who was waiting to begin lessons.

"She was asking about Lydia yesterday," the teacher recalled.

Khezmet immediately raced out to Daro and told him to take the fastest horse in the stables to look for Vashti on the northwestern road. In a few minutes, hooves crashed on the cobblestones as he rode out.

Vashti was not far from the Shahan Shah's Road when she became aware of another rider behind her. Keeping a steady pace to preserve Nzdar, she didn't look round till Daro reached for his reins. When he halted the horse, she lost her temper.

"What are you doing here?" she yelled.

"Khezmet sent me," Daro replied apologetically, his eyes darting around to avoid hers. "She wants you to come home at once. If your family finds out you have run away, they will be very upset."

She took a deep breath. "I must find the place where my cousins died," she insisted but much more calmly. "No one is going to stop me. Go back to the city."

"You should come with back with me immediately," Daro replied firmly, refusing to relinquish Nzdar's reins.

She sighed in resignation. "Follow me to the next village. We will send a messenger back to the citadel to tell them you are traveling with me to the site of my cousin's deaths and not to let anyone else come after me."

"Then we will go together," Daro conceded warily, realizing he had suddenly taken on the responsibility of being Vashti's guard.

Several days later, the riders found the cold, desolate hillside where Shawish and Artaspaya had been hastily buried by their murderers. To Vashti, the disturbed earth beneath which they had been placed in shallow graves seemed to cry out with their blood while the deafening silence helplessly mourned the lives that had so recklessly been taken. In that moment, she vowed to avenge her cousins' deaths as well as her father's.

Harpagos' conclusion that Shawish, Artaspaya, and their troop had defended themselves with daggers in brutal fights while invading Scythians targeted them with their sharp, triangular-shaped arrows infuriated her, and she kicked the lifeless soil angrily. Picturing Shawish in full pursuit of prey, his long flaxen locks streaming behind him, and his expression fixed in absolute concentration, she wondered what her life would have been like had he survived.

Thinking back over their times together, including the interlude at the waterfall, she realized she had long known that he loved her. Now she would never know how much, as their union would never be. While he had been too shy to express his feelings for her, she had not known how to respond to his advances. As her tears fell, she sorely regretted not telling him how much she admired and trusted him. She wanted to walk the site again to honor her cousins and the loyal troops who had fought so valiantly for their lives, but she couldn't; this place of defeat and suffering sent shivers down her spine like those she had experienced after the dream about her father. Turning Nzdar onto the homeward path, she wiped her eyes and face with her sleeve and vowed that such an attack would never happen again while she was alive.

That evening around their campfire, she informed Daro they were going to Lydia to try to find Shawish's and Artaspaya's murderers. When he protested, she told him she would need a dream telling her not to go to prevent her plan. But during the night, heavy rain on the roof of the shepherd's hut they had camped in woke them both from a peaceful sleep.

"We must return, tomorrow," Daro insisted, "or we might not be able to cross the river."

When the rain stopped early in the morning, Vashti relented. Eventually, the outlying villages of the capital appeared on the horizon with the citadel looming behind. Light rain was falling when the sun broke through, and a brilliant rainbow slashed the grayness. The bright curved shafts dancing across the city reminded her of Shawish's account of his visit to the Land of Karda where on Mount Judi, south of Lake Chauon, a huge legendary boat was said to be snowbound many years ago.

"The people said it housed the survivors of the great worldwide flood described in the Epic of Gilgamesh," he told her.

Cheered by her recollections of the hope-filled story and Shawish's enthusiasm for the future, she watched the bow pass over the citadel, the now misty, fading colors lightly brushing its battlements.

It is a sign that Auramazda is with us, she thought. No matter what our enemies do to us, we will survive.

Chapter 15

On arriving home, Vashti was greeted by Khezmet with a letter from Amytis. Realizing that her dear friend and cousin would now feel more isolated from her family than ever, Vashti snatched the letter, opened it quickly, and read with mixed feelings.

Dearest Vashti

Due to the tragic loss of my two brothers, my husband has given me permission to return to you, my parents, and the rest of my family for a short visit. Notification has been sent to the palace in Hagmatana with the postal messenger bearing this letter. It was hard for me to mourn alone in this foreign land; Nebuchadnezzar offered to accompany me to the temple of Nergal, his god of death, but I wished to avoid druj, so I respectfully declined.

However, I have been comforted by my conversations with my husband's chief advisor, Belteshazzar. This very wise young man captured from Yehud astounded the court with his interpretation of an important dream Nebuchadnezzar had, so I always listen to him. He said he learned from his ancestors' scrolls that his God, Yehovah, would raise his people from the dead at the end of this earth's time. I told him we are waiting for the third Saoshyant, the Savior, to bring about Frashokerti, when evil will be destroyed and Auramazda will remake everything perfect and new.

So that's enough of my sadness, I am very much looking forward to seeing you and the rest of the family. I miss you every day. Hardly a week goes by without some celebration of the Babylonian gods in one or more of the tens of temples to Marduk and hundreds of altars to the goddess Ishtar. But there is no Atashkedah temple here, so I make sure my servants keep the fire burning in the little pit I had built outside my quarters, despite Nebuchadnezzar's skepticism. After a heated discussion between us about it, during which I emphasised the value of Babylon's alliance with Media, I dared not ask for a magi priest at court, at least for a while. Still, I have my precious scroll of the Avesta and sometimes sing the Gatha songs in my chamber when my maids have lit the lamps in the evening.

And I am also thankful for my very own garden, which I wandered in for days after I heard the dreadful news about my dear brothers, seeking and finding comfort. But it does not cheer me as much as the thought of being with you and the rest of my family. Soon I will be back in beautiful, cool Hagmatana.

All my love,
Amytis

Weeks later, a large retinue was spied approaching the citadel. The *daf* beat loudly to announce the arrival of a member of the Shahan Shah's and Shahjin's family as the citadel gates were all flung open in a chorus of creaks. Second in charge of the Bears, Ferhad, formed his regiment into a mounted guard of honor in the palace precinct for the foreign entourage, and Vashti and her family rushed out of their home and stood excitedly listening to the increasingly loud clip-clopping of horses' hooves. Accompanied by a fully armed Harpagos, her parents, and Ishtovigo, in anticipation of her big sister's arrival, Shelna jumped up and down on the palace steps in excitement and waved to her cousin Parwin.

As Amytis' golden carriage breached the final gateway, the Bears raised their lances. It stopped in front of the palace, the leading Babylonian guard opened the door of the carriage emblazoned with the insignia of the lion, and Amytis stepped out, followed by her maid. Vashti stared at her cousin in awe. The unsure fourteen-year-old who had left her home ten years ago had returned in a gold-fringed fitted tunic and skirt, topped by a headdress of golden discs flashing in the late afternoon sunlight.

Shelna ran to her sister and flung her arms around her while Harpagos supervised the appropriation of the Babylonian retinue's weapons for the duration of their stay, except for Amytis' personal guard. The Bears then individually welcomed the Babylonians, who were subsequently directed to stand opposite their Median counterparts. With Shelna still clinging to her, followed by Shah Nebuchadnezzar's personal envoy and another guard carrying her belongings in a gold-plated chest, Amytis was escorted to the bottom of the palace steps by her personal guard. The Shahan Shah and Shahjin hastily descended the steps and embraced their daughter, who collapsed into their arms. Ignoring protocol, the wife of the most powerful man in the region ululated with joy.

Days of feasting followed. Free from the constraints of Babylonian court life, Amytis once again enjoyed the hunt and horse races with Ishtovigo and her cousins, including Ferhad, whom Harpagos had temporarily released from duty. With the Shahan Shah's permission, Harpagos was accompanied by Debyar, so she could observe Shelna's and Parwin's first archery lessons in preparation for their physical training tests. Ishtovigo remained his usual nonchalant self and was even a little cooler to Vashti, which made her wonder why.

Perhaps he blames me for not being allowed to go to the Mossala, she thought.

The Shahan Shah joined them when state business permitted, but it was within his chambers that father and daughter engaged in serious discussions about the Median alliance with Babylon.

"Nebuchadnezzar's second campaign in Sham was more successful than his first," Amytis explained one balmy autumn morning, as she lazed on a golden couch underneath white flax window curtains billowing in the light breeze. "In Eber-Nari, he secured oaths of allegiance from the Phoenicians. He also captured Ashkelon and its shah, plundered the city, and leveled it to the ground."

"That confirms the reports of General Taxsmaspada," Hovakhshatra replied from his silver couch. "His Lynx regiment is still stationed near the shahdom of the Hapiru," he explained, his eyes fixed fondly on his daughter. "We are very thankful for your service, dear. We know it is not easy for you in Babylonia. But with such a man as your husband on the throne, it is essential that you send regular reports of his court machinations and that we are informed of his campaigns. He could easily turn against us at any time."

"I understand, Father, but surely it is not in Nebuchadnezzar's best interests to betray us as he knows we will protect the region from the northern hordes. However, he still believes Egypt is his most powerful enemy and insists on controlling the small shahdoms in Sham and their cities. The latest reports are that he has taken Gaza, and even controls Khummu of the Hittites, which is quite close to our territories."

"Once Nebuchadnezzar decides what he wants to do and believes he can do it, he will not stop till he has achieved his goals," Hovakhshatra mused. "We are about to go into a new and different era, my dear. There will be many changes over the next fifty years."

"Father, now that you mention it, I have some information about the future."

Hovakhshatra sat up straight. "From a Magi?"

"No, from Nebuchadnezzar's chief advisor, the Hapiru, Belteshazzar."

"Does it involve Media?"

"I think so. Belteshazzar, who tells me his Hapiru name is Daniel, is a very wise prophet. He does not have a priest. He interprets dreams and visions by communicating directly with his god."

"Hmm…very unusual," Hovakhshatra remarked, stroking the curls of his gray-streaked beard as he considered the possibility. "Tell me about this wise man."

"Nebuchadnezzar has terrible dreams," Amytis went on, her voice grave. "But the worst was one he could not remember. When his magicians, enchanters, sorcerers, and Chaldeans couldn't tell him the dream, he threatened to have them torn apart and their houses destroyed. And when they seemed to be delaying, he threatened them again, even though they said it was impossible to tell the dream." She sighed heavily. "It was a fearsome time at court."

Frowning, Hovakhshatra gazed pensively out the window. "I understand Nebuchadnezzar's need to know a matter of state, but his impatience is a weakness we must not ignore," he declared, turning to her. "Tell me, who can ever know what a forgotten dream is about?"

"No one could at the time," Amytis replied, her voice wavering. "It was terrifying when Nebuchadnezzar ordered the execution of all the wise men, but Belteshazzar went to Arioch, the captain of the Shah's guard, and asked him why the Shahan Shah was so angry." Her lip trembled, and she paused from what had suddenly become a breathless recount. "I wondered if any of us would survive."

Hovakhshatra rose, approached his daughter's couch, knelt beside it, and took her hand. "But you did, dear, and here you are to tell me of these worrying events," he said, squeezing her hand. "Please continue. I am listening," he went on, shifting to cross-legged on a nearby cushion.

"When Arioch told him why the Shah was so angry, Belteshazzar requested more time to find out about the dream," Amytis continued softly. "The Hapiru then went to his three friends, who had also been brought from Yehud to work for the shah, to ask his god, Yehovah, to help them with the dream so all the wise men could be saved. After receiving understanding of the dream, Belteshazzar told Arioch, so Arioch took the Hapiru to Nebuchadnezzar to inform him that Yehovah had revealed the dream and its meaning."

"What was the meaning?" Hovakhshatra asked, still very curious.

"Belteshazzar said the Shah saw a bright image standing before him," Amytis went on more calmly.

"Sounds like one of their gods. I've heard Nebuchadnezzar has five golden statues of his most favored deities," Hovakhshatra commented dryly.

"Yes, and like most other shahs, Nebuchadnezzar believes he is partly divine, so he probably thought the image represented him. It had a golden head, arms and chest of silver, a bronze waist and thighs, and the rest of its legs and feet were iron mixed with clay," Amytis went on.

"With such a foundation, no statue would stand for long," Hovakhshatra remarked.

"Father, you are right. Belteshazzar told Nebuchadnezzar that he saw a rock fly toward the image and break it in pieces like the chaff of the summer threshing floors. Then the wind blew it all away. Nothing more was seen of it."

Hovakhshatra shook his head. "Did Belteshazzar know who threw the rock?"

"No, but it became a great mountain and filled the whole earth."

"So the rock took over the whole world?" Hovakhshatra asked incredulously.

"Yes. Nebuchadnezzar did not seem to understand this, or perhaps he didn't want to," Amytis replied softly.

"Perhaps. Did Belteshazzar explain what the different metals meant?"

"He only said the gold represented Nebuchadnezzar, who praised Belteshazzar mightily. But the Hapiru then predicted that the great god of heaven would set up an everlasting kingdom in the days of the shahs of iron and clay," Amytis explained.

"Of course, a kingdom of iron and clay could never last," Hovakhshatra replied.

"Nebuchadnezzar then fell on his face, paid homage to Belteshazzar, and praised his god as better than all the gods. The court then went into chaos as the priests of Marduk and Bel rushed in to protest," Amytis continued, her brow wrinkling again.

"Not surprising," Hovakhshatra remarked, "considering Nebuchadnezzar's changing mind and the influence of all those priests. I thought he might have settled down once he finally took Carchemish from the Egyptians and defeated the Athorayans, but it seems his moods continue."

"You are right again, Father," Amytis admitted. "But I was pleasantly surprised when he gave Belteshazzar high honors, many gifts, appointed him chief ruler of the province of Babylon, and made his three friends his assistants."

"Remarkable. Are all the Hapiru loyal?"

"Yes. They do the Shah's business faithfully. They seem to follow *asha*, never tell *druj*, and keep Prophet Zarathrustra's threefold path. I trust them fully," Amytis replied enthusiastically.

"Be careful, Nebuchadnezzar could become jealous," her father warned.

"Father, I know my husband well. He too trusts the four Hapiru. They look after the court and the province of Babylon while he is away. Nebuchadnezzar was wise to bring them into his service."

"We hope Nebuchadnezzar remains grateful to us for his clever and beautiful wife, too," Hovakhshatra replied, stroking his daughter's arm lovingly. "Were they the jewels we gave as part of your dowry?" he asked of the silver lapis lazuli necklace around Amytis's neck and matching earrings.

"Yes, dear Father. They are a symbol of my service to Media and to you and dear Mother."

Hovakhshatra leaned over and kissed his daughter on the forehead. She forced a smile but, not wanting her father to notice her sadness, cast her eyes downward. A servant appeared with chai, roasted sunflower seeds, and pistachio nuts whereupon Hovakhshatra sighed, retired to his couch, and called for wine.

"Bring a backgammon board and summon the Shahjin," he ordered.

"But, Father, I have more to tell you!" Amytis protested.

"It will have to wait until another day," Hovakhshatra maintained. "In the short time your mother and I have with our beloved daughter, we wish to enjoy her company."

The Shahan Shah spoke lightly, but privately, he wondered if Media was the silver power in Nebuchadnezzar's dream.

Chapter 16

While visiting her family Amytis often joined Vashti and Debyar's other pupils at picnics in the late spring sunshine and crisp mountain air she had missed for so long. One day after they had lunched at the hunting grounds, Debyar led them a little way up Mount Alvand and asked them to sketch one of the wildflower species dotting the slope. Handing each a charcoal crayon carved from the burnt wood of the Atashkedah fire and a sheet of beaten papyrus reed brought from Babylon by Amytis, she seated herself on a large rock to view her pupils' progress. Buzzing bees filled the silence as Vashti drew the multiple blooms of tall hollyhocks and Amytis sketched bell-like clumps of fritillaria. Parwin and Shelna copied the flowers of ranunculus, jonquil, narcissus, hyacinth, and anemone bulbs whose stems had not long burst through the warming earth. After Ishtovigo outlined the water lilies that graced the ponds in the palace gardens from memory, he drew the whole group busy before the backdrop of a snow-melt stream.

At the end of a happy, peaceful day, Vashti asked Gulah to bake walnut-honey cakes and invited Amytis to her home for the evening. The Babylonian guard stood outside, so Vashti told everyone to speak quietly.

"Dear, here are the drawings we did today," she began, passing a silk-wrapped parcel to Amytis. "To remind you of our delightful times together."

Amytis' eyes welled up as she hugged Vashti and thanked her. "They will be preserved under wax and hung on the walls of my chamber in the palace at Babylon," she promised.

"Be brave, dear cousin. One day I will visit you in your adopted city," Vashti replied. "Providing you send an official invitation."

Amytis smiled through her tears. "Of course I will, so we can ride atop the walls of the city of Babylon together."

Vashti clapped her hands and laughed. "Nzdar will love it!"

"Then it is decided," Amytis confirmed. "Now that Nebuchadnezzar has the guiding hand of Belteshazzar at court, everyone is happier, except at spring festival time," she whispered. The listeners drew closer. "It's not Norouz in Babylon, it's the festival of Akitu in honor of the god Marduk."

Everyone frowned. "Don't they have any dancing around big fires?" Parwin asked.

"No, but last year after Nebuchadnezzar had a very important dream, he made a huge statue of gold sixty cubits high by six cubits wide, just like he saw in his first very strange dream."

The listeners looked puzzled. "Ask the Shahan Shah to tell you about the dream next time you visit," Amytis suggested.

"Anyway, my husband built the statue on the plain of Dura to the southeast near the River and gathered all his officials, governors, and judges from the provinces to dedicate it. Then he asked them to bow down to it when all the musical instruments were played at once," she whispered in the palpable silence. "He told anyone who would not bow to the image that they would be thrown into a fiery furnace."

The listeners gasped. "Did anyone refuse?" Vashti asked.

"The Shahan Shah's Chaldean advisors informed him that three of his Hapiru officials were ignoring him by not serving his gods or bowing down to the statue. My husband then fell into one of his rages, called for the three Hapiru to ask them if what the Chaldeans said was true, and reminded them of the fiery furnace threat so they would obey."

"What happened then?" Parwin asked anxiously.

"The three Hapiru replied quite disrespectfully that they had no need to answer the shah on the matter," Amytis went on breathlessly, "and that their god would deliver them from the fiery furnace and the shah's hand." She then took a tattered piece of parchment from her basket and read: "But if not, let it be known to you, oh Shahan Shah, that we will not serve your gods or bow down to the image you have set up."

The listeners' jaws dropped but soon closed in broad smiles.

"Brave men," Shamin said, "to not bow down to that image."

Amytis placed the parchment back in the basket and put her finger to her lips. "We must be careful. The walls are thick, but we might be heard through the window." The listeners leaned in again. "Nebuchadnezzar's face screwed up with rage," Amytis continued. "With straw soaked in oily black tar from the seeps at Arrapkha, he ordered the furnace to be heated seven times hotter and asked his strongest men to bind the three Hapiru in their cloaks, tunics, and *kulaw-u-dastmals* and throw them into the fiery furnace."

"Did the strong men obey?" Parwin whispered in the shocked silence.

"Yes, and as soon as they threw the Hapiru into the fire, the strong men were burned up themselves!" The listeners clapped their hands over their mouths in astonishment.

"What happened to the Hapiru?" Shamin asked.

"Nebuchadnezzar got up quickly and looked in the fire. What he saw amazed him. He asked his advisors if three men were thrown into the fire, and they said they were. The advisors must have thought Nebuchadnezzar had gone mad with anger again because he claimed he could see four men in the fire, and one was like a son of the gods."

All eyes were fixed on Amytis. "My husband then went to the door of the fiery furnace," she continued. "'Shadrach, Meshach, and Abednego, servants of Most High God El Elyon, come out and come here,' he called. Then the three men came out of the fire."

"Were they burned?" Shelna asked anxiously.

"No. The Shahan Shah and all his governors, officials, and

advisors saw that the fire had not affected the Hapiru at all. Their hair was not singed, their cloaks were unharmed, and they did not even smell of fire," Amytis replied triumphantly. "I saw them myself afterwards."

"Did you bow to the statue?" Parwin asked.

"No. I told my husband I would not attend the gathering, as did Belteshazzar, but we were the only two he allowed to be absent. He knows he can't make me do what I don't want to, and that if he tries to force me, I will speak to Father about the alliance," she announced triumphantly with a wide grin.

"Brave sister!" Vashti murmured. "Who was the one like the son of the gods in the fire?"

"Who do you think?" Amytis asked.

"Asa Vahista, Auramazda's *yazata* of fire?" Vashti suggested. "Or even a Saoshyant?"

"Since I was not there, I do not know, but I think it was a powerful sign of Auramazda," Amytis replied.

Everyone nodded. "What happened to the three Hapiru afterwards?" Shamin asked.

"Nebuchadnezzar blessed their god, as he believed he had sent his *yazata* to deliver his servants who would not obey his command, and who gave themselves up to death rather than serve any god but their own. Of course, he kept the Hapiru in his service."

"Your husband really is crazy," Ishtovigo told his sister after another silence.

Amytis nodded. "But that's not all he did," she continued. "He made a decree that any people, nation, or language that speaks anything against El Elyon, whom he called Most High God because of his protection of the three Hapiru, would be torn limb from limb and their houses destroyed, as there was no other god who was able to rescue that way."

"Did Nebuchadnezzar do away with the other gods of Babylon?" Vashti asked.

"No. They are all still there," Amytis answered despondently.

Ishtovigo stood to leave. “Dear sister, is that the end of the story?” he asked, without trying to hide his boredom.

“Not quite,” Amytis replied as her brother walked toward the door. “Nebuchadnezzar promoted the three Hapiru in the province of Babylon.”

Shamin sighed. “At least the captives were not killed. I’m so thankful for the wise rule of our Shahan Shah and Shahjin. Amytis dear, have you informed your father of these events?”

“Not yet, Aunt, but I will tomorrow,” Amytis promised.

Parwin and Shelna were yawning, so Amytis took her sister’s hand, and they were met at the door by the Babylonian guard.

After Parwin went to bed, Vashti and Shamin sat quietly for some time, thinking about Amytis’ courage and fortitude in such trying circumstances.

Chapter 17

Before Amytis left to return to Babylon, her father asked her to accompany Vashti at the reception of tribute from the various representatives who had journeyed from all four corners of the Medes' shahdom. On a mild summer's day, both women preferred to be outside riding instead of sitting in the candlelit Audience Hall receiving foreigners and their advisors, all of whom Harpagos and Amytis' guards carefully watched. But they cheerfully assumed their duties.

Seated on silver couches, Vashti and Amytis received the tribute, which scribes recorded on wax-covered boards, and asked them about the welfare of their peoples. The procession passed steadily until a familiar face appeared before Vashti. Mithridates' gentle brown eyes beneath his bushy brows and neatly tied *kulaw-u-dastmal* were unmistakeable.

"Good day, Vashti of the Medes," he greeted in his Aryo dialect, his calm, reassuring tone jolting her memory of the last words he spoke before they parted in the foothills of the Alborz Range.

Vashti's heart skipped a beat. Taking a deep breath and straightening her shoulders, she replied evenly. "Welcome, most noble chief of the Parthavan."

"We have not been the same since you left our company," Mithridates replied.

"You are too kind," Vashti replied, blushing.

"No. It was you who graced us with your presence," he insisted. Harpagos was approaching, so Mithridates ordered his servant to present his tribute. With a searching glance, he then moved on. As Vashti placed her hand on her cheek to hide it, Amytis stopped speaking to the emissary she was receiving, looked over at her, and smiled quizzically.

At the end of the long afternoon, Amytis asked Vashti to dine with her that evening. Although tired and wanting to find out about Mithridates' visit, she accepted. It wasn't until servants were bringing in the dishes on which their meal was to be placed that Amytis mentioned Mithridates.

"The Parthavan chief seemed to know you quite well," she remarked casually.

Vashti's heart pounded again, and she coughed nervously. "We met on my trip to Bactria. He found us in the desert and saved us and our animals from certain death. Then he showed us the way to Baxtri. It is I who should have given him tribute," she explained, trying to keep her voice steady.

"Yes. He knew who you were, and the way he looked at you was quite familiar," Amytis noted, her curious smile returning.

"He guided and protected us for several weeks," Vashti explained. "I never encouraged him. If he thought I did, he was mistaken," she added hastily, wondering if she was telling *druj*.

"Do you want me to ask Father to invite him to the palace tomorrow?" Amytis asked.

"No, no, that is not necessary. He must leave tomorrow," Vashti replied curtly.

The rest of the evening passed with chatter about extended family members while Vashti kept thinking about Mithridates and wondering if he was only in Hagmatana to bring tribute.

Perhaps he has also come to discuss the proposed agreement I raised with the Shahan Shah on my return from Bactria, she thought and waited till the conversation lulled to ask her uncle about it. His reply that an arrangement had been made aroused her curiosity, but further questions would have been improper. She would have to wait for a private audience to find out.

That night, she dreamed a man whom she could not identify invaded her home, kidnapped her, and took her away on his horse to a desert oasis where he kept her captive in an ornate pavilion. She was released, but no ransom was paid.

She awoke next morning to the clacking of horses' hooves on the cobblestones outside. Half-asleep, she stumbled to her window and looked out. Two men, one with a *kulaw-u-dastmal* covering the lower half of his face, were heading for the golden gate. With the dream still clouding her mind, she rushed out in her night robe, wondering if the covered man was who she had seen in her dream. Suddenly, he stopped, turned, and pulled down the scarf. She gasped as Mithridates smiled at her just like he had at the oasis pool where she had so unwisely washed.

"Vashti," he called across the chilly morning, "come with me to Parthava. My people and I need you." The cold suddenly woke her up, and she stood shivering, not knowing how to reply.

Mithridates dismounted and walked toward her. Wordlessly, he removed his cloak and offered it to her. Without thinking, she took it and wrapped it round herself, the acrid smell of ganja smoke both thrilling and irritating her nostrils.

"Is that the same robe you wore in the water of the oasis?" he asked, smiling quizzically.

"Of course not," Vashti snapped. "That robe is long gone…and this one has nothing to do with you." Surprising herself with *druj*, she felt the blood rise hotly to her face again.

Mithridates stood silently looking at her, his expression blank.

"I had a dream," she blurted.

"About what?"

"Someone kidnapped me."

Mithridates looked around the deserted yard. "You are quite safe now," he assured her.

"Then I awoke and saw you outside."

He stared at her again and smiled just a little wickedly. "Do you want me to kidnap you?"

"Of course not."

"I'm glad. I would never attempt such a crime in full view of the barracks of the Shahan Shah's number one regiment. And on you, Vashti of the Medes, the maker of my most happy memories," he replied with false indignation. She stood open-mouthed until the creaking of the front door of her home alerted her to Shamin in the doorway.

"Vashti dear, who is your friend? Stop all this early morning noise and invite him for chai and breakfast," her mother called.

"Would you like to join us?" Vashti asked, a little tentatively. The Parthavan chief nodded assent and ordered his companion to tie the horses to the oak tree.

"Take them to the stables," she told the companion. "And ask the lead stable hand to feed you, too, at my request."

Inside her home, Vashti introduced Mithridates. Khezmet was waiting with a suitable gown for her, so she dressed quickly, returned to her guest, and gave him back his cloak. When he sat down on the floor rug, Vashti was instantly reminded of the sour smell of wet wool on the stormy day she had joined him in his pavilion at the oasis after being rescued.

Gulah brought chai, bread, olive paste, and boiled eggs while Mithridates answered Shamin's questions about Parthava. Still occupied with her dream, Vashti sat back and watched him charm her mother with his quaint accent and warm, fathomless eyes like he had captivated her in their many conversations. The lilting tones of his voice speaking compassion and wisdom, but holding firm strength in reserve, enthralled her. She sat motionless trying not to stare but wanting to absorb his spirit so that she might somehow keep it within her forever.

Was Auramazda trying to tell her something about this man with whom she felt such a close affinity? He seemed the same as he was on their travels—true to *asha* and with no sign of *druj*. For a fleeting moment, she thought she must go with him, but when she heard Shamin mention the deaths of Cica, Shawish, and Artaspaya, she knew she had to stay. But deep in the recesses of her consciousness, she wanted to fly away with him like a free bird to the wild land of her dream.

"Vashti…our guest is leaving." Shamin's voice interrupted her thoughts as Mithridates rose and thanked his hosts. Jumping up, Vashti led the way to the door, and he followed.

Outside, they waited in silence while Khezmet called for the horses. When they arrived, Vashti still could not speak.

"Till we meet again," Mithridates declared forlornly, removing then replacing his *kulaw-u-dastmal*. With one last glance, he mounted his horse and signaled his companion forward.

In the still, cold morning, Vashti stood listening to the steadily fading sound of the riders' passage down the citadel's paths. It wasn't the cold that shook her, it was a strangely unexpected fear that she would never see him again.

Chapter 18

Following Amytis' departure, an unusual melancholia settled on Vashti, and her cousin's note that she had arrived home safely did little to cheer her.

"Nebuchadnezzar is rebuilding the old palace of Babylon and the Esagila and Etemenanki temples," Amytis had written. "He believes they are necessary for the prosperity of his territories, but he does not know that Auramazda and the Mitradat covenant will do the same with a lot less effort on his part. I wish I could tell him, but he is not yet ready to listen."

It hardly seemed weeks since she and Amytis had discussed the future of Media, and her determination to be ready to avenge the deaths of her father and her cousins by becoming an officer of the Bears. Amytis had been skeptical.

"Do you think Father will allow a woman leader in the army?" she had asked.

"Not until I prove myself," Vashti had replied.

"In battle? But we have peace now," Amytis had maintained.

"Yes, but Uncle still suspects the Lydians are hiding Shawish's and Artaspaya's killers. If he seeks revenge, I want to be part of the regiment leading the fight," Vashti had replied firmly.

"I think Father has other plans for you," Amytis had suggested.

"What?" Vashti's reply was sharp.

"You and Ishtovigo—"

"Not before I join the army if ever," Vashti had shot back.

"Someone has to be the wife of the next Ahasuerus the Mede," Amytis replied stolidly, anticipating her brother would assume the affectionate title the people gave his father after his victorious battle with the Scythians.

Vashti shook her head. "I have no feelings for him. He is like a naughty big brother to me," she said decisively. "Shawish was different. He loved our nation, and I've always wanted to prosper it."

"I had no feelings for Nebuchadnezzar when we were married, but his gifts endeared me to him," Amytis confessed. "And I don't think Ishtovigo feels the same way about you as you do about him. He's always asking Father about you. Now Shawish and Artaspaya are gone, we must think differently about our future."

"I do not wish to be the next Shahjin of Media, and I will not tell Ishtovigo or anyone else *druj* about my opinion of him," Vashti stated emphatically.

"Because of the Parthavan chief?" Amytis asked warily.

Vashti had looked away without answering. She didn't want to argue with her closest cousin, and she knew that whatever she said would make no difference to her situation. The tight feeling in her chest returned. It was only a matter of time before, like Amytis, she would be obliged to make a marriage agreement that wasn't of her choosing.

But she would delay that time for as long as possible.

A month later, Vashti's melancholia lifted with the wedding of Harpagos and Debyar. Her teacher had refused the energetic young general at first, claiming his duties for the Shahan Shah and the Bears would take him away too much, and she would often be left to raise their children alone as her family lived in Rhagae.

"But he won me by promising to take me to my home city as

soon as the Shahan Shah permits," Debyar had admitted. "How could I refuse such a kind offer?"

Vashti could tell from the excitement in her teacher's eyes that more than the promise had won Harpagos her heart.

"He is the future of Media," she had declared. "Harpagos will do many great things for us, and I will be there to record them, especially since his writing needs much tutoring. Besides, he is most attentive."

"Do not worry," Vashti had assured her beloved teacher, smiling at the thought of Harpagos' courtship manners. "You too will become part of our family." And Debyar had hugged her favorite student tightly.

The wedding was an enormous event. Although the Tiger and Lynx regiments were on duty on the northern and western borders of Media, and the Bears were still guarding the capital, Harpagos' regiment were given leave to celebrate the marriage of their leader to the tall, willowy teacher.

Preparing the bride, Khezmet applied fragrant face oils while Vashti adjusted her green robe of crushed silk tied with a red sash, which matched the garnets set in the *sarwain* Harpagos had brought her from Urartu. "Even in his sorrow for the loss of the Shahan Shah's two sons, Harpagos remembered me, and we were not even courting then," Debyar reminisced softly with a little smile.

Vashti nodded, straightened the teacher's *sarwain*, and kissed her. "You too are the future of Media," she assured her.

Encircled by a ring of soldiers dancing with their wives and extended families, the bride and groom sat on silk-covered cushions embroidered by Debyar's pupils as strolling musicians entertained the guests. Surrounded by a sea of wild rose petals gathered by Vashti, Shelna, and Parwin, Harpagos and Debyar seemed to be their own island. Exchanging little twinkles of affection, they sometimes reached for each other's hands but never quite touched. Recalling the time Mithridates took her hand and kissed it at the oasis, Vashti again wondered if marriage plans were being made for her but privately wished her teacher and Harpagos an eternally happy union.

Several head of game procured for the wedding feast from the Shahan Shah's hunting park by the Scythian army trainers were roasted over fire cradles and eaten with bread and Mesopotamian figs, all washed down with wine from Kasir. After hours of dancing, the Bears were left to celebrate without their commander, who was hosted with his bride by the Shahan Shah and Shahjin at a banquet in the palace. By the end of the meal, Hovakhshatra had promised Harpagos and his new wife a trip to Rhagae for the following Norouz.

Accompanied by Vashti and Ishtovigo, Harpagos and Debyar then left for the Atashkedah in the Shahan Shah's carriage for the marriage formalities, after which the newlyweds returned to the general's quarters near the palace. Around the fire cradles, the Bears continued the festivities well into the night. For some, it would be the last they would have together before departing to train Bactrians on the northeastern frontier as approved by the Shahan Shah after Vashti reported the governor's request. While Harpagos remained at home for his marriage year, the Bears were under the command of General Ferhad.

Chapter 19

The winter of Shahan Shah Hovakhshatra's twenty-first regnal year passed slowly.

Khezmet's three children joined Debyar's lessons, and her students sometimes went to the city to practice the Aramean language spoken by Athorayans and others. But Debyar was even more interested in teaching her students the Avestan language by reciting Prophet Zarathrustra's hymns of the five Gathas, some of which the children learned to sing.

Once the snow on the mountains began to melt, preparations for Norouz began, including Harpagos' and Debyar's trip to Rhagae. When the Shahan Shah suggested that Vashti and Ishtovigo accompany them, the heir to the throne immediately agreed while Vashti asked for time to think about the proposal. She had long desired to see the famous city but didn't want to spend two months with her overly attentive cousin. Eventually, not wanting to miss the excitement of Debyar's and Harpagos' second wedding, she agreed.

With two guards and four donkeys carrying shelter, clothing, and food supplies, early in the month of Adar the four travelers left Hagmatana along the eastern road to Nisea. Once there, the party rested for a few days to prepare their rides before re-joining the road east to Rhagae. At the renowned horse-breeding region of Nisea, Nzdar and the other horses blissfully cropped new medicago clover shoots while Vashti and Debyar picked bunches of last season's dried stalks to tie onto their riding bags.

Progress was slow through the mountains, but villagers welcomed them to their homes carved into sheer, rocky ledges. Clustered on the sides of steep, snow-draped valleys, the stone dwellings clung to the mountains in silent refuge. Some nights, Vashti was lulled to sleep by the first tinkling trickles of snow melt in the streams that flowed down the middle of these rugged settlements.

Another two uneventful weeks later, the first peaks of the Alborz Mountains appeared in the distant north, and the travelers rode along the lee of the range.

"The Akkadians called it Alborz," Debyar explained, "but we call it *Hara Berezaiti*, the highest peak."

"And north of the ranges is Caspian," Vashti added.

"Yes, long ago it was known as *Kawkeyzhun*, the home of fair-skinned people between the Black and Caspian Seas," Debyar informed them. "It is considered the place where our women gave birth with the help of Auramadza. Many of our people still live there."

"Maybe one day we will visit that land," Vashti remarked.

Debyar nodded. "Their god was called Hu," she continued as Ishtovigo produced his *shimshal* pipe and began to play.

"Was Hu the same as Auramazda?" Vashti asked, as Harpagos' deep voice harmonized the pipe with his rendition of the Gatha songs.

"It was the early name for Auramazda," Debyar explained. "Before Prophet Zarathrustra, Prophet Mahabad called the one and only God, Hu, whose full name, Ahuramazda, represented the sun. But Prophet Zarathustra likened God to fire on earth and named Him Auramazda."

"So both prophets taught that God was light," Vashti confirmed. "Is *Aur* like the name for Ariavarta?"

"Good question, dear. The answer is yes." Fascinated, Vashti asked what else Prophet Mahabad taught.

"From his time comes 'mitra,' the agreement between the people and the creator. *Dat* was the covenant between the people and

Auramazda, the creator God," Debyar explained.

"So Mitradat was the covenant of laws between the people and creator God," Vashti concluded enthusiastically, her eyes shining.

"Yes, it is the foundation of our shahdom." Debyar beamed proudly. Prophet Mahabad also developed the seven stages of education, starting with physical training, then reading, writing, social values, and endurance of hardship. Most of my older students have completed these, except the heir to the throne," she elaborated, glancing at Ishtovigo. "You are yet to cross the desert and the mountains in one trip," she told him. "Harpagos will make sure you complete all your training." Ishtovigo scowled but recalling the hardship she had experienced on her trip to Bactria, Vashti was thankful that she had passed her test.

"There were also rewards for good behavior in the Prophet's system," Debyar continued, "and punishment for crimes."

"Did Prophet Mahabad teach about tribal life?" Vashti wanted to know.

"Yes, dear, all the principles of *asha*, including justice, friendship, and communal sharing come from him," Debyar replied.

"So we have Auramazda and His enemy Angra Mainyu. But who is Spenta Mainyu?" Vashti asked.

"She is the Spirit of Auramazda who creates life and goodness and protects the sky, water, earth, and plants," Debyar answered, her lilting tones hanging on each word.

Picturing Shamin's full figure and her fixed smile belying the apprehension in her eyes as she had waved her daughter goodbye with her headscarf, Vashti was reminded of her mother's constant love, affection, and wise guidance. Like the Spirit of Auramazda, they were the life-giving fountain of her whole existence. As if reading her thoughts, Debyar reached over, took her hand, and squeezed it.

"Let's always be grateful for the patronage of Auramazda," she said reverently.

"I'm tired of hearing about these teachings," Ishtovigo complained loudly, having exhausted his music repertoire. Then, much to the amazement of his companions, he proceeded to pull a sheet of reed parchment and a charcoal stick from his bag and began to sketch while his horse continued to faithfully follow the road.

Debyar, Harpagos, and Vashti exchanged familiar glances as Ishtovigo entertained himself in ignorant bliss.

Several days later, the party reached the outlying villages of the city of Rhagae. "Behold, the central home of the Ariavartan people," Debyar announced proudly, pointing to the fires ringing the city. "For hundreds of years in the land of fire, travelers have witnessed blazes everywhere during Norouz." Behind them, against the deepening darkness, the luminescent glow of snow on the mountains reflected from the sun's waning light lifted Vashti's spirits.

Rhagae is Media's sparkling *sarwain,* she thought.

The next day, the city was alive with preparations for the festival. In the streets, iron cradles were filled with firewood ready for the evening's celebrations while colorful banners fluttered from roof tops. Visitors from nearby villages brought animals to be slaughtered and the meat was boiled in huge copper pots.

From street chatter, Debyar learned that the governor had ordered crates of olives from the Guilan region of Caspian. The crisp, slightly tart smell of bread cakes freshly baked in tendur ovens lingered in the busy streets. Women piled high the thin, flat cakes, which waited to be topped by *mast* from clay urns kept cool in pools of crystal-clear river water. Men shouldering sacks of a new grain from the land of Hindush marveled that they had safely traveled over thousands of stades and laid them carefully on street corners. Soon the inviting aroma of creamy kernels boiling until they were soft and sweet wafted from other pots. When Vashti bought a little bag of the seeds to take back to the Shahan Shah, she wondered if it would also grow near the warm climes of Caspian.

After Debyar's family welcomed the visitors into their wood-framed stone home, special preparations were made for their daughter's second wedding during the Norouz week. While Harpagos took Ishtovigo to meet the governor to discuss the willingness of the farmers and townsfolk to join the army should Media come under attack, Vashti helped Debyar ready herself. The teacher's mother had provided a white silk robe with a golden sash, reminiscent of the magi priests' costume.

"Mother taught me all I know about the Prophets and the priests," Debyar explained. "Her father was Piree Magush of the Atashkedah in Rhagae. I have no brothers, only sisters, so she always dressed me as a little priest when I was growing up." She grinned. "My cousin has now taken Grandfather's place."

Vashti nearly dropped the palette of eyelid colorings she was holding. "Dear, I did not know you were of the Magian tribe!" she exclaimed.

"Only the Shahan Shah and Harpagos know," Debyar replied softly. "We do not tell all our secrets."

"Do you know how your cousin learned the ways of the Magi?" Vashti asked, her interest piqued.

Debyar nodded. "Originally, only those who completed stages four, five, and six of the Mitra training could become Magi. They studied the stars to interpret dreams and inform the people about the future. Those who reached stage seven acquired knowledge similar to the Prophets', which would enable them to lead the nation in the future."

Vashti sighed. She had not had any clear dreams for a long time. "Did the Magi of old tell of the future of Media?" she asked.

"Not specifically, only the Prophet Mahabad warned our people about the need for more food as our populations grew. He said that hundreds of years from now, very complicated machines would make many objects, including small flax fiber sheets to pay tribute and for exchange of goods. But he also said the evil spirits under the influence of Angra Mainyu would take all the gold, silver, and other metals and use them and the sheets stored in vaults to control our people instead of fighting wars. And that the same spirits would also rule over food and make the people fight for it. He predicted the people would be so badly hurt that Ahuramazda would have to intervene to care for those struggling to survive those terrible days."

"That is why we have this rice," Vashti replied of the new grain. "It is Auramazda's provision, like flaxseed from Egypt. We must send for some of those little brown seeds once Nebuchadnezzar controls that land. And we should warn the Shahan Shah to increase the guards on our treasury and even hide our gold and silver in secret vaults and caves in the mountains."

Debyar nodded. "You are right, dear. We must prepare now for those days for we do not know when they will come upon us."

"We will," Vashti asserted, "but now we must work out how to fix this *sarwain* on your head." Untangling its shining gold discs, she fitted the headdress snugly onto Debyar's fair hair using fine silver clasps. "Perfect," she said, "for the learned wife of a skilled warrior."

That night she dreamed of a throne on which sat a faceless shah with no scepter.

Chapter 20

The next night, as if in anticipation of the union of husband and wife, the moon rose to meet the setting sun. Before long, Harpagos' and Debyar's home wedding had become a whole city event, except for Ishtovigo, who insisted on smoking *chaudel* from a pipe heated by a small lamp. Despite his claim that the effects of the dried red poppy flowers were negligible, he soon fell asleep, and Harpagos was duty bound to rescue him from some enthusiastic dancers.

"He is tired from his journey," Vashti hastily explained to the governor, shaming herself with *druj*.

As the evening progressed, the communal energy of the dancers and the shouts of people jumping over fires merged hazily. At times, amongst the many moustached and bearded men, she thought she saw Mithridates, swinging his arms to the beat of the jingling *daf* between women shrugging their shoulders to the insistent call of the *shimshal*. But he did not appear, and she gave up searching faces until just after midnight when a firm hand touched her arm and she turned around to see him, his gentle brown eyes once more staring at her from beneath bushy eyebrows.

"It is you," was all she could gasp.

"Yes, Vashti of the Medes, I did not expect to meet you here," he replied. "But I see the Shahan Shah has you on duty again," he quipped, pointing to Ishtovigo propped up on a bag of rice. "He is his son?"

She laughed. "Yes," she answered, looking around for Harpagos, who was watching Ishtovigo from his place next to Debyar in the dance circle. "The Shāhan Shah has ordered his protection, even at General Harpagos' second wedding."

Mithridates nodded. "Come over to the big fire," he urged, grabbing her hand.

With a quick glance and smile at Harpagos, who had also kept his eyes on her and nodded consent, she followed, surprised by her guard's trust in her escort and strangely thrilled by her compliance with Mithridates' suggestion. She didn't know why Harpagos thought Mithridates was safe, but she was too excited to stop and think about it.

In the central city square, the local tribesmen had lit an enormous fire, into which they were throwing gray, hole-ridden stones wrapped in straw and oily cloth.

"The people have learned how to use the stones hurled from fiery Mount Zamawand and the oil seeps from Rey to celebrate," Mithridates commented blithely as several missiles hissed, flared brightly, and exploded in the middle of the conflagration to the ululations of women in the crowd.

Suddenly, amidst the exhilaration, she realized Mithridates still held her hand. Worried that someone would notice and object, she tried to remove it from his surprisingly soft grip, but he tightened it inside the folds of his cloak.

"No one can see it, nor do the Parthavans know who you are," he assured her. She gave a gentle squeeze back and he turned to her, smiled just a little smugly, and winked.

They watched until no more firestones were thrown, and the dance resumed. Slowly and inexorably, in celebration of a new day and new life, the repeated mesmeric steps bound the dancers together well into the early morning hours. As light crept into the eastern sky, the fire died down and the sun rose. Parents woke their sleeping children and wandered off to their homes, *dwars*, and pavilions, cocks began to crow, and dogs sniffed for stray pieces of meat. Suddenly fatigued, Vashti wondered if the night had been a dream.

"I will take you back to your people," Mithridates declared when the music had stopped. "Where are you staying?"

Vashti removed her hand from his comfortable grip and pointed to a distant house in the street. Soon they were outside Debyar's family home, and he turned to her, his eyes fixed as though trying to hold her there.

"It is…so difficult to leave you," he mumbled. She opened her mouth to reply, but before she could, he grabbed her hand, kissed it, and strode briskly away. She watched until he reached the end of the street, but he did not look back. Wiping away tears, she took a deep breath and pushed open the gate of the compound wall. On guard duty, Harpagos grunted a greeting from behind his gingery beard, and she walked slowly down the path to the front door.

Inside the house, she lay down to sleep, but her hand smelled tantalisingly of earthy frankincense, mixed with pungent oily smoke.

After a week's rest, including picnics with Debyar's family in the ever-greening countryside, the travelers set out for Hagmatana. Vashti did not see Mithridates again, which was a relief as Harpagos' questions about him probed too close to her heart. The thought that she might not have gone back to Hagmatana had she met the Parthavan chief again disturbed her, and she struggled to put it out it of her mind as they departed the city.

The return journey went quickly, and soon the party reached the purple carpeted Nisean plain where they rested the animals for a few days before negotiating the last leg of their journey. When they arrived home, the palace precinct was deserted, but soon Khezmet appeared with Shamin, who explained that the Shahan Shah was in council. Harpagos rushed into the palace to find Hovakhshatra and Ardela deep in conversation with Godel watching. Barely acknowledging their chief general, the ruling couple continued without raising the scepter.

"Our son is not ready," Ardela stated.

"If he isn't ready now, he never will be," Hovakhshatra replied.

"Then perhaps he should not succeed you," Ardela continued.

The Shahan Shah stared at his wife. "Then who do you suggest?"

"Shahan Shah and Shahjin," Harpagos interrupted, "if you are talking about the succession, there are at least two tribal chiefs who are very strong and wise."

Still not having acknowledged the return of the party from Rhagae, Hovakhshatra waved the suggestion away. "Without a blood line of succession, we will appear weak. Where is Ishtovigo? I wish to see him immediately."

"Shahan Shah he is not here. He insisted on visiting the Mossala," Harpagos replied awkwardly.

"I told you to keep him away from that place," Hovakhshatra shot back angrily.

"My Shahan Shah," Harpagos interrupted again, "please forgive me. Since Debyar was not feeling well and I wanted to stay with her, Vashti offered to find Ishtovigo and bring him back."

"The Mossala is full of *druj* and will lead my son even further from *asha*," the Shahan Shah yelled. "Go and retrieve him now."

Harpagos' face color matched his hair as he marched out. Wearily, he walked to the stables, chose a fresh horse, and descended to the Mossala, passing Vashti who told him the priests refused to admit her to the temple. At the Mossala, Harpagos was told the heir to the throne was being entertained by one of the fertility priestesses. After a heated argument with the priest, who demanded payment for her services, Harpagos drew his dagger whereupon the man yielded and went off to find Ishtovigo. When the disheveled heir appeared, through gritted teeth, Harpagos ordered him onto his horse, which he led slowly through the city as night fell, so as not to attract attention.

On Harpagos' advice, and to avoid the ire of his parents, Ishtovigo crept into his quarters through the servants' entrance after which the general went off to try to placate the Shahan Shah and Shahjin.

The following day, determined to duly address Ishtovigo's behavior, Harpagos sought him in his quarters. Reiterating the Shahan Shah and Shahjin's wish that their son not attend the Mossala because it sullied their names, he added that disloyalty to the Atashkedah was not a good example to the people.

Ishtovigo regarded his friend intently, his forehead creased in thought.

"Vashti is the only woman for me, but she does not want me," he mumbled sadly. "I've always loved her, but she infuriates me with her self-righteousness, so I go to the Mossala in the hope that she will seek me out and scold me. It's the only way I can get her attention. Most of the time our families are together, she sticks her nose in the air and pretends I'm not there."

Harpagos gazed out the window, seeking inspiration. "Be careful. Going to the Mossala will annoy Vashti more and lower her opinion of you," he advised. "That way neither of you will ever agree, and your friendship will not grow." He paused and turned to his companion. "Remember your responsibilities as the heir to the throne and prepare diligently to take your father's place. When Vashti notices the difference in you, she will want to know you better."

Ishtovigo grimaced. Vashti had captured his heart, but he didn't think he could ever capture hers. Convinced he would never be good enough for her, he grabbed his cloak and marched out.

By midday, aware that something important was happening in the council chamber, servants crept around the palace while the Shahan Shah's chief advisors were summoned and given permission to speak about the succession matter.

"My son is not fit to rule Media," Hovakhshatra admitted to the sombre listeners. "He defies the Mitradat and hardly ever shows interest in national matters."

"But Shahan Shah," Aswer, one of the advisors, protested, "Ishtovigo has proved himself in military training and could easily lead the army."

"And therefore, the whole of Media," General Taxmaspada added.

"More than military skills are needed to keep our territories," the Shahan Shah replied. "My successor must not engage *druj*. Good thoughts, good words, and good deeds are necessary for the preservation of Media."

From the corner of the room, the Piree Magush grunted his approval.

"He is young," another advisor commented. "Once he is married, he will forget the Mossala."

"And Vashti is the only one who can be his wife," the Shahjin declared.

"I've heard even she can't reform him," Hovakhshatra commented. "What do you think Harpagos?"

The young general sighed. "Although Ishtovigo completed the trip to Rhagae with us, he hasn't finished his hardship test," he replied. "This means he is not yet fit to rule."

"Shahan Shah," the Piree Magush interrupted, "Ishtovigo is still interested in rebuilding the palace at Shush. Why not put him in charge of the project?"

"Yes. He has little engineering experience, but perhaps he could supervise the construction as part of his hardship test," Ardela added, seizing on the suggestion. "And he loves designing mosaic-tiled walls. He could work on them too."

Harpagos frowned and opened his mouth to reply but was prevented by the Shahan Shah.

"Not like Shah Nebuchadnezzar's," Hovakhshatra insisted. "We are not going to spend our hard-won wealth on lavish buildings. There are no guarantees that our enemies won't attack at any time, and our military always needs costly equipment. But we will send our best engineers and builders with Ishtovigo to Shush and enough gold to finish the palace."

"And I think a worthy advisor to keep him out of trouble," Harpagos suggested whereupon Aswer smiled and offered his services.

"Yes, considering his behavior at his first visit to Shush," Ardela agreed. "Once Ishtovigo leaves, we will consult with Vashti," she added.

The Shahan Shah nodded and handed Harpagos the golden scepter, signaling the end of the meeting.

Chapter 21

Vashti began to dream again, but all she could remember was a palace of marble pillars near a garden. It wasn't the palace at Hagmatana, so what was Auramazda trying to tell her? And she still didn't know the identity of the city being conquered in her earlier dream.

She was wondering whether to consult the Piree Magush when a letter arrived from Amytis. It read:

Dearest cousin

Even though I have told Father and Mother everything, I am also letting you know my news because I trust you just as much. Do not worry, dear, all is well here. Nebuchadnezzar has not had any disturbing dreams for a long time, and Belteshazzar and I have been overseeing the court while my husband has been in Sham. Following his successes in Ashkelon and Gaza, he is back there with the army, despite rumors that his brother, Nabu-shum-lishir, might try to take the throne, and that there are some signs of unrest in the provinces. However, Belteshazzar receives regular reports from his assistants, Shadrach, Meshach, and Abednego, that the local garrisons remain loyal.

Amel-Marduk is now eight years old but too young to learn much about the court. I am thankful that Father sent a magi priest from Rhagae, which my husband finally approved, to instruct him in the ways of the Prophet, leaving his tutors to teach him the knowledge of Babylonia. However, he much prefers me reading the Avesta to him than any other writings and loves to hear the stories of his grandfathers' victories over the Scythians and the uniting of our six tribes. My only sorrow is that he has not seen the snowy mountains of Media or our green valleys in springtime. But when he is older, I will take him home, providing Nebuchadnezzar agrees to release his heir to the wilds of his mother's childhood.

Father informed me of your trip to Rhagae for Norouz. Please write and tell me all about it as I was too young to go with him and dear Mother when they visited the city. Did you see the Parthavan chief again? I wonder if such a dour man would ever dance in a celebration like Norouz. But perhaps only you can answer that, even though his familiarity with you was quite unexpected!

Please don't delay your reply, dear, so the postal rider can take it on his return trip.

I do love you,

Amytis

Wondering what her cousin thought about Mithridates, Vashti felt her chest tighten. Did she know something about him that would cause suspicion? And had Amytis concluded that she was secretly in communication with him? Her mind wandered to another dream where, in a bad storm, a figure in a dark cloak rode up and tried to pick her up. She had woken up wet with sweat, wondering again what Auramazda was trying to tell her. Her thoughts were interrupted by a knock on the door and Khezmet calling her to receive the Shahan Shah's messenger.

"Shahan Shah Hovakhshatra requests his niece, Vashti, to attend him and the Shahjin at midday in their private reception chamber," the messenger announced.

"Tell him I accept his invitation," Vashti replied, hoping she wasn't going to be asked to go on another trip. In Rhagae, Debyar's cousin had instructed her further on the teachings of Zarathrustra, and she was keen to ask her teacher more questions. She sighed.

The next lesson would have to be tomorrow.

Glinting walls flashed past as her feet slapped the marble floor of the silver-lined palace hallway. Unlike when she was younger, the long walk never seemed to end. Feeling strangely alone, she stopped to listen for the fluttering of her *yazata's* wings, but all was deathly quiet.

Outside the reception chamber, she paused and took a deep breath. Harpagos ushered her in to where Hovakhshatra and Ardela sat solemnly on their couches with the golden scepter between them.

"Please be seated," Hovakhshatra indicated of a silver chair. "We will not need the scepter today. Are you well dear?" he asked.

After Vashti replied in the affirmative, Ardela spoke. "Dear, we thank you for your loyalty to Media, you have always upheld the ways of the Prophet and your family."

"*Zors spas,* Shahjin," Vashti replied. "It has been my wish to give my nation my best service."

"We have been thinking about the future of Media," Hovakhshatra continued as Vashti's sense of foreboding constricted her throat. "The succession must be guaranteed."

She tried to swallow but couldn't. Nor would thoughts of being corralled like Nzdar in his stall allow her to reply. Hovakhshatra cleared his throat. "Dear, our son is without a wife…"

Her heart thumped.

"He must marry to continue the rule of Media and provide the next heir."

"Yes, Shahan Shah," she croaked.

"We would like you to marry him," Hovakhshatra blurted.

There was a long silence while she tried to think of a reply that wasn't *druj*. Finally, Ardela spoke. "You do not have to answer now, dear. Take a few days to consider our request," she offered, her eyes downcast.

Preferably the rest of my life, Vashti thought. A servant brought chai in fine Egyptian glasses and the Shahjin urged her to sip, but she respectfully declined. Her mouth was dry, but she could not drink.

"I am honored by your offer, Uncle and Aunt," she eventually replied, not knowing why she used the familiar titles, but desperately wanting to plead a merciful escape from an unthinkable future.

The uncomfortable silence continued until the Shahan Shah dismissed her.

She walked out past Harpagos and continued till he could no longer see her. Then she ran down the corridor, trying to suppress the cry welling up in her throat. Outside, she raced down the palace steps past the stone bears who seemed to reach out to claw her. In the stables, she found Nzdar recovered from the lameness of his Rhagae trip and quickly threw a rug over him and fitted his reins. Grabbing her riding bags and cloak, she flung herself over him and guided him toward the golden gate.

Nzdar picked his way calmly down the circular paths of the citadel, the wind ruffling his mane and her hair flowing as she tossed the silver clasps confining her unruly tresses over the wall. When she reached the bottom of the citadel, she could not decide which way to go, so she closed her eyes, tried not to think, and let the clip-clop of Nzdar's hooves decide for her.

When she opened her eyes, she was not far from the fork in the eastern road that would lead to Parthava.

Over the mountains, a lowering storm was threatening.

Chapter 22

Stade after stade, Nzdar plodded on…the shelter of Alborz was far away, but was it the only way she could avoid Ishtovigo? As the afternoon wore on, fatigue threatened, and she closed her eyes once more. Soon, sensing the onset of night, Vashti slowed Nzdar.

"Darkness will be my friend, and my enemy should robbers appear," she reasoned. Suddenly, a crack of thunder startled her, a flash of lightning lit the sky, and huge raindrops began to fall. Before long, she and Nzdar were soaked.

What a fool I am, she thought, wishing the rain would wash away her cares. I should have been looking for the road home to my tribe's lands! Surely, I will be safe there. She shivered, but when the rain stopped, Nzdar's steady hoof steps carrying her farther away from the city soon soothed her distress.

She did not know how long it was before unhurried hooves approaching set her heart racing. Recalling her recent dream about a dark figure trying to kidnap her in a storm, she searched for cover beside the road. A low rock outcrop behind some trees was hardly enough, but she quickly dismounted and led Nzdar to the outcrop, hoping that the other rider had not seen her in the fading light. Behind the rock, she signaled Nzdar to lie down as he had learned when they were training, and he sank quietly to the ground. After picking up a couple of rocks twice the size of her fist with which to ward off an attack, she lay down behind him. Soon the other horse slowed then stopped.

She held her breath as footsteps squelched sodden leaves.

This is not how I want to go to *bahasht*, she thought, but robbers usually work in bands.

Then a familiar man's voice called her name. She looked up to see Harpagos staring at her. "What are you doing?" he asked, holding out his hand. "You should not be out here alone."

"You are right," she replied flatly. "I do not have any weapons." She stood without taking his hand and shook Nzdar's reins. The horse rose, and she brushed off her wet cloak. "I am going home to my village," she announced. "Would you like to come with me?"

"Vashti, if you return to your clan, you will never be able to serve Media as your family requires," Harpagos declared, "and Auramazda is calling you to rule."

"It matters not," Vashti cried in frustration, "I will not be bound to that dog, Ishtovigo. He can marry anyone of the tribal chiefs' daughters he wants. He's probably had most of them already."

"Be careful what you say about the Shahan Shah's son," Harpagos warned.

"Out here there is no one to listen," she yelled back.

"Let us go to your people tomorrow," Harpagos suggested quietly. "We will ask the chief if he knows anyone suitable to marry Ishtovigo." Pulling the rug off his horse, he placed it over the rock. "You can sleep under this. I will stay outside. But first we must eat," he entreated, taking some bread and cheese from his riding bags. "And there is one skin of water."

After struggling to light a fire with wet fuel, the two ate silently then retired. Following an uncomfortable night on Nzdar's rug, Vashti awoke to him nuzzling her and Harpagos trying to reignite the fire.

"Just enough for chai," he explained, taking a small bronze pot and two rhytons from his riding bag. "Debyar insisted I bring these."

Ashamed that her revered teacher knew she had run away, Vashti hung her head. "How is she?" she inquired.

"Well, the baby is moving now."

"He or she will grow up free," she commented.

"Only if you are there to make it sure," Harpagos replied, throwing her a stern glance. Vashti looked toward the rising sun. The great ball of fire governed the life of the world, but men could not ensure order among people. She wasn't confident she could either but lacked the courage to tell her friend what he didn't want to hear.

Not long after midday, they found the road to her mountain village. Passing women weaving brightly colored woolen rugs with patterns of flowers, two-headed snakes, and fish bones on wooden looms, Vashti asked Harpagos to remind her to take one of the durable artworks back to the palace. When the path took them through flocks of sheep and goats with their shepherds, she knew they were not far from her village. As they rounded the last bend, tears blurred her eyes at the sight of the familiar flat-roofed houses, all huddled together near the stream, just as she remembered them. She was home!

Numerous cousins, aunts, and uncles emerged from their dwellings to greet her, lovingly throwing their arms around her, and kissing her. Embraced by her muscular Aunt Rusen, she sobbed until all around her grew silent. By the time she stopped and cast her eyes around the circle of curious relatives, her uncle, Chief Zoran, was wringing his hands in dismay.

"What have they done to our Vashti?" he asked Harpagos, rolling up the sleeves of his panther skin *chokha*. The general led him aside and quietly explained. "Come into my house and we will have chai and talk about your problem," Uncle Zoran offered, his eyes lit with a kindly smile. Aunt Rusen immediately released Vashti and marched into her house, calling instructions to her daughters.

Inside, Zoran asked about his brother Hovakhshatra's health to which Vashti replied positively with thanks. Aunt Rusen's daughters appeared with chai and honey-soaked walnuts bound in fig leather, and Vashti soon relaxed to the cheerful cries of children playing outside and the heady, yeasty smell of bread baking. When

Harpagos and Zoran went outside to consult with the village men about the safety of the region, she was besieged by cousins asking questions about the palace and the city.

On returning with Harpagos, Zoran inquired about her other family members then regarded her thoughtfully. “So you do not want to marry Ishtovigo, dear?”

“Yes, Uncle. He is not my choice.”

“But, dear, it is every woman’s wish to be married and especially to a future shah.”

“Yes, Uncle, but it is not mine.”

“Then what will you do for your family and Media?”

“Protect us from our enemies, and keep our nation strong, Uncle.”

“And how will you do that if you are not Shahjin?”

“I have trained with Harpagos’s regiment. I am as good with the bow and arrow, the sling, and the lance as any man.” Zoran glanced at Harpagos who nodded.

“But can you hold a shield and fire your weapons at the same time?” Zoran asked.

“No man can do that, but I have a special pouch and strap for the shield that allows me to turn to fire at the retreating enemy. Like the men, I have learned from the Scythians,” she explained proudly to which Harpagos assented again.

“How can my flower of a niece do this?” Zoran asked Harpagos.

“She is not big, but she is strong in her body and fast to mount her horse. If she falls, it will not be hard,” the general replied.

“But her hair,” Zoran objected.

“Will be tied up in battle,” Vashti shot back.

Uncle whistled. “Then we have two problems. A woman who wants to fight in the army and no future Shahjin.”

“Can you recommend someone suitable to take Vashti’s place?” Harpagos asked Zoran.

"My Tujela is not married, but she knows nothing of the Shahan Shah's court and living in a palace. She would have much to learn, especially as she does not know the language of the court."

Harpagos shook his head. "Then we will have to look elsewhere."

Uncle Zoran agreed. "Vashti, come with me to the stream," he entreated. "I have a story to tell you." He rose and they walked over gray, water-worn stones to sit down together beside the stream. "See the sparkles," Uncle said, pointing to gold flecks glinting on rocks underneath rushing blue-green water. "They remind me of a story told me by great-grandfather." He took a deep breath and began.

"One day, when he was riding alongside a stream with his servant, Grandfather noticed a Hapiru riding a donkey loaded with all his possessions. 'Where are you going?' Grandfather asked.

"'I have escaped from Rhagae where the Athorayans exiled me, and am returning to my homeland,' the Hapiru replied.

"Grandfather took pity on the Hapiru and accompanied him to Hagmatana then paid for him to be guided over the Zagros Ranges. When he left Grandfather, the Hapiru gave him an urn with black stones in it. The servant was disappointed, claiming the ungrateful foreigner could at least have put some honey in the container. But Grandfather said not to worry, they did not help the foreigner for a reward, but because he was a stranger in their land."

Uncle stopped and glanced at Vashti, who was still watching the gold flecks in the stream.

"When they got back to the village," he continued, "Grandfather and the servant broke the urn open, took out a handful of stones, put them in his riding bag, and threw the urn into the stream where it broke up completely and the stones sank to the bottom. In the next flood, the stones and the pieces of the urn were washed away."

"One day when Grandfather was in the jeweler's shop, he remembered the black stones in his bag and sent his servant to fetch them. The jeweler asked him where he got the stones, so Grandfather explained."

"'If you can find any more, I will give you ten times the price of gold for them,' the jeweler offered. Grandfather and the servant raced down to the stream to look for the stones but could not find any."

Zoran finished and caught Vashti's gaze. "What does the story tell you?" he asked, his eyebrows raised expectantly.

"We must take what we are offered even if it seems dark and worthless," she replied flatly, realizing what the story meant for her future.

"Yes. We cannot be sure it is not Auramazda's gift to us, but we might not receive the reward until we learn of its full value," Uncle said, his voice kind but firm.

She gazed past the stream to the forest-clad mountains looming in the distance. They seemed too high to cross, but her people often walked over them, even when the winter snows were deep.

"I will do it, Uncle," she replied, turning to Zoran. "I will marry Ishtovigo, but…but promise I will always be welcomed by you and Aunt in the village," she pleaded.

"This will be your home forever," Zoran assured her, reaching out and putting his arm around her shoulders. "And when you become Shahjin, you will have joint custodianship of the land."

Vashti shook her head but thanked him. "The land is not mine to occupy. It belongs to the Busae people. I will leave the tribe to care for it and all the living things within its borders," she assured him.

Chapter 23

Over the next few weeks, Vashti took the time to enjoy her relatives' company. Clad in Tujela's clothes, she taught the village children to write their language, played games with them, and told stories around communal evening fires about Nineveh, Nebuchadnezzar, her trip to Bactria, and the funny things that happened at horse races and weddings. But she knew she could not delay her departure forever. Once Harpagos had finished instructing the local men about how to better defend themselves and their families, and she had chosen the rug she wanted to take with her, it was time to return to Hagmatana.

The weather was again stormy, and they passed through several showers on the return journey, but the hot summer sun soon dried their clothes. From the outskirts of the city, just as the citadel was coming into view, a rainbow once again arced above the citadel walls, and the gold-and-silver-trimmed battlements sparkled as the sun broke through. Vashti wondered if they spelled bright days ahead before a dark cloud poured torrents on the capital.

"Another soaking coming up," Harpagos announced grimly.

It began to pour, and she sneezed. "At least we will be clean when we reach the palace," she joked.

Instead of joyously greeting her daughter, a relieved Shamin said little when Gulah opened the door of their home to Vashti, who surmised her mother had been talking to the Shahan Shah.

"Sit down, dear," Shamin told her a little crossly. "Please don't leave again without letting me know where you are going."

"Dearest Mother, I am sorry I did not tell you, but the Shahan Shah asked me to marry Ishtovigo, and I had many doubts," Vashti replied apologetically.

"Why, dear?" Shamin asked, not in the least perturbed. "My brother has been training you for years, and now he is giving you the chance to one day lead our nation. But it will not be for years into the future. Hovakhshatra and Ardela are still in good health."

Vashti agreed and Shamin rested her eyes on her daughter lovingly. "Is there anything else you want to talk about?" she inquired softly.

"Is Ishtovigo here in Hagmatana?" Vashti asked.

"No. Hovakhshatra has sent him to Shush to finish the palace. He will be away for several months."

Absent as usual, Vashti thought, but at least it will give me time to complete my preparations to join the army. She was shivering but hot at the same time.

"Mother, I don't feel well. I am going to bed," she announced.

"Of course, dear, I will ask Gulah to bring you some chicken soup," Shamin replied, placing her hand on Vashti's forehead. "You are hot," she clucked before calling Khezmet and asking her to take a pitcher of water to Vashti's room. After sipping the soup, Vashti fell into a dreamless sleep and woke up sweating. She arose and took a cool drink but could not fall asleep again. Reaching for her writing tablet and rod, she poured out her cares onto a sheet of parchment.

To my dearest friend,

Although the night is cool, I am burning with fever. I caught cold after I ran away when the Shahan Shah asked me to marry Ishtovigo, but Harpagos came after me and we went to my village where I wanted to stay forever. However, had I done so, the chief would eventually have wanted me to marry his son. Do you think it was cowardly to run away?

When I visited Parthava some time ago, I met another chief. I sometimes think of his tall bearing, his purposeful walk, his few words that mean so much, and the way he looks at me as if we belong together. I know this will never be, he is probably married by now and the tragedy is that within a year I will be too…to a man I do not love.

I wonder if I will ever see that chief again. Perhaps, in his mercy, Auramazda will send him here one day soon to take me away before I am lost in duties in the palace forever.

Whatever happens, I will follow the example of my cousin Amytis, who wisely co-rules the court of great Babylon when her husband is absent. She can endure anything, including her husband's moods. I will strive to be as strong as her.

Having unburdened herself, she pushed the tablet and rod under the bed and promptly fell asleep. Only the *yazatas* would ever know that Mithridates was both the subject and the intended recipient of a letter that would never be sent.

On waking, searching for inspiration, she reached for one of her Avesta scrolls. "She has not won anything who has not won anything for her soul," read one of her favorite lines, but it failed to motivate her. Ashamed of her weakness, she rolled over in bed and tried to go back to sleep so she wouldn't feel so guilty. When Khezmet tried to wake her, she groaned and murmured that she wanted to sleep.

Worried when Vashti did not get better, Shamin sent for healing herbs and oils to treat her sickness, but they made little difference. Day after day, Vashti lay in her bed, sleeping, and dreaming of leading a women's army division in between reading and memorising Gatha hymns.

Eventually, Ardela came to visit her with an invitation to attend the Shahan Shah's meeting that afternoon with the generals, all of whom had been summoned to the capital. Suddenly aware of the message from the Avesta, she thanked her aunt, jumped out of bed, and called Khezmet to bring her scarlet *chokha*, woolen *pantol*, and Bear embroidered vest. Ardela hurried out to Shamin and winked.

"Our plan has worked," she whispered. "Vashti has revived!"

That afternoon, walking to the palace once again felt strange to Vashti. Her energy was high, but she feared her strength had deteriorated, and her eyes were sore. Remembering Zoran's story, she chastised herself for giving in to self-pity far too long.

"Sit in the corner, dear," the Shahan Shah told her after Harpagos admitted her to the council chamber. "What, if any, are your concerns about our military preparedness?" he asked the generals. "You may speak freely."

"Now that Athoraya is finally no longer a contender for supremacy, our main problem is Egypt, is it not?" General Biraxeas queried.

"Considering the Egyptians supported Shah Ashur-uballit of Athoraya against us for four years after the fall of Nineveh, they cannot be discounted as a force," the Shahan Shah replied.

"But the Egyptian army was all but decimated at the Battle of Carchemish," General Harpagos recalled.

"It appears that the Babylonians are still wary of them," Hovakhshatra replied.

"Eber-Nari and the rest of Sham will soon fall to Nebuchadnezzar," General Taxmaspâda predicted with the authority of recently acquired knowledge from his posting in the region.

"Then we will uphold our alliance with the Babylonians both militarily and diplomatically," the Shahan Shah confirmed.

"Which helped them defeat Necho the Second and the Athorayans at Harran," General Harpagos reminded the councillors.

"Shahan Shah, what is our current defense strategy?" General Biraxeas wanted to know.

"We will let Nebuchadnezzar weaken Egypt while guarding against possible threats to our north and east," Hovakhshatra replied.

"Shahan Shah, do you mean the Cimmerians and the Saka north of Bactria?" General Taxmaspada asked.

"The Cimmerians ride to the beat of their own drums. Of all the Ariavartan people, they opposed us at Carchemish, so we cannot trust them. Apparently, they can call on any number of troops from the northern confederacies, and we know how they can fight," the Shahan Shah maintained. "Eventually, we will have to fully subdue Urartu to provide a buffer against them."

"Shahan Shah," General Harpagos interrupted, lowering his voice respectfully, "what are your plans regarding the pursuit of the assassins of Shawish and Artaspaya?"

"I'm pleased you asked, General," Hovakhshatra replied. "I have engaged one of my most trusted agents, Rebin, to disguise himself as a beggar and infiltrate Lydia, and its predominantly Scythian regions. He speaks the languages of those peoples and is part Scythian."

"How long will you give Rebin to find them?" Harpagos asked.

"As long as he needs, his commission will continue until he locates the murderers."

"How will you get reports on his progress?" General Biraxeas asked.

"I have asked the most prominent merchants in Hagmatana to give Rebin any information gathered from the major cities where they conduct their business. In this way, we will cover a wide area. Eventually, when the killers lower their guard and feel safe to talk, we anticipate their boasting will reach the merchants, who will pass the information on to Rebin during his travels," Hovakhshatra explained. The generals all murmured their approval.

"What are your orders for the forces, Shahan Shah?" General Biraxeas wanted to know.

"I am sending your regiment west to aid our allies if necessary. General Taxmaspâda and his regiment will replace you after a year. General Harpagos will remain here on account of the impending birth of his first child." He turned to Vashti, who had quietly listened to the proceedings. "My niece will be appointed to assist her brother Ferhad, who will be commanding the Bears at this time."

There was a long silence while the generals absorbed the news, their eyes shifting uncertainly. General Biraxeas was the first to congratulate Vashti while General Taxmaspada wished Harpagos Auramazda's blessings on the upcoming birth. Then they all marched out leaving Vashti to thank her uncle for his generosity. Hovakhshatra cleared his throat.

"Not all the men will accept you at first," he admitted. "But they will soon learn that you can fight like they do," he added with a wry smile. "Congratulations, dear!"

Hardly able to contain her excitement, she grinned triumphantly. At last, she had reached her goal of being an official member of the Median cavalry!

"Shahan Shah, I will always be at Media's service," she replied in the gravest of tones.

In her jubilation at the prospect of being able to avenge the deaths of her family members, she broke protocol and danced lightly past Harpagos who flashed his approval with a wide grin as he opened the door for her.

Chapter 24

Racing along the silver corridor, she flew down the palace steps, quickly crossed the cobblestones to her home in the citadel wall, and flung the door open. She couldn't wait to tell Shamin and Khezmet her news.

Shamin listened warily. "Dear, will you be going to war?"

"Not in the foreseeable future, dear Mother. All our territories are currently secure. And if the Shahan Shah permits, I will train more women for the army, so they too can join the Bears. Ferhad and I will prepare to defend the plains east of Lydia. As cavalry, we must use the bow and arrow better than the Lydian archers. They fought the Athorayans fifty years ago and then the Cimmerians, but they might not always be friendly toward us."

"But the Shahan Shah will never let you go there. He will not risk the life of the future Shahjin," Shamin protested.

"I and my women fighters will be as good as the men," Vashti replied boldly. "So good that the men will not want to fight without us."

Shamin nodded, but her usually cheerful face was doubtful.

Vashti's confidence belied the struggle that was going on in the barracks. Ferhad had reported that despite his sister's obvious riding and weaponry skills, her appointment as co-leader had fomented unrest in the Bears' barracks. Some said they would not train with women while others declared they would never fight alongside women. But when Vashti suggested a separate women's division, to her surprise, the men begrudgingly accepted her proposal. She successfully sought the Shahan Shah's approval, and the first women's fighting unit in Ariavarta was established.

"You will need many more battle *chokhas* and *pantol*," Khezmet remarked after hugging her mistress on hearing the news. "We will get the women weavers to make them for you."

Some days later, Khezmet found Vashti sitting pensively on the courtyard seat beneath the oak tree. "Sister, what are you thinking?" she asked.

"Khezmet," Vashti replied, turning to her friend, "would you still be willing to serve me in the palace?"

"Of course, my darling. I have told you I will serve you anywhere, providing Daro is also there."

"I just wanted to be sure. I know…that you will always be my maid."

"Anywhere, even in the darkest prison," Khezmet affirmed, and they both laughed.

In Shush, Ishtovigo was not happy.

"Father has not provided enough gold coins to pay for Lebanese cedarwood to build the palace, so we will have to use clay with a brick facade for the walls instead of stone and timber," he complained to his mother in a letter. "But there is still enough stone for the columns at the nearby village of Abiradu. I hope Father won't mind if I send to Sardis for stonecutters and woodcarvers as we might not have enough of our own."

"Your palace sounds lovely, dear," Ardela wrote back. "Don't forget we have plenty of craftsmen who can fashion gold. And I suggest you ask Amytis to send some Babylonians to make sun-dried bricks for the walls. Tell her that if Nebuchadnezzar conquers Egypt, you would like him to bring back more silverwork and some ebony wood."

"Thank you, Mother, I will be overseeing the tinting and glazing of the bricks on the walls myself," Ishtovigo replied. "Please ask Father to increase the tribute on our richest territories, so I can finish the palace. I want to surprise everyone, including Vashti, with the most beautiful building in the Shahdom of Media."

Ardela caught her breath when she read her son's remark. No one had told him about the plan for his marriage to Vashti, his father had ordered it be kept a state secret. Ishtovigo also had to pass the test of independence before he was considered suitable for marriage while she and Hovakhshatra hoped that his dedication to the palace construction would make him more fit to one day rule Media.

"I will send some porcelain tints for the internal walls of the palace," she wrote back. "I am sure your building will be one of the finest in Media, son."

A year later, with the palace completed as far as funds would permit, Ishtovigo returned to Hagmatana where, according to his father's and mother's wishes, he married Vashti.

The couple had not spoken to each other for over a year.

On the eve of her wedding, Vashti was searching in her riding bags for something she could carry the next day as a special token of her fidelity. At the bottom of the bag, she found a small leather pouch containing a piece of inscribed deerskin. With trembling hands, she read:

How can I tell your voice is sweet?

Well, it enters my heart and takes me

off in the air where I dance like a leaf.

What do I know about your body?

Well, you shake me when you are with me

And I get restless till I see you again.

And till I see your body is for me

Always for me, over and over, again.

Running her fingers gently over the deerskin, she remembered the day Mithridates had given it to her. Surely these words were not the same as those the minstrel had sung to her when they were in Baxtri! Was the poem referring to that awful moment he had seen her in a wet robe at the oasis pool?

Anyway, I am getting married to Ishtovigo, she thought, although doubts about his fidelity still plagued her. "It does not matter now," she told herself, trying to shrug off misgivings tinged with panic.

But she knew it did because many times the Parthavan chief had come to her in dreams, calling her. Each time she had said yes, he had reached out *his* hand, but she could not grasp it. There was no need to tell anyone or ask the Magush what the dreams meant; she knew that she could not enter Mithridates' world, and he could not enter hers. The pain when she admitted that neither possibility would ever be their destiny flew like little arrows from her heart to her whole body, the body that was once again flimsily clothed in an old robe with tiny grains of sand stuck in the hem.

The Shahan Shah had decreed a double celebration of the wedding and Norouz, and family and tribal members had flocked to the capital. Their fringed *dwars*, with colorful striped, star, and sun designs matching the many rare cut jewels on Vashti's wedding *sarwain* dotted the plain outside the city. Excited shouts echoed up to the citadel as she and Ferhad took the journey to the palace in the family's carriage. But as Nzdar slowly trod the few cubits to the stone bear guarded steps, she broke out in a cold sweat. She was marrying a man who did not honor the Mitradat and never had. And she didn't know how reliable he would be when the scepter of Media fell into his hands. Trembling inside, she gave her arm to Ferhad, and they walked the silver hallway toward the banquet hosted by the Shahan Shah and Shahjin.

The Great Reception Hall of the palace was decorated for the occasion with white broom, yellow daisies, and red inverted tulips. During the long afternoon of eating and drinking, Ishtovigo partook of much wine despite his father's protests. A short interval in the proceedings was called while Harpagos took him to the cold spring feeding the palace pools.

"Your last hardship test," the general informed him tersely as he dunked the protesting groom's head in icy water.

Vashti kept smiling, but her stomach was sick, and she could hardly eat.

I would rather face the Lydian army on the Halys River plain than this indolent man, she thought while the guests ignored the groom's absence. By the time the Shahan Shah had raised his full rhyton several times in celebration of the upcoming marriage ceremony, Ishtovigo had returned in vigor to the room and settled himself beside Vashti as if nothing had happened. She felt the leather pouch with the deerskin inside the sash of her gold threaded robe. Its soft pliability reminded her of true fidelity, and she smiled graciously again.

"Somehow, my life before this day will sustain me by the power of Auramazda," she told herself.

When the feast had finished, the family carriage took Vashti to the Atashkedah where Ishtovigo waited for the formalizing of the marriage by the Piree Magush. Inside the carriage afterwards, Ishtovigo placed his hand on hers.

"Do not look so worried, my love. Media has never been stronger, and one day, it will all be ours."

"Of course, my dear," she replied. "But it will always be the peoples' too."

"Yes, you are right," he conceded without looking at her.

Down in the fire dotted city, where the banner of the Blacksmith flew from the tallest buildings, the people shouted, "May Auramazda bless our great Shahan Shah Hovakhshatra and his wife Shahjin Ardela and their family," and "All praise to Kawa who rescued us from the tyranny of Azhadahak," as the leading families' carriages passed. After each chant, the music reached an even higher crescendo. Everywhere women waved colorful headscarves and men brandished multipatterned sashes. Dancers formed circles around fires all over the city while other guests shared picnics.

When the carriage appeared, and Vashti and Ishtovigo stepped out, the people erupted into a spontaneous roar. Enthusiastic revelers then seized them, and they were quickly absorbed into a huge dance circle. Harpagos and Godel immediately assumed positions next to the bride and groom, but it was impossible to protect them from the joyous well-wishers. After some hours of lively dancing to the incessant beat of the *daf* and shrill tones of *shimshal* pipes, the revelers set a huge fire. Acrobats performed a series of death-defying jumps over the fire, accompanied by continuous clapping from the crowd, but when the show was over, the people fell strangely silent in anticipation of Ishtovigo's reading of the Norouz poem:

Without the light and the fire of love,
Without the Designer and the power of Creator,
We are not able to reach union.

Light is for us and dark is against us
This fire massing and washing the heart,
My soul yearns for it.

And here comes Norouz and the New Year,
When such a light is rising.

When he took Vashti in his arms and kissed her, the crowd's roar was mixed with women's ululations.

Swept away by the happy throngs, for a little while Vashti felt as content as she had around the fire at Rhagae, but all too soon it was time to depart with her husband for their first night together in Ishtovigo's quarters. When they arrived, her cream silk wedding robe laced in fine pure gold thread was torn, and, she no longer wore her bejeweled headdress crown.

Thankfully, Khezmet had seized it at the height of the festivities, promising she would give it to the treasurer for safekeeping in the palace vault.

Much to the astonishment and delight of all, Ishtovigo proved himself a faithful husband and responsible member of his family under the watchful eyes of Vashti and Harpagos. Joy flooded the family when Vashti and Ishtovigo's first child, Darayaus, was born in the twenty-third regnal year of his grandfather. The people of Hagmatana celebrated, and each family was given a portion of finely ground flour and a cake of dried fruits by the Shahan Shah and Shahjin.

Darayaus grew and was soon running round with Debyar and Harpagos' little girl, Gulnaz. Despite Ishtovigo's objections, Khezmet's three children helped their mother care for them when their parents were on official business. Vashti continued to train the members of her women's fighting division, and when the representatives of the subject nations came to give tribute every year, she received them but never saw Mithridates. Every Parthavan she asked about him knew nothing. Worried that something had happened to him, she sent Godel to find out. He discovered that Mithridates had gone to Egypt two years previously and apparently returned, but there was no news of him, either alive or dead. Dismayed and discouraged, she stowed the leather pouch Mithridates had given her in a secret compartment in her jewelry box and tried to forget about him. Her dreams and the small piece of deer parchment remained the only reminders of the times when she was truly free and happy.

Khezmet entered her mistress's bedchamber one day when the hot late spring sun was well across its morning path and found her dozing.

"Wake up, sleepy one. Darayaus is calling for you," she urged.

Vashti yawned and pulled the blankets over her face. "But I am still tired," she mumbled. She was so mainly because the lack of news about Mithridates was still on her mind. She couldn't help wondering whether he had died and the Parthavans were keeping it secret. To distract herself, she had worked extra hard in training the day before.

"I'm not surprised after you practiced archery and trained by running up and down a mountainside carrying heavy lumps of blacksmith's untempered iron yesterday," Khezmet continued.

"I need to be strong enough to throw a lance and ride long distances with my other weapons and supplies," Vashti explained. "The Shahan Shah expects all regimental members to be tough in their bodies and highly skilled with their weapons. And I'm not going to ask my women to do anything I can't do myself," she added.

"Dear, we know the Shahan Shah won't let you fight in a real war."

"Not unless my troops and I continue to prove ourselves."

"Not today," Khezmet declared, gleefully waving a parchment scroll. "You have a letter with the lion seal."

Vashti sat straight up in bed and grabbed the scroll. It had been several months since she had heard from cousin Amytis. Opening the seal, she read:

My dearest Vashti,

After missing your wedding and not seeing my nephew grow, I hope to visit you as soon as possible with Amel-Marduk.

My homesickness has been a little worse lately, for weeks I haven't stopped thinking of everyone celebrating Norouz. Babylonia has nothing like the house-to-house visits, special Norouz foods, and fireworks of Media, even though we have plenty of oily seeps around to light up. How greatly I miss the Norouz dance! I think my feet might almost have forgotten the steps. Some practice is required. But I thank Auramazda that Nebuchadnezzar still does not expect me to attend the festivals here for Bel and Marduk.

My problem now is that Nebuchadnezzar receives frequent visits from the priests who treat him as a god. This makes him think he must protect his people as their father by expanding the shahdom to the west and stopping the Egyptians from regaining any territory. At night, he wakes in great distress and sweats, and I have no choice but to call the servants to bathe him until he becomes calm. I think he has bad dreams. The next day he goes to the priests, who cannot interpret his dreams, and his confusion and agitation increase. If only he would listen to my magi priest while Belteshazzar is touring the province of Babylon.

My darling, I am so sorry to write to you of these vexing matters at your time of such happiness. Please forgive me. You must come and stay with me for a while in autumn when the harsh heat is over. Then we will savor the fruits of the Babylonian harvest. Be sure to bring Darayaus, who must get to know Amel-Marduk.

In the meantime, I do hope Nebuchadnezzar will not experience any more bouts of his strange affliction.

It is morning and the duties of the day await, so I must leave you now.

I am still your loving,

Amytis

Sighing, Vashti asked Khezmet to request an audience for her with the Shahan Shah and Shahjin to determine their knowledge of the Babylonian court situation. Their reply indicated she should visit that afternoon.

The Shahan Shah was in such high spirits after the arrival of recent tribute in new and rare gold and silver combination coins that he appeared unconcerned about the implications of Amytis' comments regarding the machinations of the Babylonian court.

"Nebuchadnezzar has had these attacks of ill health before," he reasoned. "The Magush thinks it is most likely the symptoms of that wretched fever that plagues the marshes of Babylon."

"Amytis might be implying the priests are trying to manipulate the shah with a type of spell," Vashti suggested. "A shift in the power configurations of the Babylonian court could easily affect us."

The Shahan Shah nodded. "Keep regular contact with Amytis. Please write to her that we miss her and trust that Nebuchadnezzar's health will soon improve." Vashti agreed to his request and Hovakhshatra dictated the following diplomatic memo to an attending scribe:

Honored Shahan Shah of Babylonia

We wish you a speedy return to personal tranquillity, health, and harmony in all your endeavours. Peace and stability across both our shahdoms are still our desire.

Hovakhshatra of Media

"If Nebuchadnezzar moves again on Ursalim, we need to know beforehand, even though a power struggle in Babylon might delay it," Hovakhshatra added, sealing the document in hot wax with his bear ring insignia.

"Or the campaign is hastened as a result of a power struggle," Vashti suggested.

"True, my dear. I do believe you have your father's head for strategy," the Shahan Shah replied, and Vashti smiled just a little smugly. "And now, dear, I expect you would like to see my son," he continued.

"I would, Shahan Shah," Vashti replied. "But I fear that he might be somewhat ill-disposed. When I last saw him, he was quite merry with wine."

The Shahan Shah frowned. "We do not want to see him return to his old habits. Please monitor his consumption and encourage moderation."

"Do not worry, Uncle. I have noticed some noble changes in my husband. He tries hard to please and usually avoids *druj*," Vashti replied.

"Yes. It's just the times that he falls prey to it that worry me," Hovakhshatra confessed.

"We all must learn from our mistakes," Vashti countered.

"Agreed, dear, and I have been impressed with his work as assistant treasurer," Hovakhshatra admitted. An official entered with some parchment scrolls, so her uncle suggested she find his daughter, cousin Shelna, who he said was in some distress.

When Vashti found Shelna lying on her brocaded bed cover staring dismally up at the ceiling mosaics, she gave the youngest member of the leading family a hug.

"Why is your face so long, dear?" she asked.

"Ferhad has been at military camp in the mountains for many months," Shelna moaned. "I want to visit him."

Vashti took her cousin's hand. "Dear, you know your father will not allow you to attend such a camp until you are older. Did you know that years ago, Ishtovigo and I were friends, like you are with Ferhad?" she said, searching for ways to console her cousin.

Shelna sat up. "And what happened?"

"We had some differences, and we spent a long time apart on your parents' business," Vashti explained.

"Was that before or after Shawish and Artaspaya died?" Shelna asked, her interest piqued.

"Before, when I went to Bactria and Ishtovigo went to Elam the first time," Vashti replied, taking a brush and running it through Shelna's golden locks. "Dear, this is an important opportunity for my brother to represent the father he lost so early and to honor his name," she explained. "He is preparing to fulfill his duty to his family and his nation."

Shelna sighed. "I know but it's hard. I miss him."

"Yes, but if you want to get closer to Ferhad, why don't you join the army yourself?" Vashti suggested. "There are still vacancies in my women's division."

Shelna's eyes shone. "Do you really think I could?"

"Of course. You are young and can easily build your strength and weapons skills. We have plenty of women your age. None of them want to end up slaves to the Lydians or the Scythians."

"But first I have to finish my lessons," Shelna admitted. "I'm finding Aramaic quite difficult."

"I will give you extra time to learn," Vashti offered, "and there are some Athorayan women in my unit. You can practice your languages with them."

Vashti put the brush down and finished plaiting Shelna's hair. "Put your cloak on, and we will find Ardela and Shamin to discuss the matter," she urged. "And let's ask Debyar if we can learn about plants at the hunting grounds next week. I'm sure she would be delighted to show us the medicinal flowers and herbs."

"And we can look for plants that have the ingredients for *arayesh* coloring for our faces, and perhaps even make our own!" Shelna suggested.

Vashti laughed. "Debyar probably knows how, but you won't need to look beautiful on the battlefield unless you want to paint your face to scare the enemy."

Shelna clapped her hands. "We will do both and have a wonderful time!"

"Let's find our mothers right now and tell them the news," Vashti urged, and the two hurried out.

Chapter 25

"Now we know why Nebuchadnezzar has spent a full year at home refitting his horses and cavalry," the Shahan Shah told his council a few months later following the arrival of the ambassadorial pouch from Babylon. "Ever since his success at Carchemish, he's been determined to conquer Sham and Egypt."

"It is best that we do not help Babylonia this time," the Shahjin suggested. "We were only at Carchemish to make sure the Athorayan army would never attack us again."

"I agree," Harpagos stated firmly. "We are not in alliance with Babylonia to expand its territories."

"Yes," Hovakhshatra concurred. "We are mostly interested in northern Sham bordering our lands in Mesopotamia, which are currently secure, thanks to the troops' work on our forts. And you are right, my dear," he told his wife. "There is no need for us to consider aiding Nebuchadnezzar because Amytis also reports that his latest attempt to conquer Egypt has failed with significant losses on both sides."

"An army must confront many obstacles to get into Egypt," Harpagos informed the listeners. "Several hostile nations occupy the Sinai Desert."

The Shahan Shah nodded agreement. "Amytis further reports that Hapiru's alliance with Necho of Egypt has resulted in Nebuchadnezzar laying siege to Ursalim. She believes he's still determined to prevent Egypt having any influence in Sham as he keeps returning after only a short stay at home. He's even attacked the Shebans in the desert of Sham."

It's still difficult for Amytis, Vashti thought. Nebuchadnezzar hasn't changed even after those very strange dreams he had years ago.

"Is Ursalim still under siege?" General Biraxeas asked.

"As far as we know, yes," Hovakhshatra replied.

From the corner of the room the Piree Magush asked permission to speak, and it was granted. "Shahan Shah, Auramazda has sent me a dream about Yehud, that shahdom is full of *druj*." In the belief that the fate of every nation that defies its god or gods was destruction, everyone agreed solemnly.

"I have asked Amytis to report every two months, but while our ally is busy in Sham, we do not need to be concerned about his activities in our region," the Shahan Shah declared. "Are there any more questions?"

"Did Amytis mention whether Nebuchadnezzar has taken any captives from Ursalim?" Vashti asked.

"No, and we will not accept any more at this time," the Shahan Shah stated firmly. "The only Hapiru we have are those exiled here by the Athorayans. And unlike some of our ancestors and the other nations, we will not take slaves or women as tribute." With this declaration, he rose, raised the golden scepter, and closed the meeting.

Vashti immediately walked out to the stables to check Nzdar as Daro had reported him lame again. Inside, she found her beloved horse with a nasty sore on his leg and looking lean. After asking Daro to attend to the infection and increase his feed, she accepted his apology for being busy caring for the new herd of cavalry horses that had just arrived from Nisea for her women fighters. But as she patted Nzdar and watched Daro put olive oil and a bandage on his leg, she became aware of the figure of Ishtovigo backlit in the stable doorway.

"Still think your women can fight in the army?" he asked disdainfully as she approached him on her way out.

She turned away from his gaze. “Yes, we are ready to defend Media,” she replied coolly.

“How many other leading women have fought for their nation?” he asked.

“The Hapiru told me that many years ago, Devorah, their female judge, led them into battle against Sisera, the mercenary general of the Canaanite Shah Jabin. If the women of little Yisrael could lead male warriors and defeat a male army, so can my women and I protect Media.”

Ishtovigo scowled and opened his mouth to reply but closed it and then smiled. “Come,” he urged. “I have a surprise for you.” Guiding her to the stall next to Nzdar’s, he pointed to a dark bay horse. “He is yours. His name is Thunder, and he comes from the Qandil Mountains. I think it might be time to put Nzdar out to pasture. He is too old for the cavalry.”

Vashti wanted to protest, but Ishtovigo seemed pleased with himself, and his firm tone meant it was pointless to disagree. She thanked him for the gift and ran her hand down the horse’s silky mane. “He will look beautiful in my *golangs*,” she remarked. The horse shied away at her touch, and she jumped to avoid his hooves. “I’ve heard there’s a lot of spirit in the Qandils,” she remarked. “Let’s see if he maintains it under fire.”

“Not with all those women screaming around him,” Ishtovigo commented drily.

Vashti did not reply, and their return to the palace was tense. Later, she went back and asked Daro to put a guard on Nzdar. “Do not let anyone take him without my permission,” she ordered, realizing that “pasture” to Ishtovigo might mean a permanent place under, not on it.

Despite the wedding of Ferhad and Shelna just weeks beforehand, Norouz of that year was subdued. Amytis’ letters were gloomy, as she feared for her husband's life in his unceasing campaigns to take control of Egypt. Then one cold, frosty morning in late autumn, two messengers rode into the palace precinct, bearing the news that Babylonia's siege of Ursalim was continuing, due to Shah Jehoiakim's alliance with Egypt. Against the advice of some of his officials, including Harpagos, Hovakhshatra once again sent General Taxmaspada's Lynx regiment to Sham.

In his seventh regnal year, determined to break the siege, Nebuchadnezzar camped outside Ursalim. Shah Jehoiachin, who surrendered when the city fell, was taken captive to Babylon along with eleven thousand other Hapiru.

"Nebuchadnezzar has brought the dead Shah Jehoiakim's son, Jehoiachin, to Babylon where he and his family now eat from the Shahan Shah's table," Amytis wrote. "He has made the new vassal shah Shah Zedekiah swear an oath of loyalty to Babylonia and remit substantial tribute, a share of which he has offered our army."

"Tell Nebuchadnezzar we refuse all except what is needed to supply General Taxmaspada and his forces," Hovakhshatra replied.

"Nebuchadnezzar took the treasures and furnishings of the Hapiru temple including its golden vessels," Amytis later wrote. "I was very much saddened by the sight of the long, bedraggled lines of thousands of Hapiru courtiers, prominent citizens, and craftsmen whom the troops had driven across the desert. Secretly, I hoped that some of them would prove as useful to Babylonia as Belteshazzar and his friends."

"One family of a young man with a delicate wife carrying a pretty little girl particularly impressed me, and I wondered how they had survived the dreadful trek through the desert. Their sunburned, hopeless faces and their barely shod, bleeding feet shuffling over the Processional Way behind the troops' victory march, made me sick. I told Nebuchadnezzar to insist his men feed and water them straight away and warned that if he didn't, I would advise Father and Mother to reconsider the alliance. My husband snarled refusal, but I stared back, hands on my hips. When he ordered provisioning of the captives that hour, I was very relieved that he had listened to me and not flown into one of his rages!

I vowed to Auramazda never to forget them and their compatriots and immediately departed to find Belteshazzar to make sure the captives received treatments for their injuries before being settled by the Chebar Canal."

The report shocked Vashti, who finally realized that Ursalim was the foreign city with the beautiful colonnaded temple that was plundered in the dream she had many years ago. Seeking to discover why Auramadza had given her such a dream, she visited Piree Magush.

"You are being warned that something happened in that war, which has grave significance for you…in the future," he informed her.

Not satisfied with this explanation, she wondered why Auramadza gave her such strange dreams whose meaning couldn't be interpreted.

The following year, Amytis informed her father that Nebuchadnezzar had campaigned as far as the Ufratu River and then turned back. Later, at the Idiqlat River, he had driven the stalwart people of Elam to retreat. After returning to deal swiftly and brutally with rebellion fomenting around Babylonia and its territories, Nebuchadnezzar suspected that the Medes had traitorously influenced a defector in his palace. Only the initial interventions of Amytis had prevented her husband from disastrously attacking his Median allies. Letters were hurriedly sent back and forth between the treaty partners with Hovakhshatra eventually sending Harpagos to successfully reason with his son-in-law.

A year later, Amytis reported that the shahs of Ammon, Edom, Moab, Sidon, and Tyre had formed a union against Nebuchadnezzar in the land of the Hapiru but not attacked any of the occupying forces.

"Nebuchadnezzar's latest venture into Sham has yielded even more wealth for Babylonia," she wrote, "and my husband has begun one of his most extravagant building programs ever, including the rebuilding of the old palace and commencement of a new palace."

Chapter 26

In the early autumn of the same year, Khezmet gave birth to her third child. Two years after the fall of Ursalim to the Babylonians, with the Median military still providing a peaceful presence in Sham, the Shahan Shah and Shahjin's household was increased by the birth of Vashti and Ishtovigo's daughter, Zerena, and a baby boy, Kshathrita, to their daughter Shelna and her husband Ferhad. Kshathrita became the third male in line to the throne of Media.

While young Darayaus had firmly attached himself to his mother, Zerena was very much her father's daughter; each time she saw Ishtovigo, her eyes would light up and she would put her little hands out to him. Ishtovigo doted on his daughter, and his dealings with local and foreign merchants would often yield a trinket, a toy, earrings, a bracelet, or a necklace for her.

"She is the most decorated child in the palace," Vashti was known to comment.

In the meantime, Darayaus had learned to ride his first pony and pestered his mother to take him hunting. When she finally relented, he was horrified by the death of a gazelle and had to be quickly returned home. The incident was unsettling to say the least as everyone in the palace knew that within a year, Darayaus would be sent from his mother's care into the company of men to learn military skills. So a few months later, Vashti and Debyar began to teach him about the necessity of hunting skills in preparation to lead his nation into battle. But when left to practice his initiation prayers with *kusti* threads wrapped three times around a white *chokha*, he would sneak off to find his grandfather with the excuse that he wanted to learn more about his great-grandfathers.

Despite Ishtovigo's aversion to the servants' children being in his quarters, when he was away, Vashti would often allow Khezmet to bring her daughter Shireen over to play with Darayaus. Their innocent, high-pitched chatter as they played together happily was like a soothing balm to her parched life of endless official duties. But if Ishtovigo returned early from a trip, Shireen had to be hurriedly whisked away as Vashti did not want the children to witness her husband's display of temper. Darayaus had to learn to be content with her company only on these occasions until Zerena and cousin Kshathrita were old enough to play with him, and once more delightful children's voices could be heard echoing around the palace chambers.

Several years later, when Darayaus the Mede celebrated his tenth birthday, the Shahan Shah finally received the words from his faithful spy, Rebin, which he had waited many years to hear. The agent had ventured as far as the Halys River in pursuit of rumors from traders that the murderers of the heirs to the Median throne were hiding in Lydia. With specific information gleaned from local merchants trading over the border, Rebin located the suspects, who, true to the Shahan Shah's prediction, had boasted of their crimes around campfires. The spy immediately hastened to the border and left a message for postal riders traveling the Shahan Shah's Road.

When the news finally reached Hovakhshatra, the relief he felt from releasing years of grief and anger spilled forth into tears of joy; so much so that it took Ardela several minutes to calm him.

"We will send a company of troops straight away to retrieve those dogs who killed my sons and bring them back for trial," the Shahan Shah declared before telling his advisor to summon

General Harpagos. “Rebin must return to Hagmatana to give evidence.”

Weeks after leaving the city, Harpagos sent back disappointing news. Shah Alyattes the Second of Lydia, apparently having ascertained from his own spies that the Medes were on their way to apprehend the suspects, sent soldiers to the border to intercept Harpagos and his troops. After being refused access to arrest the murderers, Harpagos reported to Hovakhshatra and awaited his orders.

Over a year of diplomatic representations yielded little progress in the dispute despite Hovakhshatra’s claim that the accused were his subjects and had committed the crime on his territory. Alyattes in turn maintained that the Scythians were citizens without a homeland and had been adopted by and granted asylum in Lydia. Hovakhshatra’s final plea for their release so he could pursue justice for his sons fell on deaf ears.

Summoning his full council, the Shahan Shah reluctantly declared that the only course left for the Medes to avenge the death of their sons was to go to war against the Shahdom of Lydia. Ishtovigo agreed but General Biraxeas had more questions. After receiving permission to speak, he pointed out that most of the forces in Sham would have to be recalled if a successful campaign were to be mounted on Media’s western border. The Shahan Shah agreed and replied that he had already drafted instructions for General Taxmaspada.

Vashti inquired about the overall distribution of troops, reminding the Shahan Shah of the need to protect the shahdom’s eastern flanks. Privately, she wanted him to consider the toll of such a distant war in terms of men and funds.

“Couldn’t you order Harpagos to send a raiding party to find a secret way across the border and capture the offenders?” she suggested.

“Alyattes is very arrogant,” Hovakhshatra replied. “Clearly, he does not respect international conventions and is a very stubborn neighbor. This is a timely opportunity to teach him that he cannot do as he pleases with our citizens, thus violating our sovereignty. Furthermore," he stated, his eyes steely, "if we are to maintain strength on our western flanks, we will have to assume a greater position of power in relation to Lydia."

Vashti realized that apart from not answering her question, the Shahan Shah had decided. She dreaded the effects of war; the disruption, the waiting, and the losses, perhaps of some of her own family members. Even if the Shahan Shah would allow her to order her women's division to the conflict, she wondered whether she should involve them in the attempt to avenge her cousins' deaths.

The members of the council, including the Shahjin, nodded sadly in agreement. Finally, the Shahan Shah turned to the Piree Magush, who stood silently by his side.

"Can you add anything more to the discussion, honored Magush?" he asked.

The priest nodded. "The Lydians are deceiving us with *druj* and then lying about it again. They are not taking responsibility for what happens within their territory. They must learn that international deception is destructive to their subjects and the nations in the region," he replied sternly.

The Shahan Shah took a deep breath and exhaled slowly. "Do we have your blessing, Piree Magush?" he asked.

"The Prophet never advocated war, but whatever you decide, Shahah Shah, may Auramazda be with you and our forces."

Hovakhshatra looked around the room. "We are not taking this decision lightly," he declared, "but if we do not act firmly, word will spread that if attacked, we do not protect ourselves. And that," he stated emphatically, "is simply not true. Nor will it ever be while my wife and I rule Media." He then rose and the golden scepter was replaced in its silk-lined box.

Vashti and Ishtovigo made their way back slowly to their quarters. Neither of them spoke until she asked him if he would go to war.

"No," he replied firmly. "I expect Father will lead the forces, and I will take his place in his absence," he declared with a self-satisfied smile.

"Of course, my dear. You are the obvious choice to carry on while the Shahan Shah is away. But Ferhad will go"—she shivered—"and Lydia is so far away."

Ishtovigo put his arm around his wife. "Don't worry, my love. Once Father captures the guilty Scythians, everyone will be home by Norouz."

Privately, Vashti thought the campaign would not succeed; she knew because she had seen it in a dream. Now she regretted not telling the Magush, but she realized it was useless to do so as the Shahan Shah's mind was unlikely to change.

Shahan Shah Hovakhshatra duly informed Nebuchadnezzar of Babylonia of the withdrawal of most of the Median troops from Sham. With the support of Amytis, who was keen to see her brothers' deaths avenged, Nebuchadnezzar agreed.

The Median tribes mustered all able men for war, and the preparations began. In Hagmatana, blacksmiths sweated over forges while steam hissed from nascent iron and bronze shields. Cartloads of willow and pine branches rattled in from the mountains to be honed into arrow shafts and lances. Leatherworkers and bootmakers toiled for long days to make horses' reins, soldier's chaps, and knee-length boots from cowhides acquired from herds across the Zagros Tableland. More horses were brought from Nisea.

In the villages dried foods, rugs, *dwars*, and other supplies for encampment, journeys, and active service were collected and loaded onto carts bound for the capital. Many a sheep and goat appeared thinly covered as women spun and wove cloth for tunics and *pantol*. Even the children collected stones for slingshots and scraps of wool for the horses' *golangs*, and snared foxes to fur-lined boots.

When all was ready, on yet another cold morning, the Shahan Shah's family assembled on the palace steps to farewell him and the departing troops. Shamin and Parwin stood with Ardela,

Shelna, and Kshathrita to farewell Hovakhshatra and Ferhad. Darayaus held his mother's hand, and Zerena clung to her father as Ishtovigo raised the golden scepter while the Shahan Shah rode past. Clad in a long-sleeved, sheep's fleece–lined cloak embossed with green and red inverted tulips and silver bears, Hovakhshatra lifted his lance and bellowed the battle cry.

Staunch faced and holding Gulnaz, Debyar kept her composure as Harpagos waved and disappeared through the golden gateway. Only when the troops reached the city where women's ululations and men's battle cries echoed across the grand settlement and drifted up to the citadel, did those inside the upper wall cry, "huloo-lalao, huloo-lalao," in anticipation of victory.

"Do not fear," Ardela told them. "I have had a dream that we will not lose this war."

Little did she know that for the next five years, her husband would fight in a senseless conflict while his son built a luxurious palace in Shush.

But Vashti remembered her dream that the war would not be won.

Two years later, with the war in Lydia continuing, yet another disturbing letter from Amytis detailed the beginning of Nebuchadnezzar's final assault on Ursalim.

Dearest cousin

Please keep sending all news from the Lydian front. It is important because the international situation has changed much since I last wrote. Shah Zedekiah, whom my husband appointed ruler of Yehud, must have been waiting for years to try to overthrow his rule. We could not allow this because Yehud is important for the control of Sham and particularly Egypt. So when Pharoah Psamtik and then Pharoah Apries both encouraged rebellion against us, and Zedekiah, followed by Ithobaal of Tyre, refused to pay tribute, Nebuchadnezzar besieged Ursalim.

Vashti shivered as she read the letter. War was so destructive, and the Shahan Shah's venture in Lydia was no different. He had returned once to obtain funds to replenish the army, but much to his dismay, the treasury chests were almost depleted.

"Have not the provinces given tribute?" he had asked Vashti.

"Yes, Shahan Shah, but the cost of the palace at Shush has been very high," she had replied. "I have told Ishtovigo this is not your wish, but he will not listen."

"Then find another storehouse for the tribute and deposit it there with a guard," Hovakhshatra had ordered. With the stables almost empty and Ishtovigo absent, Vashti instructed Daro to dig a vault beneath them, hide the chests of coins and other tribute in kind there, and cover the floor again with straw.

"I will personally watch over the storage of these funds as they arrive," she informed Daro, "but no one else must ever know about it." Swearing secrecy, Daro went down to the city to find trustworthy laborers.

The next time Ishtovigo visited the treasury, he found the chests as empty as he had left them. In a rage, he accosted the treasurer, who explained that Vashti had accepted all tribute on behalf of the Shahan Shah.

"Where is the tribute?" he yelled after striding into her quarters unannounced.

Wary of his temper, she took a side step toward the safety of the door. "It is in storage waiting for the Shahan Shah to use it for the war," she replied calmly.

"That wretched war will ruin Media," Ishtovigo complained. "If we are to remain a recognized and respected power, we will have to show our neighbors just how strong we are with even more impressive buildings than theirs. That is how Nebuchadnezzar became number one in the region."

"By plundering Sham and spending much of the wealth on trying to take Egypt? And stealing people and using them as slaves? By building numerous temples and memorials to all his gods and himself as one of them? But when he has a peculiar dream, he devotes himself to Belteshazzar's god then proceeds to destroy the temple of that god and steal its sacred objects. It is madness," she cried.

Ishtovigo stared open-mouthed at her. "What has happened to you, Vashti? Why are you so disloyal to our ally? Father would not be happy with such words."

"And if I told him where the war funds have been going, you might never take the throne," she countered resolutely.

Ishtovigo came closer, so close she could smell his rancid breath. "On the Shahan Shah's authority, I order you to stop your treason. Where are the extra funds?" he yelled.

Vashti stepped back and held her gaze. "Under your father's orders, I will not tell you," she replied through gritted teeth. "And I will not allow Media to be weakened by the man entrusted to care for her."

Ishtovigo's hate-ridden eyes bore into her as he raised his hand and slapped her hard in the face. Her head tilted backwards, and as she lunged forward to right herself, she overbalanced and fell on her face. Then everything went black.

Chapter 27

The loud voices, Vashti's cry, and the door slamming as Ishtovigo exited sent Khezmet quickly into the chamber.

"Dear," she cried, kneeling beside her, "what has happened to you?" Gently rolling Vashti over, she gasped at the sight of her bloody nose and cracked lip. She lifted her onto the nearest couch and gently wiped the blood away with her scarf. "Wake up my darling," she urged. "Who has done this to you?"

"Ishtovigo," Vashti murmured, her eyelids fluttering.

"Bring some water," Khezmet called to a servant in the corridor outside. Trying to focus on the room spinning around her, Vashti groaned. "Do you want me to call the Shahan Shah's guard?" Khezmet asked.

"No. He is my husband's guard now…" Vashti sucked in her breath and tried to sit up, but Khezmet caught her as she sank back down. "Perhaps I will wait till my head feels better," she mumbled.

"Let me send a servant for the Magush. You are not well," Khezmet implored.

"No, please don't. No one must know of this…shame," Vashti insisted.

"It is not your shame. It is your husband's," Khezmet muttered angrily as she wiped more blood from Vashti's face. "The Shahan Shah must be informed."

"No. He is too far away and too busy with the war," Vashti insisted. "Please do not say anything to anyone. We will handle the situation ourselves. I will speak to my women's army division leader and ask her to arrange guards for my chambers."

"Yes, my darling," Khezmet replied, kneeling beside Vashti and stroking her arm. "I will go to the cold spring and get a wet cloth for your face," she promised.

"*Spas*, dear," Vashti murmured, closing her eyes to contain her tears.

"Ishtovigo will have to pay for this," Khezmet fumed on returning a few minutes later. "Daro told me he's been going to the Mossala whenever he returns from Shush."

Vashti sighed. "I was hoping he had changed."

"Once *druj* gets into someone, it is very hard to get it out," Khezmet complained. A soft knock on the door revealed Darayaus, who had been playing with Zerena in the next room. Khezmet grabbed a scarf and quickly wrapped it round Vashti's head.

"Mother, are you sick?" Darayaus asked. "Why is your nose so big?"

"I fell over," she explained. "I am lying down to make it better."

"Then I will help make it better too," Darayaus offered, kneeling beside his mother and gently rubbing her temple.

Vashti winced and Khezmet waited a short while before carefully taking his hand away. "Darayaus, please go and play with Zerena and the other children. Your mother needs to rest now," she told him.

Darayaus frowned, withdrew his hand, and got up. "Get better soon, dear Mother. I love you," he called as he left.

Tears welled again in Vashti's eyes as Khezmet placed the cold cloth on her nose. "This must not happen again," her maid declared fiercely.

"Harpagos would have stopped my husband," Vashti replied, grabbing hold of Khezmet and sitting up, "but he isn't here either. And if Ishtovigo finds out I'm guarded by my women warriors, there will be more trouble between us. He wants to restrict me to palace duties only…including dressing up to receive foreigners."

"Beauty is easy for you but being caged in the palace is not," Khezmet remarked.

"Our ancestors fought those uncivilized tribes whose men used women for their benefit only as some still do," Vashti lamented. "Now it seems that *druj* is creeping into the heart of the palace."

"But not into the hearts of the people," Khezmet declared. "Do you know when the Shahan Shah will return?"

"No. It could be in months or even years."

"I think you should inform your women warriors of the danger posed by Ishtovigo and the Mossala."

"You are right, dear," Vashti agreed, taking Khezmet's hand and squeezing it. "While the forces are away, they are our only true protection."

When Khezmet left to fill a ceramic jar with cold water, Darayaus crept back into his mother's chamber. The question he asked caused a lump in Vashti's throat.

"Mother, does Father tell *druj*?"

Vashti sniffed and adjusted the scarf over her forehead. How could she tell *druj* herself when it would upset her son?

"What makes you think Father tells *druj*, dear?" she asked.

"I heard some guards in the hallway say so one day," Darayaus replied.

"What did they say he told *druj* about?"

"His friends…some people in the city," Darayaus answered innocently.

"Did the guards say the names of those friends?"

"I think one was ... Kusha, another was Ghazem, and the other might have been Ad-Admatha."

Vashti's heart thumped at the mention of the three Parsu thieves dismissed by the Shahan Shah for stealing from the treasury who were now back from imprisonment in the fort of Arrapkha. She drew Darayaus to her and hugged him.

"Do not worry, my dear. Those men have broken the laws of Media by doing bad things to Grandfather, but they have been punished. I'm sure Father was trying to find out if they were telling *druj*, just so Grandfather won't be robbed again."

Darayaus smiled. "Yes, Mother, Father is looking after us all, especially while Grandfather is away."

Vashti took her son's hand again and patted it. "You're a good boy, Darayaus. One day you will be a kind and wise ruler of Media."

"Thank you, Mother. Now I am initiated, I am ready."

"Bless you, son," she whispered.

Darayaus smiled, bent over his mother, and kissed her on both cheeks.

Chapter 28

Instead of apologizing to Vashti for his attack on her, Ishtovigo argued with her when she suggested that she visit Babylonia. Eventually, wishing to find out more about the Babylonian court, he agreed.

"With Father away, the court here will be quiet, but do not be absent longer than eight weeks," he instructed. "A postal messenger will accompany you to send a report and return to inform you of any progress in the war."

"Darayaus is old enough to come with me," Vashti replied, "but Zerena will remain with Khezmet and you."

"But won't you need Khezmet to help you at the Babylonian court?" Ishtovigo asked, his attitude suddenly and unexpectedly agreeable.

"Amytis has many maids. I'm sure she will offer me one," Vashti replied quickly.

Five-year-old Zerena cried and clung to her father as Vashti and her party prepared to leave a few days later. Vashti had tried to explain that she was going to Babylon to help keep Grandfather Hovakhshatra safe, but Zerena was too young to understand. Her tears and tantrums tore at Vashti's heart as she waved goodbye from the carriage jolting toward the golden gateway.

Clad in their shields and rounded helmets and armed with their lances and swords, Vashti's four female guards appeared as capable of protecting her as any male warriors. She, too, carried her lance and her archery weapons. An advisor, Aswer, the postal messenger, and a maid, Yezda, whom Khezmet insisted she take, completed the party.

"You will enjoy playing with cousin Amel-Marduk in the big palace in Babylon," Vashti told Darayaus as their carriage emblazoned with the insignia of the Bear wended its way down the citadel's circular roads. "The walls are wide enough for horse races."

Darayaus' blue eyes widened. "Really, Mother? Can I ride along the walls? How long will it take to get to there?" he asked, brushing away black wisps of hair that had escaped from his fringed *kulaw-u-dastmal*.

"Dear, you are not old enough to ride alone in a foreign city. Perhaps cousin Amel-Marduk will take you there. But rest now. It might take three weeks to get to Babylon. If the weather is fine, we will be able to go faster once we leave the mountains behind."

After crossing two rivers and descending the Zagros Mountain range, the party reached the dry flood plain of the Idiqlat River. There was little shelter and approaching travelers were met by Vashti's guards, questioned briefly, and left to go on their way. Most were farmers taking their produce to market towns or herders with their animals.

In Babylonian territory, a twenty-four-hour guard was posted, which was sorely tested one evening. After making camp beside sparse bushes lining a small tributary river, one of the guards gathered sticks and lit a fire while two others built a low dam wall in the river to catch fish. Suddenly, the guard on duty cried out and pointed to a band of horsemen with scarves across their faces on the top of a nearby rise. Yezda screamed as Vashti reached for her bow and arrow and fired as the horsemen raced down the hill toward the carriage next to which Darayaus was playing with some stones. Then an arrow from the lead guard, Irdabama, hit the first rider and he fell. His companions kept coming, but

Vashti pulled her lance from the carriage roof and threw it at the closest rider. It narrowly missed him, and he was almost upon her when an arrow from another guard, Pentaya, caught him in the chest. Realizing their cavalry charge was not frightening anyone into surrender, the attackers returned fire, hitting Aswer, who was sheltering Darayaus, in his upper arm. By then the women's arrows had stopped the enemy's rear ranks, and after picking up their whimpering injured, they retreated.

Vashti rushed to Darayaus who assured her he was not hurt. But the arrow in Aswer's upper arm had to be removed. Searching through her bag, she found some clove oil, which she applied to the arrow entry point. Then two of the guards steadied him while another quickly pulled it out. His cries echoed across the plain, and Vashti held him as he gasped in shock.

"Find the oil of myrrh in my bag," she told Pentaya as she dropped more clove oil onto the wound. "And bring a clean cloth to dress his arm."

"Shall I ride to the hill and see if the attackers have gone?" Irdabama asked.

"Yes, but be very careful. And tell the others to survey all around us for movement. Shoot at anyone who appears."

With the bleeding stopped and Aswer feeling more comfortable, Vashti summoned the other three guards and the postal messenger to discuss the situation.

"We are at least a week's ride from Babylon," the postal messenger told them. "We will have to go more slowly because of our friend's injury."

Vashti agreed. "During the day, Irdabama will ride cautiously ahead looking for any danger beyond our vision. And Pentaya will guard our rear. You two others will ride either side of the carriage," she directed. "The night watch must be aware of the horses' behavior. They will sense danger before we do, especially if it comes from bandits who could be riding camels."

"Do you want me to ride swiftly to Babylon to request extra guards?" the postal messenger asked.

"No," Vashti replied quickly. "We can protect ourselves. But for now, please prepare our evening meal," she instructed the guards.

After a satisfying meal of fish prepared on hot coals with bread and chai, the first night watch was set. Aswer was given frankincense oil for his pain and directed to sleep in Vashti's dwar with Darayaus.

"I prefer to sleep in the open," she told the guards, resting her head underneath the carriage. Two of them lay down on either side of her with Yezda and the postal messenger at her feet. "At least it is warmer here than in the mountains, and we have the trickling water to send us to sleep," she commented brightly.

Only the change of the guards at midnight disturbed the sleepers, and perhaps a little soft humming from she who was on watch.

Vashti awoke in the morning with wet eyes and a thumping heart. She had dreamed she was in the arid lands of Parthava again, lost and thirsty. Then Mithridates had appeared and guided her to the most beautiful oasis she had ever seen. Date palms bearing soft, sweet fruit waved in the gentle breeze, and thick reeds grew around the waterhole where a myriad of birds came to drink. He invited her into his pavilion, but she insisted she could not follow as a voice called her back into the desert. She had turned away as Mithridates' smile faded.

Throwing off the rug under which she had slept, Vashti wiped her eyes and approached Irdabama on the second watch as she stoked the coals of last night's fire.

"*Roj bas*," she greeted as the guard placed a blackened iron pot on the coals. "We will all have to be more vigilant today."

Irdabama lowered her head in shame then quickly lifted it to focus on the faintly glowing horizon. "Yes. I should have noticed the attackers sooner," she replied.

"But your response was quick and sure," Vashti countered sympathetically, patting her on the shoulder. "And I am more than happy with all my troops' defense." Irdabama nodded and flashed a grateful grin. "Sleep now till we break camp," Vashti continued. "I will keep watch until the other guards wake up."

Aswer said he felt better, but his arm was still painful. While they were eating breakfast, Vashti remembered something else in her riding bag that Mithridates had given her. He had told her that the farmers in Parthava and Bactria picked poppy flowers when their petals had fallen then slit the seed pods and removed the milky juice from inside. Dried and ground up, it could be used for all pain, so she mixed some of the greenish powder in water and gave it to Aswer. Mithridates had told her many poor people had taken the pain relief powder to get drunk and ruined their lives when they couldn't stop. So she carefully stowed it deep in her bag.

Aswer was soon feeling much more comfortable, but Vashti ordered him to rest and not move his arm. She and Darayaus would take turns riding his horse so he could do just that in the carriage.

Just before the party left, Vashti assembled everyone and praised them, especially her guards, for successfully protecting her and Darayaus.

"Your first battle has been won." She smiled. "Now it's on to Babylon with no more incidents."

Her encouraging words deliberately avoided mention of the disaster that almost befell them.

Chapter 29

Before reaching Babylon, Vashti's party had to ford the Idiqlat River, which was high enough to swim the horses across and float the carriage on a wooden raft buoyed by inflated animal skins. Assisted by the raft master, her guards loaded the carriage onto the raft while Vashti and Darayaus rode the horses. After hitching their horses to the raft, the guards rode them as they swam through the water. Following a few tense moments when they had to dismount in the middle of the river and steady the carriage in the swift current, everyone reached the other side with their animals.

The rest of the journey continued without mishap, and soon they entered the sun-baked plain leading to the city of Babylon.

"It won't be long before we arrive at *Babali*, the gate of the gods," Vashti informed Darayaus. On the outskirts of the city, they passed a temple, and he asked what was written on the entrance sign. "According to the Akkadian Aramaic Aunt Amytis taught me, it is the New Year's House," she replied. "But you will be able to ask her yourself in a little while."

"What do they do in a New Year's House?" Darayaus asked. "Why don't we have one?" His questions came thick and fast, but the high walls protecting the city were looming before them. Halting the party at the fort on the northern entrance, Vashti's guards informed the Babylonian guards of their identities. Although hesitant about admitting women escorting a carriage with the Bear insignia, they accepted the postal rider's letter from Ishtovigo and allowed them all to proceed. After crossing a moat over a drawbridge that Darayaus reckoned was a stade long, they marveled at the many cargo-laden boats on the river.

"This place would be very hard to conquer," Darayaus remarked when they encountered a second wall.

"Every city has its weak point," Vashti countered.

"What is Hagmatana's?"

"Not enough walls," she replied with a playful grin, and they both laughed, partly in relief that their journey was nearly over.

As they passed underneath the high arch of Ishtar's Gate, fascinated by the raised mosaics of animals embedded at regular intervals on yellow trimmed, blue tiled walls, Darayaus couldn't help but ask about them.

"Ishtar is the Babylonian goddess of fertility, the people ask her for more children and to increase the herds and flocks and crop yields. Her symbol is the lion," Vashti replied, recalling her conversations with Amytis about her adopted city.

"Why don't we have walls like these in our city?"

"We worship Auramazda. We appreciate the animals he has made, but we know they are not gods."

Darayaus nodded. "Do the Babylonians also worship bulls and that other strange animal on the walls?"

"Yes, dear, bulls are a symbol of strength, and the other animal is a dragon representing Marduk, Uncle Nebuchadnezzar's favorite god. It is an imaginary animal, not living now, but thought to have roamed the fields and forests before the time of our ancestors."

Darayaus shook his head. "Uncle's mosaics are nearly as colorful as Father's," he commented. "But is there a fire temple here, Mother?"

"I am not sure. We will have to ask Aunt Amytis." Vashti lowered her voice to a whisper. "We must be careful of *druj* in this city. And be sure not to mention that our Hurrian ancestors occupied Babylonia a long time before the rise of Uncle Nebuchadnezzar's forebears. We don't want to upset Uncle."

Darayaus agreed solemnly and gave her a kiss. "Yes, dear Mother," he whispered. Settling back into the carriage, he started to count the creatures carved into the walls along the road.

"Aunt Amytis said Uncle Nebuchadnezzar is very proud of this street," Vashti remarked. "He calls it the Processional Way. I like the daisy flowers above the lions. They remind me of our mountains in springtime."

"Where does the street go?" Darayaus asked.

"Aunt Amytis told me it leads to the temple of Marduk where Uncle was a priest when he was quite young."

"That's strange. Father is not a priest."

Vashti looked at her inquisitive son. Despite the excitement, his eyelids were beginning to droop. She put her arm around him. "Don't fall asleep now, dear. We are almost at Aunt Amytis' home."

"Look, Mother, there is a very high palace with gardens like ours," he cried, suddenly alert and pointing to a huge building of several tiers dotted with trees, hanging vines, and flowering shrubs. "There are pillars and waterfalls at each level. Mother, how did the Babylonians build this?"

"Dear, we will find out from Uncle and Aunt soon as they live there. You will have to be patient as the Prophet taught us," she replied. "Look, here is the palace entrance gate." The carriage crunched over a gravel driveway before stopping in front of a huge flight of steps trimmed by stone lions. "Can you see Aunt Amytis?" she asked as Darayaus peered at the carriage's opaque window.

Aswer dismounted and presented Ishtovigo's letter to one of the Babylonian guards, who spoke to his counterpart at the huge wooden brass-hinged doors atop the steps then disappeared into the building. Soon Amytis appeared in an elaborate, feathered headdress, and full robe trimmed with silver discs. Beside her stood a tall young man with his mother's slim physique.

"My darlings," she cried, rushing to the carriage as Yezda helped Vashti out. After kissing and hugging Vashti and Darayaus, and introducing her son, Amel-Marduk, Amytis invited them into her stately home.

"Bring everyone for refreshments," she urged, beckoning the rest of the entourage. "How long have you been traveling?" she asked, tousling Darayaus' hair.

"Only about three weeks," Vashti replied.

"But we had a little trouble," Darayaus piped up.

Embarrassed, Vashti pointed to her bandaged advisor. "Would you ask one of your physicians to inspect my advisor's arm?" she requested.

Amytis looked a little worried but spoke to one of her guards, who quickly marched off. "Let us go inside so you can wash off the dust of your journey," she urged, taking Vashti's arm.

After a bath scented with Amytis' most luxurious oils, Vashti told her cousin about the bandit raid and was assured the incident would be investigated. Then she and Darayaus dressed for an informal dinner and were escorted along a gold-lined corridor to a magnificent reception chamber. The treelike bronze and silver-banded pillars crowned with blossoming lotus-shaped capitals and lotus flower mosaics supporting the chamber's high ceilings held Vashti's and Darayaus' attention until Amytis nudged her. Trying not to appear overawed, Vashti became acutely aware of Shahan Shah Nebuchadnezzar striding toward her, the gold waist chain about his long purple robe jingling.

Pleasantly surprised, she stepped back, unable to hide her admiration for his dark curly hair topped with a neat, tasselled fez, his gray-streaked beard and his aquiline nose beneath dark eyes constantly darting round the cavernous chamber. When he enthusiastically kissed her on both cheeks, the faint odour of chewed frankincense resin and the solid gold chain around his neck brushing her robe exuded an awesome presence, intensified by the self-assurance of unrestrained power.

"Welcome to my dear wife's most loved cousin," Nebuchadnezzar enthused with a warm smile. "The treasures of Babylon are at the service of the niece of our most esteemed ally and her son. How is Hovakhshatra's son, my good friend Ishtovigo?"

"Very well, Shahan Shah. Thank you for your kind welcome," Vashti replied just as jauntily.

"How was your trip?" her host inquired affably.

Vashti told him and he frowned. "This is not acceptable in my territories. I will order troops tomorrow to find the bandits and execute them immediately. Next time you visit, please send forewarning of your departure date and I will provide a unit of my personal guards to escort you."

Vashti smiled. "Thank you, Shahan Shah, but that won't be necessary. Shah Hovakhshatra will soon be home from Lydia with General Harpagos and the Median army. We are missing our full complement of troops, but my own guards soon dispensed with the enemy."

"And dear Mother helped," Darayaus chimed in.

"Thanks be to the gods that everyone is safe now. Let us go into the welcome feast for our guests," Amytis intervened hastily in response to her husband's annoyance.

Darayaus's eyes widened at the array of rich sweets and spiced meats seasoned with onions, mint, leeks, and garlic on the Shahan Shah's table, but he took his cue from his mother, who waited for her hosts to be seated then nodded, so he could sit next to Amel-Marduk. Amytis winked approval and a servant brought ceramic jugs of wine.

"Please bring freshly pressed wine for the young people," she ordered.

"How is the health of Shah Hovakhshatra and Shahjin Ardela?" Nebuchadnezzar asked.

"We receive regular reports from the Shah, and the Shahjin is well but anxiously awaits news of him and the campaign against the Lydians," Vashti replied.

Nebuchadnezzar grimaced. "It has been long. Is there any word of the killers of the heirs to the throne?"

"Not yet, Shahan Shah. Lydia is a vast territory, and Alyattes remains silent on the matter."

"Hovakhshatra is extremely patient. I would have conquered the whole region and razed Sardis if Alyattes had not yielded the murderers immediately," Nebuchadnezzar assured her. "Now Alyattes plays war games with Hovakhshatra and wears down his western front. Does he expect us to come to his aid if the stalemate continues?"

"No, Shahan Shah. There has been no mention of such a request. Our forces are still strong, and my father-in-law is determined to avenge the deaths of his sons," Vashti replied, not knowing if she had told the truth about the Median army.

Nebuchadnezzar nodded. "Yes, and many chests of gold and silver make the cost of such a war very unprofitable." Vashti smiled assent but refrained from mentioning that the Medes' motive was more personal than territorial.

"How is Hovakhshatra's building program progressing?" Nebuchadnezzar continued.

"The canal system has been more of a challenge than yours because of the mountains," Vashti replied, "but progress has been steady, and we are increasing our food production. I note the fields of green crops and date palms feeding Babylon."

"We have enough farms inside the city walls to supply the population for an extended siege," Nebuchadnezzar boasted. "An enemy will never take the city once I have completed the third wall with its moat. It will be yet another of my great works that you will see under construction when we tour the city. And Amel-Marduk is keen to show Darayaus some of the palace's secrets, aren't you, son?" he volunteered, beaming at both young men. "My darling wife hopes you will be free to attend a reception with her and her ladies, too," he added, turning to Amytis and patting her hand.

"Certainly, dear," Amytis replied, smiling broadly.

"Thank you for your kind invitation, Shahan Shah. It will be an honor," Vashti replied.

"Tell Aunt and Uncle about your women's army, Mother," Darayaus suggested.

Vashti blushed as Nebuchadnezzar raised his eyebrows. "Not now, dear. We have had a long day, and Uncle and Aunt want to hear more about the family."

Nebuchadnezzar agreed and the evening proceeded smoothly as Vashti recounted stories of weddings, newborns, and Norouz celebrations. The evening had drawn late by the time the tired travelers were escorted to the guest sleeping quarters. Having safely reached their destination, they quickly fell into peaceful rest.

Chapter 30

Vashti woke early the next morning to the sound of horses' hooves echoing across the rooves of the city. Through sleepy eyes, she looked out the window and saw Irdabama and Pentaya clad in their scarlet cloaks racing a couple of Babylonian guards along the outer wall, which had fascinated Darayaus the day before. As the Median woman finished in front of their opponents, their ululations rang out across the metropolis, which thankfully had only just begun to stir.

Jumping out of bed, she sipped the chai Yelda had served and began to pace the stone floor. "If the city officials find out, how will I explain this to my hosts?" she asked herself. "And why didn't I instruct my guards more precisely about being guests in the proud capital of Babylonia?" She was still trying to think of an excuse when Darayaus came in to tell her that he had eaten breakfast with Amel-Marduk, who had offered to take him up the mountain.

Vashti's brow creased in puzzlement. "But there are no mountains here, dear."

Darayaus grinned. "I mean to the top of the palace, dear Mother."

Vashti had just given her hearty approval when a knock on the door revealed Amel-Marduk in a long, black silk cloak embroidered with the outline of a lion. "Come, cousin, I will show you many wonders," he beckoned.

Darayaus followed Amel-Marduk happily, leaving Vashti still thinking about how she would explain the behavior of her guards.

"First, I must seek Aswer to see if his injury is healing and ask his advice," she decided.

Yelda appeared with a brightly painted ceramic cup of freshly pressed grape juice and asked what she would like to wear. "Since we could only carry a few outfits," Vashti replied, "today it will be the scarlet Mukryani robe and the green, yellow and red sash of the future Shahjin of the Medes. As Yelda rummaged in her chest for the robes, Vashti was reminded of her diplomatic obligations.

"Please also find the gifts I have brought Shahan Shah Nebuchadnezzar as assurance of our friendship," she requested.

"Of course, mistress, as soon as I have applied your face oils and powders," Yelda replied.

With his guard watching from a short distance, Amel-Marduk took Darayaus outside onto the balcony of the lowest palace terrace. "Where did these wild almond and dwarf oak trees come from?" Darayaus asked, pointing to the familiar vegetation.

"Father sent for them from the Zagros Mountains," Amel-Marduk replied. "He even brought transplanted cedars from Lebanon."

"And I see ash and terebinth trees too," Darayaus noted.

"You know much about the plants of your land," Amel-Marduk replied. "We have other botanical species from all four corners of our territories," he announced imperiously.

"Our teacher takes us into the mountains so we can learn about the trees, the grasses, and the flowers. She has drawn pictures of the plants and animals from distant places like Alborz. One day I will go there with dear Mother. She loves it, and she went to Parthava too," Darayaus enthused.

"Surely not that uncivilized place of wild tribesmen," Amel-Marduk replied.

"No. Mother told me how one of them rescued her and her guards from the desert. She says the Parthavans are kind and noble, and they have a beautiful land of many different peoples," Darayaus insisted.

Amel-Marduk grunted disinterestedly. "Let's go to the next terrace," he suggested. "Each level of the gardens rests on cubed pillars in which the trees and flowers grow," he explained as they climbed internal steps past gurgling water pipes. "Father's builders bought stone from Sinai near the Red Sea for enough slabs to place at the bottom of each cube. Then they put down a layer each of reeds, asphalt tiles, and lead and filled the rest of the cube with soil. None of the terraces underneath the gardens will leak," he added confidently.

"Those layers would also keep the roots cool in this hot climate," Darayaus commented.

"Yes, cousin, your teacher has instructed you well," Amel-Marduk agreed.

Darayaus leaned over the balcony. "Are these mud brick?" he asked, pointing to the walls.

"Yes. The whole building is clay mud brick baked with asphalt."

Darayaus whistled in amazement. "So you have oil seeps here too?"

"Yes. Oil is used to heat the brick furnaces," Amel-Marduk replied, glancing upwards, "but there is more to see in the terraces above."

Darayaus waited till they reached the top before asking his next question. "It hardly ever rains here, so are the gardens watered by the pipes we passed?"

"Yes. Look down below." Amel-Marduk pointed to the bottom of the gardens where some men were turning a handle attached to a wheel and shaft. Buckets full of water which had been collected from the river were being hauled in chains and taken upwards where they disappeared inside the palace.

"The buckets on the chains empty into channels on every terrace then a wheel at the top returns them to the bottom to be filled again," he explained.

Darayaus stood watching the continuous motion of the machinery clanging up and down. "Who are the men turning the wheel?" he asked.

"Slaves," was the answer, "mostly from the provinces. It's how Father keeps the subject peoples under control and provides workers for farms and the building of the city monuments. When the slaves are exhausted or die, we use donkeys."

Darayaus looked at the bare-chested bodies glistening with sweat. "Does this make Aunt Amytis happy?" he asked.

Amel-Marduk shrugged. "She said Grandfather Hovakhshatra wouldn't like it, but it is different here to Media."

"Yes," Darayaus replied agreeably, despite his dismay. "Thank you for showing me these mechanical marvels. We don't need them at home because the water comes down from the mountains so fast it flows easily into the palace pipes where it's heated by woodburning furnaces. When it cools, we use it for the gardens off the side of the Great Hall," he commented. Not wanting to seem ungracious toward his cousin, who displayed a measure of his father's self-assurance, Darayaus heeded his mother's warning not to mention how long ago their people had developed knowledge of agriculture, the cosmos, and the natural world in the land between the Two Rivers.

"Yes, living in the mountains has advantages," Amel-Marduk conceded.

"You must visit one day," Darayaus entreated.

Amel-Marduk nodded politely but again without interest. "Let's return to our mothers," he suggested. "The sun is becoming too hot."

Darayaus agreed and they descended the internal steps to where Vashti was having breakfast with Amytis. After confirming Aswer's improved condition and accepting his advice to say nothing about her guards' early morning indiscretions, Vashti was informed by Amytis that a tour of the city was planned for the day. Soon the door was flung open, and a heavily armed guard preceded Shahan Shah Nebuchadnezzar.

"Honored guests, please join us as we inspect the wonders of Babylon," he entreated. Vashti sighed in relief. Nebuchadnezzar's equanimity indicated he had not been told of her guards' early morning antics.

"Darayaus and I look forward to seeing your building projects, Shahan Shah," she replied.

"You and Darayaus will be traveling with my wife, our son, and I for our tour of the world's most magnificent city," Nebuchadnezzar continued, gesturing widely. "And carriages have been provided for your servants."

Outside the palace precinct, Nebuchadnezzar's guard cleared the way for his entourage's passage through narrow, mud-brick-house-lined streets. Inside the carriage, the Shahan Shah extolled the grandeur of Babylon while Amytis provided details of monuments and temples. Despite the obvious contrast between the few rich and the many poor people, Vashti and Darayaus showered their host with compliments about his busy city.

"The camels are carrying gold from southern Arabia, and the horses are bringing bags of olives from Sham," Amel-Marduk eagerly informed them of traders' caravans strung along the Processional Way.

"What's in the carts?" Darayaus asked.

"Cedarwood from Lebanon for Father's building program," Amel-Marduk replied.

"This is the compound of the Etemenanki temple," Nebuchadnezzar announced, pointing to the large building they were passing inside a substantial square wall. "We will visit there another day." A little farther along, the temple of Esagila stood behind its own protective compound comprising a large and a smaller court.

"The original temple to Marduk of Old Babylonia was surrounded by images of the gods whose cities we conquered twelve hundred years ago," Nebuchadnezzar continued, "and Abzu, a little lake representing Marduk's father, Enki, god of the waters. Now that I have rebuilt it, it is the center of Babylon. Come see inside."

Soon the visitors stood gazing in amazement at the fine wood, gold, and precious stones lining the interior of the temple. "After my father Shah Esarhaddon reconstructed the temple from the foundations, I built the gold statue of Marduk and the statue of his consort, Sarpanit," Nebuchadnezzar boasted as he led them through an anteroom to the inner shrine room, dominated by the imposing statues.

"This is truly a tribute to the ingenuity of Babylon!" Vashti exclaimed.

"How often do you come here to worship, Uncle?" Darayaus asked.

"Only on holy days," was the reply.

"Grandfather goes to the Atashkedah once a week," Darayaus commented innocently.

Amytis looked worried, and concerned that Nebuchadnezzar's mood would change, Vashti intervened.

"We very much appreciate you showing us this wondrous temple, Shahan Shah. We are privileged to be in alliance with such a strong and devout ruler," she gushed.

"I don't know how Hovakhshatra goes to war without the aid of the god Belus. He is the reason for all my victories," Nebuchadnezzar confessed. As their host gazed upwards, Vashti turned to Darayaus and put her finger to her lips. Darayaus winked and remained silent.

"Shahan Shah, my father-in-law knows he can always rely on his ally," Vashti replied.

"Yes, as we do with him and Media," Nebuchadnezzar replied confidently. "But let us now depart for a picnic at the river," he announced.

Chapter 31

"The Ufratu River rises in the mountains of Tur not far from the land of Urartu," Darayaus remarked once they had seated themselves on cushions strewn on the riverbank. Palm trees above waved in the breeze while behind them, the pillared, flora enhanced terraces of the palace loomed in overarching splendor. On the river, gaily decorated boats, their curled bows carved with figures of Babylon's gods, and their decks laden with grain, wood, stone, and flax, steadily plied the calm waters.

"Perhaps we should send our tutors to Hagmatana for instruction," Nebuchadnezzar suggested to Vashti. "Darayaus knows much for a boy his age. It seems some of our teachers lack knowledge of the lands to our east and west."

Vashti opened her mouth to reply but was prevented by Amytis who, surprised by her husband's admission, agreed. "Our children are so busy learning the wisdom and greatness of Babylon that the other lands are sometimes forgotten," she commented.

"Ah, speaking of knowledge, here comes my chief advisor," Nebuchadnezzar announced, "with the servants and our meals."

Three chariots approached. The first, also bearing the insignia of the lion, halted and out stepped a tall, graying man of assured bearing. Clad in a blue robe and wearing a gold chain around his neck resembling the Shah's, he approached the party and bowed deeply to Nebuchadnezzar and Amytis.

"Good afternoon, Shahan Shah, Shahjin, and son, Amel-Marduk," he stated in Aramaic. Then he bowed to the visitors, his handsome face creased in a smile as he straightened. "And welcome to your most esteemed guests."

After Vashti and Darayaus were introduced to Belteshazzar, Nebuchadnezzar's cupbearer ordered the placement of soft cheeses, finely ground wheat bread, olive paste, and cold meats on low tables of gold taken from the second chariot. After the cupbearer tasted the food and drink, the Babylonian family was served, and then everyone else. Belteshazzar sat down between Vashti and Amytis on one of the rugs provided by the driver of the second chariot, just as the third arrived with meals for Vashti's entourage.

"My greetings to the great women of the land of the Magi," Belteshazzar declared. "How are the rest of your family members?"

"Many thanks, Chief Councilor," Vashti replied in Aramaic. "My husband is well, but as the war with Lydia continues, he finds the responsibilities of rulership taxing. However, he has very generously agreed to my visit with my family here."

"I am sorry to hear of your husband's heavy burdens," Belteshazzar commiserated. "Are the Shahjin and your daughter well?"

"Yes," Vashti answered. "I thank you for your kind inquiries about my family."

"Shahjin Amytis has often spoken of her loved ones. They are very familiar to me," Belteshazzar admitted.

Amytis beamed. "We are all one big family. Belteshazzar belongs to us too," she said, reaching for a honey and sesame cake. The Hapiru, who had not eaten, bowed his head. When he lifted it, Vashti noticed his deep brown eyes droop with sadness. "I am also of the family of Yehovah," he replied softly, glancing at Nebuchadnezzar, who was deep in conversation with his son and nephew.

"That is the name of his god," Amytis whispered to Vashti before inviting Belteshazzar to eat.

Vashti nodded, remembering the Hapiru of Hagmatana. Perhaps

while I am here, I can unofficially inform Belteshazzar of the condition of his people in Media, she thought.

Pleasant conversation continued until the sun began to merge into the reddish orange heat haze of day's end, at which time Amel-Marduk suggested Darayaus travel the river with him to observe the sunset from the northern fortress. After farewelling their families, accompanied by two well-armed guards, the young men stepped onto one of the manned sailboats moored nearby.

As boatmen paddled the craft up the river, darkness began to envelop them, and the reflected light of oil lanterns danced on the waterway until a huge wooden spiked gate loomed before them.

"The river enters the city here," Amel-Marduk explained. "The gate can be lowered into the water to prevent any person or boat from entering. Our city is very safe."

Darayaus looked east toward the fort and the moat beyond. If an invading army were to dig a channel from the river and drain it to the marshes we saw on our inward journey, it would be easy to lift the gate and get into the city along the riverbed, he thought. But wondering if he was committing *druj*, he felt obliged to agree that the city's defenses could never be penetrated.

Amel-Marduk smiled satisfaction in the flickering light, but Darayaus had already mentally mapped Babylon's one weakness.

The next day, Amytis held a banquet for the leading women of the city. "Your yellow silk, gold-threaded *chokha* and skirt with its red and green sash and matching *sarwain* headdress is perfect for the occasion," Yezda suggested to Vashti. "And the hot weather."

Vashti sighed. "Except for being with Amytis, I would rather be riding Nzdar in the mountains where I discovered the lichens that made the orchil lichen dye for my robe," she confessed. "And I don't know any of the women of Babylonia."

"Then the banquet is your chance to make new friends for Media. Remember…good thoughts, good words, and good deeds," Yezda reminded her. Vashti inwardly castigated herself. How could she have forgotten the Prophet's maxims so easily, especially in a city where everything she did affected Media's relationship with its ally? She would have to be more careful about her words and her actions.

The full sleeves of Amytis' robe of Lydian light purple encircled Vashti in a hug before she took her place next to her cousin to greet each guest at the banquet. She didn't know whether Amytis' sweet smile or the precious stones embedded in her silk turban headdress shone more.

I wonder how many of these women are really her friends, she thought, before complimenting Amytis on her appearance.

"This was Nebuchadnezzar's gift to me when we sealed the marriage arrangement," Amytis whispered as her maid straightened her crown. "It seems like a long time ago."

All except one of the guests introduced to Vashti bowed and graciously took her hand. Remembering Yezda's advice, once the banquet was progressing smoothly, Vashti excused herself from the women she was seated with and made her way to the unhappy guest.

"My dear, are you well?" she asked.

"I am, but I do not wish to speak to you," the young woman replied.

"Why not, dear?" Vashti asked tentatively.

The young woman scowled, looked around, and lowered her voice. "I am from Athoraya," she explained, "where my grandfather built many temples for Shah Sin-shumu-lishir. My city was conquered by the Median army, and we fled to Babylon when I was a baby. We had nothing when we arrived. For years, my father worked constructing Shahan Shah Nebuchadnezzar's palace where he learned to become a master builder of houses for the rich. Now he is wealthy enough to be among the city's leading builders, but we are still captives."

Touched by the woman's plight, Vashti wondered what she could do to help her. Then she knew!

"My husband is building his palace at Shush in Elam," she replied looking the Athorayan in the eye. "He is looking for skilled workers in stone and wood. Give me your father's name, and I will pass it on to his engineer. If your father is needed, our messenger will inform Shahjin Amytis. I will speak to her about the matter."

The young woman's eyes lit up. "Thank you, m-mistress," she stuttered. "Will we be free in Shush?"

"Yes. You will be free subjects of the Shahdom of Media but not permitted to return to your homeland."

The young woman smiled her appreciation and offered Vashti her hand. "I am Shirat. I trust I will meet you again in Shush."

"So do I," Vashti replied, smiling inwardly at the power of the Prophet's maxims to resolve conflict.

Suddenly feeling fatigued, she closed her eyes and sank into the soft couch beside Shirat. The sweet scent of roses coming from the terrace garden and the soothing melodies of women playing the harp, the lyre, and the flute offered to take her to another world. Idle chatter about luxury fabrics, precious gemstones, and servant's faults faded into nothingness; and for a moment, she was beside a bubbling oasis spring in early morning Parthava. The surface reflected a young woman lithe in her sleeping robe. When she looked up, a ruggedly handsome man on the other side of the pool chuckled, and she wondered how long he had been watching her.

"Vashti, Vashti dear." Startled from her daydream, she hardly recognized Amytis' voice. Shirat gently shook her arm. "Mistress, the Shahjin is calling you."

Vashti stood and bowed to her cousin. "Yes," she answered, "I am coming."

"No women's banquet is complete without speeches." Amytis grinned. "Would you like to entertain my guests with stories of our beautiful land?" Quite unprepared and still a little dazed, Vashti stammered agreement and glanced around the chamber's chatty occupants.

"May I reintroduce the wife of my esteemed brother, Ishtovigo of the Medes," Amytis announced. "Vashti is going to tell us about the women of her land." Some of the Babylonians already looked bored and tired, so Vashti scanned her mind for something that would hold their attention.

She took a deep breath. "We are walking knee-deep in snow, carrying our weapons," she began. The women looked puzzled. "Everything is cold, white, and wet. It is harder than crossing a river," she explained. The women's eyes riveted to her. They were listening. "Our horses are exhausted and so are we, but Scythians from the north have been attacking our villages, killing our men and carrying our women off as slaves." No one in the room moved. "Night falls and we find a cave in which to shelter." The listeners' eyes clouded. "It is a cold hole in the mountainside," she added, once more grabbing their attention. "The next morning is sunny and warm, and the snow is melting, so we proceed to the nearest village and find it free. The people tell us the enemy is farther north." She paused and glanced round the listeners. Their eyes were still fixed on her, waiting for more.

Amytis tapped her on the shoulder. "Tell them who you really are," she whispered. Vashti's gaze swept the spellbound room again. "I am Vashti of the Medes, future coruler of Media and commander of Shahan Shah Hovakhshatra's women's army division," she declared. "We protect our women and our nation."

The silence was palpable. Someone coughed then Shirat stood and clapped. One by one, most of the women rose, cheered, and clapped. Only a few of the elders lifted their heads and sniffed.

"Women do not fight in an army," Vashti heard one say.

Amytis frowned and stepped forward to speak to her, but another official's wife was already walking toward them. Tall and strongly built, the woman threw her tasselled scarf over her shoulder and addressed Vashti.

"I would like to learn how we can defend ourselves too," she requested. "Would you teach us?"

Amytis quickly intervened, her brow creased anxiously. "Let me speak to the Shahan Shah first," she suggested. "We do not want him to think our confidence in the Babylonian army has waned."

The woman nodded. "I will wait for your word, Shahjin."

Once the women had resumed their seats, one of Amytis' servants rang a little bell whereupon the hostess thanked her guests and announced the close of the reception. A new warmth had pervaded the gathering, and most of them hugged Amytis and Vashti as they left, but Amytis still looked worried.

"My husband must not learn of your speech," she pleaded. "If he does, he might think we are planning a rebellion."

Vashti smiled. "Don't worry, dear. Do you really think he will believe women's gossip?"

The next day, Nebuchadnezzar ordered carriages for another tour of the city, beginning with an imposing building equal in all three dimensions. "Our father Hammurapi began the Etemenanki temple eleven hundred years ago," he informed his guests grandly. "It is the foundation of heaven and earth. My own father embedded gold, silver, and gemstones from the mountains and the sea in the foundations. Under the fired brickwork he buried sweet-scented oil, aromatics, and red earth. He taught my brother and I that it was an honor to serve Marduk and made us carry gold and silver baskets of mud mixed with wine, oil, and resin chips on our heads during the construction."

"But *I* built this wonder for all the world to see. *I* raised its top, made doors for the gates, and *I* dressed it with bitumen and bricks," he boasted. "However, I am bound to give credit to Shah

Esarhaddon and Shah Ashurbanipal of Athoraya for the extensive rebuilding programs they undertook before mine."

The guests stood silently gazing at the structure until Nebuchadnezzar asked them to follow him up a flight of stairs that climbed past three tiers of porticoes and led to more stairs ascending the next five floors. After resting on the seats provided halfway up the temple, they finally reached the seventh floor, which housed only a large, richly adorned couch and a golden table.

"It's quite different from our temple," Darayaus commented whereupon Vashti nudged him to say no more.

"The shrine at the top is for Marduk to rest in when he comes to visit us," Nebuchadnezzar explained.

The room's simplicity reminded Vashti of the inside of an Atashkedah temple, but she decided not to displease her host by saying so. While Amytis described the material origins of the bed provided for Marduk, everyone nodded and smiled politely.

When the party had descended the temple, Amytis suggested they view the full Processional Way. Nebuchadnezzar agreed and signaled the carriage drivers to proceed to the road. "I could never allow our distinguished visitors to leave our glorious city without seeing my most outstanding edifice," he enthused. "But it might still be surpassed, as many of my projects are not yet finished."

When they reached the road's richly adorned walls, Nebuchadnezzar pointed to the entrance archway where workers were fixing glazed tiles. "The New Year's parade starts at the Esagila temple, continues through Ishtar's Gate, and finishes at the Akitu temple outside the city," he told his guests. "Perhaps one New Year you would like to join us and keep my beloved company," he suggested to Vashti then glanced at Amytis, who averted her eyes.

Vashti put her arm through her cousin's and squeezed her hand. "We would be honored, Shahan Shah," she replied, immediately scolding herself for uttering *druj*. After acknowledging Vashti's reply and ignoring his wife's silence, Nebuchadnezzar insisted his guests experience more of the splendor of his city and ordered his carriage driver to cross the river. From a huge bridge, they viewed the Adad and Ea temples to the west. Turning north onto the Kumar Road, they passed the Edad Temple, finally ending their tour at the Temple of Ishtar. Inside, shocked by sculptures of the naked goddess on its walls, Vashti steered Darayaus away as soon as politely possible. "Ever since Nebuchadnezzar was high priest of her temple in Uruk in his youth, he's been devoted to her," Amytis whispered as her husband praised the goddess's powers.

By the end of the day, sick of the heat and the sight of lavish temples surrounded by thousands of poor people's dwellings crowded together, Vashti looked forward to returning to the cool, spacious palace.

Amytis yawned. "The people are all here to serve the gods," she murmured apologetically before her husband entered the carriage.

Vashti nodded. "Darayaus has fallen asleep," she replied softly.

Chapter 32

When Darayaus woke up, to ease their discomfort in the excessive heat, Nebuchadnezzar insisted on providing another carriage for his Median guests for their journey back to the palace. Within the less crowded compartment, Vashti took the opportunity to relax and close her eyes, but when she opened them a few minutes later, Darayaus peppered her with questions about the temples they had just seen.

"Where did all the gold, silver, and precious stones in those buildings come from, Mother?" he queried.

"Probably from the Athorayan palace at Nineveh," Vashti replied.

"And where did they get them from?"

"From the lands they conquered. They either took them from the people or bought them from the mines in Sheba, Egypt, and other places."

"Where did all our gemstones and precious metals come from?"

"Some from Nineveh and Athoraya but mostly from the Median triangle and our other territories. If the lands we conquered were poor, we left the people with what they had. Auramazda gave all the wealth of the earth, so we are to share it for the benefit of all the peoples of our shahdom and use it wisely," Vashti replied.

"Surely the gods don't need it," Darayaus commented.

"Nor do they need to be cared for by humans," Vashti replied dourly.

“Why are Uncle Nebuchadnezzar and his priests always trying to please so many gods?” Darayaus wanted to know.

“Like some other shahs, he believes that after the gods created the world, they lived by themselves in their own cities, but eventually, they got tired of looking after themselves, growing food, building houses, and digging canals,” Vashti explained. “The *asha* of Auramazda’s kindness and generosity was forgotten when Uncle’s ancestors began to believe that the gods created them as slaves. They thought that if they worked for the gods, the gods would care for them. That’s why so many offerings of food, animals, and even people are made to those gods.”

“How are people offered to the gods?” Darayaus wanted to know.

“I will tell you about that another day,” Vashti replied quickly, loathe to admit the reason for the senseless sacrifice of humans to appease gods of wood and stone.

“Why don’t we offer food and animals to Auramazda in the Atashkedah?”

“That is a very good question, dear. Has Debyar taught you about the Mitradat covenant?” Darayaus shook his head.

“Before Prophet Zarathrustra, Prophet Mahabad taught the Mitradat contract between the people, the creator god, and his law. Our Ariavartan people made treaties between themselves based on this law. We still follow that law, which is why we do not need all these temples and gods.”

Darayaus smiled. “Thank you, dear Mother, you are very wise. I would never want to be a slave to these gods.”

It was Vashti’s turn to beam. “We will never be slaves if we follow the Mitradat and *asha*. The Hapiru in Hagmatana told me about the covenant with their high father, Avraham. They have scrolls that tell how he left our territories many years ago and traveled west to Harran where Yehovah god told him to go to the land of Canaan. There Avraham received the covenant.”

“Perhaps Belteshazzar knows about the Mitradat too,” Darayaus remarked. “We should ask him.”

Vashti hugged Darayaus closely. “Yes, son, we will.”

The following day, Amytis took Vashti to the palace's family quarters where several women watched numerous children playing and fighting in the courtyard and gardens.

“Who are all these people?” Vashti asked as they watched from a marble seat.

“They are the Shahan Shah's other wives, concubines, and children,” Amytis explained. “We are not always friendly as each wants her eldest son to succeed his father, but they all know Amel-Marduk is the true heir. That's why Nebuchadnezzar has a special guard for him.”

Vashti frowned. “Do you think someone might try to harm your son?” she asked.

“It has happened before in Babylonia and other powerful nations, but mostly when the line of inheritance has not been clear. Nebuchadnezzar made sure it would be with me but said his subsequent marriages were necessary to ensure the loyalty of the peoples he rules,” she continued, her voice tinged with sadness. “But he has assured me I will always be his first wife.”

“And will Media remain the preferred ally of Babylonia?” Vashti asked above the noise.

“I think so, but nothing is certain.” She leaned over and hugged Vashti. “I will stay loyal,” she whispered, “and so will Belteshazzar, but there are many people in this court that cannot be trusted.”

Vashti shuddered. Amytis' confession had reminded her of Ishtovigo's Parsu advisors, and she wondered how much they could be trusted at her own court.

Before the Median party left Babylon, Nebuchadnezzar summoned Vashti and Aswer to a meeting with him and his advisors, all except Belteshazzar, who was away performing his role as governor of the province of Babylon. Nebuchadnezzar's magnificent marble columned state reception chamber shrouded in thick curtains rendered Aswer speechless until Vashti began answering her host's questions. "How long do you think Hovakhshatra will pursue the Lydians?" Nebuchadnezzar asked, his tone mildly disparaging.

"Shahan Shah, he will continue until the Lydians give up the killers of his sons," Vashti replied. "Since their deaths, he has been haunted by the story that they were murdered and parts of their bodies eaten by their enemies. But after Shah Alyattes expelled many Scythians from the Lydian region who returned to the Transcaucasia area that we control, he pleaded innocence and refuses to cooperate even though we know from our spies in Lydia that the killers have confessed."

"It is a matter of honor when one heir is killed and doubly so when two are eliminated," Nebuchadnezzar commented. "Perhaps Hovakhshatra should take another wife to produce a replacement."

"That is not necessary. Ishtovigo and Darayaus are quite well and capable," Vashti replied sharply.

"We remain strongly and confidently in control of our territories."

Aswer's strangely squeaky voice embarrassed Vashti, but she kept her expression neutral and cleared her throat in preparation for a question she felt compelled to ask.

"Shahan Shah, are your troops still engaged in the siege of Ursalim?"

"The Babylonian's fathomless eyes flickered, and she waited for his temper to flare, but his demeanour remained passive.

"We expect to take the city within a matter of months," he replied with a hint of irritation. "I will return there soon to oversee the final stages of the campaign." He paused, fixing his black eyes on Vashti. "We have been told that Media has a women's army division," he remarked dryly. "If it is true, will the fighters be stationed beyond your territories?"

Vashti's heart leaped under Nebuchadnezzar's penetrating gaze. "I do not yet have a deputy commander ready to do so," she replied evenly. "But I think soon…"

Nebuchadnezzar smiled, but his arched eyebrows mocked her. "We will see about that. In Babylonia, it is not considered proper for women to fight against men in war."

Remembering that Ishtar was also a goddess of war, Vashti was ready with her reply. "If women are in danger, we will go anywhere to protect them under my orders," she stated firmly then stopped, her heart pounding.

She had just challenged the region's most powerful man.

"We must leave before I get us into more trouble," Vashti told Yezda the next morning. "I need to know more about the war in Lydia, and Zerena must be missing us. But first I must see Amytis."

"So soon?" Amytis complained, her voice quavering, when Vashti told her. "Two weeks have hardly been enough with you and Darayaus."

"Dear, many tasks await me at home, but we will never forget the reasons why you gave up your life with us to marry Nebuchadnezzar," Vashti replied hugging her cousin tightly. "You are more precious than all the gold, silver, and jewels in the Shahan Shah's treasury."

"And I'm often comforted by the thought of your influence in the palace at home," Amytis replied, blinking back tears. "Media would have been ruined if Ishtovigo had married one of those awful Mossala priestesses like he wanted to…" She stopped and clapped her hand over her mouth. "I'm sorry, dear. I didn't mean…"

Vashti sat down. "So that's who he's been visiting all these years."

"Yes, but I think Father sent her away to Elam."

Vashti pursed her lips angrily. "And this has been kept from me?"

"Father didn't want to upset you, and he thought if you knew you might refuse his plan to marry Ishtovigo."

"Thank you for telling me, dear," Vashti replied softly, struggling to calm herself while trying to hide the hurt that stabbed her chest. "I always hoped Ishtovigo would change his ways, but…I don't think he has."

The next day, the Median carriage and its retinue assembled outside Nebuchadnezzar's palace ready for departure. The Shah himself was receiving visitors from the east, and Vashti wondered if the Parthavans were among them. In his place, he sent Belteshazzar to officially farewell his guests.

While Amytis' servants stowed presents for her family in the carriage and dried foods and bread were laden on the horses, Belteshazzar and Vashti spoke quietly to each other. When all was ready the Medes mounted their rides, and Amytis clung to Vashti and Darayaus.

"Write to me often, dears, especially about Father, Ferhad, and the war," she entreated, "and tell my dear mother, brother, and sister how much I love them."

"Stay strong, dear," Vashti told her. "We have few friends and some enemies within, but we will always resist them." She didn't know why she had mentioned the need for vigilance, perhaps because the thought of returning home made her feel both excited and uneasy. She kissed Amytis and thanked Belteshazzar for supporting the alliance.

"We welcome you anytime you are required to visit us in Hagmatana," Vashti added.

"It would be an honor to meet the leading family of Media," the Hapiru replied. Vashti and Darayaus climbed into the carriage, and the guards signaled forward. The carriage creaked into motion and, followed by an escort of Babylonian guards, headed for the Processional Way.

As they passed under the embedded lions of Ishtar's Gate, noticing his mother's tears, Darayaus assured her that *yazatas* were looking after Amytis and Amel-Marduk, and she agreed. "What were you talking about with Belteshazzar?" he asked.

"He confirmed that the covenant of Yehovah God with his people is in many ways like the Mitradat covenant."

'I thought so," Darayaus concluded happily, and his mother put her arm around him and cuddled him.

The entourage had just passed the northern fort when Vashti noticed the Babylonian guards were still with them. She stuck her head out the window and asked Irdabama why.

"Shahan Shah's orders," came the reply from the Babylonians. "We will be with you all the way to the border."

Vashti sighed and sat back in the carriage. Reaching for the parcel Amytis had given her earlier that morning, she unwrapped sheets of fine reed parchment and a curious, finely honed writing rod with a reed tip.

"Dip the tip in the black liquid in the little jar," Amytis' note instructed of the clay pot in the package. "Use it to write on the parchment. Belteshazzar showed me. It is much faster and easier than a charcoal writing rod."

Hardly aware of the sentiments she was pouring onto the fragile page, Vashti began to write the graceful notations of her favorite Avestan language while Darayaus held the little pot. After the first page, she stopped to wait for the ink to dry. Then she read:

Dear, I feel lost without you. I am the commander of an army but feel I cannot continue without the sight of you in my eyes and the sound of your voice in my ears. You are the only one I can write to about my weakness (may Auramazda forgive me). He too is my friend, but He is not flesh and blood. He is Spirit.

Dear, I need you and your spirit. It breathes life into me, just like my hand in yours, the movement of your body as we danced, and the firelight shining in your eyes. I fear we will never dance together again.

I will return soon from this hot place to the cool mountains where we last met…for such a brief time. I do not know what awaits me there, except for your absence. It has been so long since I have seen you, and I pray that you are safe.

She put down her writing rod. After replacing the lid on the black jar, Darayaus had fallen asleep holding it in his lap. She kissed him and closed her eyes.

The carriage wound its way across the baking Babylonian plain.

Ishtovigo and Zerena welcomed Vashti and Darayaus on their return with kisses, hugs, and a special feast of roast venison and new wine. The only news of the Lydian war was worrying reports of losses and an appeal for more troops from the provinces, which Ishtovigo had arranged. Cartloads of willow branches, medicinal oils, and herbal tinctures had been sent to relieve the suffering of the injured troops; and many women and girls wore dull colors in mourning for their lost family members.

Khezmet's three children had grown even bigger, and the two eldest were already riding. She greeted Vashti with the news that another baby was on the way.

"Wonderful!" Vashti cried. "I thank Auramazda that Yezda is here to help when you become too heavy and after the birth."

Khezmet grinned, thankful that her charge would be cared for in her absence.

With the need for more troops to support the war effort, Vashti visited Irdabama and Pentaya and asked them if they were prepared to fight far away from home. They cheered and whooped loudly. "We are ready they cried," the *golangs* on the shoulders of their *chokhas* rippling. Vashti hugged them both together. "I am sending you to help end the war," she ordered even though privately she still thought it should never have happened.

When she informed Ishtovigo of her decision, he replied that it was a stupid idea. "Women are not strong and tough enough to fight seasoned warriors like the Scythians, the Parsu, or the Lydians," he maintained.

"So they can plough, sow, and reap the fields but not defend our honor in battle?" she shot back.

"Defending our lands is for our men. For centuries they have guarded our mountains. Now we need to protect our extended territories so we can support a growing population," Ishtovigo maintained.

"I think my women are more than ready to do so and even to lead the army," Vashti replied, lowering her voice to contain her mounting frustration.

Ishtovigo laughed. "Are you joking? They have not been tried once on the battlefield."

"Then let them have the opportunity," Vashti pleaded in her most submissive voice. "I'm only asking that fifty join the main force. Most of my women are lighter and smaller than the men, and their shorter bows draw more quickly," she went on fervently. "They would support a rear-guard attack when the main force is under pressure. No enemy will expect to see women in the cavalry. The affect on them will be like the fear our camels gave the Athorayans' horses in the battle of Nineveh."

Ishtovigo stared at her, his dark, almond eyes narrowing. "No. I will not allow our future mothers to be put in such danger and our forces to be humiliated," he replied with conviction. "The enemy will think we are almost beaten if we bring women into the conflict."

"Nonsense. They will wear the same clothes. The only difference will be their victory ululations."

"Or their immediate surrender in terror."

"Like they do when giving birth," Vashti chided.

"Which is what they should be doing at home."

Realizing she would never convince him, she turned to leave.

"That's the last time you leave Hagmatana," Ishtovigo called after her. "Every time you return, you have another stupid idea in your head."

"Not as wasteful as your lavish palace in Shush," she shot back, "especially when we are at war." Quickening her pace as Ishtovigo tried to follow her, she slammed the door in his face and ran down the silver corridor. Outside, she hurried to the stables and found Daro.

"Prepare the women's division's horses for the journey to Lydia," she ordered breathlessly. "They will be leaving the day after tomorrow, but do not let anyone else know."

Daro nodded. "I will call the blacksmiths to attend the horses' equipment and the forces' weapons," he promised.

"Yes. Keep the doors shut so they cannot be heard," she instructed.

A couple of days later, Irdabama and Pentaya assembled their little band of warriors outside the city. "Our men need you," Vashti told the women. "They have been at war for three long years, and they are tired. More troops have been summoned from the provinces, so you will be accompanied by Parthavan forces. We expect them to arrive within the next few days."

Shouldering their bows and quivers, their brass shields shining and their chaps rapping as they stood to attention at Irdabama's command, the women warriors rammed their lances into the ground, ululated, and shouted, "*Biji* Shahan Shah Hovakhshatra and Shahjin Ardela of the Medes."

Vashti smiled. "*Zors ciwana,*" she replied. "May the light of Auramazda always shine on you. Now is your chance to prove that you can fight as well as the men." But deep down, she wondered if she was sending her precious sisters to injury and death for the stubbornness of the Shahan Shah.

A couple of uneventful days later, Vashti awoke to the distant thump of horses' hooves. Grabbing a warm gown, she ran along the silver corridor, down the stone steps, and climbed the golden gate to view a column of lightly armed soldiers entering the city from the eastern road under the red, yellow, and purple banner of Parthava. She strained her eyes to see if Mithridates was leading them, but the figures were too small.

Racing inside, she crept back into the chamber she sometimes shared with Ishtovigo, who was still asleep, and put on her riding *chokha* and *pantol*. Out in the stables, she grabbed a bridle, threw a rug over Nzdar, and rode out through the citadel gates down to the city. The column had reached the deserted marketplace by the time she met its leader. His hooked nose was Mithridates' as were his beard and moustache, but his scarf and headdress were those of another man. When he saw her, he raised his arm to stop the column, dismounted, and bowed.

"Are you Vashti of the Medes?" he asked.

"Yes," she replied. "Why do you ask?"

"You look just like my brother Mithridates' description of the most beautiful woman in the Ariavartan realm," he replied. "He sends you his warmest greetings. I am Arsaces."

She sighed inwardly in relief, and her heart jumped for joy. Mithridates was alive and well! 'Many thanks, Arsaces," she replied, trying to steady her voice. "Your brother saved my life when I visited your lands. I am forever indebted to him."

"He speaks of it fondly as a privilege," Arsaces replied. "Now I and my countrymen are here to return the favor you bestowed on Parthava with your presence."

Vashti looked at the line of travel worn faces behind Arsaces. "I trust all of you will return to your homes and your lands," she replied. But doubt tore at her heart, and she pondered how much longer the Shahan Shah would allow his grief to rob others of their lives and leave their families stricken.

Chapter 33

Reports by Aswer that Ishtovigo's expenditure on the palace at Shush was still draining the treasury after she had replenished it from the stable store worried Vashti, so she sent her advisor to Shush to find out more. Several weeks later, he returned.

"The rubble from the area cleared for the palace was used for the wall foundations, which were forty *p'anka dva* cubits deep on bedrock," he reported. "After the walls were built, Babylonians were brought in to cover them with glazed bricks featuring bear, inverted tulip, and flame symbols."

"The building will be very strong," Vashti replied, "but its cost might weaken us."

"And the local laborers are now rebelling," Aswer continued. "They claim they are still waiting to be paid and refuse to be treated like slaves. Instead of listening, Ishtovigo sent to Mylasa for black and white marble for the palace floors."

Vashti gasped. "He has told our people to go into enemy territory to do business with the Lydians while we are at war with them?"

"It seems so," Aswer replied. "The battle front is further northeast on the Halys River, so I trust they will return."

"How will the marble be brought to the building site?" Vashti asked, concerned about the mounting expense.

"Ships will bring the slabs through the Great Sea to Tyre and then ox carts will carry them overland to the Idiqlat River mouth, from where they will be taken in boats across the Makran Sea to the port of Boushehr and finally to Shush."

"Such a long and costly way to bring materials just for the floor. Why could stone not be used?"

"Stone will be used for part of the building," Aswer explained. "Ishtovigo believes the palace at Shush should be symbolic of our power, our culture, and our knowledge. He says we cannot compete with Babylon's wealth, but we can create an exceptional style of architecture. So the Hall of the Shahs will have stone columns sixty *p'anka dva* cubits high and the width of a tall man's height across their base. The columns supporting the roof will be eighty *p'anka dva* high, but the quarries are close by, so we do not have to transport them far."

"What about the entrance?"

"It will be quite simple as the Hall of the Shahs will be reached by two highly decorated stairways from the north and the east."

"So that will be the tribute hall," Vashti surmised. "Our forces have been fighting for years while my husband has been planning such opulence. If the Shahan Shah is not already dead, this will kill him. I must speak to the Shahjin. She knows we have everything here in Hagmatana necessary to display our civilization and our sovereignty over Media and our territories."

She dismissed Aswer quickly and hurried to the Shahjin's chamber. Ardela had just returned from a visit to the Atashkedah and was looking quite pale. "Dear, you look unwell. Shall I call the Magush?" Vashti asked.

"No, thank you, dear. I am not sick," the Shahjin replied wearily. "But last night I had a dream the Magush could not interpret. Our forces were fighting the Lydians near a wide river. Then everything faded away. I was afraid our army had been destroyed."

Vashti didn't want to worry her mother-in-law anymore, but she had to tell her of the problem in Shush. Ardela replied that she knew about it but didn't know how to stop her son's squandering. Remembering her violent disagreement with Ishtovigo, Vashti was reluctant to speak to him about the matter but promised to ask Aswer for advice.

Sometime later, one of Vashti's remaining fighters rode into the citadel, quickly dismounted, and asked to see her. On discovering that some farmers had found Aswer injured near the river, Vashti asked her to accompany Daro to retrieve him.

The farmers had wrapped Aswer's head in a woolen scarf, which was soaked in blood by the time he arrived at the palace.

"Who did this to you?" Vashti asked angrily before telling Khezmet to bring another bandage and some healing oils.

"Kusha, Ghasem, and Admatha," Aswer mumbled. "After I asked them about Ishtovigo's palace, they told me not to interfere and that as the future Shahan Shah he wants to build the most impressive and luxurious palace in the world so he can show the leaders of every nation."

"Parsu," Vashti muttered, "even though they've been punished for robbing the Shahan Shah, we still cannot trust them. He should never have brought them into his service. What else did they say?"

Aswer took a deep breath and shuddered as Khezmet removed his bandage to reveal a gash on the back of his head. "I went for a ride near the river," he continued, moaning as Khezmet gently dabbed oil on his wound. "I was thinking about the expenditure in Shush when I noticed three horsemen with *kulaw-u-dastmals* over their faces following me. I greeted them cheerily when they approached me, but they scowled and told me to not question Ishtovigo's plans. Then they beat me with a club and left me beside the river. I heard them using each other's names as they rode off, thinking I was unconscious, or dead," he explained, lifting his *pantol* to reveal bruises on both his legs.

"Tell the guard outside my door to send for the commander of the Shahan Shah's guard immediately," Vashti told Khezmet angrily. When he arrived with his men, she ordered them to arrest Kusha, Ghasem, and Admatha and place them in detention. "They will stay there till the Shahan Shah returns," she instructed. Then she marched to Ishtovigo's quarters with Khezmet and entered unannounced. Looking up from the mosaic plan he was drawing, he greeted her politely.

"What brings you here, my dear?" Ishtovigo inquired indifferently.

"Are they for the Shush palace?" she replied pointing to the plans.

"Yes. Do you like the floral designs?"

She nodded. "I have been speaking to one of the Shahan Shah's advisors about the building," she continued calmly.

"It is progressing well and should be ready for occupation within a year."

"Do you realize there is still not enough money in the treasury to finish it?"

"Do not worry, dear. When Father brings home the plunder from Lydia, the chests will be full."

Vashti frowned. "That is not the reason he and the troops are fighting. This is a war of honor, not expansion."

"I thought Father intended to take Sardis."

Vashti shook her head. "Have you forgotten how your dear brothers died, and Alyattes' refusal to give up their murderers?"

"Isn't that what Father is trying to avenge?"

Vashti sighed. "Yes, but our enemies attempted to weaken us by assassinating Shawish and Artaspaya. Your father is also fighting to protect us and keep us strong." Ishtovigo stared at her vacantly and said nothing. "Unless they are captured," she went on, "they or their children will try again. Shah Alyattes has shown that he wants to challenge Media by harboring the murderers. Your mother knows this. You should talk to her about it."

"Are you accusing me of disloyalty?" Ishtovigo asked angrily.

"No. But today, three of the Shahan Shah's advisors attacked my advisor, Aswer. Do you know why?"

Ishtovigo's lip curled angrily, but she held his gaze until he looked away. "Aswer answers to me, not you," he declared. "Do you understand?"

"Do Kusha, Ghasem, and Admatha always answer to you?" Vashti replied, ignoring his question.

"Of course."

"Then you won't see them for a while because they have been locked in the palace storehouse, and I have the key."

"You do not have authority over my advisors," Ishtovigo replied through gritted teeth. "Why was I not informed of this matter before you imprisoned them?"

"I have authority because of the Mitradat and the Shahan Shah's word," Vashti replied evenly. "Just like your mother does."

"While my father is absent, my word prevails," Ishtovigo yelled, "and I will not be told otherwise. Get out of here with your *druj*. Father can say what he likes now, but women will never rule when I am Shahan Shah of Media."

Vashti stepped back as he moved threateningly close, clutching a tile cutting tool.

"Very well. We will see what the true Shahan Shah has to say about that," Vashti replied coolly. "Come, Khezmet."

Outside in the hall, she signaled Khezmet to hurry with her to Aswer. "You will have to leave," she instructed him in her chambers. "It is not safe for you here. I will find a place where you will not be harmed."

Chapter 34

Not long after conflicting with Ishtovigo over the three Parsu, Vashti released them and told them to leave the city, ordering their banishment if they returned. Before her husband could retaliate, she received a disturbing letter from Amytis about the final fate of the city of Ursalim at Nebuchadnezzar's hands:

My dear Vashti

I cannot imagine the suffering of the starved inhabitants of Ursalim after two years of siege. Nebuchadnezzar told me some had killed and eaten their children. When the city's walls finally fell, my husband took the gold and silver vessels, the utensils used for sacrifices from the temple, and other treasure and objects of worship. He brought them here to the temple of Marduk to show whose god is more powerful, and that Yehud is no longer.

To keep Yehud under control, my husband appointed Gedaliah the Hapiru as governor, but after being captured while trying to escape, Shah Zedekiah was taken to Riblah in Sham where his sons were killed before him, his eyes were gouged out, and he was brought here as our prisoner. Such are the results of defying my husband. I shudder to think what evil he can do.

A month later, he sent his Chief Guard, Nebuzaradan, to burn Ursalim, including the temple, the palaces, and the great homes. So your dream about the city completely came true! Some Hapiru leaders fled to Egypt and many priests, army officers, scribes, and nobles of Yehud were killed by our forces, leaving the city desolate. Nebuzaradan then took most of the remaining people away, leaving only the poor farmers to till the land.

Once more, we received a sad train of exhausted captives, some of whose number had died on the journey. Thousands of emaciated men, women, and children were paraded along the Processional Way, and I could hardly believe such misery was happening to the Hapiru again. Again I assisted Belteshazzar's efforts to save the foreigners, some barely alive, others trying to run away at any opportunity. They too were settled along the Chebar Canal, which supplies irrigation water from the river.

It has taken nearly twenty years for my husband to subdue Yehud, which is located strategically at the crossroads of numerous other small nations. Yehud will never ally with Egypt again, so Nebuchadnezzar now has no obstacles to his goal of conquering that great southern power.

I finish this with a very heavy heart.

Amytis

Vashti immediately summoned Aswer, whom she had recalled from protection when Ishtovigo sent his attackers to Shush and told him the news.

"Are you concerned that Babylonia will now fix its eyes on Media?" he asked.

"Not yet, but we must remain vigilant. Except for Belteshazzar, Nebuchadnezzar does not have any source of *asha* wisdom like the Magi or the Avesta. His wise men can barely interpret dreams," she replied. "He relies on his own addled mind, which recognizes no boundaries except his own authority. Besides, his army is not trained to fight in the mountains."

After ignoring Aswer's suggestion that she should consult Ishtovigo, she dismissed him and wondered if Auramazda was yet to tell her about the future of Hagmatana.

Chapter 35

After another disagreement with Vashti, Ishtovigo departed for Shush, leaving her to wait for news from the Lydian war. Harpagos' eventual report of the stalemate was bleak. But following discussion of the situation with Aswer and the remaining advisors, it was agreed there was nothing more they could do, except encourage the people to prepare for the troops' return.

Debyar continued to teach the leading families' children, including her own little girl. One day, looking pale and anxious, she showed Vashti a letter from Harpagos that had arrived with the latest battle report:

My dearest Debyar,

I think of you every day in this desolate place just inside our border on the Halys River. We are encamped on a narrow plain divided by the river with mountains just behind. On his side of the divide, Shah Alyattes is well prepared with hundreds of reinforcements and granaries nearby. We are constantly replenishing our sustenance, weapons, and ammunition from the mountains while at times we run dangerously low on treatments for the wounded.

However, the nearby villagers have carefully nursed the sick and injured with their own medicines. I have requested more of these from Ishtovigo with my report, which includes a list of our brave fighters who have lost their lives. Please ask Vashti to ensure the widows and children are cared for.

My darling it is often dismal here without you, especially when it rains or the cold winds blow. We are so far from our loved ones and facing a determined foe. When the battle begins, the roar of the Lydians amidst our battle cries is deafening and the crashing and chinking of armor of both sides adds to the din. Our sturdy mountain-bred horses, though, are braver than theirs and never spook even at the height of the fray. Most exasperating for the Shahan Shah is the sight of Scythian mercenaries in their pointed hats fighting alongside the Lydians. Enraged by this insult from Alyattes, he flies into battle, so I have ordered our fiercest fighters, including commanders Irdabama and Pentaya, to protect him.

And now my beloved I believe I have described enough of the privations of war. Your face is ever before me as we attack those who have harbored Shawish's and Artaspaya's murderers and would take our hard-won territories.

It has been a privilege to be the husband of such a learned teacher and devoted mother as you my darling.

May Auramazda preserve all three of us until we meet once more.

Always your faithful

Harpagos

Debyar lost her usual composure, and tears spilled from her eyes. "It's been so long since the army left," she sobbed. "Will we ever see them again?"

When Auramazda's *yazatas* watch over his people, some record their victories and their losses. In their Book of the Mitradat Covenant, *yazatas* wrote about a battle that altered the course of Anatolian history and set the stage for irreversible change in the Medes' fortunes. It read as follows:

The winter of 586–585 before the expected arrival of a Saoshyant was a particularly harsh one with troops on both sides of the Halys River hunkered down as icy winds whipped in from the north. They were kept busy feeding their animals and shovelling snow, but supplies were dangerously low by the spring thaw. Finally, the weather relented, allowing food and medicines to be brought in and weapons to be refitted.

Consulting only Harpagos, Shahan Shah Hovakhshatra planned his last campaign, determined that if it was not successful, he would call a truce and offer to negotiate a treaty. The troops looked so despondent he feared that if his plans were made known, men who had not seen their families for five years would desert. He hated the thought but considered it a strong possibility. Commander Vashti's women fighters did not seem deterred, but they had joined the war later. Worse still, the murderers of the heirs to the throne remained at large somewhere in Lydian territory. And lastly, Hovakhshatra's strength for battle was waning. Even so, both he and Alyattes refused to cooperate with the envoy sent by Shah Nebuchadnezzar of Babylonia to broker a peace between the two powers.

By Norouz, the Medes were ready for their final series of assaults. They celebrated briefly in the evening by lighting numerous fires, sending a defiant message to their enemies. Then early in the morning, they crossed the swiftly flowing Halys River to face their heavily armored foes. The warm sun sparkled on the metal leaved armor of both Hovakhshatra's and Alyattes' forces. Horses neighed nervously and lances crashed against iron and bronze. Facing his enemy squarely, the Shahan Shah of the Medes raised his lance and uttered the battle cry. Shah Alyattes responded, and the two forces raced toward one another, the shrill tones of the Medes' pipes penetrating the expanse of the battlefield.

Hovakhshatra was almost unseated in the first confrontation with Alyattes's chief general. General Ferhad, who was right behind him, knocked the attacker off his horse but failed to injure him. The Lydian remounted his horse and set off for Ferhad, who was by now fighting another enemy. The soldier lashed at Ferhad with his battle-ax. Ferhad swerved but received a severe blow to the head, which knocked him to the ground. Realizing his general was in trouble, and with Irdabama in close pursuit, the Shahan Shah retraced his path after witnessing the double attack on Ferhad. By the time he reached his son-in-law, he was very pale, and blood ran from his ear, but Irdabama had killed his cowardly assailant.

"Shahan Shah," Ferhad whispered, "look after Shelna and Kshathrita."

Hovakhshatra hoisted the dying man onto his horse and rode through the battle, fighting enemies on both sides. But by the time he reached the shelter of the camp, the life of the youngest general of the Bears was gone.

Laying the body gently on the grass, Hovakshatra continued to water it with his tears as though they would somehow revive Ferhad.

"First Cica and now his boy," he sobbed, "How much more must be paid for Media's honor?"

While the battle raged, the Shahan Shah saw not only his men fall, but the faces of the dead of nearly five years of struggle. He had lost his own boys and many more fathers had lost theirs trying to avenge their murders.

"These bloody clashes must end," he decided. "The price that has been paid is more than enough."

The following day was a time for both sides to bury their dead. Harpagos and Hovakhshatra asked Alyattes for a truce of several days to travel deep inside Median territory to which he agreed. Ordering the men accompanying them to source branches and leaves to protect the soil from Ferhad's necessary earthen burial, they rode to Lake Chauon where they dug a grave in the sandy soil under a lone oak tree beside the water.

"Cica and Shamin's boy was only at the beginning of his life," the Shahan Shah lamented as he surveyed the tree's budding leaves.

In Ferhad's sash, he found two letters, one written by Shelna and the other Ferhad's unfinished reply. Keeping the unfinished letter for Shelna, he placed her letter to Ferhad back in the sash.

"Perhaps this will help them communicate with each other forever," he thought. For Ferhad's son, little Kshathrita, he retrieved the co-commander's silver bear insignia but left the necklace given him by Shelna.

"Such was their love that they will neither marry another," he speculated to Harpagos.

Then they slowly filled the grave and built a mound of stones to mark it.

"Somewhere for the yazatas to sit," the Shahan Shah remarked.

He and Harpagos then stood to attention and bowed as the mournful sound of the shimshal and the slow beat of the daf farewelled Ferhad.

"Until Frashokeriti brother," was Harpagos's tearful goodbye.

Little did he know that the end of the world would soon seem to come.

On the night of their return, storms in the mountains melted and washed down swathes of snow and ice. The streams at the headwaters of the River Halys filled and overflowed with meltwater, creating a brown flood that rushed down the valleys to the plain where the two armies were arrayed against each other. When the water finally reached the battlefield, it spread over the plain, causing both armies to retreat. For six weeks, floodwater lay on the wide valley, preventing military engagement. This was the first act of Auramazda on behalf of the exhausted Medes.

The second was well observed throughout the world. The Median Magi knew of its impending occurrence but declined to make the event known fearing that forewarning would cause fear of an apocalypse. But just before the predicted day, they told Vashti, who sent messengers to Hagmatana and throughout the Median triangle to inform the citizens and keep them calm. So the city was not disturbed as the moon passed across the sun, causing dense darkness over Media on the third last day of the month of Gulan, approximately 585 years before the expected birth of the second Saoshyant.

However, it was anything but calm on that hot day on the soggy battlefield of the Halys Plain as soldiers continued to dig drainage trenches while others engaged in battle. But soon, combatants and animals of both sides experienced an eerie and inexplicable lethargy. By midday, the fighting had dwindled to sporadic clashes between small bands of troops. Both sides seemed to be longing for the setting sun to bring respite. Much to their amazement, shortly after noon, their wish was granted. Slowly, the sunlight began to fade. A spot appeared over the great celestial light, which grew and eventually covered it, casting complete darkness over the battlefield. Birds flew to their nests and the earth was hushed. Shah Alyattes shook violently, believing that the gods were about to punish him for instructing his men to not always follow the rules of war. But Shahan Shah Hovakhshatra suspected Auramazda was telling him that he would withdraw his protection if he continued to pursue his war of revenge. Hovakhshatra approached Alyattes with a truce banner, and both agreed that the gods wanted them to cease fighting.

To seal the treaty between the Medes and the Lydians, Alyattes agreed to give his daughter Aryenis in marriage to Ishtovigo of Media. Aryenis was to have three months to prepare for her new life in a distant land. Other provisions included the inviolable retention of the Halys River as the official boundary between the two nations. Having counted his considerable troop losses, Hovakhshatra declined to pursue the matter of the fugitive assassins of his sons.

And so, the Medes departed the Halys Plain, having secured a pact that guaranteed peace on their western border but at great cost.

The watching *yazatas* put down their writing rods and sighed.

For weeks, lines of weary, battle-worn Median soldiers slowly toiled east along the Shahan Shah's Road. Fresh horses stabled a day's ride apart provided relief for the most exhausted cavalry mounts as messengers rode ahead carrying news for those waiting in the capital.

Finally, on a hot summer's day, a lone rider ascended the citadel of Hagmatana and informed the palace guard that he bore news from the returning forces. The Shahjin and Vashti received the message and sent drummers into the city to inform the residents. The excitement grew as people bustled around preparing to greet the soldiers. But the messenger had been told not to reveal the outcome of the war.

Three days later, another messenger heralded the imminent arrival of the forces. When all the preparations were finished, a little group of leading women and children with Ishtovigo, who had returned from Shush, gathered in front of the palace. First to breach the golden gate was the Shahan Shah, riding in a chariot. Barely able to distinguish the strong, statuesque man who had left five years ago from her diminished, haggard husband, Ardela rushed to him as he stepped awkwardly from the chariot.

"Hovakh dear," she cried, "what has become of you?"

The Shahan Shah swayed, but his driver reached over to steady him. "My dear, I never realized just how beautiful you are," he declared, fixing his eyes on his wife, stretching out his arm to greet her, and coughing harshly.

Shelna rushed to her father as Harpagos dismounted behind the Shahan Shah and greeted Debyar. "Father, where is Ferhad?" she cried.

Tears ran down the Shahan Shah's face. "My darling, his spirit rests with Auramazda."

"No, no," she cried, breaking into a heartrending, *Hulo-lao, hulo-laolao*, and raising her fists to shake them at the sky. As her cries echoed across the courtyard, Ishtovigo gently took his sister's arm and escorted her toward the palace. Alarmed by his mother's howls, little Kshathrita began to cry so Vashti scooped him up and spoke soothing words. But he soon wriggled free and ran to his grandparents.

"Shahan Shah," he asked in his clear child's voice, "what have you done with my father?"

"Kshathrita, son of the Medes, come and I will tell you the story of your brave father, General Ferhad, joint commander of the great Bear regiment." Grasping his grandson's hand, with the aid of his wife, the Shahan Shah walked slowly up the palace steps. Inside, Shamin instructed the servants to prepare a potion to quieten Shelna.

Harpagos then dismissed the remainder of the Bears, who dispersed gloomily to the barracks or retraced the path down the hill to their families where they met Arsaces' little band of Parthavans. Following the departing Bears, Vashti sought the diminished band, thanked them for serving the Shahan Shah loyally, and ordered that they and their horses to be provisioned in the barracks and the stables respectively.

After returning to the palace to find a sobbing Shelna being comforted by Ardela, Vashti raced outside to meet Irdabama and Pentaya with thirty-six of the fifty fighters she had sent to the Halys River. When Daro and his assistants had led their horses away, they shuffled around, forming lines with the injured valiantly leaning on their lances, and others peering out from head bandages. Those who could stood to attention as their commander moved among them, brushing off the dried mud from their *chokhas* and hugging and kissing each one despite the unpleasant, rancid smell of congealed blood and stale sweat.

"Welcome back," she told them as tears of joy and sadness streamed down everyone's faces.

Wiping her face with her sleeve, she called Khezmet to prepare her bathhouse so her warriors could wash in warm water from the palace pools laced lavishly with her most healing, cleansing oils.

"You have proved yourselves in battle for all to see," she continued. "Your prowess establishes the reputation of Median women fighters for the ages to come. No one can say you are not the equivalent of men in your determination and bravery. *Biji* Media!"

Strengthened by their commander's loving-kindness, the able-bodied supported the injured as all the women threw off their exhaustion and invited Vashti to join them for a ragged but still spirited victory song and dance.

Afterwards, she retired to her chamber to record the names of her precious sisters lying underneath the Halys Plain, and those of the survivors, in her personal chronicles.

Chapter 36

Young Kshathrita sat comfortably in his grandfather's lap, contentedly playing with the shiny silver bear emblem he had just received.

"Why is everyone so sad?" he asked.

"Your father has gone to sleep for a long time," Hovakhshatra replied. "Your mother is sad because she wanted to go hunting with him again."

"If my father is so brave, why doesn't he wake up and teach me to ride with Mother?" Kshathrita asked.

"He was very tired from fighting in the war," the Shahan Shah replied.

"Like you, Grandfather?"

"Yes," came the reply with a yawn and a smile. Media will be safe if this boy ever takes the throne, Hovakhshatra thought.

Just then, Ardela bustled in. "Time for a nap for you two," she insisted. The Shahan Shah nodded, rose unsteadily, and was escorted away by his wife and grandson. When he awoke, he immediately called for Vashti to attend his chambers.

"Shahan Shah," she protested after he had held out the golden scepter, "don't you want to consult Ishtovigo too?"

"Not yet. I want the truth from you. And besides, Aswer tells me Ishtovigo has been in Shush most of the time I have been away."

Vashti cast her eyes downward. "Yes, Shahan Shah."

"I am sorry he left you with so many duties."

"They are not duties, Shahan Shah. They are an honor and a privilege."

Hovakhshatra sighed, reached over, and gently patted her arm. "Your service to Media will never be forgotten, my dear."

Vashti's smile hid her dread of a question about the treasury. However, the Shahan Shah's next remark saved her from the embarrassment of having to answer.

"Aswer also tells me the treasury is nearly drained. I thought my son would do so, so I negotiated a hefty dowry in gold-silver coins from Alyattes for Aryenis. He doesn't know we already have them," he divulged with a wink. "The alliance will allow us to trade in the new coins throughout our territories and with other nations, including Babylonia. Their value will increase our wealth, so we will not have to impose taxes on our people."

"A very wise decision, Shahan Shah, but who is Aryenis?" Vashti asked warily.

"My dear, didn't Aswer tell you? Aryenis, daughter of Alyattes of Lydia, is betrothed to Ishtovigo to seal the peace between us."

Shocked, Vashti stepped back. "Shahan Shah, that is not our way. You yourself have only one wife, and Ishtovigo is hardly husband to me. How could he be to another woman?"

Hovakhshatra smiled in satisfaction. "Then you and Aryenis should become good friends. And Darayaus is and will always be first in line to succeed his father," he assured her. Although Vashti duly thanked the Shahan Shah for his promise, she wished the treaty could have been affirmed another way. Shahs in the other nations had bred many sons from multiple wives who had struggled for supremacy on the death of their father, but this wasn't the time to challenge her father-in-law's decision.

"As soon as I am well, I will travel to Shush to inspect the new palace," Hovakhshatra continued. "But now, please ask Harpagos to bring in Kshathrita. We have much more to talk about."

Vashti wanted to ask about the condition of the standing army, but Hovakhshatra was lying on his couch coughing, so she decided the matter should wait. Soon Ardela appeared with Kshathrita, who fascinated the Shahan Shah with his efforts to hide his little silver bear under cushions and behind brocade curtains until his grandfather fell asleep.

When the Median council finally met, Ishtovigo informed his father that his Parsu advisors were in Shush, a policy that the Shahan Shah questioned but seemed too unwell to oppose.

After Hovakhshatra asked why the locks had been changed on the treasury door and Vashti explained that some funds had been taken without her permission, Ishtovigo glared at her. But even more disconcerting was the Shahan Shah's disinterest in pursuing the matter. "Harpagos will now give details of the treaty with Lydia," he continued.

Glancing uncomfortably at Vashti, Harpagos described the territorial and military provisions of the treaty then announced the imminent arrival of Aryenis of Lydia in preparation for her marriage to Ishtovigo, who immediately jumped to his feet and confronted his father.

"Why have I not been consulted about this arrangement?" he roared.

Harpagos stepped over and put his hand on Ishtovigo's shoulder. "Beware of how you speak to the Shahan Shah," he warned.

"How can I ever become Shahan Shah of Media if I am not trusted?" Ishtovigo yelled before turning and storming from the room.

Vashti took a deep breath. "Shahan Shah, I assure you, Aryenis of Lydia will be welcomed to Media. Now I request your leave."

It was granted and she left quickly. She didn't know why her marriage to Ishtovigo had hardly ever been harmonious, and he had not shown interest in her for several years, but the arrival of a new wife would signify the end of her status as sole wife of the male heir to the throne.

Perhaps Aryenis will satisfy my husband and bring him happiness and peace, she thought sadly and with just the slightest tinge of jealousy.

On the recommendation of the Magush, Ishtovigo, Vashti, and Ardela assumed all the Shahan Shah's duties to allow him to recover. But too often Ardela would find her husband burning lamps late into the night with Harpagos, Aswer, and the chief priest.

"I declare that man will kill himself for Media," she confided to Shamin.

Not long after, despite Ardela's advice that it was too soon, Shamin suggested that she, Shelna, Kshathrita, and Vashti should travel to Ferhad's grave with a small troop of male and female guards. On the evening before their departure, Vashti prepared a small banner of Kawa for her nephew to fix to the stones above his father's resting place.

While they were away, Ardela quietly took the opportunity to plan the wedding of her son and Aryenis. When Ishtovigo had again attempted to protest the agreement to his father, Ardela told Harpagos to refuse him entry on account of her husband's health. The Shahan Shah was kept out of the resulting scuffle but was heard to say, "I want my son to be happy with another wife and stop visiting the Mossala."

Not surprisingly, Ishtovigo went off to Shush again but later returned with his Parsu advisors and resigned to his father's wishes regarding his marriage to Aryenis. The wedding proceeded smoothly with the Shahjin arranging for Vashti and Khezmet to visit the city on the day to make sure the war widows and orphans were being adequately cared for by their families.

A week later, when Ishtovigo's two wives finally met at the Shahjin's reception for her second daughter-in-law, Vashti offered her hand to Aryenis, who smiled nervously.

"Welcome to Media. We are so pleased you have joined us," Vashti said in Aramaic to the well-rounded, auburn-haired young woman before her. Aryenis' shoulders relaxed, and she smiled back and thanked her hostess in her own language. The Shahjin then asked Vashti to sit on her right and Aryenis on her left at the banquet table. The wives of the Shahan Shah's advisors, generals, and other city leaders then sat down; and Ardela stood to welcome them all.

After the meal, Ardela took Aryenis on a tour of the palace, following which Vashti invited Aryenis to her quarters. The new bride's remarks came more easily as Vashti described her role as second wife of the male heir to the throne until Aryenis lowered her voice secretively.

"I have some important information," she said.

"What is it?" Vashti asked in a whisper.

"When it was hot at home in Sardis," Aryenis explained, "we sometimes resorted to a small town on the coast of the Aegean Sea. Some Scythians who escaped Media live there, including those whom the Shahan Shah seeks." Aryenis' unwavering gaze signaled she was telling the truth. Vashti beamed appreciation and told her to continue.

"My maid's family home is nearby," Aryenis resumed. "She has heard the killers boasting of their conquest of the Shahan Shah's sons and knows where they are." Vashti looked pleased, patted Aryenis's arm, and thanked her profusely.

"I will send a servant to you with the details," Aryenis added, winking.

Early the next morning, Aryenis' maid delivered a small parchment scroll to Vashti's quarters indicating the location and appearances of the wanted Scythians. Vashti immediately sent for General Harpogos.

"We will need the help of the Shahan Shah's spies to complete his wish," he commented when she showed him the information. "But he must not know what we do. If the spies are captured, he can say he knows nothing of them, so the treaty with Lydia will not be threatened. We must send the spies very soon. The Shahan Shah is not getting any better."

A month later, two headless male Scythian bodies were found on the steps of the temple of the goddess Kuvava in the Lydian capital, Sardis. The following day, Alyattes of Lydia's new chief general, who had participated in the double attack on General Ferhad, died mysteriously; it was thought from poison.

Weeks later, three Median merchants crossed the Halys River into their home territory. On reaching Hagmatana, they delivered important news to Harpagos, who immediately requested an audience with Hovakhshatra as he basked in the warm autumn sunshine.

"Shahan Shah," he began, "I am pleased to show you trophies secured by the actions of some of my men." Opening the bag, he revealed two metal belts engraved with the round, indented Scythian shield and spattered with dried blood. "These were taken from the bodies of the Scythians who we know confessed to killing Shawish and Artaspaya."

The Shahan Shah sat up straight. "How?" he rasped.

"I cannot say because others might be endangered. But by the Mitradat, Shahan Shah, this is *asha*."

Hovakhshatra put his hand on his heart as his tears fell on his robe. "Auramazda be praised!" he cried. "He has seen fit to punish those devils who took my boys' lives all those years ago."

"Moreover," Harpagos continued, "General Ferhad's cowardly attacker is no longer alive."

The Shahan Shah rose with some effort. "Call the Shahjin, Darayaus, and Shelna," he ordered. "We will celebrate." Vashti rejoiced with the rest of the leading family for hours but became concerned as the Shahan Shah's color slowly drained from his face. She sent for the Magush, who regarded Hovakhshatra momentarily then shook his head.

"His life force is nearly spent," he told her sadly without Ardela's hearing. "There is nothing we can do."

Ten days later, Hovakhshatra, the first to be called Ahasuerus the Mede, but known affectionately to his people as Uvaxstra, died peacefully in his sleep after appointing Harpagos commander of all his forces and granting walnut groves to the revealed avengers of his son's deaths. Shahjin Ardela awoke to the silence of a husband who had loved her constantly and faithfully and always championed her and the women of his family. From Hagmatana to the Halys River in the west, east to Bactria, north to Azadia and Urartu, and south to Elam, riders took the sad news and once again men bawled, "*baw-ka-roo,*" ("Father is dead"). In Babylon, like her mother, Amytis could not be comforted, and Nebuchadnezzar closed the city's temples. Throughout the Atashkedah temples of the Ariavartan lands, the magi priests let the fires grow dim until it seemed they might die while the people wondered how they would live under a new ruler.

Vashti keenly felt the loss of the man who had readily taken her own father's place and had treated her like his daughter. Relegating her doubts about Ishtovigo to the back of her mind, she sought to comfort Ardela, Shamin, and the other family members while her husband consulted his council about the funeral arrangements.

But Vashti also set her mind to become Shahjin of the Medes.

Thousands of mourners joined the stades-long funeral procession of Shahan Shah Hovakhshatra as it wound its way west toward the reddish-brown tomb at Ashkawt, which he had instructed his stone masons to prepare for his burial. After crossing the river in the valley below the tomb, the leading families' carriages were followed by Shah Nebuchadnezzar and Shahjin Amytis of

Babylonia in their gold carriage, and then the rulers of nations as far away as Macedonia, Egypt, and Hindush.

For several weeks afterwards, the dark mood that had engulfed Media hung like a thick cloud over the city of Hagmatana. While Shahan Shah elect Ishtovigo met with Nebuchadnezzar, Croesus, the new Shah of Lydia following Alyattes' death, the vizier of Egypt's pharaoh, and other rulers and provincial leaders, Vashti and Amytis discussed the futures of their respective nations.

"We are both in a position of strength with our allies and our enemies, but internally Media faces uncertainty," Vashti confessed, fixing her eyes on her cousin. "Years ago, your father made me promise to look after Media when he died," she added. "I intend to keep that promise."

"My brother has the ability to rule, but not enough of father's devotion to Media," Amytis admitted sadly.

"Yes, the palace at Shush is…"

"Another monument," Amytis finished. "Ishtovigo is competing with Nebuchadnezzar."

"While the people sometimes struggle to feed themselves in very harsh winters," Vashti complained. "I wish we had Egypt's grain storehouses."

"But as Shahjin, could you order the construction of more?" Amytis suggested.

"If there are enough funds," Vashti replied quickly before reminding herself about the vault beneath the stables.

"The palace in Shush has been expensive," Amytis noted. "How is Aryenis?" she asked, switching the subject.

"Her father has trained her well. She is intelligent at court, and Ishtovigo's temper doesn't seem to bother her. There will be no problems with the alliance providing she stays loyal," Vashti replied.

"Father made another good decision." Amytis smiled, her eyes misting.

"Not with the war in Lydia," Vashti countered then castigated herself for her insensitivity to Amytis' grief.

Amytis grimaced. "It took far too long to convince Nebuchadnezzar to send a peacemaker," she admitted, her eyes now welling with tears. "If I had insisted sooner, perhaps Father would be alive today," she cried, reaching for an embroidered cloth inside her gown and wiping her eyes.

Vashti gathered her cousin in her arms and hugged her tightly. "You forget that he wouldn't listen at first," she consoled. "And it was his stubbornness that wore him out."

"Yes," Amytis sniffed. "He gave his life for the Media he created and loved."

"So now we have had enough of war," Vashti declared resolutely. "Please inform Nebuchadnezzar that we will not assist him on any Egyptian campaign."

"I will do so with pleasure," Amytis replied just as firmly.

Once all the dignitaries had left Hagmatana, a council consisting of the Magush, the Median generals, the tribal chiefs, and Shahjin Ardela formally approved Ishtovigo and Vashti as the new Shahan Shah and Shahjin of Media. The inauguration ceremony was delayed for forty days, after which Hovakhshatra's memorial stories were told, but once the capital's dense cloud of grief started to lift, the preparations began.

Determined to impress foreign visitors, Ishtovigo spared no expense on embellishments for the city, and when everything was completed to his satisfaction, he and Aryenis left for the palace in Shush. Vashti stayed to oversee the final details of the inauguration with Ardela, who remained in the lesser advisory role of the Shahan Shah's mother.

On her return with Ishtovigo, Aryenis complained of sickness. The Magush diagnosed liver disease. She recovered for a short time, soon to fall ill again. This time the Magush recommended consulting a midwife, who declared Aryenis with child. The announcement sent another flutter of excitement through the palace but left Vashti with a hollow sensation in her stomach when she realized that she was no longer the only bearer of the Shahan Shah's legitimate children.

My position is a little weaker, she thought. But Darayaus is still the male heir to the throne.

That night, tossing and turning with doubts about her future as wife and Shahjin before falling asleep, she dreamed she was riding deep into the realm of Bactria on the back of Mithridates' horse, holding fast to him and never letting go.

One unusually warm winter's afternoon some months later, while Vashti and Aryenis sat comfortably by a tendur stove embroidering baby clothes, Aryenis suddenly cleared her throat.

"My father is not trustworthy," she confided, looking down at her growing waistline. "If the child is a boy, he will attempt to kidnap him."

"Why?" Vashti asked warily.

"My father only values a male heir. It is the way in my former country. Women there have little status at home or anywhere except as convenient servants or objects of beauty. When the alliance was discussed, Father seized the opportunity to get rid of me and appease Shahan Shah Hovakhshatra. My two brothers are married, but they have no sons."

"I will have an extra guard set for you both if the child is a boy. No one will steal a child of the Medes," Vashti asserted. "Do not fear. You might have a girl."

"Then she will be safe," Aryenis sighed, "and I believe Auramazda will protect my child." Vashti surveyed the rotund young woman opposite her.

Even though she is alone in another land, she has adopted our ways readily and without complaint, she thought.

"There are other women living in the palace in Shush," Aryenis continued cautiously, glancing sideways at Vashti, "and some children."

"Yes. Ishtovigo claims his other wives guarantee peace with the provinces and our neighbors," Vashti replied evenly, but her tone bore distaste. "He has kept them in Shush because he knows his mother would not approve his disregard for the Mitradat. I fear *druj* will destroy us."

Aryenis sniffed disapproval, and both women stared silently out the window as the fire in the oven crackled and the light faded.

At the close of Ishtovigo's and Vashti's inaugural year, they were crowned by the Magush in the Great Hall of the palace at Hagmatana, which was decked in green, red, and yellow while a huge banner of Kawa flew from the roof. Afterwards, Shahan Shah Ishtovigo, now known as Ahasuerus the Second, and Shahjin Vashti took their carriage down the hill for a tour of the crowded city streets. Representatives of the Median tribal clans who had set up their colorfully woven *dwars* and fringed pavilions on the plain outside, and even brought their animals, enthusiastically greeted their new leaders. Much to Harpagos' concern, Ishtovigo and Vashti mingled freely with the crowds, including visitors from the provinces. When the entourage halted, a group of women presented Vashti with a brightly woven cloak featuring the figures of a mother and child on behalf of the widows and orphans of the city. In the evening, fires once more flared all over the city.

The following day, the new rulers hosted all the dignitaries, including Kambujiya of Anshan city, the Parsu heir to the province of Elam. Before he departed, Ishtovigo renewed the loose alliance with Elam, allowing the Medes to continue to occupy Shush as their southernmost city.

At the end of several long days of vows and well-wishes, when Khezmet removed the weighty, jewel-encrusted gold crown from Vashti's head and massaged her aching neck, the new Shahjin ran her fingers through her freed hair and wondered how many more burdens would be placed upon her shoulders.

As the summer of that year waned, Ishtovigo and Vashti executed their duties together harmoniously in public, but in private, their relationship remained cool. When Aryenis gave birth to a girl, there was great rejoicing.

"Mandane," Ardela declared, "she will be called Mandane of the Medes." And when her father agreed, Aryenis was overjoyed that her Lydian family would never lay claim to Mandane to satisfy their greed for power.

While the new member of the family was receiving much attention, Vashti consulted the Magush and Aswer on an additional law to the Mitradat enshrining Media's rule by a man and a woman. They would be the ruling family or leaders of the six Median tribes. But surprisingly, the men rejected it.

"The Prophet's word is sure. No further laws are necessary," the Magush stated. "Your own family is a shining example of unity," Aswer confirmed. Vashti shook her head, thankful that they didn't know about the disagreements between her and Ishtovigo. Her only recourse was to secretly plan to strengthen her women's army division.

As autumn cooled into winter, baby Mandane was spoiled with attention from her big sister Zerena. But in Babylon, Ishtovigo's sister was far from happy. A worrisome note from Amytis explained that Nebuchadnezzar had indeed tried to take Egypt again and had left a garrison of soldiers there claiming Pharoah Apries had surrendered to him. Then a little later a puzzling letter arrived from Amytis about another of her husband's dreams, which she recounted in detail:

After wishing all his subjects well and recognizing the blessings of the Most High god he called El Elyon, my husband had a dream which his wise men again failed to interpret, so he asked Belteshazzar to do so. In his dream, he saw the branches of a great tree spread over the whole earth. Its height reached to the heavens, and it fed and sheltered all living things. Suddenly, a yazata *came and ordered the tree be cut down, leaving a stump bound with iron to remain in the rain amongst the grass and the animals. The stump assumed a man's heart for seven years as decreed by the* yazata. *It seemed to Nebuchadnezzar that El Elyon determined who would rule the kingdoms of the world. It was all very confusing!*

Interpreting the dream, Belteshazzar explained that although the tree represented Shahan Shah Nebuchadnezzar above all the rulers of the earth, it would be cut down, and he would live with the beasts of the field for seven years until he sprouted like a revived tree. However, my husband would have to redeem himself before Most High God El Elyon by living righteously and caring for the poor.

A year later, after relatively little communication with Babylon, Vashti was about to send an envoy to the city to inquire about Nebuchadnezzar's health when Harpagos brought her a simple message from Amytis attached to the official ambassadorial report.

It read:

It is now nearly twelve months since Nebuchadnezzar's very strange dream, and he still walks round the walls of the palace, admiring the great city he has built. Belteshazzar must have been mistaken in his interpretation of my husband's dream last year.

Vashti sighed in relief, but two weeks later, another messenger bearing the lion insignia rode up to the palace entrance and immediately informed the guard he had an urgent letter for the Shahan Shah and Shahjin. On receipt of the letter from Amytis, Ishtovigo immediately summoned Vashti and his council.

"The Babylonian court is in turmoil," he declared. "Shah Nebuchadnezzar has left the palace and indeed the city of Babylon and lives in the open fields with the animals. He has not spoken words, but grunts like…a beast. He is growing long hair all over and seems convinced he is an animal."

The silence that followed was finally interrupted by the Magush. "Have the Babylonian wise men any remedies for this complaint?" he asked.

"It seems the Shah is unapproachable and unintelligent," Ishtovigo replied dourly. "Shahjin Amytis has appealed for our help. She is ruling Babylonia with the Hapiru Belteshazzar's aid." Ishtovigo glanced round the shocked council members. "The Hapiru has declared that the Shah will be sick for seven years." Remembering Amytis' account of Nebuchadnezzar's first dream, Vashti shuddered and wondered if it was coming true. But she kept her thoughts to herself as the council members considered the implications of the possible fall of Babylon.

"This situation could expose Babylonia to threats or rebellion from Egypt and Croesus of Lydia might seize the opportunity to invade Sham and join forces with Pharaoh," Harpagos warned.

"Not if Aryenis intervenes," Vashti replied.

"I don't think she has enough influence on her father," Ardela surmised, and Vashti had to concur. After further discussion, it was agreed that Media would offer every assistance possible to the court of Babylonia, and Ishtovigo dictated the commitment to the scribe.

"How will we assist when our capital cities are so far apart?" Ardela asked.

Ishtovigo looked around at the council members. "I am seeking your approval to shift the Median seat of power to Shush, which is closer to Babylon. I will propose to Amytis that from Shush I will rule both Media and Babylonia," he stated. "I believe the palace there is now fit and ready for such a role."

An audible gasp could be heard from all the council members except Aswer. "I do not wish to leave Hagmatana," Vashti replied firmly in the confused silence.

"You, Aryenis, and the children will be coming with me," Ishtovigo told her. "Aswer, Ardela, the Magush, and the rest of the council will rule the Median triangle from here. Shush is much better placed to manage both the Median shahdom and Babylonia…and…even Parsua."

Another stunned silence was followed by Ishtovigo's next announcement. "Inform Amytis and Belteshazzar that, according to our alliance, I am ready to be the acting Shahan Shah of Babylonia while Nebuchadnezzar is absent. And I will, of course, remain Shahan Shah of Media," he added.

Alarmed by Ishtovigo's presumptuousness and concerned about the practicalities of managing such a vast region, Vashti stood, acknowledged the rest of the council with a nod, and marched out.

It was pointless to disagree with Ishtovigo in public.

Chapter 37

In their private chambers, Vashti accosted him. "You are crazy to assume Amytis would agree to your proposal," she told him. "The Babylonian priests and councillors will never approve."

"We will know in a few weeks," he replied coolly. "As Shahjin, she doesn't have the authority to keep control of such a large and wealthy shahdom as Babylonia. Besides, I've heard Chief Minister Belteshazzar is more than capable of managing it, especially since he's not distracted by the needs of the Babylonian gods. I'm sure we will all work together harmoniously."

Vashti grimaced. "If Amytis approves, I insist Aswer remains with me as my advisor," she replied.

"But I thought we agreed he would stay here," Ishtovigo replied.

"There was no agreement. You stated your decision without consulting me. I was hardly going to challenge you in front of the rest of the council," Vashti stated calmly.

"Then you should have. I am not going to change my mind now. It will make me seem weak."

"No. It will make you seem wise if you follow my recommendations."

'So you think the council will listen to you instead of me?"

"It should listen to both of us."

Ishtovigo stepped menacingly closer. "You will do as I say once I am Shahan Shah of both Media and Babylonia!" he yelled, his face contorting and reddening in barely controlled anger.

Vashti stepped back. "According to Belteshazzar, Nebuchadnezzar will be sick for seven years. But Nebuchadnezzar's first dream signified that once Babylonia falls, Media will be the most powerful nation in the world," she replied calmly. "So as you say, we cannot afford to appear at all weak. Leaving Hagmatana is a sign to the rest of the world that we are divided. It's a stupid idea."

"I do not believe a madman's dreams," Ishtovigo mocked. "But Shush is the obvious choice for a world capital," he maintained.

Vashti sighed. "I will agree only if Aswer can come with me," she replied and turned to leave just as a frowning Harpagos opened the door to her husband's chambers. Stopping outside the door to listen, she heard him ask Ishtovigo if he wanted a second personal guard.

"Shah Nebuchadnezzar's illness is probably not from natural causes. Either he has been poisoned by substances unknown or a curse has been put on him," the general suggested.

But the only reply from Ishtovigo was that his ever-present Parsu advisors were enough.

Weighed down by the responsibility of ruling the Babylonian Empire, Amytis gladly accepted her brother's offer. And in Hagmatana, Vashti reluctantly began preparations to move to Shush. Since Nzdar was too old to make the long arduous journey, Daro suggested he be walked to pasture in Nisea where horse breeders would take good care of him. About this time, a deputation from Parthava arrived with tribute, and Vashti asked that she and two of her guards accompany them with Nzdar on their return journey. They gladly consented, and the party set off a few days later.

It wasn't long before Vashti's questions about Mithridates were answered by his representatives, who explained he had been crowned Shahan Shah of Parthava in Mitradatkirt, the new capital. He had not remarried, maintained he was solely dedicated to

Parthava, and did not have any women in his household apart from his mother and sister, who also acted as his advisors. Recalling Mithridates' inquiries about her marital status on her first journey east and his love for his deceased wife, she smiled inwardly.

He is indeed an extraordinary man, she thought, wondering if she had been too hasty in her reply to his veiled offer of marriage all those years ago. Many times, she had regretted the decision, but what mattered now was that the one man who truly cared for her was alive and safe. Thankful that her tears of relief and gladness fell silently on Nzdar's rug, she patted him and told him how much she loved him.

When they arrived at Nisea, Nzdar was weak and thin, but the medicago clover was in full bloom and the head horse breeder, Kikkuli, assured Vashti he would soon recover. As she prepared to leave him, happy memories of her trip to Bactria and his faithful service for over thirty years flooded back. Fixing his red, yellow, and green *golangs* for the last time, she buried her head in his gray mane and whispered a blessing for his safe journey to a *bahasht* of green pastures and cool, clear water.

"Until Frashokeriti, brother," she whispered. On reaching the bend in the road that would take him out of sight, she looked back. Nzdar lifted his head from the thick, purple-flowered grass he had been munching and whinnied enthusiastically.

He would always be her noble steed.

On the party's return to Hagmatana, Daro came out of the stables to take the travelers' horses. "Come," he said, "I have something to show you." There in Nzdar's stall was a young dapple-gray mare, with black markings. "Meet Nzdar's daughter," he enthused. "She was born while you were in Babylon and is fully trained and ready to ride. Her name is Delal."

Vashti carefully approached the neat, sturdy mare, who stamped her feet in greeting. "Delal, my darling," she said softly. The horse swished her tail and shook her head. "She is frisky," Vashti remarked, "we will need her in Shush. Send Thunder to Nisea," she instructed of the troublesome horse Ishtovigo had given her. "Tell Kikkuli he needs to complete his hardship test," she added, with a carefree laugh at the thought of the head horse trainer's dismay.

Realizing that Darayaus also did not want to leave Hagmatana, Vashti suggested he accompany her to Shush. "Dear, the Shahan Shah is going to need advisors on his new council. Why don't you ask if you can join? Now that you've completed your military training, your presence on the council would be most valuable," she encouraged.

"Thank you, Mother. I will speak to Father about it," he replied somewhat apprehensively and went off to find Ishtovigo. Vashti was left to wonder if her suggestion would lead to more family conflict, as Ishtovigo often complained that Darayaus took his mother's side when differences between his parents arose. But she had no trouble convincing Zerena to move to Shush, knowing she would never leave her father, despite the Elam fevers. Although reluctant to leave Shamin, Parwin decided to go with Vashti to Shush. But Shelna, who had become closely acquainted with a commander of the Tigers, the regiment newly assigned to protect Hagmatana, chose to remain with Ardela and Kshathrita. Without consulting Ishtovigo but recalling her dream years ago of a strange and very different palace, Vashti ordered her women warriors to prepare to decamp to Shush at a time she would specify.

Amytis continued to report no improvement in Nebuchadnezzar, who had become almost unrecognizable in his garb of long feathers and birdlike claws.

"All the incantations of the soothsayers have had no effect and Belteshazzar says he cannot do anything, as Most High god El Elyon is teaching the Shahan Shah," she wrote. "We have decided to reduce the overcrowding in the city of Babylon and prevent the outbreak of plague by making a decree to free some of the Hapiru. Please ask my brother if they can be sent to Shush. They are loyal, hardworking citizens and do not cause any problems."

Vashti replied with the following message: "Ishtovigo wants favorable inhabitants in Shush; he will accept the Hapiru."

So it was with mixed feelings that the court of Ishtovigo and Vashti separated from the other leading family members of Media and departed Hagmatana in the late spring of the couple's second regnal year.

Not long after they arrived in Shush, Ishtovigo called a council meeting and reintroduced his Parsu advisors: Kusha, Ghasem, and Admatha.

"They are needed to keep the inhabitants of the territories in the region united and loyal," he had told Vashti, who doubted the wisdom of his decision, but agreed only to keep peace with her husband.

"We will see if they are truly loyal or if they manipulate Ishtovigo against Media's interests," she wrote on the reed parchments she had asked a scribe to compile as her chronicles. "At least Harpagos' presence here with the Bears and my women's division should be enough to defend this city."

Refusing to call Shush the capital of the Medes, Vashti privately maintained Median rule would always be from Hagmatana. The Piree Magush had declared he was too infirm to relocate, but Parwin had recommended her close friend Pir Daidwand to act at the Shush court in the chief priest's stead. At the Piree's suggestion, Vashti asked Pir Daidwand to secretly contact the Median nobles in Shush about building an Atashkedah temple in the citadel.

Chapter 38

A month later, without consulting Vashti, Shahan Shah Ishtovigo made two announcements that threw the court in Shush into turmoil. With his three Parsu advisors by his side, he declared that taxes would be imposed on Media and all the provinces.

“But Shahan Shah,” Vashti protested, “the rains have lessened, and the crops are poor in some of the provinces. This will cause hardship for the people and perhaps even unrest.”

Ignoring her comment, Ishtovigo continued. “And in recognition of our sovereignty over all the lands of the Medes and the Babylonians, we will reveal our greatness to the world over the next six months. Our new and superior capital will allow our wealth to be easily viewed by the representatives of all the subject nations,” he explained. “Let these celebrations reflect our marvelous engineering and cultural achievements.” He paused for effect, but all except the Parsu were grim-faced. “Soon messengers will be sent to the provinces of Babylonia and Media that we rule inviting them to Shush,” he continued. “We must prepare to make them most welcome.”

Aswer opened his mouth to reply but was interrupted by the Parsu, Kusha, who stood closest to the Shahan Shah. “All the details will be arranged by Ghasem and myself,” Kusha informed the council.

Vashti caught the eye of Harpagos standing on the other side of Ishtovigo. He frowned and narrowed his eyes in protest. She acknowledged the gesture with a slight nod. “Shahan Shah, will the rulers and their representatives be bringing their wives?" she asked.

"Of course, and their attendants," Ishtovigo replied.

The three Parsu smirked. "We will assist you to prepare for the women's entertainment and the necessary banquets," Kusha told Vashti, "while their husbands are busy with affairs of state."

Vashti groaned inwardly. All those hours of court gossip, the antics of children, and the latest silks from the land of Sina, she thought. I hope Amytis will come.

Pir Daidwand requested permission to speak, and it was given. "Shahan Shah, will all the temples in the city be on display?"

"Yes. You will meet with the other priests and guide our guests to their places of worship."

"But Shahan Shah, the Atashkedah in the city is still under construction," the Pir noted.

"Then I will order my builders to make sure the temple is finished before our visitors arrive," Ishtovigo replied.

"You are most generous, Shahan Shah," the priest answered with a bow. Concerned that Darayaus had said nothing throughout the meeting, Vashti smiled reassurance at him. He responded with a grimace, which Ishtovigo ignored before dismissing all the council members except the Parsu. Outside the chamber, Harpagos approached Vashti and requested an urgent meeting in her chambers. Overhearing the invitation, Darayaus asked to attend.

"The Parsu cannot be trusted," Harpagos stated when they met a few minutes later, and he had received the approval of Vashti's guard.

"Dear Mother, I fear they want to take over Media," Darayaus asserted. "What can be done to stop them?"

"Do not be concerned," Vashti told both men. "We have the support of all the leading Medes in the city. After suffering Ishtovigo's duplicity while he was building this palace, they signed a *dat* of loyalty to Shahan Shah Hovakhshatra. Now they refuse to do so with my husband but have declared their loyalty to me."

Vashti glanced at Harpagos, who did not comment. She wondered why, but it wasn't the time to ask. "What is your opinion of the new council, General?" she inquired instead.

"Ishtovigo is placing us in a difficult and possibly dangerous position. We know that over a hundred years ago Achaemenes of Parsua wanted to control Media. But I think we are safe for now as the Parsu still do not have the military power to threaten us."

"It would only take one traitor," Darayaus commented.

"Or three," Vashti added in reference to Kusha, Ghasem, and Admatha. "I will ask Aswer to get the Parsu advisors' confidence to determine where their loyalties really lie. If either of you hears anything that might threaten our shahdom, please inform me immediately."

"Should we let Grandmother know?" Darayaus asked.

"No. We do not want to worry her. But I will send a message to General Biraxeas to investigate any report of suspicious activity in Hagmatana. I will also send spies to Pasargadae to determine if the Parsu are preparing militarily," Vashti replied.

Harpagos hesitated then spoke. "Shahjin, we are bound to follow the Shahan Shah's wishes."

"Yes," Vashti replied, "but not if he violates the laws of the Medes…and the Parsu. Each of us is bound first by the Mitradat."

Harpagos nodded and Darayaus agreed. "Mother," Darayaus continued, "would you give me the honor of assisting Pir Daidwand with the completion of the Atashkedah?"

"Of course, dear," Vashti replied, "that's one less responsibility for me. Since your father has now taken an interest in the building, you can keep him informed as to its progress. I only ask that it be completed in time for the wedding of Aunt Parwin and the Pir. In the absence of our other family members, I have given them permission to marry."

Darayaus offered his thanks and hurried off, leaving Harpagos to bow and ask to take his leave.

That afternoon, Vashti visited her women warriors in the barracks she had allocated them inside the citadel near the Bears' quarters. Half the troop was practicing hand-to-hand combat with new techniques learned from travelers from the land of Sina while the other half repeatedly pushed themselves up from the horizontal position in between juggling iron weights to the beat of a drum. Vashti thought she caught a glimpse of Khezmet in the back row but shook her head when she remembered she had just left her in her chambers. A surprise was Shirat, the Athorayan from Babylon, whose father Vashti had found work for at the palace. Everything came to a halt when the women realized their commander was present, but Vashti told them to resume and summoned Irdabama and Pentaya.

"Shush is less safe than Hagmatana," she told them. "Even though we seem to have the support of the Medes in Shush, I feel the need to ensure our safety here more surely. I know I can trust you both completely, which is why what I am about to ask you might put you and some of your sisters in considerable danger."

Neither Irdabama nor Pentaya looked uneasy.

"You can accept this mission yourselves or choose some of your most trusted sisters," Vashti went on. "Volunteers will be required to infiltrate the homes of Parsu leaders in Shush to find out who is loyal to Ishtovigo and who isn't."

"And what about those loyal to you?" Irdabama asked.

"Give me their names, and I will pass them on to Aswer. They might be needed in future." Vashti regarded each of the women carefully. "You could find yourselves in the households of men plotting to destroy Media. If they discover who you really are…"

There was a hesitant silence then Irdabama looked at Pentaya who nodded. "Commander, we are ready," she confirmed.

"Please await further instructions," Vashti ordered and turned quickly to leave so they could not see the tears in her eyes. Her heart thumped.

Kusha, Ghasem, and Admatha could have them hanged the same day they are caught, she thought. But now Aswer must choose men to work for us in Pasargadae.

Within a few months, the simple stone Atashkedah of Shush with its double-arched entrance was completed next to the women's barracks. Without Vashti's knowledge, Khezmet and Parwin secretly trained with her women warriors while two others, posing as Athorayan servants under Shirat's instructions, chose to embed themselves within the local community. When the two others' first report was presented by Khezmet and Parwin, Vashti was shocked.

"How do you two know the Parsu you have listed are loyal to us?" she asked.

"Darling," Parwin explained, "I could not leave you to fight this battle alone, so I joined Irdabama and Pentaya."

"And I've been training early mornings and late nights when the children are asleep," Khezmet added.

"Our strength is together," Parwin said solemnly.

Closing her eyes tightly to hold in her tears, Vashti hugged and kissed them both. "*Zors spas*, my beloved sisters. We must be very careful until we know more about the Parsu." Then she summoned Aswer, who had nothing to report but asked for more funds for the spies in Pasargadae. After writing a note to the treasury guard giving Aswer access to the funds, she was annoyed when her advisor soon returned claiming he was barred from entering by Kusha's assistant.

"We will see about that," she uttered between gritted teeth. "It is now time to approach the Shahan Shah."

Ishtovigo was entertaining Aryenis, and Zerena and Mandane were playing together at their parents' feet when Vashti asked Harpagos to interrupt him about an urgent matter of state. On entering the cool quiet of Ishtovigo's chamber, she found him lounging on his favorite silver couch. When he made a point of holding out the golden scepter to Vashti, she felt like grabbing it and throwing it back at him but decided to humor him by touching it lightly.

"Dearest wife," he crooned salaciously, "what brings you here this warm spring day? Another urgent issue I'm told. What can be disturbing your fine head and your sculptured visage on such a day?"

Wondering if he was drunk again, Vashti took a moment to consider her reply. "Shahan Shah, it pains me to inform you that I have discovered a problem with the treasury door."

"Then get the locksmith to fix it," Ishtovigo ordered.

"It is not that type of problem, Shahan Shah. Kusha has the only key, and his assistant will not allow Aswer access."

"I authorised Kusha," Ishtovigo replied.

"Then I am asking that Aswer be given a key on my behalf."

"Dear, the Atashkedah is complete. What do you want more funds for?"

"Shahan Shah, I want funds to help protect Media as I carry out my duties as coruler of our shahdom," Vashti stated coolly.

"But Media is not under threat," he countered.

"It might be if a Parsu can prevent my access to the treasury," she replied.

"Kusha only acts under my orders, and I am the first line of defense of Media," he insisted.

"Are you sure you can trust Kusha?" she asked.

"Why do you always doubt me?" Ishtovigo's voice was beginning to rise.

"I am not Shahan Shah, but I'm asking you not to let any other person or power attempt to undermine my authority," she went on coolly.

Ishtovigo rose from his couch. "No one rules Media and Babylonia but me!" he yelled. "And you will not change that… ever."

"That is not the way of your father, the great Hovakhshatra," Vashti replied calmly.

Ishtovigo rose from his couch as if to threaten her but seeing Harpagos quickly move to intervene, he abruptly sat down. "It is my way," he growled, "and you will obey it. My father is dead and cannot help you now." Vashti looked at Harpagos, who remained stone-faced. Realizing it was once again useless to argue with her husband, she turned on her heel and marched out without replying, his wine infested breath following her. "And neither will anyone else," he shouted.

Chapter 39

Vashti hurried to her chambers, called for Aswer, and asked him to get the key to the treasury door from Kusha's assistant.

"But, Shahjin, how am I to do this?" he asked, his forehead creased in puzzlement. "He carries the key everywhere in a pouch around his neck."

"Invite him to a banquet with wine and tell him how much you admire the Parsus' work for the Shahan Shah. I will ask one of my women to entertain you both with music and dance while you get him so drunk that he falls asleep. Remove the key and take it to the palace locksmith early the next day to make a copy. Bring the copy to me and ask Kusha to another banquet that night. Then place the original key on the floor of the banquet chamber where Kusha will find it when he arrives."

Aswer stared at her in amazement. "Shahjin, the key is a cubit long. What will I do if Kusha wakes up before I remove the key from him?"

"You will offer him more wine and tell him the banquet is not yet over."

Aswer shook his head and went off, wondering if he would survive the task the Shahjin had set him.

◆❦◆

A few days later, when Aswer brought the precious key to Vashti, she congratulated him and told him to use it to get a bag of silver coins with which to pay the spies in Pasagardae. But she did not venture into the treasury herself. She knew how much wasn't there, and that, besides the stables in Hagmatana, more of Media's wealth from Lydia was hidden elsewhere. Then she wrote to Amytis telling her about the planned celebrations in Shush and the influence of the Parsu at court.

Amytis's return letter stated that Nebuchadnezzar's condition had still not improved and that she was training Amel-Marduk to take his father's place should he not survive the illness that beset him. Concerned about her brother's behavior, she wrote that Babylonia was on full military alert and might choose not to help Media if it was attacked. Finally, she and Belteshazzar would decline the invitation to Ishtovigo's celebrations due to Nebuchadnezzar's illness.

Her cousin's reply brought little comfort to Vashti, who messaged back that the Parsu influence meant Media might not be able to guarantee support to Babylonia. With Ishtovigo unwilling to discuss such matters with her, Vashti asked Aswer to speak to him about delaying the celebrations until Nebuchadnezzar's predicted seven years of affliction had passed.

"Suggest that our enemies might take advantage of the festivities to attack," Vashti told him. But Aswer reported the next day that the Shahan Shah would not listen and was determined to carry out his plan.

It was time to confront her husband…again. She sent her request to meet him in the throne room without any advisors and was notified that he would see her the following day at noon. When she arrived, Harpagos greeted her outside and raised his eyebrows in warning.

"The Shahan Shah is somewhat ill-disposed today," he declared.

"Is he sick?" Vashti asked.

"No, not really," Harpagos replied, shaking his head. "Call me if there is trouble."

Bracing herself for conflict, Vashti entered the overheated room where Ishtovigo sat on his silver-covered ivory throne. Taking a deep breath, she stepped onto the lowest of the six stone bear adorned steps that ascended to both his throne and hers. Much to her annoyance, Kusha was in attendance. He handed Ishtovigo the golden scepter, which was held out to her. As she touched it, he smiled lasciviously.

"What brings you here my most beautiful wife?" he asked.

His question rankled her because Ishtovigo now openly referred to his numerous other wives, acquired ostensibly for diplomatic reasons, along with concubines who had caught his eye and now occupied his 'second women's house'. It did nothing to make her feel that she was at all worthy or attractive to him.

Ignoring the slight, she attempted to speak but reeled back to avoid the blast of his wine-ridden breath. "Firstly, I request my lawful place beside you as coruler of Media," she stated calmly.

"Cer…tainly…come closer, my love," Ishtovigo urged, leaning unsteadily toward her as she took the last few steps to the identical throne beside him.

"Shahan Shah," Vashti continued calmly, "please ask your advisor to leave us."

"Kusha is party to all my affairs," Ishtovigo replied, sitting up suddenly. "He stays."

Vashti sighed inwardly. "At least, according to the Mitradat, my husband will confirm any decisions he makes while drunk once he is sober," she reminded herself. "Very well, dear," she answered.

"What is your request, then, my most pre…cious Shahjin?" Ishtovigo asked.

"Shahan Shah, with the increase of our responsibilities while Babylonia is under our rule, do you still think it wise to expose any potential enemies to knowledge of the riches and glorious splendor of Media?"

Kusha frowned and asked permission to speak, which was given. "Shahan Shah, may I say this is the greatest opportunity Media has had since the whole region came under our control?" he queried, his wicked eyes narrowing and his thin lips curling in a sly smile. "It might never happen again."

Ishtovigo's eyes wandered as he considered the question. "Then…the cel…ebrations must go ahead," he eventually replied.

Incensed by Kusha's interruption, Vashti clenched her fists and held her breath.

"Dear, let us draw lots to decide the matter," she suggested, flashing her most winning smile. When Ishtovigo nodded, it was taken as agreement, but she wondered if he was falling asleep. "Please make the numbers even," she requested, and Kusha hurried out to get the tile lots.

Pir Daidwand was called to hold the pouch containing the tiles, and each was taken under his watchful gaze. When Kusha picked the shortest tile, he couldn't contain his triumphant grin, and immediately announced the commencement of the arrangements.

Vashti left but not before loudly insisting that the house near the palace where women were kept and prepared to serve the Shahan Shah was a shame and that it should be closed while important visitors were in the city. Harpagos and the Pir agreed while the Shahan Shah and Kusha took no notice.

Mainly because Ishtovigo had fallen asleep.

Over the next five and a half months, shahs and emissaries arrived from Lydia in the west to Hindush in the east. Unexpected was a delegation from the far-off land of Hellas on the islands of the Great Sea. The emissary's wife sought Vashti and enthusiastically informed her that the Apadana Hall above the palace near the treasury reminded her of the acropolis of Athena in her home city. Impressed by her compliment, Vashti offered to show her the Atashkedah.

When they met the following day at the home of the Magush next to the temple, the Hellene was not so gracious.

"Such a simple building for your god," she remarked after Pir Daidwand had shown her the outside of the building. "How do the people ever feel safe without protection from gods like Zeus, Heracles, and Ares who we revere?" she asked.

"If Auramazda needs help, we have our forces," Vashti replied without mentioning the Bear regiment stationed next to the palace. "The Shahan Shah's Median and Parsu advisors live in the houses," she added, pointing to the buildings surrounding the palace in another effort to impress her guest.

"I've heard you have women warriors," the Hellene woman remarked with a derisive smile. "I suppose they practice their climbing skills up the cliff below the temple."

"Six days out of seven. They are always ready to defend Media," Vashti replied coolly. She was beginning to dislike the haughty Hellene.

The woman's face fell. "We only allow men in our army. We women are expected to raise sons for Hellas' fighting forces," she sneered.

"We raise sons and daughters for peace in Media and all that are in its lands," Vashti replied firmly, reminding herself uncomfortably of the Prophet's three maxims.

"Ah, daughters," the Hellene replied, the ribbons in her fair hair fluttering as she nodded. "We understand men in Media have no less than five wives."

Vashti felt the blood rush to her face. "That is not our practice, except for the rare case of our alliances," she snapped, suddenly disconcertingly aware that she was straying into *druj*.

"Then who are the women living in the house behind the palace?"

Vashti glared at her guest. "That is the business of the Shahan Shah and Shahjin of Media," she replied, even more annoyed that the house was so visible to international guests. "You are welcome to visit the public buildings of the citadel, but other places are private. Would you like to see inside the Atashkedah?" she offered in a more subdued voice.

The woman pulled her cloak tighter over her dull peplos and sniffed. "No, thank you. I hear they have fires burning, and smoke makes me cough." Vashti signaled her carriage driver and ushered her guest into the vehicle. Nothing was said on the return journey to the Hellene's quarters beneath the Apadana.

Not all the wives of the shahs journeying to Shush with their husbands were so unpleasant. The wife of the Shah of Hindush, whose bright gown reflected the colors Vashti preferred to wear, presented her with a gift of a female goddess figure whose fanlike headdress matched her generous robe. Thankfully, the barrier between Aryenis and her brother's wife was broken by Mandane, who attached herself to her aunt with much affection. When Vashti later asked Aryenis if the Lydians had spread *druj* to the Hellenes about marriage practices in Media, she strongly denied it.

Each week, Vashti examined the guest list to see if the Parthavans had arrived, but each time she was disappointed until Aswer told her Arsaces had just presented himself. Hurrying to her window, she saw the familiar two humped Bactrian camels being led away by the emissary's servants. "Ask Arsaces to attend my chambers as soon as he has finished the Shahan Shah's tour," she directed Aswer.

That night, Vashti dreamed she was once more in Parthava and free, but Mithridates did not appear in any of her visions.

Finally, later the next day, Khezmet announced Arsaces was outside her chambers. The acrid smell of ganja smoke wafted from the Parthavan as he entered, and she was suddenly transported to a huge fire on a brilliant Norouz night. When she grasped Arsaces' hand in greeting the rippling tones of a minstrel's tanbur strings accompanying a love song came back to her, and she recalled the softness of another hand on that magical night in Rhagae.

"Most gracious Shahjin, greetings from Shah Mithridates," Arsaces declared. "He sends this small token of his appreciation and apologizes for his absence." He handed her a heavy, intricately carved sandalwood box. Although it was against protocol, Vashti opened the box to find a small carved bust of a finely chiseled woman's face topped by a slim blue cap banded in gold.

"Shah Mithridates acquired this sculpture of Shahjin Nefertiti of Egypt when he visited that land," Arsaces explained.

Vashti stood speechless while the kindly Arsaces waited. Finally, she spoke. "Tell the revered Shah the Shahjin of Media is forever in his debt," she replied softly. Arsaces assented, bowed, and left, promising to always be at her service.

Alone in her chamber with the sculpture, Vashti opened the box again to find a fine parchment sheet inscribed in Avestan. "For you I would sacrifice even the presence of your likeness," Mithridates had written. Cradling her head in her hands, she wept quietly, her tears falling on the ornate box.

The enemy Angra Mainyu stalks the halls of the palace, and I have so few allies and such a small force, she thought, but in Parthava I still have a dear and loyal friend.

Khezmet returned from the women's barracks early in the morning to find Vashti lying on a damp pillow. A dream of the sweet valleys of Ariavarta had just strengthened her for the battle she sensed was soon to happen.

Chapter 40

Throughout the celebrations, Vashti did not respond to Ishtovigo's numerous invitations to attend his all-male tours and banquets. Immediately after refusing her request to suspend the festivities, he had appointed four more Parsu advisors. With the thought of being treated primarily as his showpiece before his guests, and her wishes as Shahjin still being ignored, she continued to absent herself. Aswer's placatory messages on her behalf failed to assuage Ishtovigo's mounting anger, prompting Harpagos to advise her to attend at least some of the tours. But determined to be heard first, she kept refusing.

For the final week of festivities, Ishtovigo invited only the officials of the citadel and asked Vashti to hold a banquet in the palace for the women. She agreed but expressed her doubts to Khezmet and Aswer.

"Why has the Shahan Shah invited all, both great and small, to these celebrations?" she asked. "He has hardly shown concern for the common people and his servants before."

"Shahjin," Aswer replied, "we must be very careful. Since the Parsu have gained even more power at court, and they are strong in Anshan and Parsua, this unusual event could be exploited by them."

"Dear, there is something else you should know," Khezmet added. "As you instructed, I visited our sisters in the city. Irdabama is well but says she has not seen Pentaya for many days."

"Does Irdabama know why?" Vashti asked anxiously, regretting that she had not allowed her spies to take weapons.

"No. She only said that the Parsu Pentaya is working for is particularly harsh."

"Then I will look for her myself right now," Vashti declared, reaching for her cloak.

"I would not advise that, Shahjin," Aswer declared. "It could endanger the other spies."

"It seems they are already experiencing danger," Vashti replied sharply. "Find me some town dweller's clothes," she ordered Khezmet.

That evening, wearing plain *chokha* and *pantol* and with her hair hidden within a man's *kulaw-u-dastmal*, Vashti lowered herself down the citadel wall under the Atashkedah and entered the city in search of Pentaya. Eventually, as Irdabama had described, she found her working in her "master's" bakery. Vashti waited her turn to buy bread from Pentaya, who gave no sign of recognition of her commander.

"There will be a full moon tonight," Vashti remarked as she handed Pentaya a small bronze coin in payment. Pentaya nodded and replied that she would watch it later. It was the signal to meet outside the Atashkedah where the women warriors would gather with their commander on moonlit nights to view the celestial body in all its bright glory.

A few hours later, Pentaya arrived panting. "I must hurry back to the Parsu's house before his servants discover I am no longer in the squalid room where he keeps me," she explained. "Before I was confined there, I noticed many Parsu, other foreigners, and some of our people visiting my master's home. I heard them say they are making weapons and training soldiers."

"Where?" Vashti asked, concerned that Medes she thought loyal were mingling with Parsu.

Pentaya shook her head. "I don't know."

Grimacing, Vashti paced the stone floor.

"Find out if the Medes are really traitors or spying on the Parsu for us," she ordered.

"Vishtaspa and Hamayun the captive are the foreigners," Pentaya replied.

"Any Hapiru, Athorayans, or Babylonians?" Vashti asked.

"None that I know of, Commander."

Vashti took a double-sided knife from her sash. "Use this to protect yourself," she ordered. "And please, if it doesn't put you in any more danger, find out which Parsu are conspiring against us."

"But how, Commander?" Pentaya asked.

Vashti wanted to avoid Pentaya's innocent eyes set in her cheerily round face, but she couldn't. She was dealing with *druj* that could be deadly. "Smile sweetly at your master and ask if he has any other work for you."

"Yes, Commander," Pentaya replied readily, but her eyes blinked uncertainty. "For Media," she added, her confident tone belying any sense of danger.

Vashti hugged Pentaya's small, solid frame tightly. "Hurry back to your post, my dear," she urged, swallowing the lump in her throat. "And may the *yazatas* protect you." Pentaya nodded, turned away, and disappeared into the shadowy night.

Vashti returned quickly to the palace, entered through the servants' door, and hurried to her chambers to consider what she should do next, if anything. The oil lamps were burning low when she decided to write a note to Kambujiya of Anshan, informing him of a possible Parsu insurrection in Shush and explaining such an action would bring war between Media and Anshan.

"Kambujiya pledged loyalty to us when Aswer visited him," she told herself as she rolled the parchment and sealed it with the insignia of the bear. "This will test it."

The next morning, she asked Khezmet to deliver the letter to Harpagos for immediate dispatch to Anshan. Four days later, she received a reply sealed with the image of the falcon.

My dear Shahjin Vashti

I have no knowledge of a potential uprising either in Media or Anshan, but should I discover any such treachery, I will take immediate steps to crush it. You and Shahan Shah Ishtovigo can rely on my loyalty to Media. Together we are strong.

Your servant
Kambujiya of Anshan

He seems to follow the word of the Prophet, Vashti thought, and I have not known him to commit *druj*. Now I must wait.

Two nights later, she was woken urgently by Khezmet. "Dear, there has been an incident in the city. Pentaya is dead."

Vashti sat straight up, wide awake. "Where? Who told you?"

"Irdabama came to the barracks while I was night training," Khezmet explained then put her hands over her face and burst into tears. "She…she said she had gone to visit Pentaya at the Parsu's home and that when she arrived the servants were carrying her body out," her maid sobbed. "They…they told her they found Pentaya in her master's chamber with a two-sided dagger through her heart."

Vashti gasped as stabbing pain ripped through her own chest. "Where were they taking her?" she rasped.

"They would not say, only that they were acting under their master's orders," Khezmet replied before sitting down heavily on the end of Vashti's bed.

"We will retrieve the body," Vashti vowed, her voice still croaky, "or every Parsu in this city will be expelled…or worse. Does Irdabama know what happened to the dagger?" she asked, supposing it was the one she had given Pentaya.

"Irdabama said one of the other male servants told her he had seized it. She thinks the servant is one of us. She went back to the Parsu's house to get the dagger, but it was too heavily guarded."

"Irdabama was brave," Vashti spat. "And we must be very careful now. That servant could be an enemy spy trying to entrap us. Call Aswer," she ordered.

Within a few minutes, a sleepy Aswer arrived and was informed of the situation. "This calls for the immediate apprehension and arrest of the Parsu baker, a curfew in the city, and a house-to-house search," Vashti declared without seeking advice. "Summon Harpagos."

Khezmet hurried out again, and Aswer regarded Vashti warily. "Shahjin, I suggest you ask Harpagos to investigate further. If only a few Parsu are involved, such measures could cause unnecessary mistrust, even unrest, in their community."

"Aswer," she replied sternly, "a member of the Median forces has been murdered. We will not take this lightly. And we should be on the alert for a possible attack."

"But Shush is hardly of strategic value, considering it is quite distant from Babylon and Hagmatana," Aswer replied warily.

"Precisely," Vashti replied tersely. "Shush is midway between both cities. Control of it is key. And despite the apparent neutrality of Arsamnes of Parsua, I believe the Parsu advisors' influence on my husband could threaten the security of Media."

"Shahjin," Aswer continued calmly, "the Shahan Shah's tours and feasts have strengthened relations with all the provinces, including Babylonia, but they have been tiring. Let us patiently and cautiously wait for the results of Harpagos' inquiries. We don't want to upset those like Shah Arsamnes whom we would wish to make allies."

The door opened, and a fully armed Harpagos burst in, just a little more slowly than usual. After Vashti explained the situation and Aswer gave his advice, Harpagos was of one opinion only.

"Arrest the Parsu baker immediately," he declared. "Once he is in our custody, we will find ways to make him tell us where

Pentaya's body is and the location of the rest of the conspirators and their weapons."

Vashti nodded. "Take Irdabama with you," she commanded. "Report to me immediately after you have carried out my orders and make sure you retrieve the dagger that killed Pentaya." Harpagos strode out, and Aswer was given permission to leave after being cautioned to tell no one of the attack on Pentaya.

Khezmet stood gazing at Vashti. "Dear, I must tell you something else," she said, her voice shaky."

"Yes, dear, what is it?" Vashti replied, struggling to keep her own voice steady.

"Uh, Irdabama said P-Pentaya's *pantol* was torn, and she was badly beaten."

Vashti shook her fist at the ceiling. "Any man who so defiles a woman of Media must answer to me," she vowed through gritted teeth. "I will find him myself and personally make sure he takes no more breaths once my dagger pierces *his* heart."

"No, sister," Khezmet pleaded. "Pentaya would not want you endangered to avenge her death. We do not know how strong the Parsu here really are."

"Her death is a loss for all of us," Vashti yelled, shaking her fist again. "The women of my regiment will want nothing less than full retribution."

Khezmet grabbed Vashti's arm and gently lowered it. "Dear, you are right, but we are in a delicate position," she replied calmly. "You must think clearly now. Much depends on your decisions… and your actions."

Vashti stared back at her maid and breathed in deeply. "Dearest Khezmet, you are right. I must keep my temper."

"Yes. It is what the Prophet would do," Khezmet concurred, grabbing a cloth, and wetting it with cool water from the chamber's spring water fountain. "So you must," she urged, placing it on Vashti's forehead.

The two women sat in silence until Vashti began to sob. When Khezmet put her arm around her mistress, the two wept together until, unable to restrain themselves any longer, they gave themselves up to ear-piercing wails of grief.

Nearby, their unseen *yazatas* lowered their wings in mourning.

Chapter 41

Harpagos returned the next day with Pentaya's body. To keep the loss secret from any conspirators in the city, Vashti ordered her earthen burial close to her living sisters in a secret tomb beneath their barracks. Vashti and Irdabama solemnly wrapped their precious sister's body in one of Vashti's silken robes. Then they stood two arms' lengths from her and held each end of a white cloth over the body to keep the spirit connection of *paiwand* between them all.

Then, with uplifted hands, Pir Daidwand prayed: "We beseech, O Mazda, first and foremost this, the abiding joy of Spenta Mainyu, your holy mind. Grant that we perform all actions in harmony with the righteousness of your divine law and acquire the wisdom of the good mind so that we may bring happiness to the Soul of the Universe."

Then Vashti and her women warriors returned silently to their quarters before breaking into the deep wails of mourning.

For three days, Vashti did not eat nor did she sleep in her bed. In between dozing on her couch and pacing her chamber, she awaited the results of Harpagos' investigations. The city remained eerily quiet under the dark of the moon as the Bears searched every building. Finally, Harpagos reported that he had apprehended Pentaya's Parsu master who, under "considerable persuasion," eventually admitted to murdering her.

"How was he persuaded?" Vashti asked. Harpagos hesitated and Vashti raised her eyebrows in query.

"We applied the thumb screws."

"For how long?"

"Until he confessed."

"We do not torture our captives," she retorted.

"Not like the Athorayans, at least the Parsu still has his skin," Harpagos replied dourly.

"Never again," she ordered. "Did you find the other weapons?"

"The killer told us of two hiding places apart from the house where Pentaya was killed. One in the city and one in the mountains. We have seized all the weapons in the city and are still searching for those in the mountains. A Hapiru named Hegai is assisting us. He gave me this." Harpagos took Vashti's dagger from his sash. "He said it was used to kill Pentaya."

"Give it to me," Vashti demanded.

"Is it yours, Shahjin?"

"I gave it to Pentaya for her protection."

Harpagos opened his mouth to speak then closed it momentarily. "Shahjin, your women are not ready for such a weapon."

"General Harpagos, as the co-commander of all the Median forces, I will decide how my women warriors are armed. Irdabama and Pentaya proved themselves more than capable of fighting for Media on the Lydian front. There is no reason why they cannot protect us here."

"How many of your regiment are you willing to sacrifice to solve this Parsu problem?" Harpagos demanded far too impertinently in the presence of his commander.

"No more because your men are going to capture the rest of the rebels," she cried. "And remember, every one of my fighters is a volunteer. Irdabama and Pentaya chose to accept the mission I offered them as did two others who are still in the city. They were not ordered on such an assignment. Now I'm ordering you to choose members of the Bears to patrol the city and report any suspicious activity."

Harpagos nodded. “As you wish, Commander,” he replied, but his tone lacked conviction. “I remain at your service but ask to be informed about threats anywhere else in our shahdom.”

“Of course, we will stay vigilant and in daily communication. Find out if my three women in the city know who Vishtaspa and Hamayun the captive are, if they are connected to Ishtovigo’s advisors, and what they are doing that might endanger us,” she ordered. “Have you interviewed Hegai?”

“No, Shahjin. We were concentrating on finding the weapons.”

“Bring Hegai to the palace for an audience with me as soon as possible.”

“Certainly, Shahjin. I will do so tomorrow.”

“The day after, Pentaya’s murderer will face judgment. If found guilty, he will be executed by my regiment,” she instructed, dismissing Harpagos with a wave of her hand.

Hegai the Hapiru shook in his sandals. He had been told by his Parsu master that the Medes were a harsh, vicious people, ready to execute captives at the slightest sign of rebellion. The Parsu had also told him and the other servants that the Shahjin was the worst of the two rulers, and that when on her throne she would lance anyone who approached her if she decided not to hold out her silver scepter.

Hegai thanked Yehovah god for his life and that he had no family to leave behind should he not survive his meeting with Shahjin Vashti then followed Harpagos down a marble floored corridor. When the guard opened the door, Hegai saw no throne nor was a scepter visible. The beautiful woman who stood gazing out the white curtained window of her pink plaster-lined chamber turned and smiled at him. When her smile faded, little lines on her forehead and below her cheeks appeared, and her green eyes were edged with sadness.

Surely this cannot be the Shahjin, he thought.

"Thank you for coming to see me," Vashti began. "Are you Hegai, who found my Pentaya dead?"

Hegai trembled again. Was she going to accuse him of the murder? "Y-yes, Shahjin," he stuttered on finding his voice.

"And did you give General Harpagos the dagger that killed her?"

Hegai nodded, desperately hoping he was not digging his grave.

"Did you see your master kill Pentaya?" Vashti continued.

"N-no, Shahjin. I was about to bring my master more wine when I heard a cry from his chamber."

"Go on," Vashti urged softly.

"I…I raced in to see him standing over the w-woman who worked in the b-bakery lying on the floor w-with a dagger in her chest," he gabbled. "The P-Parsu, h-he was known to have used her." Hegai hung his head. "I am s-sorry, Shahjin."

"What was my Pentaya wearing?" Vashti asked.

Hegai looked away and gulped. "The cl-clothes she was killed in were bloody and torn. My master was lying still, cut, bruised, and groaning. I closed the door, but my master yelled for one of the women servants. The servant shrieked when she saw your fr-friend and ran away. So I…I put a rug over her." He lowered his eyes. "The master's wife was not home, so I carried her out with the help of another male servant," he went on, finally lifting his gaze.

"In the courtyard, we saw a strange woman watching us who left quickly." His voice shook again. "Sh-Shahjin, this was a terrible crime."

Vashti wiped her tears away with her hand. "Thank you for looking after my dear sister, Hegai," she replied softly. "Did you see or hear your master harming her?"

"I did not see him, but I heard cries and thumps coming from the room…then the woman's scream," Hegai continued, more composed. "She was usually very quiet in the house, but she was absent for days at a time. I thought she went back to her family. She never even told me her name. Is that because she was your sister, Shahjin?"

"Yes. She was my sister in arms, but not born of my family." Hegai looked confused. "The women of Media are all sisters," Vashti explained. Hegai nodded, but his glazed eyes reflected puzzlement.

"I am going to ask the Shahan Shah to take you into his service as a reward for your honesty," Vashti announced.

Hegai's heart leaped. He would escape the Parsu's horrible grip! "Sh-Shahjin, I am forever indebted to you," he blurted.

"No. It is I who am indebted to you, Hegai. Return to your master until an officer of the regiment is sent for you. If you notice anything suspicious while you are still in his home, remember what it is and tell the officer as soon as he arrives. My guard will escort you out now."

Hegai mumbled thanks and marched out to the waiting Harpagos, his head held high as he praised his god.

After calling Khezmet to touch up her tearstained face, she summoned Aswer to inform him of her decision and arrange for the new servant's admission to the palace. Then she sent Khezmet into the city to find the women spies and make sure they were safe. It wasn't enough to entrust the welfare of her precious three to Harpagos' men.

Chapter 42

When Khezmet entered Vashti's chamber the next morning with her breakfast, she found her mistress entwined in her Egyptian flax sheets and still sound asleep.

"Wake up, Shahjin," she urged, placing a tray of barley bread, citron fruits, and *mast* on the silver table beside Vashti's bed. "It's banquet day."

"Did you find our three sisters in the city?" Vashti asked sleepily, rubbing eyes that had not enjoyed much sleep.

"Yes. They are back in the barracks awaiting your command about Pentaya's murderer."

"That will have to wait until after the banquet," Vashti commented, surprised that they had returned without her orders but understanding why. Still disturbed by a dream that her crown headdress could not be found, she yawned, rolled over, and asked how many women were coming to the banquet.

"At least thirty," Khezmet replied.

Vashti grimaced. "Except for Aryenis, I do not fancy sitting down with my husband's other wives."

Khezmet frowned. "Yes, but it is only for one day. Tomorrow you will be free. And Aryenis will assist most amicably while Debyar can easily make conversation with anyone. Today is also important for Zerena. She will be attending her first women's banquet."

"Forgive me, dear. Against the word of the Prophet, I am afraid my thoughts are sometimes not good," she confessed before reaching for her sacred parchments on the shelf above her bed. "But yesterday, I clearly informed Ishtovigo I would not entertain his concubines. It is beneath my station to do so," she added vehemently.

"This shows that your words and deeds are good," Khezmet replied with a reassuring smile.

Vashti sat up, beckoned Khezmet to come closer, and hugged her. "Thank you, my darling and my closest friend. What would I do without you?"

"Without me, you would still be strong," Khezmet replied confidently.

Vashti sighed. "This is the last day of my husband's festivities. Tomorrow, I will take a ride in the mountains outside the city." Still uneasy about her dream, she stopped leafing through her parchments. "Khezmet, please take my crown headdress from its box. I wish to make sure it is ready."

"Of course, dear. I cleaned it yesterday."

Khezmet removed a carved wooden box from a cedarwood chest. "Here it is." She lifted the lapis-lazuli and garnet-studded headdress from its silk-lined bed. "Bright as new."

Vashti sighed again; this time in relief. My dream must not have been important, she thought. For three years, the crown had been the sign of her rulership, which had seemed secure until recently. To further quell her anxiety, she asked Khezmet to summon Darayaus, who had been assisting his father with the foreign visitors but had refused to attend the last week of celebrations due to the raucous behavior of those who overindulged in wine.

After Khezmet left to prepare her bath, Vashti still couldn't forget her dream. She didn't know why, but it reminded her of a story Father Cica told her when she was a little girl about the legendary rescue of young girls held captive in a mountain cave. She was still deep in thought when Khezmet called her to the bathhouse.

As she followed her maid down the long corridor, her uneasiness almost dissipated. The chief cook shouting instructions over clanging pots and pans, the savory aroma of herbed lamb, and the sweet smell of sesame and honey date cakes wafting from the kitchen assured her preparations for the banquet were progressing steadily.

Trickling water echoing through the pristine marble bathhouse relaxed her, but the lingering fragrances used by the women who had preceded her, and would soon enter after her, were another reminder that she was no longer first in the eyes of her husband. Left to laze peacefully in rose-scented water, she closed her eyes and tried to think good thoughts. Soon she was riding through the noisy, busy streets of Baxtri beside Mithridates, laughing as he told her about the funny little disputes he had solved as chief of the Parthavan towns and villages.

She was wondering if she would ever see him again when Khezmet returned and commented on her radiant appearance. Luxuriating in the oil of myrrh being massaged into her skin, she was reminded of her imminent role as banquet host by the faint chink of goblets and thump of platters on the heavy wooden tables coming from her official reception chamber.

This will be my most prestigious feast, she thought.

By the time she returned to her chamber, Darayaus was waiting. After kissing his mother on both cheeks and inquiring after her health, he commented that he had not seen her looking so beautiful since their arrival in Shush. She thanked him, and mother and son took chai and sweets together on floor cushions.

"Father has not ordered everyone to drink wine throughout the week," he informed her. "I hope he will allow each guest to make their own choice today and choose wisely himself."

"Yes," Vashti sighed. "When the week is over, we will have our own celebration."

Darayaus reached over and hugged her tightly. "Let's picnic in the mountains tomorrow," he suggested.

When he had left, Khezmet brushed Vashti's hair and wrapped the dark strands in hot strips of beaten flax stems. Then she folded and secured her Shahjin's Mukryani scarlet robe with an intricately molded silver brooch, over which her silver-threaded coat was fitted. In a light moment, Vashti joked that her robes weren't quite as heavy as her battle armor. Laughing, Khezmet straightened the robe's tiny golden discs and tied its gold embroidered sash before applying kohl to her mistress' eyes and a dash of red poppy powder to her cheeks.

After winding the silken bejeweled crown headdress atop Vashti's cascading dark curls, Khezmet clasped a deep jade stone necklace around her neck. "Shahjin Nefertiti would have praised you," she enthused, stepping back to admire her work.

"And I praise you, my very dear sister," she added fondly with a hug. "Please inform Harpagos that I am ready to receive my guests and ask him to bring Zerena and the Shahjin's silver scepter to my official reception chamber. Once they arrive, we will depart for the banquet."

Khezmet left, and Vashti took her thrice knotted *kusti* cord and knelt to pray. She was still kneeling when her maid returned. "Harpagos will escort you himself, dear," she said. "He has informed your personal guard."

Trying to shrug off the unease that still bothered her, Vashti stepped into the cool corridor where Harpagos was waiting. After standing to attention a little longer than usual, then bowing low to his sovereign, he turned smartly; and they set off for the banquet. But Vashti was already regretting the dismissal of her personal guard for the occasion.

In her reception chamber ambient lamp lighting cast a golden glow on the silverware and goblets, and platters piled high with grapes, pomegranates, and figs barely enticed her tight stomach. Assuming her position in front of a silver couch, she encircled the scepter of power with her hennaed fingers and waited while Harpagos confirmed the identity of her guests.

Then, with Khezmet behind her, she began to receive them. Firstly, Aryenis, then Zerena and Debyar kissed her on both cheeks, and were followed by Ishtovigo's other wives and those of the palace and city officials. Lastly came Kusha's wife, who refused the kiss, claiming she was a little unwell. Vashti smiled, held out the scepter, wished her a return to good health, and decided to think nothing more of the Parsu's ungracious manner.

Hours of laughter and chatter about the availability of luxury silks and linens, the shortage of wine from the southern provinces, and the need to train daughters to be obedient and sons to be daring were interspersed with expressions of sympathy for Shahjin Amytis and her husband. Vashti had just congratulated herself on a successful banquet when the wife of Hamayun the captive, who had been accepted at Ishtovigo's court, made an insulting remark about the Hapiru people. Reminding herself that the obnoxious woman was of the same blood as the Athorayans, Vashti lifted her head and smiled.

"We do not discriminate between the captive peoples in Media," she stated clearly, "and we do not expect our guests to either." The woman opened her mouth to reply but soon closed it in response to Vashti's cold stare.

Hardly had harmony been restored than her guard entered and whispered to Khezmet who relayed his message. "Mehran wishes to speak to you, Shahjin," she informed her. "He did not explain why."

Wondering what Mehran, who was one of her husband's personal servants, wanted at this late stage of his festivities, she told Khezmet to ask the guard to admit him. When he entered after Vashti offered the scepter, she ushered him away from her guests.

"Shahjin, the Shahan Shah requests your presence at his feast. You must wear your crown," Mehran stated officiously.

Feeling uneasy again, to give herself time to think, she told him to wait outside. A couple of long minutes passed before she stepped out into the corridor and was shocked to see Ishtovigo's other personal servants. But the clashing of rhytons resounding from the distant Apadana garden and the intimidating retinue of Ishtovigo's servants prompted her decision.

"Please thank the Shahan Shah and tell him I cannot accept his invitation as my guests are still present," she informed Mehran coolly.

"But the Shahan Shah sincerely wishes to show his officials your beauty, Shahjin," the servant insisted. "He has informed them you are the crowning glory of Media and Babylonia. If you do not attend, his honor will be tarnished."

"Inform the Shahan Shah that as his coruler and equal, I will not display myself at his feast like one of his concubines," Vashti replied through gritted teeth. "My crown represents the honor of Media and its women, and I will not wear it before such a disorderly gathering."

It was Mehran's turn to be shocked. Turning away angrily, he and his fellow servants marched toward the noisy Apadana garden, muttering.

Chapter 43

Once her guests had left, Vashti summoned Aswer and Pir Daidwand and explained Ishtovigo's request.

"I fear the Shahan Shah is losing his grip on the court," she added.

"Shahjin, do not judge your husband on one mistake," Aswer pleaded.

"His celebrations have elevated his greatness in his own eyes, but he still allows the Parsu too much influence," Vashti replied firmly.

"What sort of influence?" the Pir asked.

"It was Parsu who brought me the message," Vashti replied. "I think they are trying to unseat me."

"But Shahjin, the people adore you," the Pir replied. "Why don't you give them the pleasure of your company?"

"Dear brother-in-law, appearing like one of my husband's concubines at such an occasion is beneath my position in the Shahdom," Vashti replied angrily. "If I did, I would be seen to approve of women being kept in the Shahan Shah's two women's houses, which is *druj* of enslavement. It casts the dark shadow of Angra Mainyu and the *daevas* across our shahdom."

The Pir frowned. "Yes, this is clearly against the Mitradat. What must we do about such corruption?"

"We must act before more women are captured," Vashti replied angrily. "I have long wanted to do so, but my situation at court has become too tenuous."

"Yes, Shahjin, I will speak to the Shahan Shah about these violations as soon as his celebrations finish," the Pir replied.

"Thank you, dear Daidwand, but I fear the Shahan Shah has chosen a path from which he will not depart," Vashti cried.

"This is not our only problem," Aswer added. "We must call the loyal Medes of the city to our aid before the Shahan Shah's Parsu advisors persuade him to expel us all. Then there will be nothing to stop them getting Kambujiya of Anshan or Arsamnes of Parsua or both to rebel against us."

Vashti agreed and told Aswer to summon Harpagos. When Aswer returned a few minutes later with the general, she explained Ishtovigo's request, but Harpagos seemed unconcerned.

"Shahjin, this is essentially a domestic matter," he opined.

"Not if the Parsu are trying to dethrone me," Vashti replied, her heart thumping. "Will you stay loyal to the Shahan Shah no matter how much he defies the Mitradat?"

"My dear Shahjin, this is not new for the Shahan Shah. We must learn to deal with his ways," Harpagos maintained, looking sideways.

"Do you know if the Medes in the city are still loyal?" Vashti asked.

"No, but I guess they are fewer than the Parsu who support the Shahan Shah's advisors," was the reply.

Vashti frowned. "I will deal with the enemy later," she declared, picking up the silver scepter. "Until I understand more about the situation, this will remain with me."

Harpagos nodded, but a flicker in his eyes made her wonder who he would choose in an open conflict between her and Ishtovigo.

"Wait until tomorrow to visit the Shahan Shah," Vashti told the Pir. "He might be in his right mind by then."

"Yes, Shahjin, may Auramadza bless you as you seek to guide Media in the ways of the Prophet," the priest declared before touching the scepter and asking permission to leave.

Vashti turned to Aswer. "Do you think any of my husband's Parsu advisors will speak openly to you?"

"Shahjin, it is very risky to ask. I have heard them mention Vishtaspa, who has family connections throughout our territories," he replied.

Khezmet, who had been listening from the other side of the room, stepped forward. "Sister, I will go into the barracks and ask Irdabama and our other spies about Vishtaspa."

"We still need to know more about the Parsu connections to the Shahan Shah," Vashti replied to her maid, "but be careful. And before you go, ask Irdabama to choose some sisters to imprison Pentaya's murderer while he awaits judgment by the Pir," she ordered.

Flashing the victory sign, Khezmet nodded and quickly left.

Stalking the garden of the Apadana after the Shahan Shah's feast, Angra Mainyu drove Ishtovigo's fury as he aimlessly roamed the neat, geometrical paths over which he and Vashti had walked quietly in their more congenial moments, discussing their rule of the vast shahdom of Babylonia and Media. But now, like the shooting pomegranate bushes and blossoming cherry trees hidden behind tall cypresses, he was blinded to the future, and the fragrances of budding roses and curled lily flowers lining the garden's central rectangular pool evaded him in the suffocatingly still air. Worse still, the apparent lifelessness of dormant olive and fig trees left him hopeless. Fearing an outbreak of the illness afflicting Shah Nebuchadnezzar in Ishtovigo, his Parsu advisors watched anxiously and worried about their own futures.

All Ishtovigo could remember about Vashti was her opposition to his every wish. From hunting in their childhood to building his magnificent palace, she was there to question, object, and refuse. Worse still, he suspected she had stolen and hidden much of the wealth acquired by Media from Athoraya and Lydia. Having convinced himself that it was funding and building her women's army so she could go to war with the Median regiments, he could only conclude that she was plotting to overthrow him and rule alone. With these thoughts running through his mind, he came to a terrible conclusion. There was only one thing he could do to save himself and Media from the threat of Vashti and her women warriors. Striding toward the marble steps of the Apadana Hall, he called his Parsu advisors.

"What shall be done to Shahjin Vashti according to law because she did not obey the command brought to her by my servants?" he asked the huddle.

Manuchehr stepped forward. "Shahan Shah, Shahjin Vashti has not only wronged you, but also the governors and all the people who are in the provinces ruled by you. All women of the shahdom, especially the noble women, when they hear that Shahan Shah Ishtovigo commanded Shahjin Vashti be brought in before him, but she did not come, will do the same to their husbands. Thus, the women will hold excessive contempt and wrath toward their husbands."

Ishtovigo's heart leapt. At last others understood his lifelong predicament! Born third in line to the throne, not trusted by his father, and rejected by Vashti, as the Shahan Shah who had enchanted the rulers of the region with his new capital, he would now prove his ability to rule without the woman who had dishonored him before his house and his officials.

"If it pleases the Shahan Shah, let a royal decree go out from him," Manuchehr continued, emboldened by Ishtovigo's sudden change in mood. "And let it be recorded in the laws of the Medes and the Parsu, that will not be altered, that Vashti shall come no more before Shahan Shah Ishtovigo and let him give her honorable position to another who is better than she. When the Shahan Shah's decree, which he will make, is proclaimed throughout all his territories, all wives will obey their husbands, both great and small."

Ishtovigo gazed up into the sunny sky. The celestial bodies were not visible, but surely Manuchehr's suggestion meant all his star signs had aligned! Suddenly, his garden had come alive. It beckoned him to return to his favorite pavilion where, followed at a distance by his advisors, he ensconced himself on a carved stone seat. Propping his chin in his hand, he sat quietly for a few minutes, then smiled.

"Call my scribe," he ordered Manuchehr, "and repeat the law you have just proposed to him. Bring it to me when it is finished. I will seal it immediately. Then send it to all the provinces in their own languages so that each man should be master of his own house and speak in the language of his own people."

Rejoicing that he had reached a resolution to the problem that had vexed him for so long, Ishtovigo rose and strode away in renewed vigor. His advisors heaved sighs of relief then sniggered triumphantly. Admatha was the only one to cringe as he followed them out of the messy Apadana garden.

Vashti hardly slept that night as Khezmet had not returned, and she wondered whether she had sent yet another of her beloved sisters into danger or even death. Early the next morning, she rose and walked down the silent corridor to the kitchen where the cook was heating water in a bronze kettle hanging inside a large clay oven. He stopped immediately, bowed, and asked what he could do for his Shahjin. When she requested breakfast, he served bread, olive paste and *mast* with chai. The man kept his eyes downcast, so wondering if he had a burden, Vashti asked him about his family's health.

"They are all very well, Shahjin," he replied, "but the palace is sick with sadness."

"Why?" Vashti asked, wondering what Ishtovigo had done in his drunken condition.

"We have been told you are no longer our Shahjin," the cook declared, tears running down his face.

Her heart missed a beat. "Who told you?"

"I cannot say," he replied, his fingers trembling as he shelled hard boiled eggs.

Vashti placed her hand on the man's shoulder. "You must. Media may be in danger," she insisted.

"M-my cousin Admatha just came for his breakfast. He t-told me," the cook spluttered. "But please don't tell anyone else. I am sworn to secrecy."

"How did this happen?" Vashti demanded.

"Manuchehr and the other advisors—"

"Except Admatha?"

The cook nodded.

"When did the Shahan Shah make the decree?"

"Last night, but it is not yet sealed."

At least one of the Parsu is with me, Vashti thought, gulping the last of her chai. "I must find Aswer."

Quickly, she retrieved her silver scepter and ran down the corridor to the Apadana garden, hardly thinking. On reaching the reception hall of the enclosed garden, she stopped. A myriad of different golden rhytons, silver cups, and pieces of jewelry littered the alabaster, turquoise, and black marble floor, along with food scraps squashed on the mother-of-pearl shell and costly stone surface.

Even his servants are too lazy to clean up after Ishtovigo and his guests, she thought, stepping carefully over one of the fine linen purple cords that had fastened the white-and-blue linen curtains hanging limply from the walls. Peacocks' plaintive calls drifted eerily from the peaceful garden as she weaved her way through overturned gold and silver couches. But in the exhausted silence, she didn't notice her husband seated on his throne at the garden's entrance.

"Looking for someone, my dear?" he rasped from his golden jewel-encrusted seat of power.

Then she saw it or rather didn't see it. Her throne was gone!

She took a deep breath. "Aswer."

"He is not here. He is doing my work with my other advisors."

Her heart raced. "What work?"

"The decree to end your wrongdoing."

"What wrongdoing? It is you who practices *druj*."

"*Druj*? The lie that a woman can rule Media?"

"We have been birthed from our women and sustained by their farmwork. Shahan Shah Hovakhshatra and his fathers honored their wives by making thrones for them. Now will you tear all that down, deny the Mitradat, and lead Media to ruin like the other nations, including Babylonia?" she cried desperately.

"Media cannot have a misguided, irrational, and uncooperative woman on the throne. It needs a firm hand," he yelled.

"Firm enough to gather many women into one house and hold multiple rhytons of wine?" she countered.

Glowering, Ishtovigo rose, lurched down the steps, and tried to grab her silver scepter; but Vashti drew it away only to have a hand from behind snatch it. Kusha passed the silver orb to Ishtovigo, and he and the Parsu with him each touched it. Vashti gasped when Aswer did the same.

"Aswer," the Shahan Shah called, "Vashti of the Medes is seeking you."

"Shahan Shah," Aswer replied, "tell her I am with you."

Vashti turned to see Khezmet running toward her.

"Sister," she cried, "what have they done to you?" Sensing danger, Vashti grabbed Khezmet's hand and together the two women ran to the end of the Apadana Hall from where Vashti turned to see Manuchehr holding a reed parchment scroll on which Ishtovigo was indenting his signet ring in hot wax.

Chapter 44

"Did you find Irdabama?" Vashti asked as they hurried down the corridor leading to her chamber.

"Yes. She has heard Vishtaspa is in Bactria," Khezmet replied. "And she wanted to inform you that Pentaya's killer has been found guilty and executed."

Vashti nodded. "That's one less enemy to attack us," she spat. "And it seems Vishtaspa is not behind the bid to dethrone me."

"He might be, but from afar. We do not know if he has allies here," Khezmet reminded her breathlessly.

"It must be just these Parsu and Ishtovigo who are trying to depose me," Vashti replied, panting. "Go quickly to my chamber, take my crown, and deliver it to the women's barracks for safekeeping. My husband has taken my throne, but he will not have my crown."

Khezmet ran up the corridor and slipped inside the chamber just as Harpagos appeared at the other end. As he approached, Khezmet ran toward Vashti with the crown box. "Hurry," Vashti urged as she passed. "Take the servants' entrance that leads to the Atashkedah."

Accompanied by four guards, Harpagos halted at her chamber door. "Vashti of the Medes," he called out to her, "I am authorised to arrest you under the orders of Shahan Shah Ishtovigo."

Determined to keep her dignity, Vashti walked calmly to her chamber, opened the door, and stepped inside. Harpagos followed, leaving the guards outside. "On what charges?" she asked quietly when the door had been closed.

"Treason."

She laughed. "For not attending Ishtovigo's drunken celebration? Is he going crazy like Nebuchadnezzar? I have always been loyal to Media and have never harmed it, the Shahan Shah, or its people. Under the Mitradat and the decree of my husband's father and mother, the thrones are to be occupied perpetually by the Median heir and his wife of our people until their deaths. I cannot be deposed for such a frivolous reason. Give Ishtovigo some time to regain his mind, perhaps he will review the decree and change it."

"I tried to persuade him last night, but the Parsu were too strong," Harpagos confessed. "I have come to warn you that your life may be in danger."

"From whom?"

"Vishtaspa has assassins in the city."

"How do you know? I have been informed that he is in Bactria."

"Admatha is a true Mede who has infiltrated the Parsu community. He has reported that the Shahan Shah's advisors have paid them."

"Have you confirmed that this Vishtaspa is working with the Parsu?"

"No, but we assume so."

"Then give me your protection."

Harpagos shook his head. "I must aid the strongest party in this dispute. If I do not, Media could be weakened by division and come under attack along with Babylonia. Ishtovigo is the only shah whom most of the Median chiefs and the shahs of the other nations will honor. I am sorry." He faced her, but the general whom she had long known and trusted would not meet her eyes. Instead, his usual warm, hearty smile was frozen in a grim line, and streaks of tension creased and distorted his handsome face.

"Nonsense. Do you think forces like Kambujiya's and Arsamnes' would attempt to take all the territories of Babylonia and Media?"

"With Vishtaspa, perhaps. Apparently, he has an army in Parthava equal to the Parsu."

It all sounded very strange and even quite improbable, and she wondered if Mithridates knew of such machinations. "I do not believe they could conquer General Nebuzaradan's forces, even without Nebuchadnezzar leading them," she stated. Her head was light, but her heart was as heavy as stone. "Allow me to consult the Pir now," she demanded.

"I will escort you to the Atashkedah," Harpagos replied dispassionately.

"Please give me some time to prepare," she requested, and he stepped into the corridor.

She did not know how or why, but suddenly her mind was clear. Collecting the leather pouch with the worn note Mithridates had written her, the bust of Nefertiti, and her copy of the Avesta, she placed them with her *kusti* beads in Cica's battle bag, which Shamin had given her before she left Hagmatana. Over the shabby robe she had worn in the oasis near Mouru, she put on her riding *chokha* and *pantol* and her purple sash then grabbed her heaviest cloak.

After informing Harpagos that she was ready to leave, she followed him down the hall to the servants' entrance to the palace and then to the Atashkedah. The four guards waited with him while she entered the cool, dimly lit quiet of the temple with its ever-present, reassuring flame. Parwin appeared with Pir Daidwand, and Vashti silently sank into her arms.

Parwin sobbed and the Pir dabbed his eyes with the lappets of his headdress. "We are to expect this work of Angra Mainyu," he said quietly, "but he will not triumph through your husband. Another will take his throne before his time," he predicted.

"Do you mean Vishtaspa is trying to kill him too?" Vashti asked.

"This is not clear," the Pir replied. A figure appeared in the entrance to the temple. Khezmet stepped into the light of the fire and hugged Vashti tightly.

"It is safe," she declared of the crown, "in the bowels of the barracks."

"Tell Irdabama to prepare our women for battle," Vashti whispered to Khezmet, "but do not let Harpagos know." Taking the bust from her father's bag, she gave it to Khezmet and told her to hide it with her crown. "One day I will regain them both," she vowed.

Khezmet took the bust, and Vashti hugged her long and tight. "Be careful, my darling. Many thanks for your loyalty," she breathed. "Go now and ask Daro to bring Delal. I believe I am going to be taken away."

Khezmet began to weep. "Sister, let me go with you," she pleaded.

"You too might not be safe, dear," Vashti replied calmly, gripping her maid's shoulders and holding her gaze intensely. "But I promise to regain my place in Media's rightful seat of power." Khezmet sniffed, nodded, and stepped into the bright light outside, turning only to give the victory sign. A short conversation between her and Harpagos was followed by silence.

"To further answer your question, Shahjin," Pir Daidwand resumed, "the Prophet predicted Media would be strong for but a short time until it collapsed under the weight of *druj*." He sighed and shook his head sadly. "My dear Vashti, only you can carry that burden now."

"Media has only been truly free for just over forty years," she lamented. "And surely the Shahdom of Ishtovigo and I will not end so quickly. What can be done to save us?" she cried, turning to the Pir in desperation.

"Return as soon as you can to Hagmatana with Darayaus. Help him reestablish *asha* in Media," Daidwand replied, a note of urgency in his voice.

"But Harpagos has the Bears under his command. He has indicated he will remain loyal to Ishtovigo. We cannot fight our own forces," Vashti replied, inwardly scolding herself for even hinting at defeat. Despite her jumpy mind, she had to make logical decisions.

"Then we will raise up an army from our Busae homeland," Parwin suggested optimistically.

"One tribe cannot stand against the rest if they do not join us. Disunity will destroy the shahdom more than anything else," Vashti replied firmly. "We must hold it together."

Harpagos appeared in the doorway and nodded to Vashti. "It is time to go," he said, his voice strangely lifeless.

"Tell Darayaus to go back to Hagmatana and care for Ardela and Shamin. Zerena can make her own choice," Vashti whispered to Parwin. And to the Pir, "I promise you Media will not fall to *druj* as long as I am alive," she maintained fervently.

Outside, Debyar was waiting. "Dear, I have found a law that should soon set you free. I will travel to Anshan to consult Kambujiya and return with his answer within a week. Then you should be reinstated."

Vashti hugged her beloved teacher tightly. "Thank you, my darling. Do not be concerned. I have upheld the Mitradat. I will be exonerated."

Debyar smiled through her tears then turned to her husband. "My dear Harpagos, I have not had any reason to doubt your loyalty to me or to Media and the Mitradat until now. Please consider carefully where your allegiance lies. If anything happens to my Vashti, I will hold you responsible and will return with Gulnaz to my people in Rhagae." Speechless, Harpagos stared at his wife through misty eyes, grimaced, and mounted his horse.

As she took Delal's reins from Daro, Vashti slipped a note into his hand addressed to Amytis informing her about Ishtovigo's decree.

"Do not intervene," it warned, "or there could be war."

Chapter 45

Unable to find Vashti the next day, and disturbed and perplexed by palace rumors that she had been dismissed, Darayaus stormed into his father's quarters.

"Where is my mother?" he roared.

"Calm down, son," Ishtovigo replied, his tone smugly placatory. "She is being taken to a secret place to protect her life from that villain Vishtaspa, who has allied with the Parthavan Shah Mithridates. Apparently, she told Mithridates some of our military secrets many years ago when she was on my father's business in Parthava and Bactria. Your mother will be kept safe until we know more about Vishtaspa's work with Mithridates, especially since some of the provincial governors are very angry about her insult to me on the last day of my feast."

"Who informed you of the activities of this Vishtaspa, Father?" Darayaus asked. "As far as I know, Mithridates is an ally of Media. This story sounds like one of those you tell when you are merry with wine."

"My loyal Parsu advisors report that their spies in the city and throughout the provinces are afraid of unrest caused by Vishtaspa and his forces," Ishtovigo continued coolly. "Your mother's defiance of me would have created even more trouble in the homes and villages of the peoples of our territories and weakened our control everywhere had I not responded quickly."

Darayaus laughed. "Now you have sent messages about it to all our territories, there will be uprisings because Mother has been dismissed," he complained. "And how will you manage both Babylonia and Media without her? She is the backbone of our shahdom. Now tell me where she is so I can get her back and save Media from your stupidity."

Ishtovigo's face darkened. "You would speak to your father, the Shahan Shah of Media, like this?" he yelled, brandishing the golden scepter as if to strike his son. Godel rushed in. "Arrest him too," Ishtovigo ordered, "and take him away. Like his mother, he has no respect for me."

"So you have had my dear mother arrested?" Darayaus yelled back. Godel tried to grab his arm, but the younger man wrenched himself free, tripped his assailant, and jumped over him to freedom. Godel sprang up, but Darayaus was already out the door and running down the corridor. In hot pursuit, Godel called for more guards, but Darayaus raced into his mother's empty quarters and quickly exited through the window to the roof below. Godel watched him run across the roof, climb down the Apadana wall, and disappear into the stables. By the time he reached them, Darayaus was on the road through the city that led to Hagmatana.

Arriving in the capital several days later, Darayaus conveyed the dreadful news to Ardela, Shelna, and Shamin. Ardela immediately suggested Darayaus declare himself coruler in Hagmatana in place of his mother, assisted by his grandmother.

"But first you must get the support of the Tiger and Lynx regiments," she added, glancing at Shelna, who nodded.

"Dear, such division might lead to internal war," Darayaus warned. "We cannot have Mede against Mede. Does Aunt Amytis know of the apparent plot to destroy Media?"

"I doubt it," Ardela replied. "But I believe your mother would have sent her a message as soon as she learned of your father's treachery. Hovakhshatra was never happy about Ishtovigo succeeding him. We should have asked Kambujiya to do so," she moaned, blinking back tears.

"Do we know who the real enemy is?" Shamin asked, putting her arm around her sister-in-law, despite her own shock and distress.

"Father mentioned Vishtaspa and Mithridates of Parthava," Darayaus replied. "I doubt that the Parthavans would turn on us as they need our protection from the Saka to their north. Vishtaspa is a mystery, neither Kambujiya nor Arsamnes have mentioned him in our previous communications. I suspect Father is using him, whoever he is, as an excuse."

"How could those men be behind Vashti's dismissal from such a distance?" Shamin queried.

"Perhaps they are friends of the Parsu who are advising the Shahan Shah," Shelna suggested.

"We must send a message to Mithridates informing him of the situation. His reply will tell us where his loyalty lies," Ardela told Darayaus. "And write a letter to Kambujiya asking him to intervene with Ishtovigo on Vashti's behalf. Surely such a disagreement can be resolved without endangering the shahdom," she added.

"Hurry. We need someone we can trust," Shamin urged, her voice breaking as the tears she had struggled to restrain began to run down her cheeks. "We don't know where Vashti is or even if she is alive."

"Admatha is a Parsu who left Father's service when he realized the other Parsu were plotting against Media," Darayaus explained. "He told me after the banquet that something would happen to dear Mother, but I never thought Father would be so severe. Admatha has promised to send information as it becomes available. Meanwhile, it seems Harpagos has declared himself and the Bears loyal to Father," he added, the tremor in his voice indicating how this development had shaken him.

"A wise move considering the main seat of power is still Shush," Ardela commented, and Darayaus had to agree. "Do you think Admatha can be trusted?"

"He is the only one of Father's advisors we can rely on. Aswer is no longer with Mother and has joined the Parsu," Darayaus replied.

Shamin gasped. "My poor Vashti," she cried. "If she has been betrayed by him and murdered by the Parsu…"

"Dear, the assassination of a foreign ruler is an act of war. Anshan and Parsua would not want to fight Media and Babylonia," Darayaus maintained, pacing the worn marble floor of his father's former throne room. "And Admatha told me Mother's own forces will probably begin the search for her in the Shush region. Nevertheless, I will send an emissary to Mitradatkirt to request Mithridates' assistance," he assured his grandmother who expressed her heartfelt thanks.

"Perhaps Vashti's forces are already looking for her," Shamin said more calmly. "And once they know of Ishtovigo's betrayal of my daughter, the people throughout our territories will also be wondering where she is." She paused and sniffed. "But I believe they will find my darling girl and bring her back to her rightful place."

Ardela turned to her grandson. "You must send a messenger to Parthava immediately," she urged.

"Yes, Grandmother, but please summon the Piree Magush," Darayaus requested. "I must consult him."

Several minutes later, the aged priest shuffled on his walking stick toward a silver couch in the former throne room and sat down heavily. "Auramazda will not prosper a wicked ruler," he declared firmly after Darayaus told him of his mother's dismissal.

"Then should I seek to depose my father?" Darayaus asked.

"No. Even though he has broken the Mitradat, he must recognize his error and be given the opportunity to change his ways. And your mother is still the rightful coruler of Media."

"But how can she rule when we don't even know where she is?" Darayaus asked in frustration.

"Together, Auramazda and your mother will protect us."

"Honored Piree, this seems impossible."

"Nothing is impossible for Auramazda."

Darayaus sighed. "What might the future of Media be under my father?" he asked, frowning his doubt of the priest's pronouncement.

"He will rule with wise help until his time. Your father's Parsu advisors possess the words of the Prophet and the Mitradat. If they don't keep them, Auramazda will find another way to preserve Media."

"What wise help and what time?" Darayaus demanded.

"I must wait for the heavenly bodies to move to know the time. Wise help will come from the captives."

"Which captives?"

The Piree looked out the window. "I cannot tell, but like us, they have only one god."

Finding it difficult to remember the gods of all the foreigners in Media, Darayaus sighed. "What is your advice to me as heir to the throne, Honored Piree?"

The Pir struggled to his feet. "Your mother is safe, but it is not known when we will next see her," he remarked as he hobbled toward the door.

Without any obvious solution and not knowing what more he could do, Darayaus collapsed onto the nearest couch, unable to hold back his sobs any longer.

Chapter 46

Much to Vashti's horror, before she mounted Delal, Harpagos tied her sash over her eyes, an act that would have seen him condemned to the gallows under any other circumstances. "I have sent my second-in-command to inform Arsamnes of Parsua that Media is ready to withstand any threat from Parsua," the general told her as they rode off. Realizing she might never know the reply was little comfort.

From the sounds of their horses' hooves, she assumed there was one other guard besides the one leading Delal. Outside the city, the sun's warmth on her cheeks indicated a northerly direction, and soon Delal's gait changed as the road tilted upwards. Ignoring her, the guards talked about their families and their home villages, and she occasionally managed to lift the sash over her eyes and sneak a look at the mountainous countryside. Recognizing the voice of one guard who had accompanied her and Darayaus on a family picnic only weeks before, she wondered how those who had so loyally served Shahan Shah Hovakhshatra could betray the niece he had trained to rule alongside his son. Harpagos remained ominously silent.

As the party's progress slowed on the mountain paths, spring smells of earth warming in the weeks after Norouz assured her of the eternal and brought a measure of peace. Crossing a very cold river, the zigzag path continued in the same general direction. At nighttime, in the shelter of a mountain cave or under a horse rug spread beneath low branches, Vashti was thankful for her woolen cloak. Removing the sash from her eyes when the guard on duty fell asleep, she would gaze up at the sign of the Great Bear in the starry sky, hoping he was watching over her and wishing he would take her safely to his heavenly den.

Every morning and evening, Harpagos and the guards made a fire, boiled water for chai, and ate bread and cheese with their charge until the food ran out, after which they caught fish from a waterway or shot rabbits, hares, or other small game to roast on fire stones.

Only the greetings of a few other travelers walking or leading donkeys along the steep paths broke the monotony of the journey. To comfort herself, Vashti silently sang the Gatha songs and tried not to mourn what she had left behind. But her family, her women warriors, and Admatha's efforts to secure the support of the loyal Medes of Shush against the Parsu were never far from her thoughts. Even more painful was Aswer's betrayal.

Then one night, she glimpsed what she thought were the torchlights of a city's guards, but when Harpagos announced they had arrived at their destination, it was pitch-dark and very quiet. He removed her sash, and she looked around. Surrounded by four square stone walls receding into the dim light of the guards' torches, she could not recall such a building being constructed by Shahan Shah Hovakhshatra.

"Clearly, this is not meant just to house troops," she concluded of its forbidding walls merging into the black night.

Quickly, she loosened her father's bag from Delal's flank and shoved it inside her cloak. After ordering her to dismount, one of the guards grabbed the horse's reins and led her away before she had time to farewell the last living vestige of her life. Sensing the parting, Delal shied away, and the guard struck her with his lance.

"Stop," Vashti yelled, but the man aimed the weapon at her, and she ducked.

"You stop, fool!" Harpagos shouted, grabbing the lance. "She is still the Shahjin of Media."

"Not for long," the other guard jeered. "The Shahan Shah has others waiting to replace her."

"Now you are insulting the Shahan Shah himself!" Harpagos yelled. "Be careful of your words. We are charged with the safe arrival of the Shahjin," he reminded the guards sternly as a lamplight appeared in the fort gateway. "Here are the keepers."

An elderly couple appeared in the soft light of the lantern the man carried. He led the woman, who blinked nervously.

These people do not look like prison guards, she thought, wondering if Ishtovigo had asked her to attend his banquet not only to get a reason to dismiss her, but to banish her permanently.

Harpagos acknowledged the couple with a muted greeting and handed the man a jangling bag. The man opened it, took out a handful of silver coins, then replaced them.

"Make sure she stays here," Harpagos instructed. "If anything happens to her, you will both lose your lives."

"How long will the prisoner be kept, master?" the man asked.

"According to the Shahan Shah's pleasure," the troublesome guard replied, grabbing Delal's reins again. This time she reared and attempted to paw him. Quickly, the old woman seized the reins and spoke soothingly to Delal, who immediately quieted. "Leave her mount with me," the woman said. "We will keep her for meat."

"Nooo!" Vashti cried in anguish, but no one took any notice.

"Make sure her life is shortened too," the more malicious guard jeered, pointing to Vashti. "Such stubborn mules do not deserve to live."

"I warned you to watch your words!" Harpagos yelled, striking the offender with his lance.

"We will ensure the prisoner's safe captivity," the elderly man assured him.

"The Shahan Shah will reward you more if you follow his orders," Harpagos told the old man as he mounted his horse. The man nodded and informed Harpagos of accommodation in the village near the fort. Without a word of farewell, Harpagos turned his horse and led the guards away into the night. Her heart pounding, Vashti struggled to accept what seemed like her friend's final act of betrayal. She couldn't tell whether his stony expression caught in the keepers' lamplight expressed sorrow or anger. It was a stunning blow. The one man in Media she thought she could always rely on had failed her.

Listening to the sounds of hooves fading into the night, she clung to the forlorn hope that Harpagos would eventually rescue her. And having estimated the distance he had brought her from Shush, she concluded that Hagmatana wasn't far away.

Surely by now those in the capital will know of the betrayal, she thought. And Aunt Ardela will order the other generals to look for me.

The female keeper led her to a ground-level cell lined with animal feeding troughs and littered with dried manure. Determined not to show fear, Vashti said nothing. While the man waited outside the cell, the woman left and soon returned with a tattered black woolen blanket. Vashti kicked away the dried manure, arranged some straw from one of the animal troughs to make a bed, placed the blanket on it, and turned to stare defiantly at the couple, who both shamefacedly left. In the darkness, she began running her fingers along the cracks in the walls of the high-ceilinged cell. The stones were all closely laid.

Loosening these would be impossible without tools, she thought.

After Ishtovigo's anger cooled, he missed his first wife's presence in their quarters and her advice at court, musing that neither Aryenis nor any other woman was as clever, diligent, and reliable as Vashti. But Angra Mainyu and his *daevas* kept his mind locked in perpetual aversion to Vashti's power, even when his sister visited from Babylon some days later.

Without any announcement, Amytis strode past Harpagos into the throne room at Shush, ignored the golden scepter, told others present to leave, and began to admonish her brother.

"Why was Vashti dismissed?" she demanded.

"Greetings, sister dear," Ishtovigo replied calmly, waving the even more vigilant Harpagos away. "This is an unexpected visit. Are there more problems in Babylon?"

"Not yet, but there will be if you don't bring Vashti back," Amytis declared. "What bad spirit possessed you when you drove her from your capital? Father would never have allowed such troublemaking."

"This has nothing to do with Father, you, or Babylonia," Ishtovigo snapped back.

"You are wrong, brother dear. Belteshazzar and I have authority over the Babylonian army, and if our ally is weakened by hostile forces, we might decide to intervene. Have you visited the nearby provinces lately? Women with their hair cut lined the streets of every town and village I passed through along the road to Shush, and they were not mourning the dead."

"What do you mean? Of course, Vashti is not dead," Ishtovigo replied, his brow wrinkling in confusion.

"At least my brother is not a murderer," Amytis remarked cynically. "Then where is she?"

"She is under my protection in a secret location."

"Why? Who, besides you, is threatening her for not attending one of your raucous banquets?"

"I cannot divulge state secrets."

"Why not? All Media knows Vashti is the true ruler of the shahdom."

"She might have been," Ishtovigo admitted quietly, "but she is no longer. Be careful, sister. I do not wish to have to ask you to leave my presence," he threatened, his eyes shifting to Harpagos. He paused, doubt darkening his face. "Why am I not considered the true ruler of Media?"

Amytis was silent for a minute. "Dear brother," she continued calmly, "it pains me to say, but if you continue *druj* against Vashti, there will be unrest in Media. The people do not believe their Shahjin would commit a crime worthy of dismissal."

Ishtovigo surveyed his sister thoughtfully. "What is the real reason for your visit?" he asked.

"I am here not only for my sister-in-law but also for Babylonia. Unrest in Media could spread over the border into regions with many captives. And with Nebuchadnezzar ill and absent from the court, the people fear the god Marduk might not protect their crops. I'm also afraid that the priests might tell them that injustice will inevitably prevail." She paused and softened her expression. "Our hold on power in the court is only ever tenuous."

Ishtovigo waited before replying. "According to the law of the Medes and the Parsu, I cannot repeal the decree I issued against my first wife," he confessed. "And if I do, I will appear weak before the Parsu and our people."

"One Mede ruler sacking the other is against the Mitradat," Amytis retorted. "And Media does not need Anshan or Parsua. With Babylonia, Media could destroy both those minor shahdoms in a very short time."

"Not if Parthava were to join them. And I have word of a conspiracy against us from the east that might involve Vashti," Ishtovigo countered.

"Who informed you of this…conspiracy? Did you discuss it with Vashti?" Amytis asked.

"No. She does not respect those who told me of the threat," Ishtovigo replied testily.

"Why do you keep those Parsu advisors? Father was too kind to them, especially after they robbed him," Amytis cried in exasperation. "Are there not suitable Medes in the city to advise you?"

Ishtovigo stared for a while at the flowering bushes and palms planted around the ornate pavilions in the Apadana gardens then shook his head and turned back to his sister, his eyes full of regret.

"All the leading Medes except one declined my invitation to join my council..."

"Because they did not respect or trust you," Amytis replied. "Babylonia knows nothing of a Parthavan conspiracy, and our spies are everywhere. Did the Parsu persuade you to dismiss Vashti?"

Ishtovigo shifted his gaze. "What would Nebuchadnezzar do if you didn't attend one of his banquets as expected?" he asked.

"I believe he would take Belteshazzar's advice and be reminded of his confession of Most High God El Elyon, who hates *druj*, deceit, betrayal, and lawlessness," Amytis replied without hesitation. "Your refusal to answer my question tells me the Parsu were involved in Vashti's removal," she added. "It is *they* who should be dismissed, not her."

"I do not have such an advisor as Belteshazzar," Ishtovigo admitted forlornly with a hint of loneliness, even helplessness.

"Because you have driven Vashti from her throne and her home," Amytis shot back unsympathetically. "Forget your fanciful delusions and the Parsus' advice and bring back the only one who can restore the people's confidence in the Shahdom of Media," Amytis pleaded. "I remind you that under the Mitradat, you can make another law to reinstate Vashti. And doesn't the Avesta state that a good ruler may be either a man or a woman?"

Snapping out of his self-pity, Ishtovigo frowned and blinked, then smiled resolutely. Reaching for the golden scepter, he called for Harpagos.

Frustrated by the conversation's abrupt end, Amytis stepped back, bowed to her brother, and summoned her guard, who waited beside Harpagos.

"We are leaving now," she declared and swished her way out. At the doorway, she halted and turned to Ishtovigo sitting askew on his throne. "May Auramazda keep you," she declared solemnly, "because one day the people of Media might not."

Outside, Amytis turned to Harpagos. "Where is Vashti?" she demanded.

"I cannot say," Harpagos replied, his face reddening in shame. "Shahan Shah's orders." He cupped his hand close to Amytis' ear, and she waved her guard away. "It seems there is a conspiracy against the throne," he whispered uselessly.

Amytis sighed and ordered the preparation of her carriage for her return to Babylon. "Make sure Ishtovigo brings Vashti back," she ordered. "Otherwise, Babylonia might not continue in alliance with Media." Privately, she intended to use Babylon's spies to find her sister-in-law.

Harpagos nodded empathically. "I assure you, I will fight to keep Media secure, Shahjin."

Chapter 47

Light was beginning to creep through the narrow slit in the wall above her when Vashti finally fell asleep. In a dream, she saw early morning sunbeams dancing over the surface of an oasis pool and a smiling figure watching from the other side as she waded cool waters. When she looked closer, the figure disappeared. She awoke to cold water dripping onto the hem of the bedraggled sleeping robe she had worn all those years ago at the oasis near Mouru. Crawling out of the cocoon she had made of her cloak and her keeper's blanket, she wondered if the leaky fort had always been a gaol.

Her decision to refuse Ishtovigo's invitation had been hasty, and she questioned whether her honor was worth the loss of her throne. In the previous months, she had increasingly complied with Ishtovigo's will for the sake of unity, and she wondered if her weakness had contributed to his assumption of complete power.

The questions swirled through her addled mind, till she could no longer think of any answers. Pleasant hunting trips and the births of their children were some of the few happy times she could remember with her husband, but at Norouz in Rhagae, she had laughed with a tall Parthavan chief as fireballs exploded over a huge blaze. Exhausted, and shivering in the early morning cold, she lay down on her damp bed and prayed for wisdom and strength from the guiding spirit of Spenta Mainyu.

As she lay looking up at the mossy ceiling, the smell of musty straw mingled with dried horse manure reminded her of the day Cica had taken her to the stables to meet her first pony. But the memory intensified her fear that she might never see Delal again. Slapping her legs and arms to try to kill whatever was biting her, she peered through the dim light to find the culprits. Fleas crawling over the old woman's blanket made her wonder if imprisonment in such a squalid cell was Ishtovigo's punishment for her opposition to his grandiose plans.

She had just dozed off again when the heavy door to the cell opened and her female goaler appeared with some bread and boiled meat.

"I'm not supposed to give you this," she confessed in hushed tones, "but as it might be your last…"

Vashti looked into the woman's frightened eyes fringed by stray gray hairs. "Why might it be my last?" she asked tenuously.

"I have been told to give you water only," the woman admitted, her hand shaking as she placed a tin kettle on the filthy floor. "If you do not die in four weeks, they will kill me."

"Who will?"

"I do not know, but their language is not from here. They speak only to my husband."

Perhaps this is part of a planned attack on Media, Vashti thought. But it's unlikely to be from the Athorayans or the Scythians, and the Babylonians still need our friendship. She shivered again. The Parsu might be plotting to take Ishtovigo's throne too, she reasoned, her chest tightening. Much to her shame, she felt the first tears of despondency leak from her eyes.

The old woman coughed, and Vashti thanked her for the food. "My Shahjin, I have no choice. This is the work of Angra Mainyu," she confessed, her eyes softening,

She knows who I am, Vashti thought. This has been well planned.

"Who arranged for you to be my keeper?"

The old woman trembled. "I do not really know, but I think it is those who have been stealing from us," she cried. "They came to our village months ago dressed like warriors. They said they were on the Shahan Shah's business, but they left with some of the young women, promising to find them rich husbands, as our village is poor. We are waiting for the women to return with those husbands, but they have not."

"Which way did they go?"

"They took the road to the south."

Recalling those held captive in Ishtovigo's first women's house, Vashti shook her head. "Those men probably *were* on the Shahan Shah's business," she spat.

"Yes, Shahjin," the old woman replied, wiping sweat from her lined brow.

"Do you know someone who would deliver my messages?" Vashti asked. "I will pay them well when I am free."

The woman looked away. "No, Shahjin. The Shahah Shah's men were very fierce. They said if anyone helped you, they would destroy our village."

Vashti pursed her lips, angry that her people had been threatened and robbed. How she wished she could summons her women warriors!

Her keeper's mouth twitched nervously. "I must go now. My husband is waiting," she insisted. "I have said too much. I cannot say more." Vashti desperately tried to think of another appeal to her keeper's sympathy, but the old woman slipped out soundlessly, and the heavy cell door clanged shut.

Savoring each mouthful of the meat, assuming it would be her last, she realized she had to formulate her own plan.

"According to the laws of the Medes, I must be given the opportunity to plead my case against Ishtovigo's decision," she reasoned. But recalling the look of rage and hate in his eyes when she had left the Apadana Hall, she assumed he would never agree. "And with his Parsu advisors against me, my banishment could be permanent," she concluded. Determined not give up her throne without a fight, she wondered how the battle would be fought.

Kneeling on the dusty floor, she asked the *yazatas* to show her.

Irdabama and Aferin surveyed Vashti's angrily noisy forty-five women warriors, including Khezmet, Parwin, and Shirat, seated on the floor of their barracks and waiting eagerly to hear about the fate of their commander. After ordering silence, Irdabama spoke.

"We have trained for the defense of our people, but we never thought such an attack would come from within," she stated vehemently. "Our Shahjin has been banished and we don't know why."

"Has the Shahan Shah gone mad like Nebuchadnezzar?" one asked.

"No. The Shahan Shah still rules Media, and he has plenty of women imprisoned in his first women's house any one of whom could take Vashti's place," Irdabama replied.

Scowling, the women threw their hands in the air in disgust. "We must free them," another yelled, "now!"

"Not yet," Irdabama replied, "first we must free our commander."

"Does anyone know where she is?" another woman asked.

"We have been informed that a party of four was seen on the northern road the day after the Shahjin's dismissal," Khezmet replied. "It must have been my darling and her captors."

"Then let's go after them," the women chorused, jumping up.

"Wait," Irdabama shouted. "We cannot let the enemy know our movements. Khezmet and Parwin will take command while Aferin and I try to locate the party. We will find our beloved Shahjin and bring her back to her rightful place," she vowed.

All the women cheered and formed a dance circle where they rhythmically stomped and ululated the battle cry, *Jin, Jiyan, Azadi* - *'Women, Life, Freedom.'*

❧

Mist was swirling round the two mountain peaks that guarded Shush when Irdabama and Aferin rode out before dawn the next morning. Following the main road toward Hagmatana, they passed several paths leading farther into the mountains, but Aferin, from the local Bakhtyari tribe, rejected them all, insisting that she knew the way. The next morning, they were awakened by the clip-clopping of a donkey laden with freshly shorn wool. On questioning the man leading the animal, they discovered they were on a road that led to a fort. Irdabama asked him if the fort was occupied.

The man looked down. "I cannot tell," he answered. "Only Angra Mainyu lives there."

Irdabama frowned. "Where in the fort does Angra Mainyu stay?" she asked.

"Inside. His friends took my daughter away."

"Which friends?"

"Men with weapons. They came from that direction," he said pointing toward Shush.

"Can you lead us to the fort?" Aferin asked.

"I am sorry," the man replied. "I live in the village over the mountain and am taking my wool to sell in Shush. I cannot go all the way back now. But keep following this road. You won't miss the fort. It can be seen a long way off."

"*Zors spas*," Irdabama replied. "Shahjin Vashti is indebted to you. We will look for those men and your daughter." The man mumbled his appreciation as he led his donkey away.

The two women proceeded along the road, traveling a few more days before a stone building rising out of a huge, smooth rock appeared in the distance. "Kanhavara fort," Aferin announced triumphantly.

"Our commander might be there," Irdabama suggested. "We must find a place where we can watch the fort, day and night, perhaps from there." She pointed to a rocky knoll covered in low trees.

After riding cautiously through the forest undergrowth toward the knoll, the two women halted. The fort was in full view not far below, so they set up camp. Early the next morning, they observed an elderly couple approach the fort, the male of whom opened the gate with a key to admit his female companion. The couple came the next day, as did a flock of sheep, which grazed on the young spring grass beneath the fort walls. But their shepherd was nowhere to be seen.

Vashti looked forward to the visit of her keeper every morning, even though the poor woman still trembled and said nothing. But she always accepted her water ration gratefully. Then one day, she decided to try something different.

"Chai?" she asked, holding up the kettle. This time the old woman's face creased in a smile. She nodded and hurried out. The next day, she arrived with a clay cup and lifted the lid of a kettle from which the comforting aroma of chai wafted through the stale, musty air. Vashti wanted to hug her keeper but decided not to risk upsetting her anymore. Her hearty thanks resulted in a wide smile from the old woman, who bustled out happily.

Although the chai had little nourishment, it strengthened Vashti during the long, dank days in the silent cell as she waited for something other than losing her senses and slipping away into darkness. Anxious thoughts tormented her more than hunger pains, and she wondered whether Ishtovigo was starving her because she had denied him the affection and admiration he had craved during their youth.

"Perhaps I should have attended some of his tours in Shush for his guests, too," she thought, regretting her stubbornness. Scolding herself for not investigating the Parsu influence on her husband, she worried that they might become a threat to her women warriors. Thoughts like these sent the cold dark finger of doubt creeping up her back, and she feared she would lose her mind.

Then one day, she thought she heard the bleating of sheep outside. Standing on tiptoes beneath the slit window, she strained to listen. Yes, they were sheep! Their plaintive murmurs sounded like the rippling waters of a mountain stream, quenching her thirst for live company and reviving hope. She kept listening, but as night fell, the soothing noise slowly faded.

Each day afterwards, when she heard the tinkling bell of the flock's lead sheep, in her mind, she saw ewes nibbling fresh spring grass, while young lambs drinking from full udders wagged their tails. She imagined herself playing with the lambs as they jumped over rocks and congratulating the mothers on the cleverness of their little ones. But the shepherd was a mystery, he was as silent as the fort.

A few days later, she was praying about her ebbing strength when something brushed her elbow. Thinking it was a very bold member of the rat family she heard scratching sometimes at night, she opened her eyes to the dim sight of an almost sheer white object landing on the floor. It was a feather! She picked it up and gently stroked the scrap of sheepskin poked through the quill. Slowly, her fingers traced the outline of the freedom symbol of Kawa etched into the hardened skin.

The feather could only have come through the slit of a window that barely aired and lit her cell. Clutching it and the sheepskin to her chest, she felt hope rise again. Someone else knew where she was! In her excitement, she had not noticed that the feather was attached to a white woolen cord hanging from the window. Picking up a stone she had uselessly sharpened against the wall, she laboriously scratched the woolen under side of the sheepskin to loosen the strands of wool. It took the rest of her energy to pull them out. Then she gently tugged the cord twice. Miraculously, the feather and its message bearer crawled across the floor then slowly rose and disappeared through the window.

Chapter 48

Irdabama and Aferin watched the fort for two days, but they did not see the shepherd of the flock pastured beneath the fort. So, wishing to avoid the old couple's visits and villagers of unknown loyalties, they decided to investigate at nightfall of the next day. On circling the fort, they found a young shepherd leading his sheep along a path toward the village and asked him who was inside the fort. He shrugged then handed them a crumpled piece of dirty sheepskin. Recognizing the symbol engraved on it, Irdabama pointed to the fort.

"Is Shahjin Vashti in the fort?" she asked. The young man shrugged again and tweaked his ear. Realizing he might not have been able to understand, Irdabama made signs indicating a crown *sarwain* and elaborate jewelry. The young man tipped his head to the side as if in thought, then nodded, his eyes blinking understanding.

"She must be there," Irdabama said and thanked him. Behind him trailed a long white cord with a feather attached. "And perhaps he knows more about her," she added, trying to gesticulate a question about the cord to the shepherd who mumbled incoherently. "We will not put him in danger," Irdabama decided. "We will return to Shush for our sisters in case the other villagers are hostile. Nothing will stop us from freeing our Shahjin."

"We must hurry," Aferin urged. "We do not know what is in the kettle the old woman is taking to her."

In Hagmatana, Darayaus and Ardela were still grappling with the situation.

"We must bring Mother and Father together again, but how?" Darayaus asked.

"First, Vashti must be found," Ardela reminded her grandson. "But where should we look? She could be anywhere." She stared out the window, her perfectly oval face etched with worry lines. "This conflict has been happening for many years," she groaned, wringing her hands. "Had I spoken to both Ishtovigo and Vashti about it sooner, such terrible events might not have happened. Only a real peacemaker can mend this rift."

"Shah Mithridates is still trusted by many tribes," Darayaus ventured. "Once he arrives, I will ask him to journey to Shush to speak to Father about restoring Mother to the throne."

"Yes, dear," Ardela agreed. "This is most wise, especially considering Hovakhshatra's agreement with Mithridates."

"It is settled, Grandmother," Darayaus replied. "Please excuse me while I summon my chief advisor to choose an emissary fluent in the Pahlawanig language of the Parthavan court."

After the advisor left, Darayaus' guard entered and asked permission to speak.

"Shah Darayaus, the village chief of Kanhavara is here to see you. I told him you were busy, but he insists."

Darayaus sighed, thankful that he was not Shahan Shah. "Send him in."

"Honored Shah," the distressed chief began, "there is much trouble in my village. Our daughters have been stolen."

Darayaus frowned. "By whom?"

The chief's explanation of the village's stolen daughters raised Darayaus' immediate ire.

"This is against the laws of the Medes," he replied testily. "I will summon General Biraxeas to investigate, but first, my guard will take you to him so you can explain this alleged crime."

After giving the order, Darayaus dismissed the bowing chief and wondered who else was causing trouble in his father's shahdom.

In Shush, Aswer answered the Shahan Shah's summons quickly. "How many loyal subjects do you have for the first women's house?" Ishtovigo asked.

"My men have secured chosen ones from both Media and Parsua and even as far away as Parthava," Aswer answered obsequiously.

"Make sure these poor women are brought secretly to their new luxurious home," Ishtovigo directed. "We must keep our plan from meddlers like my wife and her ridiculous little band of women with their lances and shields. My men are looking throughout the shahdom for beautiful wives because women like them do not look after their appearance and think they can take the place of our valiant men in war. It is against the word of the Prophet."

Anticipating the success of his shah's campaign, Aswer smiled in satisfaction as Ishtovigo held out the golden scepter.

Stopping only for a few hours' sleep each night, Darayaus' emissary rode for a week to reach Shah Mithridates. On arriving, he fell in exhaustion at the steps of the shah's palace in Mitradatkirt and was revived by his guard. A little later, the emissary was received by Mithridates. On hearing the news about Vashti confirming information recently supplied by a Babylonian spy, Mithridates remembered the agreement he had made with Shahan Shah Hovakhshatra to aid Media should it come under any form of attack. Calling his council, Mithridates explained he was leaving immediately to attend to a problem in Media in honor of the agreement. Although one of his advisors volunteered, Mithridates insisted on going himself. He departed that evening with one guard, and they rode by day and into the nights, resting only for a few hours at a time. But on nearing the boundary of his own territory, Mithridates was met by local chiefs complaining that raiding parties were capturing women from villages, and they weren't Saka.

Angered by the complaints, Mithridates rode on to Hagmatana where he found Darayaus in distress.

"Media is under attack, but I do not know by whom or why," the younger man explained. "First, my mother and now some village women. This must be the work of Angra Mainyu and the *daevas*. Since the appeals of our representative to Kambujiya of Anshan have failed, my grandmother and I ask you to request that the Shahan Shah of Media make another law to bring back Shahjin Vashti."

Mithridates regarded the agitated young man before him. "Where do you think she is?" he asked.

"Admatha, a Parsu loyal to my mother and Media, has messaged that she might be somewhere in the mountains between Hagmatana and Shush."

Mithridates blinked. "That is a very big area. It could take years to find her."

"And women are disappearing…"

Mithridates stiffened. "From where?"

"Kanhavara and other villages in the Median triangle."

Mithridates spat in disgust. "This must be an organized plot," he surmised and explained his recently acquired knowledge of kidnapped women in his own territory. "Perhaps it is connected to your mother's dismissal."

Darayaus stepped back in shock. "You think my father is aiding those who kidnap women?"

"Possibly. I advise you to immediately send troops to search the region toward Shush," Mithridates replied evenly. "They must find and apprehend those who are committing these crimes. Tell them to search every village thoroughly for unusually high amounts of gold and silver coins. The kidnappers are most likely being substantially rewarded."

"I have already sent my general to investigate," Darayaus replied more calmly. "And who is this Vishtaspa? He is supposed to be plotting insurrection against Media from as far away as Parthava."

Mithridates smiled. "He is a baby, son of the governor of Parsua, he is not a threat, and neither is Parthava. We must find your mother first then I will deal with your father and any other of our common enemies."

Darayaus nodded and asked his guard to summon the Tiger regiment's second-in-command. When the soldier arrived, he was told to leave the next day to join General Biraxeas with two hundred extra troops to widen the search.

Encouraged by the message on the feather, Vashti reached for the parchments of the Avesta she had stowed in Cica's bag. The bag's worn leather brought back memories of her father, and she struggled to summon some of the courage that had driven him into battle on the last day of his life. Now, lying condemned to death in a filthy cell, she might never avenge his demise.

"O Auramazda," she read. "When will I attain insight of you? When will I attain insight of reality?"

Dimmed by precious tears, her eyes strained to read the words dancing across the crinkled sheet. She would not have enough time to explore more of the glorious mysteries of Auramazda.

Suddenly, a stone landed on the ledge of the narrow slit above, and the white feather fell through, attached once again to the white cord. But instead of a scrap of leather on the quill there was a piece of very dry bread. She grabbed the feather, pulled off the bread carefully, took a small bite, and swallowed. Unaccustomed to food, her stomach heaved, and she retched. She clutched her belly and willed the precious morsel to stay. After a few minutes, the heaving stopped, and she realized that somebody else outside still knew she was there and was trying to communicate with her.

Strengthened by hope more than the bread, she picked up the tatty pieces of Avesta parchment.

"I give my heart to you," she read, her throat lumpy. "My mind to *asha* joyfully. O *asha* give me *Yazata* Vohumanah's good thoughts."

Perhaps there is still time, she thought, to know all the *asha* of Auramazda.

"Righteousness is the best way of being," the faint script continued. "It is blissful, blissful is the one who has purity of mind and consciousness."

She couldn't stop thinking of Ishtovigo in his throne room with only Parsu and a Mede traitor to advise him. She could only hope he would soon send for her and restore her rightful place beside him.

"And always righteousness for the sake of *asha* itself," the dancing words read. "Think of good thoughts, speak with good words, act with good deeds and love everybody, spread the motto of humanity universally."

Stifling a sob, she told herself to put her feelings aside and order her thoughts as Piree Magush had advised before she was inaugurated. "If the bread keeps coming, I will survive to defeat *druj* and re-establish *asha* in Media," she vowed.

The old woman was only bringing her chai every second day, and the other days were interminably lonely. Not only did hunger eat into her body, but she was always thirsty. It was on one of those days that she remembered Mithridates's crumpled deerskin. She couldn't recall the last time she read it, or why she had forgotten it till then.

How can I tell your voice is sweet?
Well, it enters my heart and takes me
off in the air where I dance like a leaf.
What do I know about your body?
Well, you shake me when you are with me
And I get restless till I see you again.
And till I see your body is for me
Always for me, over and over, again.

Despite the warm day, she shivered in the cold prison that would soon become her tomb. She could not voice the reply Mithridates had asked for in the song nor might she again experience the touch of the one who knew her better than any other, but her inner eyes still saw a darkly cloaked man farewelling her with his hand on his heart. Clutching the deerskin, she fell into a restless asleep.

On waking a few hours later in diminishing light, she noticed something white lying on the floor. She blinked, wondering if it was another piece of bread. Reaching out, her fingers grasped a bone arrowhead around which some bread was indeed wrapped! Thankful for the skills of her provider, she pulled the bread from the arrowhead and nibbled slowly. Half dozing, she waited for more strength. When it came, she decided that even though the arrowhead was a useful weapon, if she didn't return it, there might not be any more bread. Fighting dizziness, she stood, shuffled closer to the far wall of the cell, took a breath, and aimed the arrowhead at the slit. It thudded on the floor, and she crawled painfully over to pick it up. Gathering all her energy, she reaimed the arrowhead, jumped, and threw it. This time it flew out the slit. The thrill of using the weapon enervated her for a few short moments until, collapsing onto the floor, she reached for the rest of the bread and nibbled slowly until sleep overtook her.

Scratching sounds woke her. She gripped the bread, but all her fist could feel was a few crumbs. Moaning in anguish, she scanned the cell perimeter for the thief. And there it was! In the corner, two beady eyes and a row of yellow teeth stared at her in a triumphant grin. Howling in rage, she pulled off her boot and threw it at the rat, which ran squealing up the wall to the hole that usually dripped water. Anticipating the rat's return, she reached for the old woman's kettle, curled her fingers around the handle, and waited, her dry mind deranged enough to think she could bash the rodent to death if it reappeared.

She lost consciousness as the new moon shone a sliver of light on the wall opposite the window. Then she began to dream.

She saw Ishtovigo yielding in battle to the likeness of Kambujiya of Anshan with Harpagos by his side. Then Medes brought tribute to Parsu. Soaked in sweat, she cried out and her cry escaped the slit in the wall and echoed across the hillside beyond the fort. But no one in the sleeping village heard. Only a young shepherd tending his lambing ewes in a pen on the outskirts of the village cast his eyes occasionally toward the slit in the fort wall.

Chapter 49

She awoke the next morning desperate to escape and warn Ishtovigo about her dream of the Parsu threat. But without food or weapons, it seemed impossible. In desperation, she prayed the first of her seven daily appeals to Auramazda. By the time she had finished, her mind was clear. An answer had arrived, and the plan she had been refining was finally ready.

After the old woman brought her chai, refreshed by the drink, Vashti asked about the sheep outside the fort, but the woman still said nothing.

"They must have a shepherd, but I never hear him calling the sheep," she probed cautiously.

The old woman's eyes darted around the cell. "He is mute," she replied, "but he knows many secret things."

So there was a shepherd outside the fort! He is probably bringing the bread, Vashti thought. "Can the shepherd hear anything?" she asked cautiously.

"Only a little. He is my grandson." The woman smiled proudly, picked up the kettle she had left two days before, and announced stiffly that she had to go.

Vashti thanked her keeper for the chai and beamed in return. For the rest of the day, she dozed and reread the song Mithridates had asked the minstrel to sing all those years ago in Rhagae. Late in the afternoon, just as she was wondering whether the shepherd would return, the long feather attached to the white woolen cord shot through the slit, this time with a piece of dried meat stuck through the quill. She chewed the morsel slowly then lay down to rest and read the last piece of Avesta parchment. When a little energy returned, she realized this might be her final opportunity to implement her plan. Slowly and deliberately, she inserted the dirty quill of the feather into her wrist so that blood ran. Then she smoothed out Mithridates' deerskin and shakily outlined the symbol of Kawa on the back with the bloody quill. It didn't matter if her pierced arm bloated and caused high fever, she would be dead soon anyway.

As the little rush of energy began to fade, she banged the chai kettle against the cell's window wall as hard as she could. Soon the feather and its bloodstained passenger began to move across the floor. Picking the feather and deerskin up, she shuffled to the wall and assisted their perilous climb toward the window. Then she crumpled to the floor and watched as they disappeared to freedom. Outside, the faintest rustle sparked hope that the shepherd might have received the message. Encouraged, she sipped the last of the day's chai and closed her eyes, dreading sleep and more dreams.

But she did not dream that night. Instead, she awoke when the narrow rays of light coming through the slit were high. Outside, distant shouts and chinking of metal on stone coming from the village made her wonder whether the old woman would bring her chai again or if the shepherd would bring his sheep and her only solid sustenance.

She waited and listened, but the noise soon faded.

In the village, the chief had returned and told the villagers that Shah Darayaus was sending soldiers to investigate the kidnappings. Not satisfied, the angry villagers vowed to capture the kidnappers if they came again and imprison them in the fort until their women were returned. Then they informed the chief that they were placing guards armed with farm implements on the hill near the road that led to the village. The chief agreed, and the first guards were posted.

That night, Vashti dreamed again. She saw Darayaus seated on the thrones of Media and Anshan. Standing nearby was a general bearing an Achaemenid shield. Then the same shah who had defeated Ishtovigo released captives from Babylonia and Media to return to their homelands. They took their gods and temple artefacts with them. Soon after, another Parsu trampled two others on his way to the throne. Riding across all the lands of Media and west toward Hellas, then Hindush to the east, he conquered lands as far south as Egypt, with Medes by his side. She woke in a terrible sweat, consumed by thirst and a vague recollection of Nebuchadnezzar's statue dream of many years ago. Fearing another dream worse than the vision of fallen Media, she struggled to stave off sleep.

Irdabama and Aferin led Khezmet, Parwin, and the rest of Vashti's fighters over the mountain road toward Kanhavara; their keenest-eyed archers constantly scanning the countryside for armed bands of men. After several days, only a few bags of bread remained with the donkeys they had laden with food, and the hungry but still eager faces of the women prompted Aferin's assurance that Kanhavara was not far. Minutes later, some who had ventured out to hunt for game returned triumphantly with slain hares, bunches of wild roots, and leafy plants for their evening meal.

"When we reach the village, we will make camp on the hill near the fort and plan our rescue strategy," Irdabama told her warriors as the skinned and gutted hares were thrown onto hot fire stones. "Eat then rest. Soon we will free our Shahjin."

After Mithridates left Darayaus he went down to the Parthavan quarter of Hagmatana to search for a guide who knew the region between the city and Shush. On being directed to a Bakhtyari man, who told them of the fort at Kanhavara, he immediately paid him in gold to lead the way to the village by the shortest route. The guide agreed that if Vashti was somewhere in the mountains between Hagmatana and Shush, and if there was a connection between her dismissal and women disappearing from Kanhavara, then this was as good a place as any to start looking for her. They retired early in preparation for joining a widespread, intensive search.

The next morning, they set off before sunrise in a southerly direction, hours before General Biraxeas' second-in-command departed the Hagmatana palace precinct accompanied by a select unit of the Tiger regiment.

Vashti's dreams haunted her lucid hours and came so often that she hardly noticed the old woman bringing her chai. Nor did she observe the arrows that flew in carrying the life-sustaining bread she pushed into her mouth. She no longer heard the sheep outside.

When she slept again, she saw the armies of another conqueror invade Media, flying a blue banner with a yellow sun. With his flowing mane of tawny hair and his mighty bronze armored forces, their fearless leader seemed unbeatable. He and his army overcame all the lands and peoples in their path, and her mountain people were powerless against them. When he disappeared, Media was ruled by one of his generals. But soon other huge armies of iron bearing the eagle banner of Romanus passed through cool fertile lands to the isles of the Great Sea. They swept into Yehud, toward which Magi priests were journeying, following the bright planet, Enlil.

On the fifth day, she prayed for death, but it wouldn't come. In a dream, she saw a Saoshyant teaching and healing in Yehud, but he too disappeared; and while some of her people were still ruled by

Hellenes, others came under the flag of Parthava. Saoshyant had not freed the peoples of all the conquered lands nor had he brought about Frashokeriti or taken anyone to *bahasht*, but her people who met him in a rebuilt Ursalim took his message of *asha* back to Media and Parthava.

Day merged into night and day again. All around was darkness.

Chapter 50

She dreamed again. The Median tribes joined the Parsu and there was peace, but the resistance in the mountains never stopped. Then a great warrior from the desert land of Sheba threatened them all, his massive armies of the black banner sweeping through like lightning. The blood of many Median and Parsu warrior men leaked into their lands, and the mouths of women taken captive to serve the desert men of Sheba and Egypt opened in soundless cries. The black banner overshadowed many lands to the east and the west.

But that was not all. Waves of short, narrow-eyed, sallow men on stocky horses rode through from the east, destroying the people's villages, dishonoring the women, and stealing the children. From deep in the recesses of her tortured mind, the Prophet Mahabad's warnings surfaced but brought no relief from the pain that gnawed down into her dying bones.

For a fleeting moment, the terror stopped, and peace ruled after her people's chiefs surrendered to their conquerors. The Atashkedah temples were destroyed, and Prophet Mahabad's predictions streamed through her visions. But the men and women of the mountains still resisted. Then many light-haired men appeared with big shiny horseless chariots on black wheels. Sitting in the chariots were long weapons on metal mounts, and they threw fire everywhere. The light hairs dug wells for the oily tar from Arrapkha, Rey, and other wells and took it away; and even though there was plenty left for Norouz fires, they took more. And when they pointed their fiery weapons at her people who would not surrender, they died instantly.

The fighting started again. Her people from Urartu to Eber Nari in Sham were attacked by hordes of barbarians under the banner of the crescent moon. The defenders shot small fiery weapons from their horses, but there were too many sallow, flat faces with long, thick pipe weapons firing big metal balls that killed many people at once. At times, great noisy metal birds dropped barrels from the sky that exploded like Hellas fire. Hungry, burned, injured, and bloody, her people fled into the mountains. But many could not escape and were imprisoned. And those in Media who fought the Parsu were hung from tall metal towers by strong ropes.

Next came a new red, white, and green striped banner with a yellow many-pointed star. Black-bannered Shebans drove her people from their homes, farms, and villages as those of the yellow-starred banner defended them to the death. The blood of her people poured onto their hills and fertile plains. Again, the survivors fled to the mountains, without boots or horses, to struggle through the snow and die—mothers, fathers, little children, and animals.

Another banner arose with a five-pointed red star. Men and women fighters roamed the mountains and could not be driven out by mechanical birds dropping fire from the sky or monstrous green chariots on multiple metal wheels flattening everything before them. Tumultuous noise muted cries of the imprisoned and the tortured. In the cities of Media, black-clad, heavily armored men of Angra Mainyu fired metal pellets from small pipe weapons that injured or killed her people whose banners read, "Jin, Jiyan, Azadi" in the streets. Anyone who opposed men in very tall houses wearing strange flat-topped black helmets and black gowns was arrested and imprisoned, and the streets ran with blood.

❧

Vashti's dirt-encrusted, cracked fingernails scratched the rocks embedded in her own prison floor, trying to dig a grave like the pits she saw her people thrown into alive. Unable to join them, she cried out in frustration, and her piercing cry sent the boy shepherd running toward the gray walls of the fort, his face contorted in fear and confusion.

Unaware of the stones he was frantically throwing at the wall, she moaned at the sight of barrels in her dream falling from the sky toward her people, releasing something invisible, which caused them to vomit, laugh, and finally expire. If only she could die like them.

Mithridates and his companions were halted by the village guards of Kanhavara and immediately taken to the chief's house, outside which a crowd of curious villagers soon gathered. After curtly answering the chief's questions about his identity and the reason for his visit, Mithridates asked if a woman was being held in the fort. The chief shrugged his shoulders.

"I know nothing of this woman," he replied, "but there is a couple who keep the fort for Shahan Shah Ishtovigo. They are here with the villagers." The chief pointed through the window to an elderly couple in the middle of the crowd. "Would you like to speak to them?"

Thanking his host, Mithridates followed him out and marched straight to the couple.

"I am looking for the Shahjin of Media," he declared, his sharp words laced with impatience. The old woman grimaced and turned to go, but Mithridates grabbed her arm. "Take us to the fort," he growled. The old man tried to free his wife, but Mithridates pushed him away and ordered his guard to arrest him while the chief stood by, his mouth agape in horror.

From amongst the crowd, a young man stepped forward and handed Mithridates a worn, crumpled piece of deerskin. Mithridates unraveled it, glanced at the blood-etched symbol, and turned to the old couple.

"Now you will show us where the woman is in the fort," he roared. The old woman clutched her throat, but her husband kept trying to wrestle free of the guard.

"The fort is that way," the chief cried, pointing to the forbidding building in the near distance. Hoisting the female keeper onto his horse, Mithridates ordered his guard to lift the protesting male keeper onto his mount, and they raced toward the fort.

All was silent within the prison walls. "Where is she?" Mithridates yelled again at the disheveled couple. Sobbing, the woman pointed to one of the bronzed barred doors, and her husband took the key from inside his sash.

Irdabama's forces halted above a wide valley. In the distance, the village of Kanhavara clustered not far from the fort.

"We will approach the village from the east before making sure it is safe to survey the fort from the hill nearby," she instructed. "Beware of other riders. Our commander's captors will probably be armed."

On the other side of the village, General Biraxeas's scout reported that men stationed at the approach to the village were not the shah's guards.

"Advance cautiously," he ordered, "if they are armed, force them to surrender." But as they drew near, he realized the guards weren't bearing military weapons, so Biraxeas led his forces to the village where he sought and found the chief, who bowed low and asked how he could be of service. The general explained that he was on Shah Darayaus' orders to find and capture the kidnappers of the village women.

"But, General, the Shah of Parthava is already here," the chief replied. Frowning, Biraxeas asked where the Shah was. "He has gone to the fort," the chief answered. "Be careful," he warned. "He is very angry."

Mithridates flung open the door of the cell to find Vashti unconscious on the floor and quite still. Kneeling in the drops of sticky blood beside her, he unraveled the tangled hair around her pale face, listened close to her mouth and nose for the sound of breath, and felt her neck for a heartbeat, but there were no signs of life. Cursing, he pinched her nose, placed his mouth over hers, blew twice, and watched for her chest to rise. His guard and the guide watched silently as Mithridates kept breathing and observing, but she lay completely still. Touching her neck, Mithridates cursed again and began to breathe and watch until his guard reached across and tapped him gently on the shoulder.

"Shahan Shah," he said, "she cannot be brought back to life."

Mithridates looked around, his eyes wild. Shaking his head, he returned to Vashti, his tears dripping onto her face. There was still no beat in her wrist, but in her neck, he felt a faint ripple of life and saw her chest rise imperceptibly. As she breathed shallowly again, Mithridates called for water, and his guard ran out to the horses, returning with a skinful. Mithridates spoke Vashti's name softly, and her eyelids fluttered.

"Father Cica, you have come back," she whispered.

Lifting her head, Mithridates carefully tipped a little water onto her tongue. "Ride fast to the chief and tell him to bring the midwife and her best medicines now," he ordered his guard. "Shahjin Vashti is very sick."

Mithridates told the Queen of Media who he was, but she did not recognize him.

"Father, Father," she insisted softly, "the enemy has killed our people." After covering her with his cloak and tipping a little more water carefully into her mouth, he cushioned Vashti's head with Cica's riding bag, gently stroked her hand, and told her to rest.

Outside, horses' hooves crashing on cobblestones sent Mithridates' guide into the fort yard. He soon returned to inform Mithridates that a party of Median soldiers was asking for the Shahjin.

"Tell them she is with me and invite the commander to see what has been done to the Shahjin of Media," he instructed as Vashti's breathing became more regular.

Shocked at the sight of Vashti but assured of her survival, Biraxeas immediately instructed two of his men to return to Hagmatana to inform Darayaus.

"We still do not know who has committed this crime against your mother, but my Shah, I will not stop until I have found them and brought them to you for punishment," Biraxeas' note explained. Then he ordered his troops to question the villagers about the kidnappers.

But Vashti kept wondering if the man beside her was really Father Cica.

For the third time that day, the Kanhavara guards encountered strangers seeking entrance to their village. But this time, they were relieved to see that these strangers were women, whom they could not consider kidnappers. Irdabama identified herself and her troop and asked if they could camp on the hill before attempting to find their commander, whom they believed was imprisoned in the fort. The guards replied that they knew nothing of such a commander, but that the Shah of Parthava and some Median soldiers were in the village, searching for a woman and some kidnappers.

"We seek permission to send a delegation to meet your chief and the visitors," Irdabama requested, and the harried guards agreed.

After permission was given from the chief to enter the fort, Irdabama, Khezmet, and Parwin hurried there, leaving Aferin with the rest of the women warriors on alert. At the fort gate, they met Mithridates carrying Vashti, who lay limply in his arms. Khezmet rushed to her.

"My darling," she cried, "what have they done to you?"

Parwin followed, tears of joy mingling with horror at her sister's colorless face and sunken eyes. "Ishtovigo will pay for this," she vowed fiercely, "by the word of the Prophet, I will make it sure."

Still disoriented, Vashti continued to call for her father. "I must tell you what has happened to our people," she insisted weakly.

Back in the village, Mithridates placed Vashti in a warm bed in the midwife's house. Khezmet encouraged her to sip spring water while the midwife prepared a special *danola* soup.

"Where is the shepherd?" Vashti asked softly after swallowing a little soup. "He brings me bread."

"We will find him," Irdabama promised, "and bring him to you."

Vashti tried to sit up but sank back onto her bed with a groan.

"Rest, my darling," Khezmet urged, stroking her mistress's forehead.

"Where are my warriors?" Vashti asked, staring at Irdabama but not realizing who she was either.

Irdabama knelt by Vashti's bed and took her hand. "Do not worry, Shahjin, they are nearby, waiting for your command," she replied gently. Vashti shivered, and Parwin took off her cloak, lay down beside her sister, and placed it over them both.

"Are you Admatha?" Vashti asked Mithridates, gazing intently at the man standing at the end of her bed. "Ishtovigo must be warned that the Parsu are plotting to conquer Media."

"Dear, you have been in Kanhavara fort. Now you are safe in the village with us," Khezmet explained, pointing to Parwin and Mithridates. "General Biraxeas is here, too. Ishtovigo and the Parsu cannot harm you."

"Ahh…the fort, the kettle, the white cord, the feather…," Vashti mumbled, still staring at Mithridates. "The song…you gave me the song."

Chapter 51

Before long, the guards General Biraxeas had placed near Kanhavara reported a small group of unknown riders approaching the village. Biraxeas ordered their arrest, and they were brought for questioning before the village chief, who identified them as those who had taken their women away. Imprisoned in the fort and denied food and water in the hot weather, they soon yielded to Mithridates' persistent questions, revealing the names and locations of kidnappers under the command of a leader whose identity they had sworn never to reveal.

"You will die tomorrow if you do not tell me who has ordered the theft of the women of Media and Parthava, including the Shahjin," Mithridates told them.

After he shot and killed three kidnappers the next day, the fourth pleaded for his life and declared he was willing to give information. "Parsu give the orders," he confessed. "Kusha, Ghasem, and Aswer the Mede planned the capture and detention of women in Media to be taken to Shahan Shah Ishtovigo's first women's house."

"Are they taking victims from Anshan and Parsua?" Mithridates asked, holding a clay cup of water in front of the thirsty man.

"The Shahan Shah's other Parsu advisors sent raiding parties into those territories," was the reply, "but I do not know their names."

Mithridates threw the cup onto the dusty fort ground and the man collapsed and tried to slurp up the muddy water. "You will be fed when you tell me who has been capturing the women of

Parthava," he growled.

"Shahan Shah, I do not know," the man cried.

"Who persuaded Shah Ishtovigo to send Shahjin Vashti to Kanhavara?" Mithridates continued, drawing his bow, and aiming at the kneeling kidnapper.

"Kusha the Parsu," he rasped, shielding his face with his hand. "That is all I know, merciful Shah."

Mithridates slackened his bow. "Take him to the prison cell formerly occupied by the Shahjin," he told his guard. "When he reveals where the captured women of Parthava are being held, tell the chief to order the boy shepherd to feed him."

Following more details received from the villagers, and some locations revealed by the fourth kidnapper, General Biraxeas sent troops throughout the Median triangle to track down his accomplices and bring them to Hagmatana for Shah Darayaus' judgment. Irdabama's warriors were instructed to hold offenders captured locally in Kanhavara fort before escorting them to the capital.

Vashti was transferred to the village chief's house where Khezmet and Parwin cared for her. One day during her recovery, a weathered young man appeared beside her bed with a white feather in one hand and a long white cord in the other. On the feather he had placed a morsel of bread, which he silently offered her. She took the bread with trembling fingers and ate, relishing the coarse grain. From his shepherd's pouch, the young man then produced a sheaf of thin, flat cakes. Vashti reached out and hugged him.

"Many thanks, dear brother," she whispered.

Once Vashti understood that she had been confined to Kanhavara fort, she asked to speak to Mithridates alone.

"When I realized Ishtovigo was spending much of Media's wealth, I instructed Aswer to hide some chests in a secret place not far from Hagmatana," she informed him. "He is the only one who knows where they are."

Mithridates raised his bushy eyebrows. "If the chests are here, let's hope Aswer comes looking for them." He grinned. "We will be waiting for him."

Beneath a trapdoor in one of the fort's cells, Vashti's troops found the chests full of gold and silver coins. Concerned that Ishtovigo might send some of his troops for them, Vashti urgently messaged General Biraxeas, asking for his most trustworthy men to transport the treasure over the narrow mountain paths to Hagmatana.

When her commander was strong enough, Irdabama ordered her warriors to prepare for Vashti's transport back to the capital in a litter cover woven by the village women from the wool of the shepherd boy's sheep. Beneath the gray walls of the prison that had nearly become her tomb, the villagers assembled to farewell their Shahjin. The old couple who had kept her in the fort and whom she had pardoned insisted on kissing her on both cheeks. Last to say goodbye was the shepherd boy who declined Vashti's offer to become chief herdsman of Shah Darayaus' flocks in Hagmatana. The young man's eyes glistened as he mumbled his gratitude, and Vashti rewarded him with the bag of silver coins Harpagos had paid her prison keepers.

Word had spread throughout the Median countryside that Shahjin Vashti was returning to her home, and Irdabama and Aferin guarded her closely as Delal pulled the litter out of the village. Vashti did not look back as the party passed the hill outside where armed villagers still protected the little settlement. At the rear of her escort, Mithridates and his guard followed a line of kidnappers roped together.

A few days later, Shamin looked out her window as several unrecognizably dusty soldiers, their horses laden with heavy, bulging bags, breached the golden gateway. The lead soldier approached the palace guard, spoke to him urgently, and passed him a written message. The guard quickly disappeared into the palace and a few minutes later an official emerged and instructed the rider. The soldiers then proceeded to the treasury, leaving Shamin wondering who had brought such generous tribute.

Several days later, on Mithridates' request, the guard at the golden gate admitted a dark-colored litter with an unknown occupant, but Shamin soon recognized Vashti's escort of women warriors. Rushing to the litter, she drew back its curtain and gasped at the sight of her daughter's drawn face.

"Vashti, my darling girl!" she cried, tears of joy running down her face. "What has happened to you? Where have you been?"

'Dear Mother, I am recovering, thanks to the villagers and many others, including Mithridates," Vashti replied softly. "In his wisdom and mercy, Auramazda has preserved me."

"What villagers? Have you been living with our tribal people again?" Shamin asked, hugging Vashti tightly after Khezmet carefully helped her out of the litter.

"No, dear, but I was close by all the time. A shepherd boy rescued me," she explained, winking at Mithridates.

"What a tale," Shamin cried. "You must tell more later, dear. But first, we will get you something to eat. You are so thin," she lamented, stroking her daughter's arm. Parwin emerged from the women's warriors' ranks and embraced Shamin in a long hug.

"We have brought our Vashti back to you, Mother," she said as Irdabama instructed the rest of the members to dismount and Daro appeared to take their horses.

"Tell Gulah to prepare for Vashti and our visitors," Shamin told Khezmet. "Then ask the palace guard to inform Shah Darayaus his mother is home."

After a joyous reunion with Darayaus and Ardela, and a bowl of Gulah's *terkhena*, Vashti lay on the familiar cushions of her childhood home and listened quietly while her warriors and Mithridates told of her dethronement, imprisonment, and rescue. After falling asleep before they finished, she dreamed that she was once more riding freely through the tall spring grasses of the Zagros Mountains.

The palace servants rejoiced to have their Shahjin back, and Darayaus declared seven days of celebration throughout the Median triangle. To show his appreciation for the efforts put forth to find his mother, he gave gifts to the chiefs and the people, paid for with the coins retrieved from the fort.

On learning of his wife's rescue and repatriation to Hagmatana, Ishtovigo's anger was reignited, and he insisted she would remain Shahjin in exile with no legitimate power in Media. However, Darayaus continued to refer to his mother as Shahjin and coruler of Media. Still unable to convince Kambujiya of Anshan and Arsames of Parsua to insist Ishtovigo make a law against the dismissal of Vashti, Debyar recommended they address her as Shahjin in all official business, which they duly did. Noting the two southern rulers' intransigence, Mithridates declined to pursue the matter further.

When Vashti told Debyar of her dreams in Kanhavara, the teacher shook her head sadly and remarked that some indeed confirmed the Prophet Mahabad's predictions.

"The division of Media is only the beginning," she commented on learning that tribute from Media's western and eastern territories would be received at Hagmatana while Ishtovigo's court would benefit from the southern territories' wealth.

"Perhaps the end is closer than the Prophet thought," she added.

Vashti's own army guarded her and continued the search for those capturing and selling women to local and even foreign powers. During a battle with kidnappers near Rhagae, Irdabama was killed. Stricken with sorrow, Vashti sought her family and offered them a small portion of her lands, but they declined, maintaining their daughter's blood was shed freely for all Media and its peoples. Aferin and Parwin continued to train women warriors throughout the Median triangle to protect and defend the shahdom both internally and from cross border attacks.

Khezmet remained in service as Vashti's maid, and Parwin and Pir Daidwand returned to Hagmatana where Daidwand succeeded the Piree Magush. The new Pir brought with him Vashti's bust of

Shahjin Nefertiti, which she placed once again on the shelf in her quarters. But her crown headdress was never retrieved from the women's barracks at Shush.

Based on information gained from the fourth kidnapper at Kanhavara, Mithridates sent a message ordering his chief general to search for and apprehend kidnappers of women in Parthava and to repatriate the victims. With Vashti comfortably settled in the palace, he announced his imminent departure but not before asking her to become chief advisor in his capital, Mitradatkirt.

"There are many oases in Parthava we have not yet explored," he added, his eyes resting on her with the intensity she had experienced so many times before. "Come with me to those beautiful places."

She took a deep breath and cast her eyes out the window to the teeming city below, wishing she wasn't about to refuse this man who haunted her dreams and was never far from her thoughts. Exhaling slowly, she turned to face him.

"My answer is as always…dearest of friends," she replied haltingly, the quaver in her voice wanting to him to stay. "Although your people are most welcoming and your richly endowed land entices me to return, Media is closest to my heart. I cannot leave now that we have this division."

She scolded herself. Her answer was part *asha*, part *druj*. Media *was* closest to her heart, but since her imprisonment, life and Mithridates had become even more precious. A sudden panic ran through her body, and she shuddered. How many more times could she refuse him before he stopped asking? Unable to bear the hope and anticipation in his face, she looked away again as duty and desire fought fiercely.

The choking feeling of their first parting on the Parthavan border constricted her throat, but this time, she knew the longing in his eyes would be more heartrending. And as he bowed before her in supplication, she deeply regretted the pain of their devotion to each other.

He rose and hesitated as if willing her to change her mind. But the heavy silence still hung between them, and he departed wordlessly, leaving only the faint, woody smell of frankincense. His absence, made final by the rhythmic slap of his feet marching down the corridor outside, overshadowed her like a cold, dark cloud on a windy winter's day. Closing her eyes tightly to suppress prickly tears, once again she stood listening to his horse's hooves descending the citadel.

Three years later, Nebuchadnezzar regained his human mind and body and resumed his throne as Shahan Shah of Babylonia. There was much rejoicing in Babylonia and Hagmatana, especially when Amytis and Amel-Marduk visited the original Median capital. Under Nebuchadnezzar's new mind and recognition of Most High God El Elyon, whose shahdom he declared supreme, Babylonia experienced a welcome period of peace and stability, allowing Nebuchadnezzar to truly claim the title of the greatest ever Shah of Babylonia.

The following year, after a vicious campaign in which Kusha again sent Parsu and other foreign agents to kidnap beautiful young virgins from all the Median territories, Ishtovigo gathered candidates for the new Shahjin of Media into the first women's house at the palace in Shush. Prepared for a year to be chosen Shahjin by the Shahan Shah according to their appearance and their abilities to entertain him, they were to bestow on him all their womanly virtues. Eventually, a foreign captive was crowned with a new *sarwain* of silver and Median jade, and named after the goddess Ishtar.

Even though Darayaus married a daughter of Kambujiya of Anshan, Vashti remained Shahjin of Media in the hearts of her people. Soon after Ishtovigo divorced her, she married Mithridates of Parthava and went to live with him in Mitradatkirt, also becoming Shahjin of Parthava. Her crown headdress of rubies, emeralds, tourmalines, and lapis lazuli was never surpassed in all Ariavarta and Babylonia.

It was not until Vashti and Mithridates were alone at the end of their wedding celebrations that she told him about her dreams in Kanhavara. Fastening his gentle brown eyes on her, he listened carefully.

"Dear, it is many years since I watched you at the oasis after we first met, and I too have had dreams, but mostly of you," he admitted when she had finished. "Now it is time for us to dream together."

"I have a confession," Vashti replied. "When I was in the fort, I dreamed you were kissing me. Then my pain stopped, and I fell deeply asleep." She paused. "Was it really you?"

"I cannot tell *druj*, as there were two witnesses." Mithridates grinned. "I found you dead on the floor of that filthy prison, and after so many years alone, I could not accept that I had lost you."

"And when I was lying on that floor exhausted and without sense or feeling, I dreamed I was in the desert and you were giving me water," she added. For the first time she saw tears in his eyes. Wiping them with her fingers, she kissed him. "Thank you for giving me the breath, and the water of life," she whispered.

Not long after, Vashti dictated the dreams she had in Kanhavara to her scribe and asked him to copy them into the Chronicles of the Shahs and Shahjins of Media, which were stowed in the vault of the palace at Hagmatana and left to posterity.

In the following years, Vashti and Mithridates had two children with whom they traveled east and west throughout the sixteen perfect lands of Ariavarta. At every oasis, they celebrated their enduring friendship, their devotion to each other, and their allegiance to the Mitradat. Their descendants built the great Parthavan shahdom, which fought Romanus for hundreds of years and never was defeated.

Neither was Media.

The battle for the Shahdom of Media and its provinces still rages.

References

Zondervan. 2017. NKJV Cultural Backgrounds Study Bible.

Llewellyn-Jones, Lloyd. 2022. Persians: The Age of the Great Kings.

Gershevitch, Ilya, ed. The Cambridge History of Iran, Volume 2, the Median and Archaemenian Periods.

Rawlinson, George. 1862–67. The Seven Great Monarchies of the Ancient Eastern World (Sixth Monarchy), Volume 2.

Hamarash, Soran. 2022. The Lost and Untold History of the Kurds (first edition).

Glossary

1. **Characters - historical, fictional, peoples**
2. **Median/Kurdish words**
3. **Clothes and accessories**
4. **Foods and drinks**
5. **Musical instruments**
6. **Supernatural beings and religious/cultural terms**
7. **National/Ethnic/geographical regions**
8. **Cities and Towns**
9. **Natural features**
10. **Man-made items/names**

1. Characters

Historically and/or biblically known:

Vashti - first documented in the Old Testament book of Esther

Ishtovigo - (adaptation of Median Istumegu), known as Ahasuerus in Hebrew and English, also Astyages in English

Hovakhshatra (adaptation of Median Uvaxstra), Cyaxares in Latinised English

Shah Azhdehak - oppressive mythical enemy of the Medes whose defeat was/is symbolised in the Norouz spring festival

Amytis, Alyattes, Arsames, Aryenis, Belteshazzar and his three friends, Croesus, Darayaus, Harpagos, Kambujiya, Nebuchadnezzar, and Vishtaspa (otherwise known as Hystaspes)

Legendary or fictional:

The rest of the characters

Peoples

Athorayans - ancient Assyrians

Hapiru - Hebrew, later known as Jew

Hellenes - Greeks

Hurrians, Mitanni, Mannaeans, Hittites, Amorites - ancient Middle Eastern peoples

Kikkuli - horse trainer

Medes, Parsu (Persians), Parthavans (Parthians), Dahae were all Ariavartan tribes

Nefertiti - Egyptian queen

Phoenicians - sea peoples who settled on the eastern Mediterranean coast

Salmat Qaqqardi - Akkadian name for first Sumerians (thought to be forebears of Kurds), located in the southern part of the land between the Two Rivers (today's Euphrates and Tigris) region

Scythians, Cimmerians, Saka - ancient Caucasian tribes from the area north of the Black Sea and further east

Shahan Shah - king of kings

Shahjin - queen

2. Median/Kurdish words

asha - the truth

biji - long live

ciwana - beautiful

druj - the lie, falsehood

jin, jiyan, azadi - women, life, freedom
roj bas - good morning
zors spas - many thanks

3. Clothes and accessories

Akandys - most likely official battle cloak of Median kings

Chokha - shirt/jacket

Fez - small, neat cap worn by Babylonian kings

Golangs - colourful woollen ribbons used to decorate a horse's mane

Kulaw-u-dastmal - men's cloth wrap-around headdress

Mukryani - official robe of Median queens

Pantol - long pants or trousers

Sarwain - women's fabric or animal pelt headdress trimmed with small metal discs and/or jewels, and tassels

4. Foods and drinks

Ceci peas - chickpeas or garbanzos

Chai - black tea, possibly spiced

Chaudel - ancient name for opium

Danola - thin soup of ground wheat

Ganja - type of cannabis

Mast - yoghurt

Shire-ye-korma - date syrup used as a kind of yeast in bread

Terkhenah - thick soup of ceci peas and vegetables

5. Musical instruments

Daf drums

Shimshal pipes

Tanbur - stringed instrument with a bulbous body

6. Supernatural beings and religious/cultural terms

Angra Mainyu - evil being opposed to Auramazda

Atashkedah - Zoroastrian temple

Auramazda - supreme God of the people of ancient Ariavarta, associated with light and fire, the emblems of truth, goodness, and wisdom

Avesta - Zoroastrian holy book

Bahasht - paradise/heaven

Bansom wands - sticks of tamarisk bushes used to find out the meaning of dreams or supernatural information

Daevas - evil spirits

El Elyon - Most High God

Faravahar - visual representation of fravashi

Frashokeriti - Zoroastrian doctrine of a final renovation of the universe, when evil will be destroyed, and everything else will then be in perfect unity with Auramazda God

Fravashi - personal spirit of an individual

Avraham - prophet of Hapirus, commonly known as Abraham

Magi - priest

Magush - chief priest

Mitradat - set of laws derived from Mithra, god of covenants

Mossala temple - fictional temple of polytheistic worship

Norouz - spring festival, still celebrated throughout regions of Ariavarta

Pir - senior priest

Prophet - Zoroastrian Prophet Zarathrustra or Mahabad

Saoshyant - Messiah figure in Zoroastrianism

Spenta Mainyu - benevolent spirit of Auramazda

Urvan - can be understood as the soul of an individual sent into the material world to fight the battle of good versus evil

Yazata - divine being, good power of Auramazda, angel

Yehovah - name of Hapirus' God

7. National/Ethnic/geographical regions

Akkad, Akkadians - Empire based between the Tigris and Euphrates Rivers

Anshan - northern part of Persia

Ariavarta - traditional name for the ancient lands ruled by the Median dynasty stretching from the Hurrian region in the west to Bactria in the east

Athoraya - Assyria

Azadia - fictional name used to denote the region of today's convergence of Iran, Turkey, and Iraq that rose after the Sumerian civilisation

Bactria - eastern Ariavartan land

Baxtri - ancient capital of Bactria

Eber-Nari - ancient Syria

Elam - south-western part of Media

Hellas - Greece

Hindush - India

Kiengi - ancient name for Sumer

Media - ancient kingdom of the Medes in western Ariavarta, today called Rojhelat (East Kurdistan)

Parsua - Persia

Parthava - Parthia, today's eastern Ariavarta

Romanus - city and state of Rome

Shahdom - kingdom

Sham - region east of the Mediterranean Coast known later as the Levant

Sina - China

Susiana - region of Elam between Media and Persia

Urartu - Armenia

Yehud - Region of last two tribes of ancient Israel, taken into captivity by Nebuchadnezzar of Babylon in 588-587BC

Yisrael - originally 12 tribes of prophet Abraham's descendants, reduced to two after the Assyrian invasion and exile of 722 BC

8. Cities and Towns

Aspadana - ancient city in Median triangle, today's Isfahan

Ashur - key ancient Assyrian city

Arrapkha (Sumerian Nuzi) - today's Kirkuk, Iraqi controlled city

Carchemish - site of battle fought between the Egyptian and Assyrian armies against the Babylonians, Medes, Persians, and Scythians

Gavareh - surviving city of Median Ariavarta

Hagmatana - capital of ancient Media, also called Ecbatana, Achmetha, today's Hamadan

Hawler - today's Erbil, capital of the Kurdish Region of Iraq

Kanhavara - imaginary Median village

Median triangle - region of the most powerful Median tribes in western Ariavarta

Nineveh - capital of ancient Assyria

Rajaw, Medaktoo, Gawar, Sherwaina - cities of ancient Media

Rey - settlement near Rhagae

Rhagae - today's Teheran

Sardis - capital of ancient kingdom of Lydia

Shush (Susa) - surviving city of Median Ariavarta

Ursalim - ancient Jerusalem

Zadraka - imaginary Median city

9. Natural features

Enlil - planet Jupiter

Halys River - boundary between ancient Media and Lydia

Indigna and Ufratu Rivers - Tigris and Euphrates Rivers

Lake Zrebar, Lake Chauon - lakes of Media, today's Lake Marivan and Lake Van

Mount Behistun - archaeological site of ancient Median/ Persian history

Ninurta - planet Saturn

Nowshahr Pass, Mount Alvand, Alborz Mountain, Zagros Mountains - mountains of Ariavarta

Piree Magroon mountain of the magi - ancient cultural site on western flank of Zagros Mountains

Qandil Mountains - area where today's Iran, Iraq and Turkey meet

Regulus - brightest star in the Leo constellation

Seeps - oil wells bubbling up to the surface in pools

Sherwan River, Sefid River – waterways of Media

Shiraz region, Nisean Plain, Mahi-Dasht Plain, – flat areas of Media

Great Sea – Mediterranean Sea

10. Man-made items/names

Arayesh – red powder from a poppy plant used to make cheekbone tints

Bears – biblical title for the Median shahdom

Caravanserery - inn

Cubit - ancient traditional length of a man's arm from middle fingertip to elbow

Dwar - tent of goat's hair and/or sheep's wool

Galyan pipe - water pipe, used by smokers

Gatha songs - hymns of Zoroastrian writings

Gosan minstrels - travelling minstrels

Kayaniam Shahs - mythical kings of eastern Ariavarta

Kevci - game of chance with a board and dice

Medicago clover - pasture plant like today's alfalfa/lucerne

Nisan, Gulan, Adar, Sexwerban - Median months

P'anka dva cubit - Persian cubit, slightly longer than Sumerian, Egyptian and Israeli cubits

Qanats - underground irrigation channels

Stade - Greek unit of measurement, 150-210 meters long, depending on the time and place

www.ingramcontent.com/pod-product-compliance
Lightning Source LLC
Chambersburg PA
CBHW011218190726
48287CB00008B/2661
9781764405201